MW00625754

Copyright

This is a work of fiction. Names, characters, places, and incidents are either the product of the author's imagination or are used fictitiously, and any resemblance to actual persons living or dead, business establishments, events, or locales, is entirely coincidental.

The Wild Mustang & The Dancing Fairy © 2021 by Saffron A. Kent
All rights reserved. No part of this book may be used or reproduced in any manner whatsoever without written permission of the author except in the case of brief quotations embodied in critical articles or reviews.

A Gorgeous Villain © 2021 by Saffron A. Kent
All rights reserved. No part of this book may be used or reproduced in any manner whatsoever without written permission of the author except in the case of brief quotations embodied in critical articles or reviews.

Cover Art by Najla Qamber Designs
Editing by Olivia Kalb and Leanne Rabesa
Proofreading by Virginia Tesi Carey

June 2021 Edition
Print ISBN: 9798512370803

Published in the United States of America

Other Books by Saffron A. Kent

Dedication

For all the brokenhearted girls.
And for my husband, thank you for always being careful with my
heart.

Author's Note

This edition includes the prequel, THE WILD MUSTANG &
THE DANCING FAIRY. If you've already read it, please skip
to A GORGEOUS VILLAIN, the full-length conclusion to
Reed & Callie's story.
Also note that it is highly advisable to read the prequel first in
order to enjoy the full-length book.

PS: Please note that in order to fit the plot and the timeline
some things such as high school soccer season and Juilliard
admission process have been altered.

THE
WILD MUSTANG
& THE
DANCING FAIRY

USA TODAY BESTSELLING AUTHOR
SAFFRON A. KENT

A Gorgeous Villain Prequel

Chapter 1

Two years ago…

Bardstown High

He has beautiful gray eyes, gunmetal gray that sometimes glow in the night.

So much so that people call them wolf eyes.

His jaw is sharp and angled, a true V, and his skin looks like priceless marble. Again, so much so that people say he's got wintry, vampire skin.

They say he's got magic, dark magic, running through his veins.

If a girl so much as looks into his pretty wolf eyes, no one can save her from falling for him.

No one can save her from getting her heart broken either.

Because *he* never falls. He is mighty. Everyone knows that.

He's a heartbreaker. A player.

People say he doesn't even have a heart, or if he does, it's pitch black.

But he knows how to toy with yours.

He knows how to play with it. How to toss it up in the air just for fun and how to tie it up with strings and play with it like a puppet. And when he gets bored, he knows how to let it slip through his fingers and drop on the ground, breaking it into tiny little pieces.

Yet girls can't help but come back for more. Over and over and over again.

They can't help but come back to the Wild Mustang.

Or the Mustang for short.

That's what people call him. That's his soccer nickname.

He plays soccer, yeah.

Soccer is quite popular in our town. In fact, he's the soccer legend of Bardstown High. And he's as majestic and magical as an un-tamed mustang. As reckless and edgy and completely mesmerizing.

Although I don't call him that.

The name that *I* get to call him is something completely different, something that I've come up with after a lot of deliberation and thought: a villain.

That's what I call him.

A Gorgeous Villain, actually. Because well, he is gorgeous, but he's a villain, and I have good reason to believe that.

Four good reasons.

Four overprotective, overbearing, *older* reasons. My brothers. Who hate him with all the fire in their hearts.

Well, not all of them hate him with *all* the fire in their hearts. Only one of my brothers does, Ledger. The other three just hate him a normal amount.

Why does Ledger hate him the most though?

Because the Gorgeous Villain is Ledger's soccer rival.

My brother plays soccer too and he's a legend in himself. They call him the Angry Thorn, because my brother is a hothead and our last name is Thorne.

Anyway, they both play for the same team. And should potentially be friends and have the same agenda.

However, they aren't–friends, I mean. And they *don't* have the same agenda, at all.

Probably because they're both forwards for Bardstown High. One is left wing and the other is right and basically, they're supposed to help each other.

But they don't because they have this ongoing, age-old contest, where whoever scores the most goals in the season wins.

It's a matter of pride and honor and a whole lot of testosterone.

I don't know how it got started, this contest, rivalry, whatever you want to call it, but they both take it very seriously. Their whole team, which is divided into my brother's camp, the Thorn camp, and *his* camp, the Mustang camp, takes it seriously as well.

So does the whole town.

Whoever wins this unofficial contest becomes the reigning champion. This year it's my brother – he won by one measly goal last season – who also happens to be the captain of the team.

The whole town treats him like a king.

Which means free drinks, free food at local restaurants, posters on park benches and light poles. Back pats from people on the street and of course, all the attention from girls.

Trust me when I say that these two will go to any lengths to be the winner.

They'll do anything to mess with each other, ruin each other's game on and off the field just so they have a better chance of scoring goals.

And for years I've heard about it, about their rivalry, about *him*.

I've heard how corrupt he is, how evil and twisted. How he'd do anything to win at soccer. How much of an asshole, douchebag, bastard, motherfucker, and all those things he is.

But of course, I can't call him that. I can't call him all those names.

I'm a good girl.

I don't curse.

Besides, my brothers curse enough for all of us.

Hence the name: A Gorgeous Villain.

Anyway, it's game day and I'm at the soccer field right now.

A little personal confession: I don't like soccer. Not at all.

I think it's boring and I'd rather be home right now, either baking cookies or cupcakes, or knitting in my favorite armchair by the fire. Two of my favorite things to do.

Another personal confession: I don't understand this rivalry either. I don't understand this whole need to win and be the best at any cost. I mean, they play for the same team, don't they? If the team wins, they win, correct?

But as I said, I'm a good girl and so a good sister.

I'll always support my brothers. No matter what.

They're my whole wide world. I love them to pieces, and I know they love me to pieces too.

So here I am, sitting on the bleachers, watching a game I don't really care for, just so I can support Ledger and cheer for him.

And also Conrad, my oldest brother, who happens to be the coach of our high school soccer team.

So soccer is not only this town's sport, it's also our family sport; my other two brothers, who are away at college right now, played for Bardstown High as well.

This kind of makes me soccer royalty by extension.

But anyway, good. That's what I am. A good girl. A good sister.

Good. Good. Good.

Are you, Callie? Are you?

Are you really a good sister? Are you really cheering for your brother, Ledger, or are you also cheering for him?

Oh my God.

Blasphemy.

I'm not cheering for *him*. I would never ever cheer for him.

He's the enemy.

Yes, he is.

He is. He is. He *is*.

My agitated thoughts come to a halt when someone – a frazzled-looking girl – stumbles and almost falls on me. My arms automatically shoot up and clutch her shoulders to help keep her balance.

Even though I manage to save her from falling, the tub of popcorn in her arms tips and a flurry of kernels falls on my lap and my feet.

"Oh my God, I'm so sorry. Are you okay?" she asks as she manages to straighten up.

"I'm fine," I assure her, brushing popcorn off my dress. "Are *you* okay though?"

"Yeah. No," she replies, and clutching the huge tub of popcorn to her chest, she raises her finger in a gesture for me to wait. Looking back, she shouts at someone, "Asshole." Then she sighs and plops down on the empty seat beside me. "Ugh. I hate this. He wouldn't move his leg. Idiot." She rolls her eyes before fixing her gaze on the field. "And I was so excited for the game tonight. Am I late? I'm late, aren't I?"

"Maybe a little." I shrug. "But nothing's happened yet. It's 0-0. It's the day of the defenders. So, you're good."

She smiles. "Thanks." Then she thrusts the tub of popcorn toward me. "Want some? I already spilled on you, so."

"Sure, yeah. Thanks." I pluck out a few and pop them in my mouth. "I'm Callie, by the way."

"I'm Tempest. Nice to meet you." Her smile is bright and friendly. "So I'm assuming you go to school here?"

"Yup." I nod. "And I'm assuming you don't?"

There's something familiar about her. I can't put my finger on exactly what though. But I'm pretty sure I haven't seen her before.

She shakes her head at my question. "Nope, I'm just crashing the party. I go to school in New York."

"New York? That's exciting."

"Meh. I completely hate it there. I miss home too much." She shrugs. "But anyway, I wanted to be here for the game. I'm supporting someone. He's gonna completely freak when he sees me. He has no idea that I'm here. You? Are you supporting someone too?"

"Oh yeah. I'm…"

My words get swallowed up when she bends to set down the container of popcorn.

Because I understand who she's talking about. Who's going to completely freak when he sees her.

It's written in the back of the t-shirt, or rather soccer jersey – in school colors, green and white – that she has on. The name and the number.

In bold black letters, Jackson, 11.

She's here for him.

The Gorgeous Villain, my brother's rival.

Reed Jackson.

Actually, Reed *Roman* Jackson.

That's his full name. And all us freshmen call him by his full name.

Well, except for me. I already call him something else, but yeah.

To freshmen, he's a celebrity. A shiny star to admire from a distance. An awe-worthy creature.

And she's here for him.

"You're here for R-Reed?" I blurt out instead of answering her question.

I not only blurt it out, but I stumble on his name too.

Like it's a roadblock in the dark. A jagged rock on an otherwise smooth trail in the woods.

Something that trips you. Makes you fall.

Something that you don't see coming, not until you've already fallen.

"Yeah." Tempest gives me a quizzical look. "Why?"

Avoiding her eyes, I clear my throat, feeling embarrassed. It doesn't matter that she's here for him. Lots of girls are here for him.

He's a playboy, remember?

"Nothing. I just noticed, uh, his name on your t-shirt."

"Do you know him?"

"Not at all," I say quickly. A little too quickly and it only increases her suspicion. So I immediately follow it with, "I-I mean, except for the fact that he plays for the team. My brother plays too."

That seems to distract her. "Your brother?"

Okay, good.

I don't want to talk about him. I don't even know why I got so jarred at the fact that this girl, Tempest, has specifically come down from New York to visit him.

It's none of my business.

"Yes," I say proudly. "Actually, my other brother is the coach."

"Other brother?"

"Yes. I have four."

"Holy shit. I can't handle one."

I chuckle. "I know, right? Brothers can be…"

"A pain in the ass with all their protective shit?"

"Yes." My chuckle turns into a laugh. "Exactly. They can be a little overprotective."

"A little? My brother is the very definition of overprotective. He is *insane*." She rolls her eyes. "If he had his way, he'd lock me up somewhere and wouldn't let me out until I was thirty or something. A thirty-year-old virgin. Imagine that."

She fake shudders, making me laugh. "Your brother sounds like my brothers."

Which is the truth.

My brothers are overprotective and it can be annoying sometimes.

But I don't begrudge them that. I don't begrudge them their overprotectiveness and all their rules and curfews, their genuine worry about me.

Mostly because we don't have parents.

Our father took off just after I was born and our mother died of cancer when I was four.

So they've brought me up, you see.

Together, they've taken care of me, loved me and protected me more as my parent figures than my brothers.

Especially Conrad.

"But I guess they do it out of love," I continue, "since we're all we've got. I don't have parents, so we take care of each other."

That makes Tempest smile. A sad sort of smile but a smile nonetheless as she says, "Me too." Then, "Well, I do have parents but they're as good as nonexistent so my brother takes care of me and I *try* to take care of him."

I smile then too.

I've never met anyone who has understood this, understood what it feels like to have no parents and only siblings.

But I guess this new girl gets it.

What a fun coincidence.

"So your brother," I chirp, wanting to know more about her. "Does he go to school in New York too?"

Oh and does he know Reed as well?

How do you know Reed?

Why are you here for him? Do you like him? Are you...

God.

I need to stop.

It's none of my business.

She isn't the first girl to be in love with him and she won't be the last. If anything, I should probably warn her about him.

I should tell her that he's never ever going to reciprocate her feelings.

Because all he does is break hearts and makes girls cry.

"Nope. He goes to school here. He's a senior," Tempest replies.

"Oh! Who is he?" I ask. "Maybe my brother knows him. He's a senior too."

Before Tempest can answer though, there's a roar around us and we both get distracted. The crowd is cheering and the reason for it is apparent as soon as my eyes land on the field.

It's him.

He's the reason, the Wild Mustang.

He has the ball in his possession and he's not giving it up. The players from the opposite team are chasing him. They're almost crowding him in from all directions, all their defenders against one Reed Roman Jackson.

And for a second it looks like they might be successful.

They might take the ball away from him.

The whole stadium is expecting it. All the people who are watching, they expect Reed to lose the ball. It's in the way that they've all gone silent and the way the announcers are talking with a rapid-fire speed and a louder tone.

But they're all wrong. Every single one of them.

Like the way they're wrong about the fact that Reed is a mere athlete.

He's more than that.

He's not only an athlete, he's also a dancer.

Look at his footwork. It's exquisite. It's impeccable. It's graceful. It's the envy of every dancer, especially a ballet dancer. And I'd know because I'm a ballerina. Have been since I was five.

Reed Roman Jackson has the kind of footwork that would make any ballerina fall in love with him.

It would make any ballerina go down on her knees and weep at his feet.

Not me though.

I can't.

What kind of a sister would I be if I did?

Therefore, I can't widen my eyes at the rapid swipes and the swings of his legs as he zigzags through the closing-in crowd, still somehow keeping possession of the ball. I can't wring my hands in my lap when he nearly crashes into a guy from the opposite team. I can't lose my breath when he almost loses the ball but at the last minute, with a fake pass to throw them off his scent, he saves it.

And neither can I hop up from my seat and clap and scream when he finally, *finally*, sends the ball flying with such force that it feels like it's slicing the air itself in two before hitting the net and scoring the goal. The first goal of the game.

I can't do any of that.

I can't.

But I can't deny the rush in my chest or the puff of relieved air that escapes through my parted lips.

I can't deny that my veins feel full and bursting.

They feel full of music, of the notes of a violin, and my feet are restless. So restless to just... dance.

"*That's* my brother."

Tempest's voice pierces through and I jerk my eyes away from Reed, who's getting thumped on the back by the Mustang camp of the team while the Thorn camp is simply going about their business of getting back into their positions, including number twenty-three, Ledger.

"Um, sorry. Who's your brother again?" I ask because I completely missed who she was pointing at.

She throws me a sly smile. "The one you've been watching."

"What?"

She bumps her shoulder with mine. "The one who scored the goal just now and you got so excited that I thought your eyes would pop out of your head."

"I didn't."

Did I?

She laughs. "You so totally did. Even I don't get as excited as you did."

My heart is a drumbeat in my chest. "I —"

"It's fine. I won't tell." She mimics a zipping motion on her lips before pointing to the back of her jersey. "But anyway, Jackson. I'm Tempest Jackson. Reed's my brother."

She's Reed's sister.

Sister.

"That's why you look familiar," I breathe out before I get a hold of myself. "I'm sorry. I just thought you looked familiar."

She wiggles her eyebrows. "You also thought I was his girl-friend, didn't you?"

"What? No." I shake my head, squirming in my seat. "I... It's none of my business."

"It's okay. He has a lot of girlfriends. Oops. Not girlfriends. Girls. My brother doesn't do girlfriends."

"Oh yeah, I know."

Tempest stares at me for a few seconds. It's not long but it's enough to make me slightly uncomfortable and self-conscious. "But that doesn't mean that he won't ever have a girlfriend. You know, when the right girl comes along. He's just being an idiot right now."

"O-kay." I nod. "That's good to know."

"Is it?"

"What?"

Tempest completely turns to me then. "I like you. I think you're cool. And I think…" She lowers her voice. "You have a major crush on my brother. And –"

"Oh my God. Stop."

I look around to make sure no one's listening in on our conversation.

Although the stadium is so loud and people are so engrossed in the game, I highly doubt anyone could eavesdrop even if they wanted to.

But still.

I can't take any chances. If someone so much as got a whiff of the fact that I was talking about him, that Ledger and Conrad's sister was talking about having a crush on the enemy, I don't even know what would happen.

Ledger would definitely kill Reed. *Definitely.*

And then he'd lock me up somewhere for who knows how long for betraying him, and I wouldn't even blame him.

Because it is a betrayal, isn't it?

"What?" Tempest asks confused.

"Don't even talk about it."

"Why not?"

"Because you can't. And because *I* can't."

"You can't what?"

I look around again. I even go so far as to lean in toward her and lower my voice. "I can't like your brother."

She leans in as well. "What? Why can't you?"

"Because I can't."

"Yeah, you said that. But what does that mean?"

"It means that I can't. I'm not..." I look for a suitable word. "*Allowed.*"

"You're not allowed?"

"Nope."

"Well, who is it that's not allowing you?"

I stare at her a beat before saying, "Look, you don't live here so you don't know."

"What don't I know?"

"There's bad blood between my brother and yours." She frowns and I explain, "My brother hates your brother and the feeling is mutual, okay? So don't even talk about these things."

Her confusion has only grown. "What? Why?"

I go to explain the whole thing to her but turns out I don't have to.

When I can show her.

Because what happens at every game is already happening on the field. The two star players of Bardstown High are facing off against each other.

You'd think that ever since Ledger became the captain, he would try to steer clear of all kinds of fights and arguments. At least on the field. But no.

Because Reed doesn't let him.

Ever since Ledger became the captain, Reed's aggressiveness on the field has only grown.

I'm not sure what brought on the current argument but they're standing toe to toe.

I can't see their expressions from here so all I have to go on is their body language and it is not looking good.

There are tense shoulders, rigid backs. Wide, battle-ready stances and folded arms.

I can read my brother like a book and I know he's angry. I know that the vein on his temple must be pulsing as he says something, or rather, snaps it at Reed.

Who, on the other hand, appears completely relaxed.

Reed looks like he doesn't care that Ledger is almost up in his face. He doesn't care that Ledger looks like he might hit Reed at any point.

But I think it's all for show.

It's all to provoke Ledger, to show him that he can't get to Reed, to mess with his head.

Reed's successful too because in the next second, Ledger shoots his hand out and pushes Reed back.

Oh God.

And finally, we have a reaction.

It pulses through Reed like a current, obliterating his relaxed persona, making him rigid and unforgiving. And when Reed takes a threatening step closer to Ledger, Ledger does the same, bringing them back to standing toe to toe, their bodies sweaty, their heads bent toward each other as if they're exchanging confidences rather than threats.

The two beasts, the Mustang and the Thorn.

Just when I think that they're going to start punching each other, someone steps in.

My oldest brother and their coach, Conrad.

He absolutely hates this rivalry. *Hates*. He hates Ledger's anger. He hates Reed's recklessness.

He hates the fact that every high school team in the entire freaking state knows about this. About how the two star players of Bardstown High can't quit measuring their dicks on the field — his words, not mine — and they always take advantage of it.

My oldest brother gets between his two players, plants one palm on each of their chests and pushes them away.

When he's managed to break the two heavily panting, angry-looking guys apart, Conrad wraps his large hands around the backs of their necks and pulls them in again, giving them a piece of his mind.

When he's done Conrad straightens up and pins them with his hard gaze for a few seconds before letting them go. And just like that the game resumes.

"So that's *my* brother," I tell her, repeating her words. "The one who was clearly trying to beat your brother up. Ledger. And the one who got between them? The coach? That's my brother too, Conrad."

"Oh wow," Tempest breathes out.

"Yeah." I nod. "See? You can't even joke about it. Not in Bardstown."

She keeps staring at the field for a few seconds before turning to me. "So… I don't think you're gonna like what I'm going to say next."

"What?"

"That I think *I* have a huge crush on *your* brother." Her gray eyes — so unmistakably like Reed's — pop wide. "I've never seen someone stand up to my brother like that. Ledger."

She breathes out his name in a dreamy voice.

"I don't –"

"Oh, and you're coming with me," she speaks over me.

"Coming with you where?"

"To the party."

"What party?"

"The aftergame party that Reed always throws."

Chapter 2

I'm going to a party.

But that's not important.

That's not even on the list of top three important things.

It's not as if I haven't been to parties before. I have. A few times.

But between school and my dance classes, I don't get a lot of free time so I'm not that experienced with them either.

The ones that I have been to were loud and overcrowded and had really bad music.

Not to mention, they sort of freak my brothers out.

They don't show it though, no. For my sake, my four overprotective older brothers try to hide their worry.

They try to hide the fact that every time I go to a party, they're all always watching the clock. They're always watching the door too – well, Con does because he likes to stay home, the rest of them are usually out and about with their friends – and texting each other to see if I'm back.

I think they have a group chat together.

I mean, we have one where all five siblings are included but I think they have a secret four-person chat where they sort of obsess over if I'm okay.

I guess even though I'm in high school now, I'm still their baby sister.

The one who followed them around while growing up. The one whose ballet recitals they all went to. The one who couldn't fall asleep by herself for the longest time when our mom died, so all my brothers would take turns during the night and stay with me in my room.

I don't really remember that part, about not falling asleep by myself, probably because I was only four when Mom died, but every time I think of it, I can't stop crying and smiling.

I can't stop the rush of love I feel for my big brothers.

So over time I decided not to go to parties at all.

I don't want to worry them for something I don't really have the time for and don't like to begin with anyway.

But I'm going to this one.

And I'm going without telling my brothers.

That's their *one* rule – to keep them updated about my whereabouts.

They'll let me go to parties, or to the movies with my friends, but they need to know where I am at all times.

They don't know where I am right now.

They *think* they know; I texted them saying I'm studying with one of my friends and that I'll be back by my curfew.

They don't know that I'm here.

That I'm going to a party thrown by Reed Roman Jackson.

My brother's rival.

The guy I'm supposed to stay away from.

And I have.

I *have* stayed away from him.

I have been extremely careful never to be in the same place as him.

If he's in the courtyard with his friends, I'm in the library. If he's in the cafeteria, sitting in his usual spot, I know to stay on the opposite side of the room.

If I see him sitting inside his Mustang in the parking lot after practice, listening to music with his eyes closed, I turn around and walk through the soccer field to get to the bus stop.

Basically, I have done everything in my power to stay away from him.

So I don't really know what I'm doing here.

I don't even know how it happened. How I got pulled into going. By his sister, no less. Who I met only a little while ago.

But one minute we were watching the game and I was explaining to her about the rivalry, which I'm so glad to say that she doesn't really understand either. And the next, the game is over and Tempest is pulling me away from the field, telling me that we shouldn't be controlled by our brothers' stupidity.

That I should ignore all the rivalry stuff and go to a party with a friend — *her* — if I want to. And besides, if I don't like it, I'm free to leave.

So here I am.

Going to a party with a friend who has promised me that I can leave if I want to.

And I want to, I think.

Because as soon as I see the crowd, I realize that this is even stupider and more dangerous than I originally thought.

This party, which is happening in the middle of the woods that border Bardstown, is full of people from the Mustang camp.

The soccer players who worship him, the students from Bardstown High who are in awe of him and girls from all over town who want to be with him.

All of them are either laughing or talking or swaying with the music with red cups in their hands. I even hear people chanting his name off to the side.

Of course, Callie. This is his party.

This is his territory.

Everything here is his.

Except me.

I'm the trespasser. I'm the one who doesn't belong. I'm the anomaly here.

And what if someone recognizes me, the sister of his rival?

What if they tell Ledger about it?

Oh Jesus Christ, I haven't thought this through, have I?

I have *not* thought this through at all.

What if he uses this, me being here, as something to rile Ledger up in the next game?

He's done it before.

I mean, he hasn't used *me* to rile my brother up. But he *has* used things against Ledger. And well, Ledger has done the same, but yeah.

I need to get out.

I need to leave.

I grab Tempest's hand and try to stop her from getting into the thick of the crowd. "I think I'm…"

Going to leave.

That's what I was going to say before I left my words hanging.

Because just then the crowd parts, the horde of swaying bodies falls apart, and there opens a direct line of vision.

To him.

The guy who owns everything around me.

Reed Roman Jackson.

He's sitting on a log, his powerful thighs spread, his demeanor casual, his body leaning forward with his elbows resting on his knees.

And as usual, he's not alone.

There's a girl draped over him — I think she's from school — and she's talking to him, whispering something in his ear.

It's not the fact that a girl is hanging off his arm that makes me pause, no. I've seen this before at school, multiple times. I mean, it would be more of a shock to see him *without* a girl.

It's not the girl. It's him.

It's the fact that despite very meager lighting in the space — the moon and headlights from parked cars — every single thing about him is so clear, so vivid.

So *alive*.

Like his hair, for example.

His spiky, dark hair. The strands of which have little droplets sitting on the tips, making me think that he just had a shower, right after the game.

And maybe he was in a rush to get to his party.

Because he didn't bother with a shave and his jaw is stubbled with a five o'clock shadow.

I don't think he likes it though.

Because I always catch him touching it, rubbing and scratching it as if irritated.

A gesture that's more like a habit to him. That he's performing right now even, as he talks to the girl, his face turned toward her, a smirk lurking on his ruby-red lips.

A gesture that makes me think that maybe he likes smooth things. Soft things.

Things like his hoodie.

His white hoodie, to be precise.

So his hoodies are famous around school and in town. They're always white or cream colored and they always seem thick and cozy.

And of course soft.

Also, his hoodies are his favorite thing to wear.

Because he always has them on — well, except in summers but still. That and his dark jeans.

Black and white.

And needless to say, girls around town are obsessed with his hoodies.

They stare at them. They talk about them. They want to touch his hoodies and play with the strings. They want to wear his hoodies too.

Which from what I've heard is a privilege.

Not every girl gets to wear them, only the special ones, and so it's a coveted thing: Reed Roman Jackson and his hoodies.

Even now the girl who's wrapped around him is tracing the fabric, pulling on the strings, fingering the edge of his sleeve at his wrist as she laughs at something he's said.

Stop staring, Callie.

Right.

I need to stop staring. But the thing is that it's very hard to do.

See, that's his magic I think.

The dark magic that I was talking about.

It makes him glow.

Like his very skin absorbs whatever light is in the vicinity, leaving the rest of the world in darkness.

So much so that the only thing you can see, the only thing that you *can* focus on, is him and nothing else.

But.

But, but, but.

I'm one of the Thornes. I'm my brothers' sister. I know better.

So I should look away, and I do.

Well, I try to.

Because the moment I make the decision to look away, *he* decides to look up at me.

And I step back.

As if someone has pushed me. As if *he* has pushed me. He has put his hands on me and I had to step back, *had* to, under the weight of his touch.

The strength of his gaze, his wolf eyes that land right on me.

And now that he has found me, he's not letting me go.

He's absolutely *not* letting me leave. My legs won't even move. They won't.

Because they somehow, the traitors, know that he wants me here.

It's in the way that he slowly straightens up, the way he completely abandons interest in the girl beside him. It's in the way something breaks open on his face, on his gorgeous, *gorgeous* face made up of sharp, smooth, fascinating lines as soon as he sees me.

Something that looks a lot like interest. Curiosity.

Something that makes his pretty eyes go slightly wide followed by a tiny smirk on his lips.

It's like... he's excited that I'm here.

It's like he's thinking, *now the fun begins...*

I'm not sure how I know all of this. But I do.

It's not as if I'm an expert on Reed Roman Jackson.

I mean, we haven't even talked before.

This may be the first time that he's looked at me, and this morning when I woke up, I had no idea that today would be the day he'd look at me for the first time ever.

So yeah, I have no clue how I know all this except that I feel exposed under his eyes. I feel vulnerable and fragile. I feel like I've somehow walked into an evil den.

His evil den.

Which isn't that far from the truth.

I *am* in his evil den and I need to move. Right now.

I need to run. I need to…

Suddenly there's a commotion and Reed's attention breaks away from me. And I think I draw my first breath since he found me in this chaos.

It's Tempest. The source of commotion, I mean. She's running toward Reed.

Yikes.

I'd completely forgotten about her. I don't even know when she broke away from me and made her way through the crowd to go to her brother.

Who definitely looks surprised right now.

He even stands up from his kingly perch just as Tempest launches herself at him. Squealing, she wraps her arms and legs around him and hugs him tight.

And right in front of my eyes, I see a new side of Reed.

A side that hugs his sister back just as tightly. A side that smiles — a true smile — and laughs when his sister moves away and doesn't stop talking. A side that looks at her with a fondness that I've never seen before.

Or rather, that I've only seen on *my* brothers' faces when I surprise them with a new pair of knitted socks or some chocolate chip cookies.

Right in front of my eyes, I discover that Reed Roman Jackson, the gorgeous villain, my brother's rival and enemy, loves his little sister.

Something moves in my chest at this.

Something achy and swollen.

And God, I have to leave now.

I have to.

The longer I stay here, the more restless I feel. The more likely it becomes that someone might recognize me and tell Ledger.

It bugs me to leave Tempest like this because I really like her. But I have to go.

So taking a deep breath and with a last look at Tempest talking to Reed, who's chuckling, I turn around and start walking.

I hunch my shoulders and duck my head, trying to make myself as invisible as possible so no one pays me any attention. Although I'm not sure that I'm walking in the right direction or the direction that I came from.

But it's okay.

I'll find my way out.

So I keep walking, my feet crunching the leaves, until I leave the party behind and get deeper into the trees.

It should be kinda scary to be walking around the woods in the dark. But I grew up here, in this town. Even though I've never really ventured into these woods, I know I'll be safe.

Well, I know that until I hear a noise.

A series of noises actually.

They're not loud or anything. It's just that the woods are quiet and so they *seem* loud. They seem urgent and needy.

And oh my God I come to a halt.

My heart is banging inside my chest. The hairs on the back of my neck are standing up because what the heck is going on?

What...

A twig snaps next. Then a moan comes, followed by heavy breathing.

A second later though when I hear a grunt — a manly grunt — everything becomes clear.

Oh my God.

Someone — a *guy* — is doing something to a girl.

Isn't he?

This is what's happening. A stupid drunk guy is doing something to an innocent girl and I need to go help her.

That's why my brothers are always worried. Because this is what happens at high school parties. Guys drink and go crazy and think they can do whatever they want to a girl.

Well, not on my watch.

He doesn't know what's coming for him.

Me.

I'm coming for him and I know how to punch.

Yeah, that's right. I know how to throw a mean, *mean* punch – four brothers, remember? – and he's getting it.

Right in his face.

Swallowing down my fear, I start to walk toward the noises.

I'm trying to be as quiet as possible.

I don't want that *animal* to know that I'm coming for him. I'm gonna take him by surprise. That's the best way to do the most damage. That's what my brothers taught me.

But as it turns out, I don't think I'll be using any of the punching skills that I learned from my brothers.

Because there is no drunk guy and no innocent girl.

I mean, he could be drunk and she could be innocent but he's not doing anything to her that she doesn't want. In fact, she seems pretty into it, what he's doing to her. Which is kissing.

He's kissing her and she's kissing him back.

They're standing under a tree and there are a couple of candles around them. A blanket, beers.

Oops.

I think I crashed a date. Which is completely escalating right now.

Now that I'm close and thankfully hiding behind a tree of my own, I can hear more noises. Chuckles, rustling of their clothes, a few murmurs.

And gosh, I can see stuff too.

Their hands and legs and their mouths. It's like they're attacking each other — happily but attacking nonetheless with their lips and limbs.

I don't think I've ever seen anything like this before.

What I mean is that I have seen people kiss before even though I've never been kissed myself. But this is something... else.

This is passion and lust and rawness and holy God, I can't stop looking and I know...

My thoughts break when I hear another noise.

Or rather a *voice*.

I hear a voice.

A voice saying, "You like that, huh?"

It's rich and smooth. *Deep.*

God, so deep.

It makes me think of taking a dive off a skyscraper. It's strange that a voice can invoke such imagery and such a reckless, dangerous image at that. But I swear I feel the rush of air on my body, the adrenaline pumping through my veins as if I'm really flying.

Just because I heard a voice. *His* voice.

It's his. I know.

Even though it has never been directed at me, I've heard it before, and without volition, memorized it. And now it's here.

The voice. *Him.*

And before I can think anything else, assess the situation or even absorb it, I spin around.

As if a string is looped around my body, and he holds the other end. And he's tugging it viciously, making me spin like the ballerina that I am.

And there he is again.

A lot closer to me than he's ever been.

Reed Roman Jackson.

Chapter 3

The first time I saw him, off the soccer field I mean – I'd seen him play plenty of times before that – was my first day at Bardstown High.

It was during my lunch period.

I was trying to find the administration office without having to bother either Ledger or Conrad for every little thing, and despite being given very explicit directions leading to it, I think I took a wrong turn somewhere.

I ended up in a deserted sort of hallway with only a few lingering students in it.

I was trying to find my way back when I stumbled upon an empty classroom.

Well, empty except for two people.

One of which was him.

That was the first time I'd seen him out of his green and white soccer uniform, without sweat dripping from his brows and without a vicious flush covering his features from running across the field.

In fact, it was the first time I'd seen his features clearly and not from a distance.

The first time I'd seen how breathtakingly beautiful he was. How his features, sharp and angled, were designed to make your heart ache as soon as you looked at him.

Heartbreakingly beautiful. That's what I thought in that moment.

Also, tall.

It was something I'd never realized before, his towering frame.

I remember thinking that Reed Roman Jackson was the tallest guy I'd ever seen. Taller than even my brothers, and my brothers are some of the tallest people I know.

In his white hoodie, something else that I saw for the first time, Reed stood leaning against the wall by the whiteboard and God, the top of his head almost reached up to the edge of it. His head was slightly thrown back, exposing the masculine bulge of his Adam's apple and the strained veins running down the side of his neck.

Oh, and his eyes were closed and his jaw was tight.

At first, I didn't get why.

I didn't get why he'd be standing there with his eyes closed like that, his jaw tight before loosening up and his mouth parting on a quiet breath.

At first, I also thought that he was alone.

But then I heard a sound — a moan — and I realized that there was a girl in the room with him. And she was on her knees, almost hidden by the teacher's desk, in front of him.

That's when I knew.

That the girl he was with was… you know, doing stuff to him. And before I could stop myself, I gasped.

I gasped loudly and as soon as I did, they heard it.

The girl stopped doing stuff to him and a frown appeared between his brows.

To this day, I *know* he was going to open his eyes a second later. And when he did, his gaze would land directly on me. So I ran. I didn't wait for them to figure out that someone was watching them and that it was me.

I ran and saved myself that day.

I don't think I can save myself now.

I don't even think I can run. And it becomes even harder when another moan comes from behind me.

This one particularly loud and needy and like an idiot, *idiot*, I gasp like I did the first time I saw him.

But unlike that time, I'm not hiding behind a door and his eyes aren't closed.

They are open and they are on me and at my gasp, his eyes, those pretty wolf eyes, glint. His lips, ruby-red and plush, tip up slightly too.

And I don't think I've ever felt more exposed in my life.

More seen and vulnerable and trapped and… thrilled, all at the same time, and I think I almost explode with all the jumbled emotions when I hear, "Oh God, Justin. Stop fucking around and put it in already."

And I think *he* knows it.

The guy who's standing in front of me and watching me through all this.

Because out of nowhere he jars every cell in my body when he calls out, "Hey Justin!"

This time I don't even bother stopping myself or castigating myself for doing it, I just *gasp*.

Nor do I stop myself from widening my eyes and questioning him with them: *What are you doing?*

He seems to hear my unspoken question and he answers me in the most non-traditional sense ever.

Without breaking our gaze, he calls out again, "Take it some-where else." He pauses for a few seconds as squeaks and curses break out. "You're corrupting good little freshman girls."

I wince at his description and his smirk grows.

That was not fair.

I'm *not* a good little freshman girl.

I mean, I am. But he didn't have to say it in such a conde-scending manner. In a manner that makes me feel like an innocent, inexperienced flower.

Which again, I am, but still.

"Freshman?" A male voice – Justin – answers. "How'd a fresh-man get in here?"

Reed's mouth twists into a sardonic smile as he answers Justin while still looking at me. "Maybe this year's crop's sneakier than we thought."

This time the girl speaks. "Well, kick them out! They're boring. And God, they're so easily shocked."

My mouth falls open.

That is *not* true.

We're not easily shocked.

Reed finds my reaction highly amusing and a small chuckle escapes him. "Yeah, they are. Aren't they?" I glare at him but that only makes him chuckle once again. "So that's why you need to take your X-rated show somewhere else. Let them dream about birds and bees for one more night."

I'm outraged at this.

Outraged and offended.

Who does he think I am? And why the heck is he talking about me like I'm not even here?

Justin doesn't find it offensive, however. He thinks it's funny, and so does the girl, who giggles and replies, "Hate to break it to you,

Reed. But as annoying as freshmen are, I *think* they know how babies are made."

Somehow, his animal eyes grow even more potent and I'm forced to take a step back.

Not that I have anywhere to go really.

My spine is pretty much stuck to the tree I was hiding behind. And he knows that.

His eyes flick to the ground to gauge the distance between us before lifting back to my face. "Yeah? Well, this one looks a little too daisy fresh. I'm not sure she can handle your sex ed class without passing out. So fuck off."

I think I just pulled a muscle.

Because this is the hardest that I've frowned and glared and pursed my lips at someone, the hardest and the longest.

Meanwhile his friends, who still don't know that I'm standing here, listening in, chuckle and laugh and make crude comments from behind me.

When they're done though, they scramble off.

Leaving me alone with him.

The guy who's staring at me like I'm the most interesting thing he has seen tonight. The most interesting thing he's ever seen, actually, and now that I'm in his clutches, he can't wait to play with me.

He can't wait to open me up, unravel me, take me apart.

He can't *wait*.

"I'm not daisy fresh," I say and regret it soon after.

This is what I say to him, *this*.

Of all the things I could've said, like *how dare you talk about me while I was standing right here* or *how dare you sneak up on me* — because he did sneak up on me, right? — I say the most asinine thing ever.

I go to take it back.

But no words come out of my mouth because he chooses that very moment to move his eyes.

Which makes me realize that he hasn't looked anywhere else except my face ever since he got here.

He's changing that now though.

He's slowly making his way down my swallowing, hiccupping throat, my heavily breathing chest.

Even though there's very little light, I know he can see me clearly.

I think it's his wolf eyes; they can see in the dark.

They can see everything: my cardigan that I knitted myself – it's early February and unusually un-winter-like weather that only requires a light sweater – and my dress.

When his eyes move over it, I realize something else too.

Something both silly and important.

Daisies.

I'm wearing daisies.

My dress has printed daisies on it. That's why he said that.

Oh, and it's white, my dress.

Holy crap.

Lost in the woods, I'm dressed in his favorite color — white — and he's staring at me in a way that makes him look like a predator. Part human, part wolf, who hunts unsuspecting girls like me.

Girls foolish enough to wander alone at midnight.

"I beg to differ," he drawls when he finishes his perusal and comes back up to my face. "You look daisy fresh to me."

See?

Predator.

Beautiful, gorgeous… predator.

I fist my dress and press my back into the tree. Raising my chin, I try to look more experienced even though I'm anything but.

"And I'm not a freshman either."

"Is that so?"

Look at that tone, so condescending.

God, I hate him.

Also, I hate myself for saying that.

But now that I have, I'm going to stay the course, because backing down would be even more cowardly.

"Yes," I tell him. "I mean I am. But I should've been a sophomore. I repeated a year. And so I'm older and hence wiser. I'm about to turn sixteen in three months."

All true.

I did repeat a year. Back when my mom had been sick and eventually died of cancer.

Everything had fallen on Conrad, who was only eighteen at the time and a freshman in college. He had so many, *many* balls to juggle back then, what with my mom's deteriorating health, getting a job, keeping the house, taking care of my brothers and me – well, all my brothers chipped in and helped with me, but they were all kids themselves – that perfect attendance wasn't very high on the list.

So my teachers thought it would be best if I repeated a year.

"Sweet sixteen, huh," he murmurs, his eyes all glowy and intense.

I swallow. "Yes. So you shouldn't have said what you said. To your friends."

"What'd I say to my friends?"

I fist my dress harder.

I know what he's doing. He's provoking me. Because this is what he does.

He, Reed Roman Jackson, provokes and I, Calliope Juliet Thorne, make good choices.

So I should make a good choice here and backtrack.

But something in his eyes, in his casual but also tight demeanor, makes me say, "That I don't know."

"You don't know what?"

I lick my dry lips. "That I don't know how babies are made."

"And how *are* they made?"

Stop. Just stop, Callie.

But you know what, I hate that he's so amused right now.

It makes me want to say it, throw him off, shock him.

So I widen my stance and throw back my shoulders as I say, "They are made when you f-fuck."

What?

What did I say?

Oh God.

I think I've shocked myself. I've never ever said that word before, never.

I've heard it though. A million times. I have four brothers, of course I've heard it. But I've never said it.

Not until tonight.

Not until *he* made me say it.

The guy who has gone slightly still. Like he wasn't expecting me to take the bait.

Well, good.

There. That'll teach him not to underestimate me.

"Is that the first time you've said that word?" he asks mockingly, with his eyes narrowed.

I hate that he makes me feel so breathless and young. "Why, are you proud that you made me say that word for the first time?"

His jaw moves, that stubbled, sharp thing. It tics for a moment before he says, "Not particularly, no."

"Well –"

"Don't ever say it again."

"What?"

"It doesn't suit you."

I'm so confused.

Did he just… tell me not to say the F word?

He did, didn't he?

But that's…

Who is *he* to tell me that? Who is he to tell me anything?

"Yeah, I don't think you can tell me what I can or can't say," I tell him, raising my eyebrows, which only makes his jaw tic even more. "And while we're at it, you shouldn't have talked about me with your friends like I wasn't here. That's bad manners."

"What about crashing someone's party? Does that also fall under bad manners?" he shoots back.

My lips part.

Okay, he got me.

I *am* crashing his party. I wasn't really invited, was I?

"I wasn't… I was leaving," I say. "I just got lost."

"Lost."

"Yes."

His eyes glow again and something flashes through his features that I don't really understand. "You do that a lot, don't you? Get lost."

"I don't… what?"

"In the woods. In the hallways…"

He leaves that sentence hanging but I get his meaning. I get it and oh my God.

He knows.

He knows it was me. That I saw him. Months and months ago, on my first day at Bardstown High.

He *knows*.

A rush of heat fans over my cheeks. My throat, my entire body actually, and can I just dissolve into this tree?

Can I just please disappear?

"I'm… I didn't think you…"

"Knew?" He smirks. "I did."

"But I was… quiet."

"You weren't as quiet as you think you were. Besides…"

"Besides what?"

He leans forward slightly, the strings of his hoodie swinging, as if confessing a secret. "I didn't mind. Being watched by you. The Thorn Princess. And if you hadn't run away, I would've gotten rid of her."

"You would have?"

"Yeah."

"W-why?"

"So I could focus all my attention." Then, with a lowered voice, "On you."

My heart bangs against my ribs, bruising them. Battering them, making them throb.

In fact, my whole body throbs.

I can feel it. I can *hear* it even.

Even so, I try to hold on to my composure. I try to hold on to the authority in my voice. "As if."

"As if what?"

"As if I would've… let you or even stayed."

"I think you would've." He keeps his gaze steady and unwavering, both intense and slightly amused. "And I think you would've enjoyed it too. Girls love it when I give them my attention. They're known to even beg for it. On their knees particularly."

My knees tingle at that as if zapped by a current. They buckle too.

As if they're going to bend. As if I'm going to fall.

But I won't.

"I'm not like other girls," I tell him. "I don't beg."

Something about that makes him smirk. "Every girl begs. She just needs the right thing to beg for."

I narrow my eyes at him. "My brothers would kill you."

I'm the Thorn Princess, as he said.

That's what they call me. I'm the princess, the little sister of four legendary soccer gods who so completely hate him.

"I think I can handle myself," he says, all casual like.

"You should be afraid of my brothers, you know."

"Why is that?"

"There's four of them and only one of you."

"So?"

"So you shouldn't talk to me this way."

He gives me a once-over before asking in an amused voice, "Why, does it make you want to beg me for something?"

"It doesn't –"

"You shouldn't worry about me too much. As I said, I can handle myself."

I think so too.

He looks so cavalier, so fearless. *Reckless.*

My brothers could crush him if they wanted to.

My brothers could crush *any* guy if they wanted to and everyone in this town knows that. Everyone in Bardstown is afraid of them.

Not him though.

Not Reed Roman Jackson.

He never was and he never will be.

I mean, look at what just happened on the field. What happens every time on the field and also off it. And before I can stop myself, I ask, "Why do you hate Ledger so much?"

"Who says I hate him?"

"You're always fighting with him, provoking him. Like you did today. On the field."

"So you were watching, huh?" he murmurs instead.

"Of course. I watch every game. For Ledger. And for Con."

He stares at me for a beat before chuckling softly. "Of course. Well, your *brother* makes it easy. To provoke."

"Why can't you just get along? You're on the same team."

"You tell him to quit the team and we will."

"He's the captain," I tell him like he doesn't know.

"Not for long."

"What is that supposed to mean?"

He shrugs, his mountain-like shoulders rising and falling. "It means that he must be getting tired."

"Of what?"

"Of doing a shitty job of it. Of losing to his forward."

Right.

Of course.

The stupid contest.

So after Reed provoked Ledger, he lost his head for a while and in that while, Reed scored and won their contest, along with winning the game.

"Your *team* won," I say, exasperated. "So he didn't lose. And neither did you."

"You're right, I didn't."

"You know it's a stupid contest, right? It doesn't mean anything," I say.

He nods sagely. "Yeah, you should say that to your brother. It might help him sleep tonight. After losing, I mean."

I study him a beat, all proud and handsome.

Arrogant.

A wrecking ball really.

"Is winning that important to you?"

"Winning is everything," he replies gravely.

"And what about team spirit?"

"Fuck team spirit."

"And love of the game?"

He scoffs. "Yeah, the only thing I love is being the best. *And* my Mustang. I love that too."

Oh, his Mustang.

How did I forget about that?

The other reason why people call him the Wild Mustang is because he owns one. A Mustang, the car. Obviously in white, and rumor has it that he loves it.

It's his most precious possession.

Which is why one time, Ledger and guys from the Thorn camp slashed his tires before an important game, just to mess with Reed, and I have to admit that I didn't like that.

I felt bad for Reed.

But then I found out that Ledger did it in retaliation against Reed sleeping with a girl he liked, again before a big game, to mess with Ledger's head.

So yeah, that killed my sympathy.

"Your Mustang," I repeat in a flat voice.

"Yeah. It goes from zero to sixty faster than a girl can strip. What's not to love?"

I'm... disappointed.

I don't know why.

I mean, it's not something that I didn't expect.

For years, Ledger has been telling me the same thing. He's been telling me that Reed doesn't care about the team. That Reed is selfish. He only looks out for himself.

Conrad has been saying it too.

That's why he picked Ledger as the captain instead of Reed. Even though they're both excellent. Even though Reed's even better on some occasions.

So I've got no clue why I'm disappointed at hearing this from his own mouth when I already knew what his answer was going to be.

Reed Roman Jackson is exactly what they told me he'd be.

A villain.

Sighing, I duck my head. "I'm leaving."

I don't even manage to take a step before he says, "Not so fast."

My head snaps up. "What?"

As if that wasn't jarring enough, him stopping me, he decides to make me hyperventilate by starting to approach me.

So far we've been standing at a respectable, comfortable distance. Like twelve feet or so. But now he's closing that distance, one step at a time.

Each swing of his legs is almost a foot long and makes the powerful muscles in his thighs bulge. Makes his boots crush the leaves noisily.

I press myself to the tree as I watch him approach me. As I watch him watch me.

He knows I'm afraid.

I can see it on his features.

His beautifully relaxed mouth, the lines of satisfaction around his eyes.

"What are you doing?" I ask, my fingers digging into the bark of the tree.

He stops probably one arm away, so solid and towering, as he muses, "I'm assuming your brothers don't know that you're here."

His low voice makes me swallow. "Why?"

"Just a hunch." He dips his chin toward me, bringing us ever so slightly closer, as he smiles, sort of evilly. "And I also think they're not going to like the fact that you've wandered into the enemy camp."

I'm not sure if it's his nearness or what but I think that every part of his body is dangerous. That his blade-like cheekbones could cut and his teeth could rip.

His fingers could squeeze and hurt and that he could somehow make me like all of that.

He could make me *like* the way he'd hurt me.

I raise my chin, trying to look brave. "Are you going to tell them?"

Those sharp teeth of his come out to play when he smiles again. "Now that's an interesting thought, isn't it?"

"Please don't," I blurt out before I can stop myself. "As I said, I was leaving. You don't have to say anything. You could just… keep this between us."

Great. Just great, Callie.

Tell the villain that you want him to keep a secret.

As expected, his eyes glow.

Like he was waiting for me to slip up.

Like he was waiting for me to fall into his trap and only God can save me now.

Maybe not even Him because when he speaks in a low, raspy voice I have to press my legs together as his words drop down and sit somewhere low, very low in my stomach.

"What do I get in return? If I keep it." He tilts his head to the side. "Between us."

Run, I tell myself.

Just please push him away and start running.

But all I do is stand here, staring up at him, even when it becomes difficult, even when it strains my neck because he's so tall and big.

So beautiful that I don't know where else to look.

I also don't know how to stop myself from asking, "W-what do you want?"

This is what he wanted, isn't it?

Yeah, because his features grow warm with satisfaction before he drawls, "You."

"What?"

Slowly, those eyes of his travel all the way down to my white ballet flats. "I hear you're a ballerina."

My right foot tries to climb on to my left under his scrutiny. "Yes."

He lifts his eyes. "Then I want you to spin like one."

"I-I'm sorry?"

He shifts on his feet, making himself bigger somehow, pushing at the very fabric of the air, as he explains, "You like to dance, don't you? So I want you to dance. For me."

I blink at him.

I think I heard him wrong. He cannot possibly be asking what I think he's asking.

Just to be sure, I question, "You want me to dance for you?"

"Yeah."

"In exchange for you keeping this between us?"

"That's the idea."

My mouth falls open. "You're insane."

"I'd like to think of myself as someone who sees an opportunity and seizes it."

"What opportunity?"

"I was bored and then a ballerina fell into my lap. A good one too, from what I've heard." Again, he gives me a once-over. "So I want you to entertain me."

I ignore the flush of pleasure at his off-handed compliment. Mostly because it's *off-handed* and followed by a very presumptuous demand.

And also because, as I said, he's insane.

"What do you think this is?" I ask, exasperated. "A movie from the fifties or something? Where you're a cigar-smoking villain and you're blackmailing me into dancing for you."

"A cigar-smoking villain." He's amused. "I'm known to smoke a cigarette here and there and I usually prefer the term asshole but I like that. It has a certain flair to it."

"I'm not going to dance for you."

"Well then, I'm going to enjoy watching Ledger lose his shit in the next game when I tell him how pretty his sister looked, standing before me, begging me to keep her secret."

I clench my teeth in anger.

Have I said that I hate him?

I really, really do.

"Fine. *Fine*," I snap at him. "I'll dance for you. But just for making me do that, you also have to apologize to my brother."

"Apologize."

"Yes. You provoked him on the field today. I don't know what you said but you're going to apologize to him when you see him next."

A flash of irritation tightens his mouth. "Just so you know, I don't do well with orders."

I go up on my tiptoes then.

Because he's so tall and I want to get up in his face, which of course he notices, my feet arched up and my calves strained.

And something in my struggle to appear all strong in front of him turns his gaze even more molten.

"Well, you're gonna have to start," I tell him, "because I'm not dancing until you promise me."

He watches me silently for a few moments before stepping back.

And I think it's over.

I've called his bluff.

But then, he fishes something out of his back pocket, his cell phone, and presses a few buttons on the screen.

Suddenly, the music that was a dull sound in the background flares to life. The air fills with heavy bass and people back at the party cheer.

He commands in a husky voice, "Make it good."

Just like that, he's called *my* bluff and I'm supposed to dance for him.

How did this happen? How is this my life?

When I woke up this morning all I wanted to do was get through my classes, go to the game, and go back home to the scarf that I'm knitting for Conrad.

But somehow, I'm here, about to dance for my brother's rival.

That's not the worst part.

The worst part is that I want to.

I *want* to dance for him.

I've been *wanting* to dance for him ever since I saw him play for the first time three years ago. When both he and Ledger made the team.

God.

I'm so embarrassed to admit that. So ashamed.

But the thing is that the way he plays soccer, the way he moves across the field, with grace and beauty and a certain recklessness, fills me with music.

Not to mention, the music that he's put on… is gorgeous.

It's a mix of hip hop and rock and when the word *ballerina* flutters in the air, I let go of the tree that I've been clinging to and step forward.

When the guy in the song calls me his – his ballerina – it feels like *he's* calling me that.

The Wild Mustang who's asked me to dance for him.

And when the guy follows it up with how his ballerina drops her body like a stripper, I have to lick my dried lips and wipe my sweaty hands on my dress.

I should be offended – this song reeks of dirty, filthy sex – but I'm not.

I'm not even nervous.

There isn't the slightest bit of hesitation in me.

My body is buzzing with excitement, with shooting stars, and when I close my eyes for a second, I see light behind my eyelids.

I can't see anything on his face though.

It's expressionless, tight.

But when I take a deep breath and raise my arms, his features change.

They become somehow sharper and more chiseled but also fluid.

I think it's his lips that part slightly when I take my first spin and his eyes that shine like diamonds when I begin to sway my hips to the beat.

And after that my eagerness to dance for him knows no bounds.

I'm dying, actually *dying*, to spin for him, to sway and move.

To rock my hips and bite my lips.

To look him in his wolf eyes that grow alert with my every leap and jump. More on edge.

In fact, his whole body seems on edge, excited even.

His whole body moves to keep me in sight as I circle around him.

His feet spin when I do.

His fists clench when I throw my arms in the air.

His mouth parts when mine does to take in a shaky breath.

God.

Reed Roman Jackson is just as eager as me.

Just as tightly wound and I've never seen him this way.

I've never seen him *excited* for anything.

The knowledge of that, the knowledge that his heart might be racing just as fast as my heart and that the beads of sweat on his forehead match the beads of sweat on mine, makes me dizzy.

It makes me drunk and drugged and so high on his attention that when the song crescendos and I do my last spin, I stumble.

The world tips and I lose my balance. The ground seems to have vanished from under my feet and I have no choice but to fall.

He catches me at the last second though.

His arm goes around my waist and instead of crashing down to the ground, I go crashing into his body. My hands land on his ribs and my fingers clutch onto his hoodie.

A thousand thoughts, a thousand sensations, explode in my mind, but the very first that jumps out is that it's soft.

His hoodie.

It's the softest, coziest, plushest thing I've ever touched. Even more than the sweaters that I knit for my brothers.

The thought that immediately follows is that no wonder he loves it, his hoodie.

No wonder he wears it all the time, because everything else about him is hard and harsh and sharp.

His strong arm that's wrapped around my waist. The power in his thighs that are pressed against my stomach.

Panting and looking up into his animal eyes, I whisper, "I know that it might not matter, coming from me, but…" I swallow, gripping his hoodie tighter, my brain foggy and my tongue spewing words I don't understand. "But I think you're amazing. O-on the field, I mean. You're just so gorgeous and reckless and feral, the way you… play. It's no wonder that they call you the Wild Mustang. It's no wonder…"

I trail off, embarrassed.

What the heck am I saying?

Why am I telling him this?

I shouldn't. These are my private thoughts. *Traitor* thoughts that I shouldn't even entertain.

"No wonder what?" he rasps, his strong, muscled arm squeezing my waist.

I can't stop the words from tumbling out of my mouth then. "No wonder why girls can't stop watching you."

No wonder why I can't stop watching you.

A blush fans over my cheeks as soon as I say it and I lower my eyes.

"It does," he says.

I look up. "What?"

He squeezes my waist again. "It matters. Coming from you."

"Oh."

"And you're not a princess."

"I'm not?"

He shakes his head slowly, his eyes all intense and piercing. "You're a fairy."

I lick my lips then and his wolf eyes flare and I open my tingling mouth to say something — not sure what — when there's a shout.

"Jackson!"

My eyes pop wide at that voice and my fingers in his hoodie tighten even more.

Because I know it. I know that voice too.

It belongs to someone I know and someone I love and someone I'm completely betraying by being here.

My brother, Ledger.

Chapter 4

My brother is here.

Somehow, he's found me, and I'm wrapped around the guy he hates the most.

The guy who should be worried right now.

Very, very worried.

But he's not.

He's sweeping his eyes over my face as if memorizing it before he smiles slightly and steps back, easily getting out of my grip.

My fingers feel empty without his hoodie but I don't have the time to dwell on it because I hear Ledger again.

"Get the fuck away from her."

At this, I finally gather my wits and turn to look at my brother.

He's charging at us, rage flickering over his features.

Like Reed, my brother is tall, not *quite* as tall as Reed, and is muscled and strong. He's slightly wider in the shoulders and chest than Reed, and with the way he's glaring at Reed, I feel like he's going to use his size to his advantage.

But I really wish that this was it.

That the threat of Ledger practically bulldozing Reed, who believe it or not *still* does not look worried about it at all, was the only threat to contend with.

It's not, though.

Because I have not one but four brothers, and somehow, they're *all* here.

All of them.

How are they here? How did they know where to find me?

Even the two who're supposed to be away at college, Stellan and Shepard, the twins.

They're identical to each other and are also tall – again, not as tall as Reed – and built like Ledger, slightly wider in the chest and shoulders.

The biggest one though is my oldest brother, Conrad.

He's the tallest – definitely as tall as Reed – and the broadest too.

He isn't charging the scene like the other three but walking with authority, with a purpose that's even scarier than the pure rage radiating out of the others.

That's what makes me break into action and step in front of Reed.

"Ledger, stop," I say, raising my arms.

He's still a few feet away from us and at my voice, he finally focuses on me. "What the fuck are you doing? Get away from him, Callie."

"Ledge, I –"

"Did he do something to you?" he spits out before glancing back at the object of his hatred, standing behind me. "Why the fuck were you wrapped around him? Tell me he didn't touch you."

I shake my head. "No, he didn't –"

"Or what?" Reed says from behind me, his voice a mixture of

amused and provoking.

"Or we can turn this into one of the more fun nights than we've had in a while." That's Shepard, who stops right beside Ledger and shrugs casually.

"Fun for us. Just FYI. Not sure if it would be fun for you but still." This comes from Stellan — he's the more serious twin — who comes to stand right beside Shepard.

I can't believe they're here, Stellan and Shep.

They're supposed to be in New York. In college. Nobody told me that they were coming home this weekend.

God, what are they doing here?

Even though they're all standing right in front of me, I *still* can't believe that my four overprotective older brothers somehow figured out that I'm here.

Instead of where I told them I'd be.

See, this is what happens when you lie, Callie.

Not to mention, they all look intimidating like this, making a wall of muscles and dark glares.

They're all almost the same height and build and they all have thick, dark hair and brown eyes except for Conrad.

His hair's dirty blond with a few golden strands and his eyes are dark blue.

He's the brother I'm closest to in appearance and he's the brother I'm most afraid of. Maybe because he's more like a father figure than an older brother.

Although right now, I'm afraid of every single one of them.

Not Reed, apparently.

Because he walks closer to them, thereby rendering the meager protection I was giving him moot. "Well then, you've come to the right place. Let the fun begin."

And from the looks of it, the fun is definitely going to begin because a crowd has gathered around us.

Someone has turned off the music and most of the people have made sort of a semi-circle around us. They're still at a distance, but they're definitely watching.

Great. Just great.

My brothers don't care about that though.

Reed's cavalier words have made them frown and they each take a threatening step toward him.

Except Conrad.

Conrad, who stands a little farther away from the rest of my brothers, says, "Callie, come here."

I breathe heavily, glancing from my three ready-to-fight brothers to my oldest one. "Con, please. He didn't do anything."

"Callie."

"He didn't –"

"Get over here."

I wince and start walking toward him. And as soon as I do, the rest of my brothers shift and sort of make a boundary out of their bodies, a line between me and the rest of the world, *him* more specifically, in a very obvious display of protectiveness.

As soon as I reach Conrad, I tell him, "Please, Con. He didn't do anything. I promise and –"

"You lied," he says.

Not loudly or bitterly or in anger.

He says it in a matter-of-fact way and my heart twists.

It's not as if I've never lied to my brothers. Of course I have, but this is something big. Something serious. I know that.

As I said, they only have one rule: they need to know where I am at all times. So they know that I'm safe.

They give me everything that I ask for.

Even though they can be controlling and dominating – as ev-

idenced by this display – they try to be reasonable. They try to understand where I'm coming from. They respect my freedom.

So I'm at fault here.

"I'm sorry," I whisper.

Conrad's chest pushes out on a breath and instead of anger,
there's disappointment. "Let's go home."

I look at my three angry brothers, who still appear ready to
fight, and turn to Conrad. "I'm sorry. I'm sorry that I lied. Just please
tell them not to fight. H-he didn't do anything."

At this, I see anger though.

I do see his broad features going tight. "Come on."

"But Con –"

"Not a word right now."

I snap my mouth shut.

Then glancing over my shoulders, Conrad calls out, "Just one.
No more."

I don't know what that means or which brother he's talking to.

Until I hear a thump and a crunch. And loud gasps and murmurs from the crowd.

At which point, I spin around and see that Ledger has punched
Reed in the face, and Reed's wiping his mouth with the back of his
hand, somehow with his smirk still in place.

And he's *bleeding*.

Oh God.

Despite everything I try to go to him, but Con grabs my arm,
stopping me.

Thankfully though, there's someone else out here who cares
about him.

His sister, Tempest.

She breaks away from the crowd and dashes over to her brother who in turn does the same thing my brothers are doing to me: he

frowns at her first before sort of stepping in front of her as if to say that the world will have to go through him in order to get to her.

My heart squeezes again at this brotherly display of protectiveness, this whole other side of Reed Roman Jackson.

And I'm embarrassed that his sister is witnessing all this hatred, but at least she's here for him. Also now she *really* knows how bad the blood is between my brothers and hers.

When our eyes clash, I mouth, *sorry.*

She smiles sadly and mouths, *my fault.*

Well, not really.

I mean she didn't put a gun to my head to bring me here. She insisted and I agreed. I could've said no and avoided this whole debacle.

But apparently not.

Anyway my brothers aren't satisfied with one punch. Because all three of them take a step toward him, but Con puts a stop to that.

"Enough. Let's go."

They hate it, of course.

But they don't disobey him.

Out of habit, I guess.

He's not only my father figure, he's theirs too.

He's the one person who's stayed for us. Who's protected us and loved us, fought to keep us together and be our guardian.

He's the reason we're still a family.

So they back off and I breathe out a sigh of relief.

But when the time comes to walk away, I look at *him.*

I look at Reed.

I've been avoiding looking at him directly. I've only thrown him passing glances ever since my brothers got here – I still don't know how – and they caught me in his arms.

But now I look at him.

Only to find that he's looking back.

That his wolf eyes glint and shine as much as his split lip that's bleeding.

I don't know what I see in his gaze but whatever it is makes my heart spin in my chest. Makes it race and pound and squeeze.

This is it, isn't it?

I'm never gonna see him again.

Well, I will see him at school but I'll never *see* him like I did tonight. Or talk to him or be near him or touch his hoodie.

I'll never dance for him either.

I bite my lip at the thought.

The *rogue* thought.

I shouldn't want to anyway but I do.

I do and I...

"Hey, Ledger!"

For the second time tonight, Reed jars the breath out of me when he calls out, this time to my brother, while still keeping his eyes on me.

Ledger, who had started to walk away, comes to a halt and turns around to face him.

Reed isn't alone anymore. Along with Tempest – who's staring at Ledger with wide gray eyes – others from the crowd have joined him now.

And I fist my hands at my sides as I hope and wish and pray that this isn't going to get out of hand.

"I'm sorry," Reed says, jerking his chin at him.

"For fucking what?"

"That you lost tonight." Then, "Even though you deserved it."

Around me, my brothers seethe and I watch some of the players from the Mustang camp snicker.

But Ledger still obeys Conrad's rule and simply flips him the finger before turning around and striding away.

But I can't move.

Because Reed is back to looking at me.

His wolf eyes home in on me for a few seconds before doing a final sweep of my body and then looking away as he's submerged by the crowd.

And I realize that he kept his promise, didn't he?

The one I forced him to make before I danced for him.

He apologized to my brother.

***

It was someone from the party who told.

Someone from the party who texted someone else. Who in turn texted another someone else and that's how Ledger got the news about where I was.

He tried to call me first.

To confirm, I think. Because he gave me the benefit of the doubt, but when I didn't pick up and when the friend that I'd used as an alibi told him that she never saw me after school ended yesterday, he got pissed.

I'm guessing Conrad came along to calm Ledger down and to rein in the situation if it got out of hand. He's been a witness to many such situations over the years he's been coaching the two.

And when my other two brothers, who were trying to surprise us with a weekend visit, found out where I was, they came along in case Ledger needed reinforcements.

At least that's what I'm guessing from past experiences – Ledger is the youngest brother and like they are with me, our older brothers are protective of him as well. Not that they'd tell him or that Ledger would like that since he's all grown up and everything but still.

Anyway, they never told me why or what except how they

found out where I was.

They never told me anything actually.

Last night when I tried to say something as soon as we reached home, they didn't let me either.

Con told me to go get some sleep and the rest of them just dispersed without having a conversation with me.

Now it's morning and they're still not talking.

Con is shut up in his study and we all know not to disturb him when he's working. One of the ground rules he set up for us when he quit college to come back and take over everything.

The rest of my brothers, I have no idea about.

They're not home.

So I'm upstairs in my room, trying to get my homework done before my ballet class in the afternoon.

But ugh, I can't focus.

They won't even let me apologize to them. They won't even talk to me. They won't even...

There's a knock on the door and I sit up straight; I've been lounging around in my bed with my books spread out in front of me, but now I close them, cross my legs and call out, "Yeah?"

The door opens and I see Con.

He's got a slight frown on his forehead as he says, sort of roughly, "Hey."

"Hey," I say eagerly.

"You got a second?"

"Yes. Yes, absolutely."

I say this with even more eagerness and my oldest brother, who is so freaking tall that he has to slightly hunch his shoulders to get inside my room, enters.

Without volition, my mind goes to *him*.

My mind goes to the fact that he's just as tall, isn't he?

Would he also have to hunch his mountain-like shoulders to get inside my childhood bedroom?

God, Callie. Not now.

I'm all ready to beat my stupid thoughts into submission but I don't have to. They vanish on their own because as soon as Con enters and moves away from the doorway, I see the rest of my brothers.

They were hovering behind him and one by one, they enter too.

First Stellan, who almost has to hunch but not quite. Then Shepard, who enters with a slight grimace on his face because he thinks my room is too pink for his manliness, and finally, the brother who's closest to me in age and hence has always been my best buddy, Ledger.

It takes them a few seconds to situate themselves around my room and from experience I already know where they're all going to end up before they do.

Ledger leans against my desk, which is located by the white door. Shepard, the noisiest one, drags my desk chair out, spins it around and sits on it backwards with his arms on the backrest.

Stellan goes to stand by my window on the far side of the room. And the reason he does that is because Con is going to sit on the armchair right beside it, which he does a second later, and Stellan is Con's right hand.

Maybe because Stellan is the second oldest – three minutes older than his twin Shepard – and so Con has always trusted him the most. Even though Stellan and Shepard are eight years younger than Con.

When they're all situated and are still not talking, I open my mouth to apologize but I notice Shep elbowing Ledger and as if waking up, Ledger mutters, "Right."

He brings something out from behind him and offers it to me.

It's a giant baby pink box with satin pink ribbon wrapped

around it and despite everything, my arms shoot up to grab it.

On the top in a darker shade of pink, is written *Buttery Blossoms*.

It's my favorite, *favorite* bakery in town and they have the best cupcakes ever.

In fact, I even have a picture of it, my most favorite cupcake from there – Peanut Butter Blossom —taped up on my wall.

I have pictures of all my favorite things taped up on my wall actually. My ballet recitals, my pointe shoes, Bardstown High.

Excitedly, I look at Ledger and then all my brothers. "You guys bought me cupcakes?"

Ledger shrugs. "Yeah."

Shep shrugs too. "They're your favorite."

"And you don't get to have them enough, so," Ledger adds.

That's true, I don't.

Mostly because I'm a ballerina and I have to watch my weight. Healthy living and healthy eating and all that but oh my God, I have a giant addiction to these.

It's toxic but I don't care.

I hug the box, my heart feeling full. "Is that where you guys went this morning? Because I was looking for all of you."

Shep is first to reply with his hands in the air. "I will not set foot in that pink shop. Under any circumstances, so no. I went to see a friend."

Before I can reply, Ledger rolls his eyes. "By that, he means Amy."

My eyes pop wide. "You guys are back together again?"

Amy is Shep's on-again off-again girlfriend from high school and I really, *really* like her. She loves dancing and knitting just like me and I would love to see them end up together.

But Shep is an idiot and he broke up with her when he left for college three years ago.

I always feel bad when I see her around town; she's still so in love with him.

"Fuck no," Shep says.

"Why not? She's amazing, Shep. I really like her."

"Never said I don't like her." He smirks then. "I like her. I like her a lot."

"Yeah, her and that hot tub in her backyard." Ledger snickers.

Shep's smirk only grows. "Oh yeah, definitely. It's got jet sprays, dude. You can't compete with that. That hot tub can do things you can't even fathom, little brother."

"Oh, I can fathom. I can fathom a lot." Ledger playfully kicks at the legs of the chair Shep is sitting in. "In fact, I fathomed it last week with her little sister, Jessica."

Shep turns to Ledger then. "For real? You and –"

But before he can go on, I squeal, "Ew, gross. Both of you."

While at the same time, Stellan speaks up. "Enough. All right? You can exchange your glorious war stories later."

Ugh.

They're such players.

Sometimes I think that's why they hate Reed so much. Because they know he's exactly like them.

Ledger and Shep shut up and before anyone can say anything else and sidetrack the conversation again, I ask, "Why are you guys bringing me cupcakes?"

Ledger side-eyes Stellan and Con. "Because you're our sister."

Getting serious, Shepard nods. "And we love you."

"We also respect you," Ledger says.

"And your choices." Shep goes next.

"Also your independence," Ledger adds, making me think that they've memorized their lines.

Shepard proves me right in the next second. "Yeah, we respect that too." Then frowning, he tilts his head toward Stellan. "Wait, is that what it is? We respect her independence." Looking at me, he explains, "*Stella* here said something this morning that totally went over my hungover head."

Ledger snickers again at *Stella*, I'm sure.

It's my fault really.

When I was a kid, I couldn't say Stellan so I'd call him Stella and, well, it caught on. And now every time Shep wants to annoy Stellan, he calls him Stella.

I glance at Stellan apologetically, who's watching Shep with a flat look. "You like your face, don't you?"

Shepard chuckles because they're identical twins. "Not on you though."

"Yeah, keep talking and I'll rearrange it for you." He glances at Ledger who's still snickering. "Yours too."

When the most mischievous of my brothers, Shep and Ledger, go quiet again – not happily though – Stellan speaks up, looking at me. "Look, what these morons are trying to say is that we acted like giant asses last night. We shouldn't have barged in, like an army or something. But you scared us, all right? It's not like you to lie and we thought something happened to you. We thought –"

Ledger bursts out then, as if he's been holding it all on the inside. "We thought he did something, okay? We thought you needed our help." He shakes his head angrily. "You needed us to rescue you from him and…" He goes quiet for a second before saying, "You need to be careful."

"I know and I am. And –"

"No, it's… you need to be really careful. *Really.*"

"O-kay," I say, frowning at Ledger's grave tone. "I am."

"You don't get it." He sighs sharply. "The thing is… fuck it.

The thing is that he's attractive. Good looking, handsome, whatever. Not more than me, but still."

"What?" I'm so confused.

Shepard snorts.

Stellan's lips twitch as well.

"Yeah, and also the thing is, Calls, that our little brother wants to say that he's got a big boy crush on him," Shep adds with raised eyebrows.

Stellan chuckles as Ledger swats Shep's head. "Fuck you, dude. I'm trying to explain something."

"No need. We get it," Shepard says, hitting Ledger in the stomach with his elbow.

"The point I'm trying to make is, he takes advantage of that," Ledger continues loudly, rubbing his stomach. "Of his looks. Girls become stupid when it comes to him and he uses their stupidity against them. And you're my sister. He's bound to mess with you. Because he's smart enough to know that I'm going to win this season. Like last season. So you need to stay away from him, Callie. He's a fucking asshole, all right?"

I bite my lip as I finally get my window to apologize. "I know and I'm sorry. I don't want to ruin your game and –"

"This is not about the soccer rivalry."

That's Conrad's voice.

He's been sitting in his spot, all quiet so far, letting the rest of them talk and joke around. But I guess his patience is running thin now, because he pins Shep and Ledger with a hard gaze before turning to me and leaning forward, putting his elbows on his thighs. "I can tolerate a lot. I *have* tolerated a lot over the years. Rebellions, phases, tantrums. But I will not tolerate lies that involve your safety."

He pauses for his words to take effect, and they do.

Because he has.

Tolerated, I mean. A lot.

Obviously from Shepard and Ledger, who are the more rebellious of the bunch. All the times Shepard was suspended from school for playing a prank or making out with girls in the school closets. All the times Ledger got into trouble with his anger. Even Stellan has had his moments, not as frequent or severe as the other two, but still.

And then there's me.

I'm a girl.

A whole different species for my brothers to understand, but they've done their best.

Especially Conrad.

All the times I cried because of ballet and how I wasn't good enough. How even though I love ballet, it didn't leave me enough time to make friends and so I was always excluded from fun sleepovers and tea parties. So all my brothers would entertain me at home, play with me, drink imaginary tea with me.

Not to mention all the things a girl goes through.

That Conrad never even thought about before but had to because we had no one else to turn to.

Tampons and bras and hormones and serious talks about puberty and sex.

So he *has* tolerated a lot.

And I hate that I lied to him.

"We might have come down on you harder than we thought," he continues, his serious dark blue gaze on me. "But it was because we were worried. As Stellan said, it's not like you to lie and I'd like to think that I've given you enough freedom that you don't *have* to lie."

"I know, Con," I say, contrite. "You have. I was scared that you'd be mad if I told you I was going to his party and —"

"Fuck yeah, we would be," Ledger cuts me off.

Con glances at him. "Ledge."

Ledger quiets down then and Con turns back to me. "The reason we don't want you to go to his party or anywhere near him is not because of some useless, unnecessary soccer rivalry. It's not about a game. It's because Reed Jackson is a punk."

Con's jaw clenches and tics for a few seconds as if he can't even bear to talk about Reed. He can't even bear to say his name in front of me.

"He's a rich punk who only cares about himself. I know him and I know guys like him. Guys like him are selfish, untrustworthy, and reckless. Guys like him don't care about rules or people. They only care about themselves. Guys like him can't handle responsibilities. They leave without so much as a glance back at what they're leaving behind."

I don't know why, but it feels like Con is speaking from experience, but before I can ask him, he goes on, "So the reason we want you to stay away from him is because he's not good for you. He's not worthy of you. He doesn't deserve you. Do you understand what I'm saying to you, Callie? He's not the guy for you. You need to stay away from him because you deserve better and because you're smart. You're smarter than the rest of the girls who fall victim to him."

Chapter 5

I'm running from him.

Well, not exactly.

It's not as if he's chasing after me or anything. He's not.

In fact, if you look at him sauntering down the hallways, being worshipped by guys and girls alike, you'd think that Friday night never happened.

That I never went to his party. He never caught me while I was trying to duck out. And I never danced for him.

The only evidence of that night is that nasty split lip and the bruise on his jaw.

Even after four days, it looks just as angry and red as it must have when Ledger laid it on him.

Every time I see it, my heart twists in my chest.

My legs itch to go over to him and touch it. Touch him.

But I can't.

That's why I'm running.

The second I see him, I turn around and leave, which I usually did anyway, but these days I'm ruthless. If he comes in my line of vision, I duck my head. The second I start to think about him, I shut it the eff down.

Besides, it's not as if *he* is thinking about me.

As I said, looking at him, you wouldn't even know that Friday night happened.

Not to mention, there are girls taking care of his bruise. In fact, I saw a girl from junior year caressing it out in the courtyard today.

I think she even reached up and kissed it. I'm not sure. I didn't wait to see what she would do once she'd gone up on her tiptoes.

So yeah, I need to move on and consider Friday night an anomaly and focus on what's important.

The upcoming dance show in which I'm the lead.

Yes, I am.

I don't even know how it happened. Because I'm a freshman and they never pick a freshman. They usually go for a junior or senior.

I'm actually very proud.

If only this wasn't so hard.

I mean, it's a fairly easy routine. The dance itself is a mix of classical ballet and contemporary choreography. There's nothing here that I haven't done before.

But.

I cannot nail down the last part of it. I'm having trouble with holding the positions, with my calves being steady, with my toes bearing my weight.

So I'm basically having trouble with everything and I just want to give up and cry.

I mean, what kind of a ballerina am I if I can't get my toes to cooperate with me?

A sucky one.

School's been done for hours but I'm in the auditorium, trying to get it right.

I can't though.

Because I'm tired now. My limbs are exhausted and I want to go home and just soak in a bathtub for hours, clean up the scrapes on my toes, bandage my ankle and take a bucketful of painkillers.

So I pack up my things, unplug the stereo and bring it to the storage closet located backstage. Opening the door, I switch on the light and set the heavy equipment down on one of the shelves on the far end.

The moment I do though, I hear something, a creak and a footstep, a click, and I spin around already knowing — *hoping* — who it would be.

And I'm right.

It's him.

He's leaning against the now closed door of the storage closet, his gray eyes glued to me. And just at the sight of him, at the fact that my secret, dangerous wish has come true, I stop breathing.

I don't need to breathe anyway because euphoria is bursting in my veins like firecrackers.

He's here.

Here. Finally.

My heart races as if it's been waiting and waiting for him to come find me.

Even though I've been making every effort to stay away from him and to run.

Even though the words that come out of my mouth are the exact opposite of what I'm feeling. "Y-you can't be in here."

Good.

Good, this is smart.

This is what I should be saying to him.

He's a bad guy, remember?

It doesn't matter what I feel.

It doesn't even make sense that I feel these things.

In response, Reed shifts on his feet and settles even more against the door like he has no plans to go anywhere. "Yeah, why not?"

"Because Ledger is here," I tell him, my own feet doing what they've been doing for the past few days, itching to go to him as soon as I see him.

But I dig my toes into the ground and stop them.

"So?"

God.

Why is this so appealing? His reckless, daredevil, *rule-breaking* attitude.

Maybe because I've never broken a rule myself.

Maybe because I've never *seen* anyone break a rule with so little care where the repercussions are so dire, AKA getting beaten up by my brothers.

I bring my arms back and grab hold of the shelf behind me. Just so I'll stay put. Even though it's getting harder and harder to do that.

"He's at the library, waiting for me to finish up so he can take me home. And I can't be late. Not after…" I trail off, glancing at the bruise, still so fresh looking and red, sitting on the left side of his jaw.

His jaw that is shadowed with a light stubble that he must hate.

Under my gaze, he thumbs it. "Friday night."

He remembers…

Like a fool, I think of that first.

It doesn't matter whether he remembers or not.

What matters is, he needs to leave.

Nodding, I whisper, "Yes."

"So they're keeping an eye on you."

Not them.

As I said, my brothers have given me all the freedom. They've always trusted me.

This is me.

I'm trying to make up for last Friday.

After how they all came to apologize and bring me cupcakes, I'm doing this to make up for the lying.

It might be too much for some girls – teenagers lie, right? – and I get that.

But then those girls don't have awesome brothers like mine. They don't share a unique bond with their siblings like I do.

I shake my head. "It's me. I lied to them."

He hums thoughtfully. "And found yourself in the clutches of a villain."

My heart skips a beat when he says it, the term I called him that night.

And it's a perfect term too.

He does look like a villain. A gorgeous villain.

With beautiful wolf eyes and marble skin. A jaw so sharp and cheekbones so high. Broad shoulders and a massive chest that tapers into a slim waist.

Every part of his body looms large and threatening.

Even that bruise adds to his danger.

"You should go," I tell him, breathless.

"But here you are, aren't you? In my clutches again," he murmurs, completely ignoring my statement.

I am.

I have no escape either. I glance at the door behind him, which believe it or not is difficult because he's covering it all up with his towering body.

"Why's the door locked?" I ask him.

"You've been running from me," he says.

"I'm not," I lie, wondering how he even knows when he's been too busy with his awesome life.

"And I'm not letting you run from me again."

His words hang in the air menacingly and I ask, "*Letting* me?"

"Yeah."

I frown at him. "Isn't that… criminal?"

"Is it?"

I exhale sharply. "Yes, it is. You can't lock a girl in a closet against her will. Just because you don't want her to run."

Something like amusement passes over his features. "Right. I think I heard about something like that."

"You –"

"But also, I don't think I'm holding her against her will. Am I?"

I swallow and grab hold of the edge of the shelf tightly. "Why don't I scream and you can find out if it's against my will or not?"

It only makes him smirk. "Why don't you? Let's see if it reaches your brother and he comes to save you." He flexes his fist by his side. "I'd love to give him a matching bruise for last Friday."

My heart jumps. "You wouldn't."

"Wouldn't I?"

"No. Because… Because you apologized to him that night," I remind him, trying to tamp down shivers at the thought of him keeping that promise to me. "You kept your promise."

"And that means what?"

"It means that maybe you're not as bad as they say you are."

"Yeah, no. I'm exactly as bad as they say I am." He spreads his hands as if in a magnanimous gesture. "I'd be happy to show you if you like. All you have to do is scream."

I study him for a long, careful moment before saying, "How did you even know that I was here?"

"I saw you dancing through the window," he says.

"You did?" I ask, surprised.

"Uh-huh." His eyes grow heated, and all my ire seems to be on the verge of melting. "You were spinning. So fast. And I stopped."

"Why?"

He licks his lips and I'm reminded of how excited he looked that night when I danced for him.

When he called me a fairy.

God.

God.

He called me that, didn't he?

I've been trying not to think about it. Not to think about his words, the words no one has ever said to me before.

Fairy.

"Because apparently when you spin, I stop. When you dance, I have to watch," he says in a low, slightly rough voice.

And suddenly I feel the same way. As I did that night.

All hot and restless. My limbs buzzing.

"I sucked," I say.

He frowns. "What?"

I'm not sure if I should tell him this. But I'm going to.

I don't know why but I have to tell him the truth.

So swallowing, I whisper, "My routine. I can't do it. I-I mean, I can. But I'm screwing it all up."

His frown only grows. "Someone tell you that?"

I shake my head. "No. Everyone has been super kind so far. But I-I'm supposed to hold this pose, a developpé écarté devant, at the end for like eight counts before coming down on my knees, but I could only do it for like four or something. And even then, my calves were shaking, and do you even know how big of a crime that is? Not being able to hold straight and still. A very big crime. Huge."

It is.

And if they don't kick me out then I'll just quit myself because this is a disgrace.

For some reason, his lips twitch. "I don't think anyone would notice how long you stood on your toes."

I narrow my eyes at him, at his amusement. "Why not?"

"Because they'll be too distracted at the sight of you down on your knees." He tips his chin at me. "Especially in that."

All of a sudden it hits me that I'm in costume.

I've been wearing this for three hours now and I completely forgot. I completely forgot that this is the first time Reed is seeing me in this.

A white leotard and a light green tutu.

Not to mention, I also have wings.

They are heavy — although after wearing them for so long, my shoulders have gone numb so I don't feel their weight anymore — and made of white fur. They're slung over my shoulders with white ribbon-like strings and rustle across my spine and arms.

Like a fairy…

I've been wearing leotards and tutus all my life so until he looks at me from top to bottom, I don't realize how revealing it can be.

How tight the costume is and how it fits me like a second skin. How it highlights every lithe muscle, every delicate bone in my body.

How exposed I am.

Even more than I was back in the woods.

And before I can stop myself, I say, "It's my tutu."

When he lifts his eyes back to my face, they're the darkest that I've seen them.

Liquid and fiery.

"Yeah?" he rasps in an almost indulgent tone.

I bring my trembling hands forward and trace the frilly fabric.

"It's like a skirt."

"And what are those?"

He points to my feet and I look down. "Uh, they're called pointe shoes." I chuckle as I look up. "You know, people say that ballerinas have the ugliest feet. They're all swollen and bruised and cut up and –"

"People are stupid."

"But –"

I stop talking because something makes him move.

I don't know what it is but he straightens up and I'm wondering what the chances are that he'll stay put where he is, by the door, when he starts walking toward me.

It's not a big space so by the time I gather my wits to ask him what the heck he's doing, he's already here.

He's already touching me.

Not me, per se.

He's touching my wings. Or one of them actually.

Standing over me like a threat or something, a delicious, gorgeous threat in a white hoodie and a pulsating bruise, Reed reaches out and brushes a finger along the edge of my wing. Crazily, my spine arches up at the touch. As if he's touching my skin instead of my fake wing.

His eyes drop to my bowed body and if he couldn't see the shape of it before, he can sure see it now.

He can see the bones of my ribs, the hollow of my stomach. My really small but jutting out breasts.

"What are these wings for?" he asks, bringing his eyes up to mine.

"F-for my character."

"What character is that?"

"I'm a fairy."

Somehow his eyes grow all heated even as a slight lopsided smile pulls up his lips. "So I was right, huh?"

"I —"

He rubs the fur between his fingers as he continues, "You *are* a fairy. You dance like a fairy." His eyes flick over my face, my bun. "You look like one too."

I lose my breath for a second.

I also lose my heartbeats. My rational thoughts.

That's the only explanation for why my legs stretch up and I get closer to him. "I'm a stupid fairy though."

"How so?"

"Because I fall in love with my enemy. In the song."

"Your enemy."

"Yes, a human. He's supposed to hunt fairies."

"And what about him?" he asks, his fingers still playing with my wing and his eyes going back and forth between mine. "Does he fall in love with you too?"

"Yes." I swallow, my own fingers fisting my tutu. "Or I think he does. But he's lying."

"Why?"

"Because he's using me. He wants to trap me and bring me back to his family. I'm supposed to be his first hunt."

"What a fucking asshole."

"Everyone warns me about him. All my fairy friends and my family. But I don't listen to them. I think he's a hero."

"But he's not, is he?"

"No, he's the villain in my story."

A fire rages in his eyes, hot and so vivid that it burns me. "Yeah, I know something about villains."

My heart twists in my chest for some reason. "His name is Romeo."

"Romeo."

"Yeah. In the song."

"And you must be Juliet then."

I nod. "I'm actually Juliet." Then, "My name. Calliope Juliet Thorne."

"Calliope Juliet Thorne," he repeats in his rich deep voice. Also smooth.

And it feels as if instead of plucking at the edges of my wing, he's swirling the ends of my nerves with his long fingers. And he's doing it somewhere in the small of my back so that my spine bows for him even more.

He appreciates my efforts too.

He runs his eyes over my stretched-out body once more.

"And you're Reed Roman Jackson."

"You know my name, huh?"

"It's not a secret. Your full name. Girls chant it pretty often. Like a prayer."

He smirks. "Do they?"

"Yes," I answer, slightly irked. "They also call you Romeo."

His eyes narrow. "What?"

I nod. "Because everyone knows that Roman is just another version of Romeo."

"Yeah, bullshit."

It's my turn to smirk at his irritation. "It's okay. They do it with love. But you should be careful."

"Of what?"

"Of coming anywhere near me." I raise my eyebrows. "I'm Juliet, remember? Our names are tragic. Shakespearean. We're bad luck together. So maybe you shouldn't lock me up in a closet and should stay away from me instead."

"Or what?"

I eye his bruise then. "Or you get beaten up by my brothers."

"I told you I can handle myself."

"You know –"

"Besides what does Shakespeare know anyway?"

"What, Shakespeare knows everything."

"Does he?"

"Yes."

He cocks his head to the side as he says, "Well, how about we do something about that then?"

"Do something about what?"

"Our names."

"What?"

Instead of giving me an explanation, Reed moves his eyes away from my face and focuses on my wings. My white fur wings that are suddenly growing too heavy and too light all at the same time.

"How about I call you by my name and you call me by yours?" he asks huskily.

"Your name."

"Fairy," he murmurs, his eyes coming back to my face and burning me alive yet again. "I get to call you Fairy."

I swallow.

Fairy.

He wants to call me Fairy.

I don't... I don't know what to say.

So I just repeat his words. "You want to call me Fairy."

Instead of answering me though, he roves his wolf eyes over my face once more before stepping back and taking his touch away.

"See you around, Fae."

With that he begins to leave.

As if he didn't just obliterate my breaths, my balance with that one word.

Fae.

A second later though, he stops and fishes something out of his pocket. Keeping his eyes on me, at my heaving, shuddering body, he puts it on the shelf by his side.

"Almost forgot about it," he says. "It's for you."

It's hard to drag my eyes away from his penetrating ones but I want to know what he brought me. It's an envelope, purple and pretty, and looking out of place in this dark closet.

"What is it?" I ask, glancing back at him.

"An invitation."

"To what?"

"A party."

"You're inviting me to a party?"

"No." He explains, "My sister is. It's Pest's birthday this weekend. She wanted me to give it to you. I'm just the messenger."

Finally he leaves, and this time he doesn't stop or turn back.

Tempest.

His sister.

The girl I met at the game last week and who dragged me to his party.

I've been thinking about her, wondering if I'd get to see her again. I really liked her.

And now as her brother is unlocking the door and leaving, I'm thinking about the fact that he calls her Pest. And how he came here to do her bidding, to give me the invitation, which I'm pretty sure she must've bugged him about until he relented.

And *God* I have to go to him right now.

Snatching the envelope and clutching it in my hands, I run after him.

He's almost at the edge of the stage and I call out, "Roman."

He stops then.

Slowly, he turns around and looks at me.

I know that I should let him go. I know that I shouldn't have stopped him.

I know that doing this is foolish. And maybe I am that.

Foolish.

But I don't care.

Staring into his piercing eyes, I hug the envelope to my chest and say, "If you call me Fae, then I get to call you Roman."

Chapter 6

Tempest and I are awesome friends now.

Best friends even.

It didn't take us long to become that. In fact, I think we became good friends as soon as we met at the game. But our friendship was sealed at her birthday party.

Which I made sure to attend and which wasn't an easy thing to do.

I knew it wouldn't be.

I knew my brothers would freak out. Already me going to that one party has created so much drama and now I wanted to go to another one.

But I was going and I wasn't going to lie about it.

So I told them and, well, it didn't go well.

Definitely not with Ledger, who kept grumbling about it for that whole week, pacing and stomping and cursing.

We had four family meetings about it. *Four.*

So family meetings are a tradition in our house.

Conrad established it long ago, so whenever there's something that might be important– from where to go on vacation over the summer or Ledger getting a new truck to switching from whole wheat pasta to spinach pasta – we all get a say.

I think it's his way of keeping all of us in the loop and functioning as a family.

So that whole week, leading up to the party, there were long discussions over dinner where Ledger would just curse and say no to everything. Stellan, who would join us over the phone, would try to reason with him and tell him that I'm not a child and at least I didn't lie like the last time.

While Shep, again over the phone, would make stupid jokes all the while siding with Ledger.

Until Conrad put a stop to it all and declared that Ledger would go with me.

"It's not that I don't trust you. I don't trust where you're going. So if you want to go, Ledge will go with you."

That seemed to satisfy all my brothers and so that was how I went to Tempest's birthday party, with Ledger – and some of his friends, who he invited along without even telling me – as my bodyguards.

Which was fine.

I mean, it was an overkill but I understood where Ledger was coming from. The party was going to be full of people from the Mustang camp and he wanted some of his own friends there.

I was just glad to go and to hang out with Tempest, who was glad to see me as well.

Together, we made every effort to forget the fact that our brothers and their respective friends were glaring at each other from across the room. Or that tensions were running high.

At some point during the night, our brothers made a pact: sisters are off-limits.

Meaning they would continue to fight and be at odds with each other but none of them were allowed to bring their sisters into it. So Reed can't use me to provoke my brother, and Ledger can't use Tempest to provoke Reed.

As weird as this pact was, it came as a relief.

Because I do think that Tempest is into my idiot brother and I don't want her being used in the name of their stupid rivalry.

If a pact keeps her safe, then I'm all for it.

Besides, I do want to be her friend.

And ever since her birthday party, Tempest has been coming down from New York every weekend to hang out with me at my house and she always looks for ways to talk to Ledger.

Who always looks for ways to avoid her because she's a Jackson.

And he hates all Jacksons.

Especially the one by the name of Reed Roman Jackson.

Or just Roman.

Not that I've gotten a chance to call him that after the first time.

Because while Tempest is trying everything to tempt Ledger, her brother is trying everything to stick to the pact.

Yup.

Who would've thought that Reed would be so good at keeping promises?

At school, he goes about his normal business.

And by business, I mean he always has girls around him. He's always surrounded by his friends who also happen to be the loudest of all, attracting all kinds of attention. At practice and at games, he provokes my brother and my brother retaliates and vice versa. They stay on opposite sides of hallways and the cafeteria like they always have.

Most of all, he ignores me like he's always done.

He passes by me in the hallway without sparing me a glance. If we happen to find ourselves in the same place at the same time, he hardly knows that I'm there. In fact, when I go to his house to see Tempest like she comes to mine to visit me, he's never there.

I know it shouldn't bother me, but it does.

That's the only reason why I'm letting Tempest do this.

She's got it in her head that I'm perfect for her brother.

I've told her a million times that I'm not. Her brother isn't even interested in girlfriends. Not to mention, my brothers – Ledger specifically – would kill him if I ever got involved with him. But she hasn't listened so far and up until now, I've shot down all her ideas to get me closer to Reed.

Until today.

I mean, this isn't a plan to get close to her brother per se. Her brother isn't even home; I'm at Tempest's this Saturday afternoon.

It's a plan to give me more confidence in my own skin. To make me think that I can be sexy too.

Like all his girlfriends, or girls.

Who somehow are masters at smoky eyes and sultry make-up. Also all of them have dark, sexy hair, unlike my stupid blonde good-girl tresses.

No, don't think about that, Callie. This is about female empowerment. This is about you, not him!

Anyway, I'm wearing one of Tempest's dresses. A black mini-dress that also happens to be strapless, which hits me mid-thigh, along with her heels. On top of all this, she's done my make-up and curled my blonde hair.

All in all, I do think that I look sexy.

After Tempest dresses me up like a doll, we venture out to go to the mall like this. I was happy to stay home and lounge around all dressed up but she says that if I want confidence, then I need to go out and get it myself.

And I do get it.

Because guys have been leering at me, at us, ever since we stepped out of the house. And it is great at first but as time passes, I start to get tired.

My feet start to kill me and after pulling down my dress a million times, I don't think I like this all that much.

All this unwanted attention and guys staring at my butt so openly.

I tell Tempest that I want to go home and relax and so she calls for her driver to come pick us up.

It's a good thing because I don't think I can walk in these shoes anymore.

Only my happiness is short-lived because instead of a driver, her brother shows up in a white flash, his Mustang.

He takes one look at the both of us and his wolf eyes grow furious as he growls, "Get in."

Which we do.

Tempest and I are in the back seat while Reed drives in a seething silence. When I catch Tempest's eye in the darkened interior of the car, she winks at me happily and that's how I know.

That's how I know that she never called the driver. She called *him*.

That *scheming…* non-friend.

Because we're not friends anymore. She lied to me.

Not only that, as soon as we reach their big, sprawling house, she jumps out of the car with a happy goodbye thrown at me.

Although her brother doesn't let her go so easily.

"Straight to your room," he growls again, the only words he's spoken after his commanding *get in*. "Now. And put some fucking clothes on, we're going to have a talk."

Her shoulders droop and she mumbles something before turning to me, winking and running away, leaving me alone with him.

Oh my God.

Oh my *God*, I'm gonna kill her. I'm so gonna kill her right now.

Actually, I'm so gonna kill *him*.

For being so... authoritative and angry.

Only he also makes me want to rub my legs together in restlessness when he talks like that, in his deep commanding voice.

But whatever.

I throw open the door and jump out, totally charged up to go after Tempest and make her pay for this. But I don't get too far. In fact, I don't even get to take more than a few steps away from his Mustang because there's something stopping me.

Or someone.

How he made it out of the car and over to my side so fast, I don't know. All I know is that I can't go anywhere as long as he stands before me.

Or rather, as long as he's backing me up into his car.

As soon as my spine hits the cold metal, I shiver and words jar out of me. "Let me go."

He doesn't.

Frankly, I didn't expect him to.

But then I also didn't expect him to lean forward. I didn't expect him to put his arm on the roof of his car, just by my side, effectively stopping me from leaving.

Although I should have. Expected it, I mean.

If he can lock me up in a closet so I don't get to run from him, he can do anything.

"What are you doing?" I ask.

In response, he runs his eyes all over my body, slowly, methodically, as if making a point before raising them back to my face. "Looking at you."

Again, I get the urge to rub my thighs together at his low, heated tone. "Why?"

"Because that's what you want, don't you? You want me to look at you."

"I do not," I lie.

When did I become such a liar?

I thought I was the good girl.

He knows I'm lying too because a smirk breaks out on his ruby-red, crescent-shaped mouth. Only it has a dangerous edge, a humorless quality. "Yeah, you do. Why else would you be wearing something like that? Something that…" He looks me up and down again, a cursory and yet lingering glance. "Leaves very little to my imagination."

My imagination.

As if.

I put my sweaty palms on his Mustang so my balance doesn't falter. "That's extremely arrogant of you, don't you think? To assume that. That I'd wear something just to get your attention."

Never mind that I did. I mean, subconsciously.

Okay maybe a *little* consciously but whatever.

He dips his chin in a condescending manner. "It's the truth though, isn't it?"

In response, I raise mine, just to look defiant. "No, it's not. And this is a perfectly normal dress."

"Is it?"

"Yes."

I'm not sure what's happening tonight but everything that I'm saying is making him angrier and angrier.

And none of that is even remotely bothersome to me.

Not even when he leans further down, shaking the car at my

back and bringing his wolf eyes, which I cannot look away from, even closer.

"Because I don't think that a *perfectly normal dress* would highlight every fucking curve of your tight ballerina body," he says with clenched teeth. "Would it? Or that when you walk in it, your perky tits would be dangerously close to jiggling out. And the whole world could see the cheeks of your juicy, tight ass."

For a number of seconds after he's finished talking, I'm unable to believe the things he's said.

For a number of seconds, I simply blink up at him.

I've never ever heard anyone talk about my body in such graphic, derogatory terms. Because it is all derogatory, isn't it?

I should slap him in the face. I should.

I shouldn't feel a rush in my chest that beads my nipples to achy points or shift on my feet just to rub my butt against his Mustang.

And the fact that he can make me feel and do all these inappropriate, less than respectable, *bad* things makes me say, "You're an asshole."

At my curse – which was so effortless for me, dangerously effortless when it comes to him – he flinches slightly before growing even more furious.

"I am. And in case your four older, overprotective brothers forgot to mention it to you, assholes like me don't play by the rules. Assholes like me take whatever they want, whenever they want. And I'm probably the worst of them all."

My breaths have gone haywire so my next words come out thin and breathless. "What does that mean?"

"It *means*…" He pauses to bring his other arm up as well, putting it on the roof of his Mustang and making a cage around me. "That I'm the kind of asshole that keeps your brothers up at night. I'm the reason girls like you have a curfew. I'm the reason your mommy sits you down in your room and warns you about boys. She tells you how rotten they can be, how corrupt. How they'll lie and cheat and do anything to stick their hands under your dress. I'm the reason your daddy locks your door at night. And he puts you in a bedroom on the top floor so no one can climb in. He bars your windows. He stands guard outside of your door on the off chance that I somehow still find a way in. And I fucking do. You know how?"

"H-how?"

He shakes the car again, making me teeter on my heels, unbalancing my world. "Because I'm the kind of asshole who'd break down any door. I'd climb a thousand stories. I'd climb a fucking tower. Just to be able to get into your room at night. Just to be able to see you. And I bet you wear those lacy white nighties, don't you?"

"Yes, sometimes."

"Yeah, I'd pull apart all the bars in your window. I'd fucking go to war with all four of your brothers just to be able to see you in one of those. Just to be able to get a peek of your creamy, dancer legs in something like that. Just to see if I can catch a glimpse of something else too, in your thin white nightie." He leans in another inch as he continues, "You don't want me to do that, do you? You don't want me to force my way into your room at night, while your brothers are sleeping down the hall somewhere just so I could look at you, at your tight little body, in your white nightie."

I do.

I so do.

I want him to force his way inside my room just so he can look at me.

And as soon as this thought flashes through my mind, I shake my head. "No."

"Yeah. Because let's face it, I get a peek of you in that thing and I won't be able to stop myself from taking it too far."

"Too far."

His eyes are glowing now. "Yeah, I get a peek of you in your nightie, I'll be doing everything that I can to fucking touch it. To somehow push the hem up your thighs or pull the straps down your shoulders, just so I can get my hands on your naked body. But again, you don't want me to do that, do you, Fae?"

Oh God.

How is it that I feel both relieved and restless that he called me that? How is it that I've been waiting and waiting for him to call me by his name one more time?

It's a wonder that I can still shake my head and say what he wants me to say when all I want to say is yes. Yes, yes, yes.

"No," I whisper and arch my body, up and toward him as if offering him to touch it.

"Yeah, that's what I thought. And why not?" he asks, the strings of his hoodie oscillating in front of me in a hypnotic rhythm. "Tell me why you don't want me to touch you, to grope your fucking body like the villain that I am."

I can't remember.

I can't remember anything right now.

But I guess all of this is so ingrained in my brain that I don't even have to think about it, about the rivalry and soccer and hatred. My lips move on their own. "Because of my b-brothers."

Satisfaction bursts over his features even as his jaw tightens for a second. "You wouldn't want to betray them now, would you?"

"No."

How many times have I said no now, I wonder?

And how many times have I wanted to say yes?

I'm a fool.

A fool, a fool, a fool.

But he makes it so easy. He makes it so easy to be stupid and reckless and thoughtless.

He makes it so easy to be foolish.

"Good." He approves with a short nod. "So you're going to be careful now, aren't you? You're going to wear your daisy fresh dresses and your ballet flats. You're going to braid your hair like a good girl and you're going to stop begging for my attention. You're going to *stop* making me look at you."

His words, almost snarled from his mouth and dripping in condescension, penetrate my drugged-up mind and make me frown. They make me stand a little taller in my stupid heels when he moves away from me.

And I tell him with as much authority as I can muster right now, "Then you have to stop watching me."

Reed was in the process of taking another step back and dismissing me. But my words stop him. They make him frown. "What?"

Good.

I'm glad.

If he can give me ultimatums, then I can issue them too.

I raise my trembling chin and say, "You have to stop coming to my practice every day."

Because that's what he does.

He comes to my after-hours practice and he watches me dance.

Every day after school, when I practice in the auditorium because I still haven't nailed down my routine, he comes in.

He sits in the third row, not too far away from the stage and not too close. I don't know why. And he watches me spin and turn and leap around the stage with my wings on my back.

He watches me like he did the first night at the party.

All eager and intense and at the edge of his seat.

And I dance for him in the same way as well. All restless and excited.

After the pact I was afraid that he'd stop. I was afraid that he wouldn't watch me dance anymore. But he didn't and thank God for that.

Because somehow, I've gotten addicted to dancing for him.

Somehow, I've become addicted to the way he looks at me. Addicted to the way his shoulders seem to loosen up the longer I dance. How he sits back and sprawls out on the seat as if this is the best part of his day, me dancing for him.

So sometimes I dance for him just because he wants me to.

I abandon my practice, pick a song that I love and spin for him like the ballerina I am.

His ballerina.

But it's stupid, isn't it? And dangerous.

He's right.

He's the worst asshole of all, the biggest villain that my brothers have warned me about.

And I can't betray my brothers – Ledger – no matter what my heart keeps telling me.

So this is the best course of action, staying away like we always have.

"And why's that?" he challenges.

I press my hands harder on the Mustang. "Because you're right. This is stupid. I never should've worn this *stupid* dress."

Yeah, everything happened because of this stupid freaking dress.

If I wasn't wearing this, then I'd be safely tucked away inside Tempest's room, watching something silly on her laptop instead of standing out here in these torturous heels under his *torturous* scrutiny.

"Why did you then?"

"Because I wanted to see what it felt like…" I trail off when I realize what I was going to say.

Of course, he hones in on that and his features grow alert. "Felt like what?"

Well, I was stupid enough to bring it up, wasn't I?

I can be stupid, stupid, *stupid* enough to finish it too.

What do I have to lose anyway?

I fist the dress and stand tall in my heels. "I wanted to see what it felt like to be sexy. To be tempting for a day. To feel like all the girls at school. All the girls you hang out with."

There. I said it.

It's over. My humiliation is complete.

Can I just go home now and never ever come back here, to his house?

"You wanted to feel like the girls I hang out with."

Oh, so it's not complete yet. My humiliation.

Fine.

Whatever. I can deal with this.

"Yes." I sigh. "I wanted to feel sexy and confident and, I don't know, just not like a good girl all the time. But I *am* a good girl, aren't I? Because I hate this dress. And I hate these heels and I hate you too. So from now on, I'm not going to dance for you and you can't come watch me like it's your right or something. I'm not for your personal entertainment, okay?"

Then I throw my hands in the air and snap, "In fact from now on, you should ask one of your girlfriends to dance for you. I'm sure they'd be happy to accommodate your every whim like they always are. So, is there anything else you need to say to me, because I'd like to leave now."

He stares at me and stares at me with an inscrutable expression until I start to feel like a freak show for going off like that.

But he deserved it, didn't he?

He…

"They're not my girlfriends," he murmurs after a bit.

Something about his casual answer irritates me even further and I snap, "Yeah, do they know that?"

"They do, yes." He shrugs then but there's this wild, wild intensity on his face, in his body too, looking all tight and strung up. "With me, they always know. I don't do girlfriends."

"And why? Why are you so special that you don't do girlfriends?"

"Because I don't. It's not my style. I don't believe in love and shit."

Of course.

A typical guy. I have four brothers and two of whom are complete players like him; I know.

They're the same.

Wild and untamable.

And I don't know why he's watching me like he's performing some kind of experiment. "Well then, as I said, you should ask your other girls to dance for you and leave me alone."

His scrutiny isn't over yet.

Not for another five or six seconds, and then, "You sound like you're jealous, Fae."

I gasp. Almost.

How dare he?

How freaking dare he?

I shift on my stupid heels again.

"You'd know, wouldn't you?" I raise my eyebrows. "Because you sounded like you were jealous when you thought that the world was looking at my juicy, tight ass, *Roman*."

It's his turn to blink.

Not that it makes him look intimidated by me or something like that.

In fact, I'm the one who loses all the air in her lungs because I've been dying, *dying*, to call him that. And to say it like that, blurting it out, makes me stumble on my heels.

He's just taken aback, I think.

Not by what I said, but what he says next, almost to himself, as if he's surprised by it. "I was."

"You were?"

He looks into my wide, shocked eyes. "Yeah. And I don't like that."

"Being jealous?"

"Yes."

His frown is so... adorable. It's such a tame word for a guy like him who's made of all sharp and dangerous edges.

But that's what I feel right now.

That he's so vulnerable and adorable in this moment with his honesty and so I have to be honest too. "M-me neither."

He opens and closes his fists as if he can't decide what he wants to do with his fingers. He can't decide what he wants to do in a situation like this and I can't wait to see what he *does* do.

Then with a sharp breath that pushes out his massive chest, he becomes himself.

He becomes dark in his intentions and dangerous in his beauty.

He looks me up and down in his villainous way before taking a couple of steps closer to me and I go a couple of steps back.

"So how about I make you another promise?" he offers like the devil he is.

"What promise?" I ask, looking up at him.

But not for long because right in front of my eyes, he does something incredible.

He does something that I never even imagined he would do.

Right in front of my eyes, Reed Roman Jackson slowly comes down on his knees.

The sight of it is so shocking that my hand sticks out on its own and grabs hold of his shoulder. His hoodie.

"I don't know... what you're doing," I whisper, looking into his eyes, which are on level with mine.

Because he's so, so tall.

His answer is to smile lopsidedly and grab my ankle.

Before I can even utter a word, he's taken off my shoe and given me my breaths back. When he goes for the other one and brings me back down to earth, taking off the added four inches of my height, I want to hug him.

I don't even care that now he reaches the top of my head easily.

I don't even care that the stark difference in our sizes makes me look all helpless in front of him.

"Tell me about your promise," I whisper, putting my other hand on his shoulder as well and clutching his soft hoodie.

His gaze turns liquid. "You take off that dress and braid your hair."

"And?"

His fingers still circle my ankle, squeezing. "And you dance only for me."

"What would I get in return?"

"And in return, I won't ask any other girls to dance for me." Another squeeze of my ankle and I bite my lip. "Only you."

Only me.

He just said that.

And maybe it's not exactly what a girl hopes to hear from a guy. It's not a declaration or anything. Just a little promise. And for now, it seems like enough. It seems enough to make me smile and wiggle my free toes on the ground in happiness.

It seems enough that I step closer to him and my bare feet graze his bent knees. "On one condition."

"What?"

I dare to touch the ends of his dark hair; they're as soft and silky as his hoodie. "I hear you love your Mustang."

His eyes narrow in suspicion. "I do."

I want to touch his stubble as well, the thing that appears every evening to bother him, but I'm not that bold so I satisfy myself with playing with his soft, soft hair.

"People say that she's your baby."

His hands go to my waist. "She is."

I suck in a breath at how easily he can span my slender torso. "I want you to give me a ride."

He digs his thumbs in the soft flesh of my stomach. "Ride to where?"

I don't even have to think about the answer, and good thing too, because all my thoughts are gone except the one.

He's touching me so possessively, like how a sculptor touches their creation maybe, with authority, with a sense of ownership. "Back to those woods where the party was that night."

He studies my face for a few seconds. "You want me to take you back to the woods."

"Yes."

"Alone? At night."

I nod, biting my lip.

"What do you think your four older, overprotective brothers would say about that? About me breaking the pact."

Oh right.

The stupid pact.

"I won't say anything to them. Ever," I promise, so easily falling into his trap.

"You won't."

"No. And my curfew isn't until eleven."

That brings a smirk on his face and makes him grip me tighter, like he's never letting me get away now. "Curfew."

I grip him tighter too because I'm not running away either.

I don't know when it happened, but I've become reckless now.

A girl who wears provocative dresses for a villain and asks him to take her out to the woods at night.

"Uh-huh." I nod. "You can bring me back here before that and no one will ever know."

"Are you asking me to keep another secret, Fae?" he rasps, looking all wild and wicked. "Because you know my price, don't you?"

"Yes. And I'll give it to you."

"You will, huh."

"Yeah, I'll dance for you. For as long as you want."

Because I'm his Fae, the dancing fairy and he's my Roman, the wild mustang.

Chapter 7

I imagine telling my brothers about him.

About Roman.

I daydream about all the things I'll tell them. I'll start with how amazing he is with Tempest. This is something my brothers will definitely relate to, him being an older, overprotective brother like them.

I'll tell them that last month when Tempest got really sick and she made one call to Reed, he abandoned his classes and his practice for the day and drove up to New York City. He argued with the teachers, with the headmaster even, and got her out of the dorm within the hour. He brought her back home and for days, he took care of her.

I saw that myself.

That week, every day after school, I went to visit her and he'd be there, reminding her about meds, feeding her soup, *hovering* with a big frown and a grumpy face when she'd disobey.

I'll tell my brothers that it reminds me of how they take care of me when I get sick.

Then I'll tell them that like them, he buys me Peanut Butter Blossoms.

One day we were driving by Buttery Blossoms — he gives me a ride in his Mustang almost every time I go to their house to visit Tempest on weekends; at first, I thought she'd be mad at me for ditching her but she encourages it, me spending time with her brother — and I pointed it out through the window and told him all about it.

"So the special thing about them is that the crumb is peanut butter and the frosting is chocolate. When usually people have a *chocolate* crumb and *peanut butter* frosting. See? Special, right? But I can't eat too many. Ballet and all that. And the other day my partner told me that I was getting too heavy for him to lift. Can you believe that?" I chewed on my lips. "Maybe I should go on my juice fast this weekend. I can easily –"

I stopped talking when the car suddenly came to a halt and in a flash, he climbed out of it. I climbed out after him and watched him stride over to Buttery Blossoms.

A minute later, he came out holding a familiar pink box.

"Your partner is a pussy," he growled, thrusting it into my hands. "And juice fasts are fucking stupid."

And like an idiot, I hugged that box to my chest, blinked up at him and whispered, "You know, you shouldn't really curse this much, Roman."

His jaw clenched at that and his eyes grew all hot for a second before ordering, "Just get in the car."

And I did.

Yeah, I'll tell them about that.

All my brothers would love it because they think my juice fasts are stupid too.

And maybe if I tell them all this, they won't hate him so much.

Maybe Ledger won't fight with him.

Like he does one day at practice.

I'm not sure what happened because I wasn't there but when

Reed shows up at the auditorium with a nasty split lip, I know.

That something happened between the two of them.

But the worst part is that he won't take care of it.

He absolutely *refuses* to take care of it in the coming days. Every time I ask him to, he goes, *it's fine.*

So one day I decide to take matters into my own hands and after *my* practice, as he's helping me pack up, I lock the door of the storage closet like he did that first time.

It's a bad idea, I think.

Because when he turns at the sound, glances at the door before glancing at me, the space shrinks and grows darker.

"Did you just lock the door?" he asks, his wolf eyes alert and pretty.

"Yes."

He leans against the shelf, folding his arms across his chest. "What about your brother who's waiting for you in the library?"

His hoodie's off and so I try not to look at the tiny hills that his biceps make under his light-colored t-shirt. "Well, he can wait another ten minutes. I don't care."

A smirk appears on his lips, all split and still pretty. "Ten minutes, huh. Living on the edge, are we?"

I stand on the stepstool to get my hands on the first aid kit on the storage shelf by the door. "Yeah. He'll be fine."

"I don't think ten minutes is enough."

When I get it, I step down and turn to him. "Oh, it's enough. Trust me."

He hums, almost thoughtfully, still looking at my face. "I mean, sure. I could take care of you in ten minutes."

"Take care of me?"

Licking his lips, he nods. "Yeah. *Twice.*"

"Twice what?"

"Fair warning though," he goes on, ignoring my confusion. "I'll want to do it one more time just because I think I'll be fucking addicted to your taste. I'm already fucking addicted to your scent. Jasmine, is it? But you'll be trembling, and you'll tell me to stop so I'll decide to have mercy on you. Just this once."

Taste.

What...

My eyes go wide when I understand, when I get what he means.

And when I *do* get it, his features grow sharp, dangerous... seductive. "But then it'll be my turn, Fae. And trust me when I say that ten minutes is not going to cut it."

"It's n-not?"

He shakes his head slowly. "I'm not so easy to take care of. When you're done taking care of me, you'll be going home with scraped up knees and swollen, dripping lips. Your brother will take one look at you and call the cops on me for doing bad things to his sister's pretty mouth in a storage closet. Not that I mind. But yeah, your math is slightly off there. I don't think ten minutes is enough."

The first aid kit's digging into my ribs by the time he finishes.

And I think I already have bruised knees and a swollen mouth, just because of the picture he's painted with his dirty words. I think my brother would know it anyway, that I was with him in a storage closet.

"It's geranium. And sugar. M-my scent."

"Geranium."

I nodded. "Yes, it's rare. It says on the bottle. I like rare body oils."

"I bet."

I hug the first aid kit to my chest even more tightly. "I..."

I don't know what to say except, *I'll do it.*

Oh my God, that's what I want to say, isn't it?

I want to tell him that I'll take care of him for as long as he wants.

I'm a ballerina. I'm not afraid of a little pain in my knees and bleeding skin.

I'll take care of him just like I dance for him in the woods when he puts on the music in his Mustang and sits on the hood to watch me.

Like he's the king of the world and I'm his slave girl.

Like he's my villain and I'm his ballerina.

But then he moves away from the shelf and approaches me, taking away all my thoughts.

He glances down at the first aid kit and my blinking, blushing face. "Do it."

My heart stops beating. "What?"

"You want to take care of my split lip, don't you?"

"Yes."

"Do it then."

Then without me having to say it, he drags the stepstool over with his foot for me to stand on. So it'll be easier for me to reach his injury. And all the while I take care of his bruise, my knees feel sore and my mouth feels swollen.

But I guess most of all, I want to tell my brothers how he helps me with my routine.

They all know my love for ballet and my ambition to go to Juilliard once I graduate from high school. It's my dream to dance for the New York City Ballet Company one day and all four of them have always been supportive of it.

So I know they'll definitely approve of the fact that Reed helps me practice.

Sure, it takes a little convincing on my part to get him to agree because when I first proposed the idea, his exact words were, "I'm not fucking twirling."

"Hey! That's extremely offensive," I told him from the stage. "Ballet isn't just twirling. There's like a hundred different things, *techniques*, that you do –"

"Well, you can call it whatever the fuck you want. I'm still not fucking twirling."

I stood there, staring down at him in his seat in his favorite third row, all sprawled-out thighs and large chest, masculine and stubborn.

And gorgeous.

In that moment, I hated how gorgeous he was.

"I can't believe that you won't help me. I can't." I threw my hands up in the air. "And for what? Because ballet threatens your masculinity? That's it, isn't it? You think twirling will make you less of a guy. You think twirling is feminine. Meanwhile, you don't even care that chivalry is dying. That you've killed it. You've killed chivalry, Roman. Today. Right here, in this auditorium. And this is a crime scene. *Crime*. Scene. *Murder*. So –"

I went quiet when he stood up and started to walk toward me.

Before I knew it, he'd crossed all the rows and, putting his palms on the edge of the low-rising stage, lifted and swung himself onto the stage in one smooth motion. Just like that.

Without breaking a sweat or even taking a breath, he approached me and I asked, "What are you doing?"

"Showing you how chivalrous I can be."

"What?"

"Usually I don't mind being the bad guy, but I don't like to be accused of crimes I haven't committed. So if you want me to twirl, I'll fucking twirl and save you from distress and be your knight in fucking armor."

"Knight in shining armor," I said as soon as he finished.

He narrowed his eyes at me dangerously. "What?"

"You said knight in fucking armor. But it's knight in shining armor." I peered up at him through my eyelashes. "So you're my knight in *shining* armor."

"And if you want to be rescued, Fae, you need to start talking really soon and tell me what the fuck you want me to do before I change my mind."

And since then, he has helped me with my routine.

He has lifted me, assisted me with jumps and leaps.

He's made me better.

Surely if I tell them all of this, they won't hate him, will they?

They can't.

I mean, yes there's this rivalry and years of hatred between him and Ledger, years of them sabotaging each other on the field and at practice just to have the top spot.

But can't they move past it?

Can't Conrad see that Reed isn't as selfish as he thinks he is?

He's so much more than just a villain.

He's an amazing big brother. A protector.

A guy who keeps his promises. First by apologizing to Ledger that night, and then, by not even looking at another girl.

Because he hasn't.

Not since he made that promise to me, the night he took me for a ride in his Mustang for the first time.

I haven't seen him with a girl in the hallways. I haven't seen him flirting or taking any interest in them. In fact, the other day I overheard a few girls talking in the restroom during lunch. About how Reed has seemed distant and distracted over the past few weeks.

See?

He can be a good guy, if he wants to be.

Only he doesn't want to be.

Not right now at least.

Not as I watch him on the soccer field, practicing with the team.

Well, there's no practice going on right now because the two star players are currently facing off against each other.

It's the same scene from that game weeks ago, the one that started everything.

Ledger is all angry and bunched up and Reed is cool and relaxed.

I know I should move on and not get involved. I never have before.

I was actually on my way to my own practice at the auditorium.

Tomorrow is my show that I've been practicing for for months and we're doing a full dress rehearsal.

Actually, tomorrow's also the day of the championship soccer game for Bardstown High and I'm still trying to figure out how I can both watch the game and make it to my own show.

But anyway, right now my plan was to just watch him play for a few minutes, hidden away behind the bleachers, and then leave to get to my own rehearsal.

But now I'm walking toward them, toward the crowd, the two camps, the Mustang and the Thorn.

Conrad and his assistant coaches are trying to settle everyone down. But when Con glares at Reed, snaps something at him and points to the bench, I know that it's only going to exacerbate the problem.

Reed glares back at Con and I grimace, thinking that he's going to say something to my brother and his coach, something disrespectful. But thankfully all he does is spit on the ground and wipe his mouth with the back of his hand and leave.

Or is about to, when something happens and it's Ledger.

Just as Reed is about to turn away, Ledger taunts, "Hey, Jackson! Can't wait to beat you tomorrow. Once and for all. You're going to regret not taking your dad's advice and quitting the team. You pollute everything you touch anyway."

Oh crap. Ledger!

He was leaving, *leaving* and my brother had to go and ruin it.

Reed's dad is a touchy subject.

I know that.

So apparently, his dad, the famous builder who owns everything in this town, hates the fact that Reed plays soccer. According to him, it's a huge waste of Reed's time because he wants his son to take over the business.

"My dad is an asshole," Tempest told me one day. "Like, a complete asshole. A negligent father. Bad, cheater of a husband. I'm glad I live far away from him. Though I miss my brother. I hate that he has to deal with our dad alone. And mom's no help. She lives in her own la-la land. But honestly though, Reed wouldn't let me deal with him anyway. He likes to protect me from stuff."

So I know there's tension between Reed and his dad.

I don't know the extent of it because Tempest was right, Reed *doesn't* like to talk about it, and I've tried to get him to only for him to shut down and grow angry.

Even right now, after Ledger's unnecessary taunt, he's done the same.

He's turned angry and rigid. Like stone.

Which only lasts for maybe two to three seconds before he fists his hands at his sides.

And then I already know what's going to happen.

I already know that Reed is going to hit my brother, and when he lands a mean punch on Ledger's face, I flinch.

I flinch even more when Ledger goes in for a payback punch.

Suddenly the crowd that had calmed down grows heated once again and somehow everyone is on everyone. There are shouts and curses and thumps and grunts.

And in the middle of it all are Ledger and Reed.

They're grappling, beating each other up. There's so much malice between them. So much pent-up aggression, years of trying to best each other, to come out on top, to bring each other down.

Years of hatred that are just pouring out on their last day of practice together.

Suddenly I realize that it doesn't matter what I tell them, my brothers, or what I tell *him* even. They're never ever going to get along.

Not if they can help it.

Chapter 8

He's sitting on the hood of his car, facing away from me, staring at something in the near darkness.

He doesn't have his hoodie on – it's May now so he shouldn't feel all that cold, but still – and through the thin material of his light-colored t-shirt, I can see the slabs of his muscled back shifting with each breath he takes.

I knew he'd be here.

At this spot, in the woods.

Located at the edge of town, where his party was that night. This is also where we usually end up when he takes me out on rides.

He looks so still, so deep in his thoughts, that I feel like I'm intruding. That I feel like I should leave him alone.

But I can't.

He hasn't said it but I know he needs me.

I know he needs *someone* by his side.

So here I am.

As it turns out, it's too late to leave anyway. Because I already have his attention.

He already knows that I'm here and he turns abruptly, his eyes zeroing in on me.

I suck in a breath then.

The moment I get to see his face.

All bruised and battered, covered with cuts. So much so that he's using his half-bunched up hoodie to put pressure on his jaw.

Back at the field, when their fight continued to escalate and a crowd was gathering, teachers were called in. They made us all leave while Conrad and the group of coaches tried to break up the fight. In the chaos of it all, I couldn't see him. I couldn't see Ledger either.

I'm pretty sure he looks the same.

My heart squeezes painfully as I study his bruises in the rapidly vanishing evening light.

Stupid soccer.

I *hate* soccer.

My thoughts break when he moves.

He takes a huge sip from the bottle that I didn't know he was holding — a liquor bottle, I presume; the liquid inside it looks as transparent as water though — and slams it down on the hood.

Throwing his hoodie aside, he springs up on his feet. "What the fuck are you doing here?"

I hug the backpack to my chest. "I came to –"

He doesn't let me speak. "Shouldn't you be at rehearsal?"

"Rehearsal is done. I –"

He fires off another question before I can finish, his eyes searching something beyond my shoulders. "How in the hell did you get here?"

"I, uh, got a ride from a friend."

His gaze comes back to me, all belligerent. "What friend?"

"From dance. Her brother was picking her up and she said that she could drop me here. It was on her way back."

His gaze grows even unfriendlier. "Her *brother*."

"Yeah. You know him. He's a senior too. Jonathan Andrews."

This piece of information makes Reed's jaw so tight that I have to bite my lip at the force.

"Andrews gave you a ride."

"Yes. I've talked to him some and he seems nice. He's in the drama club and –"

"Fuck drama club. And fuck Jonathan Andrews." His nostrils flare. "You're going to stay away from him."

"What?"

"Stay *away*. From him," he growls angrily.

"Why?"

"Because he's got a fucking hard-on for you. That's why."

Is that why he agreed so easily?

To not only give me a ride but also to keep it a secret at school. Sophie, his sister, isn't going to be so accommodating, I know. But I'll deal with that later.

My only aim was to get to Reed.

I blink. "I didn't... He didn't... He was just trying to help me."

Reed shifts on his feet as if getting ready to do battle. "Yeah, I don't think so. What he was *trying* to do was lay down the groundwork so he could make a play for you later. So you stay away from him, you understand? He's a fucking asshole."

"And if I don't?"

His chest pushes out then and again I can see the carved muscles of his pecs, his ribs shifting under his t-shirt, making him look even more dangerous than usual.

I think the hoodie takes away from his danger, cloaks it in false softness.

Without it, he's all dense muscles and hard bones.

His hands are fisted, veins standing out on his wrists and the backs of his hands. "Then I'm going to fuck him up so badly that he won't be able to drive for the rest of his life."

I hug my backpack tightly and rub my arms, trying to chase away the goosebumps that arose at his threatening, possessive tone.

Trying to not lose my breaths all at once.

"You sound like my brothers," I say. "When they talk about you."

"For once, I agree with them." His glowing eyes narrow. "Although what *I'd* like to know is where in the fuck were they when you were getting into Andrews's car? How could they let this happen? What goddamn use are they if they can't keep you safe?"

My thighs clench together and I tell him in a breathless tone, "They don't know. I texted Con and told him that I'd be staying late as usual. He thinks I'm at the auditorium practicing like I always do."

I did.

It was easy too.

He was expecting it even, after weeks and weeks of lying and telling him that I needed extra hours for practice.

I did need those hours.

But mostly it was because I wanted to spend them with him.

This guy who's glaring at me and who I knew wouldn't be showing up at my practice like he usually does.

"So, you lied to them," he concludes. "Again."

I nod. "I wanted to come see you."

And in this moment, I realize that even though I hate lying to my brothers and keeping secrets from them, I'll still do it. I'll still lie for him now and forever.

I'll lie and hide. I'll seek and run and stop.

I'll go wherever he is.

"You've become quite the liar, huh? For me."

"I –"

"I think you should go," he commands in a low, determined voice.

His words make me move.

But I don't do what he tells me to do.

I don't leave.

I walk toward him, bridging the distance between us.

"Did you fucking hear what I just said to you?" he asks, agitated, watching me walk toward him.

I don't answer. I just keep walking, my backpack in hand, my eyes on his gorgeous face. Gorgeous and familiar and so achingly dear to me.

"Go home," he growls, and I keep ignoring him.

And when I finally, *finally* reach him, his face dips and his words become thick. "Get the fuck away from me, Fae."

Does he know that even when he's being all growly and stubborn and an idiot like he is being right now, he still calls me Fae?

His fairy.

And if he does that, calls me by the name he's given me, how can I ever leave?

How can I ever stop my heart from flip-flopping in my chest when I crane my neck to look up at him, at his tall form?

I shake my head. "No."

"What part of *you should go now* don't you understand? I'm –"

"I brought first aid. For your injuries." I speak over him.

"I don't need your fucking first aid."

I knew he'd say that.

So I say something else that I wanted to say. "I'm sorry."

"What?"

"For what Ledger said." I take a step closer to him, to his heat, to his violently breathing chest. "He provoked you and he shouldn't have done that. You were leaving."

He stares down at me for a moment. "Yeah well, he wasn't lying, was he?"

I raise my hand to touch his jaw where he was pressing his now discarded hoodie. But he grabs my wrist to stop me. "And I'm sorry about your dad. I don't know the why or the how or any of that stuff. But Tempest shared a little bit of it with me and –"

"Tempest should keep her mouth shut," he says with clenched teeth and his thumb mashing into my pulse.

Even so, I'm not deterred. "I-I'm here though."

"You're here for what?"

"If you ever want to talk about it."

Reed goes silent for a second as if he can't believe I said that. As if it hasn't occurred to him that *anybody* would say that. "You want me to talk about it."

"Yes." I throw him a reassuring nod. "Talking helps."

Again, he goes silent for a few seconds before he replies, "Yeah, no. Talking isn't what I had in mind. So, you should really call yourself a cab and leave."

He lets go of my wrist then, ready to dismiss me.

But he doesn't know that with nothing stopping me, I have free rein.

I have free rein to get even closer to him, free rein to put my hand on his body.

His chest.

Smooth and muscled and hard under his cotton t-shirt. Radiating heat.

As soon as I touch him though, he stops breathing. His chest ceases all motion and he lowers his eyes to look at my hand on his body.

"What is it then?" I whisper and he looks up, his wolf eyes flashing. "What's on your mind?"

The anger in him, the agitation, is palpable and when he resumes breathing, he becomes even scarier somehow.

It's like touching a wild animal, petting his hard, lethal body.

But I'm not afraid.

Because strangely I think I can tame him.

Strangely I think I'm the girl to tame this wild mustang.

"Are you sure you want me to answer that?" he asks.

His challenge only makes me caress his chest gently, tenderly, and he clenches his teeth. "Yes. Tell me."

"I'm warning you, Fae, you need to leave now."

His muscles buzz under my fingers.

As if his cold, black heart is trying to bust free from the cage of his ribs but doesn't know how yet.

"Why?"

He leans down over me, his chest pushing back against my hand. "Because my head is all fucked up right now. And this here is my second bottle of vodka. So I'm not exactly *thinking*."

In retaliation, I push him back with my hand and close that last inch between us.

So far my backpack was acting like a wall between us but I let it go now. It slips from between our bodies and crashes on the ground with a thud.

Neither of us even spares it a glance though, no.

I'm too busy finally meeting his tall, hard body with mine and he's too busy being shocked that our bodies are touching.

This isn't the first time that we've touched like this.

Of course not.

He helps me with my routine. He lifts me, assists me in my leaps and turns. He knows what my body feels like. I know what his body feels like too, all hard and smooth.

Powerful.

Like he could push mountains away to make space for his tall self and rip the earth open with his bare hands if he wanted to.

I know all that and yet I've never felt his body like this.

Just because I want to. Just because I *can*.

And neither has he.

For all his bad reputation and villainous intentions, he has not once tried anything with me. He helps me and that's it.

He's always been controlled.

Restrained.

Respectful even.

I wonder if I tell my brothers about this, about Reed's careful nature, what their reactions would be.

"I don't want you to think," I say, my neck craned up.

His stomach contracts with a large breath that he exhales as he stares down at me. "You do realize you're in the middle of nowhere, don't you?"

"Yes."

"Miles away from civilization."

"I know."

"So if you scream for help, no one is going to hear you. Not even your four older, fucking *useless* brothers whose one job was to protect you but they can't even do that right, can they?"

His rough tone makes my heart race faster. "I won't scream."

Another breath whooshes out of him. "You will. If I want you to." His eyes grow all dark just like the sky around us. "If I *make* you. And I can make you do a lot of things. In these woods, I'm the god, Fae, and my word is the only word. So if I tell you to get the fuck away from me and out of these woods, you need to do that."

I don't listen to him.

Of course I don't.

He should know by now. Just because he tells me to do something, I'm not going to do it.

Not if I don't want to.

I'm not the good girl Callie for him.

I'm his Fae and so I put my other hand on his chest too, as if to show how bad I can be, how eager.

"I'll do it," I whisper. "Whatever you want me to. I've been p-practicing."

That throws him off, my excitement, eagerness. The little tidbit of information that I let slip. I can't say that I did it accidentally. Or that I had no intention of doing it.

I had every intention.

I've had this intention for days now but I didn't know how to bring it up.

I didn't know if I *should* bring it up or not.

Given the fact that I shouldn't have been practicing at all what I've been practicing for days now.

"What?" he bites out.

If I tell him then there's no going back. Then there's no two ways about what I feel for him.

He'll know.

Reed Roman Jackson, the Wild Mustang, the soccer god, the heartbreaker of Bardstown High will know that my good girl, not-so-freshman, just turned sixteen-year-old heart beats for him; my birthday was last week and he bought me cupcakes and new knitting needles and so much yarn.

Before I can make up my mind either way, my lips seal my fate as I blurt out, "You told me the other day, in the storage closet that… that you're not so easy to take care of…"

Despite my determination in telling him, my courage falters when I actually say the words.

And I have to lower my eyes.

I have to fist his t-shirt and bite my lip as a flurry of butterflies swoops around in my stomach.

"What about it?"

His gravelly voice makes me clench my stomach. "You said that if I took care of you, I'd have bruised knees, so I…"

God, why can't I just say it?

I should be able to say it.

I started this, didn't I?

"You what?" he asks in a strangled whisper.

Finally I look up and all my fear and shyness just melt away.

He appears as he does when he watches me dance. All on edge and intense and excited. "So I get down on my knees. At night."

"On your knees."

"Yes." My knees tingle from all the abuse of the past days. "We've got hardwood floors at home. So I get down and I… I stay there."

His lips part then.

Only slightly, but I know it's because he's started to breathe heavily. His entire body is moving with it.

"For how long?" he asks gruffly.

"A long time. Until I…" I press my knees into his legs. "Until they start to feel all numb. And sore."

They do start to feel sore, after being like that for what feels like minutes and hours and days.

They do start to feel bruised up after what feels like worshipping.

Like I am praying to God.

Only my god is a devil.

A villain with wolf eyes and vampire skin.

And I feel his villainous heart skipping a beat under my fist. "You made your knees sore. For me."

"Yes," I whisper, pressing myself into him. "But that's not all. I practice something else too."

"What?"

"You said that you could... you could take care of me twice. But then I wouldn't let you. So I practice so that I will."

"How?"

My thighs clench together. "I touch myself."

"Where?"

"I... in my... you know where."

At last, he leans his face toward me, all bruised up and swollen in places, making him look like a criminal.

A thug I should run away from. But I press myself closer to.

"Pussy," he chokes out. "You touch your pussy."

I'm doused by a flood of heat at the dirty word and I nod. "Yes."

But he won't let me go so easily.

By telling him this, I've unleashed something in him. A beast, a predator, and so all I can do is revel in the fact that he finally chooses to touch me.

He not only touches me, he crushes me to him.

With his hands on my waist, his fingers digging into my soft flesh, he bends down even more, darkening the world around us.

"Say it," he growls.

"I..."

His fingers on my body grow insistent. "Say '*I touch my pussy.*'"

My own fingers dig in his chest when I obey him. "I touch my p-pussy."

"'*And I make myself come.*'"

"And I make myself come."

"For Roman."

"For my Roman."

"How many times?"

I have to gather my breaths first before I can tell him. "T-two, sometimes three."

His eyes shoot fire. "Three."

"Yes."

"Because you were practicing."

My ballerina feet can't stay still so I go up on my tiptoes. "Yes. I wanted to be… ready."

"Ready, yeah," he whispers as well. "Because you know that if I get anywhere near that thing, it's game over, don't you? You know that I'd lick her and suck on her and fingerfuck her like I've never fucked a pussy before."

"Y-yes."

"And I'd eat her out, bang her with my tongue until she gets all sore and hurt like your knees. You know that, don't you?"

I want to say that he shouldn't curse so much.

That he shouldn't use such dirty language.

But then I'd be lying because I want him to.

I want him to say these things, I want him to talk to me like that, like he's the filthiest guy in the world and I'm the most innocent girl who's never heard these things before, the girl that he wants to corrupt.

"Yes, I know," I tell him.

"Yeah, you know that I'd become what they call me. That if I catch even a whiff of her scent, I'll go wild. I'll become an animal and I'll snap my teeth and I'll snarl. And nothing would calm me down except her, except the sight of her, the taste of her. You know I'll become a villain for your fairy pussy."

My hands creep up his chest and my fingers cradle his bruised jaw, my thumbs rubbing his stubble. "A gorgeous villain."

He presses his fingers on my waist, almost picking me up off the ground. "So you were getting her ready. Like the good girl you are. You were warming her up for me."

I wind my arms around his neck. "Uh-huh."

"In your bedroom."

"At night," I continue.

"And what were your brothers doing?"

"Sleeping."

"Where?"

"Down the hall." Something violent passes through his features so I explain, "But it's okay. Because I'm quiet. I bite on my pillow. When I come."

His jaw moves back and forth before he somehow opens his mouth and grunts, "So they don't know."

"No."

"They don't know that every night their innocent little sister touches her innocent little pussy for me. For the guy they hate."

"I don't want them to hate you," I confess.

He ignores my words and continues, "They don't know that she gets down on her knees for him. She rubs her pussy until she drips and then she bites her pillow to keep quiet. So no one ever knows what she does when she locks her door at night. And she does it all to get herself ready for the guy they've warned her about. So he could abuse that pussy and make her like it."

"I would. I would like it," I tell him as if he doesn't already know.

He swallows then. "I know you would. Because I'd make it good for you. I'd make it so good that you'd be addicted. You'd become a junkie and you'd beg me for a fix. I told you that, didn't I? I told you that every girl begs and you will too."

My spine arches at his tone as if he's pulling on all my strings and I nod.

"Yes. I will. I'll do anything you want me to do."

"You'll beg me to spread your legs. To use that tight little fairy hole and stick it to your brothers. You'll beg me to destroy you in your good girl bedroom while they sleep just down the hall. While I make you moan in your lacy pillow and make you betray your brothers every night. And then, ask me, what will I do?"

My breaths are all but gone right now but I somehow wheeze out, "What?"

"I'll tell them," he says with a cold, humorless, half smile. "I'll tell them how pretty their sister looked when she opened her legs for me last night. I'll fucking brag about banging their sister under their noses."

"You wouldn't." I shake my head. "I trust you."

Maybe it's the stupidest thing I've ever said, even stupider than all the things I've been saying tonight, but I do.

I do trust him.

He had all the opportunity, didn't he?

He could've told them.

He could've used me against Ledger. He could've bragged if he wanted to.

But he didn't.

He kept our secret. Day after day, night after night.

I know he's trying to scare me away but I'm not going anywhere.

He scoffs. "Yeah, that's what a stupid little girl says before she gets into the car with a stranger who takes her away and locks her up in a room for the rest of her life."

"I —"

"So you need to go home, understand?" he says, letting me go. "You need to leave me alone because as I said, I'm not thinking straight right now."

"Do it," I tell him, ignoring his command for the thousandth time. "Make me do things. Everything you said. All of them. Please."

"Fae —"

"Please. Destroy me, Roman," I beg like he told me I would, and a shudder passes through him and through me too.

I stretch myself up then, as much as I can, and put my mouth on him.

On his Adam's apple.

I lick the bulge, his rough stubble, and I would've gone on to do more if he hadn't wrapped my braid around his wrist and pulled my head back.

If he hadn't made me look at him.

I shiver at the look on his face.

I shake with fear and anticipation.

His eyes have gone all dark like the night around us and his jaw has morphed into a true V. With his angry bruises, he looks so dangerous, so gorgeous that I whisper again, "Please, Roman."

At my plea, his gaze falls down to my lips and I think I hear a growl.

I can't be sure because it's low and thick and in the next second, I don't have the mental capacity to think about it anyway.

Because his mouth is on me.

His taste, all spicy and vodka-laced, explodes on my tongue and God, it's so delicious that I want to keep tasting him.

I want to keep analyzing other nuances of his flavor and his soft, warm mouth but just then, the sky opens up.

With no warning or forecast whatsoever, it starts to rain and we break apart.

Panting, we look at each other and I don't know what he's thinking.

I don't know if he's mourning the loss of my lips as I'm mourning the loss of his.

But again, he takes away my ability to think when he picks me up.

He lifts me off the ground and because we've done this move a thousand times before during my dance practice, I don't even hesitate to wrap my legs around his slim waist. And as soon as I do that, he puts his big hand on the back of my head and makes me huddle into his chest.

He makes me seek shelter from the rain in his big body.

And all I can do is take it and hug him tightly.

My Roman.

My gorgeous, *gorgeous* villain.

As he begins to move, I mumble, "My bag."

I wouldn't usually care about it, my backpack.

But it has something inside it. For him – not the first aid kit – and I don't want it to get wet.

Smoothly, while still carrying me in his arms, Reed bends down to pick up my bag. When he has it, I thank him and kiss the pulsing vein on the side of his neck. I hear him inhale sharply as he walks me to the back door of his Mustang.

He opens it and carefully deposits me inside the car, away from the rain, before getting in himself. He throws my backpack on the floor and I don't even wait for him to shut the door properly before I crawl over and straddle him.

It's such a bold move but I don't care.

I don't really care about anything tonight except being close to him, taking care of him.

Taking all his pain from the fight and his loneliness away.

My hands are on his shoulders, fisting his damp t-shirt, and his find their way back to my waist, clutching onto my wet dress. I stare at the water droplets that sluice down his dark, rain-slick hair to his beautiful face. They stream down his cheeks and the side of his neck, disappearing into the V of his t-shirt.

And God, I was right.

He's got muscles for days.

I can see them through his t-shirt, the ridges of his ribs and the hills of his chest and the cut planes of his stomach, and I squirm on his lap.

Wait a second. I'm on his lap.

How did I not notice this before?

My spread thighs, even though covered by my wet dress, rub against his damp jeans and oh my God, it's glorious, the rough fabric and my smooth skin. And so I squirm again but before I can do it one more time, he stops me.

He *physically* stops me by putting pressure on my waist and pinning me in one spot, commanding, "Hold on to your dress."

I frown. "What?"

He glances down at the hem of my dress. "Your dress. Hold on to it."

I pull at his t-shirt. "Why?"

"Just do it. Now," he says with clenched teeth, his body pulsing with his words.

I immediately let go of his t-shirt and grab the hem of my dress. He doesn't like how I've done it though, so he lets go of my waist and positions my hands.

He carefully puts my hand —*both* hands — in between my legs and makes me fist the fabric. And he makes me do it so tightly that my knuckles jut out with the force.

When he's done, he looks up. "Don't let me push it up your thighs."

My heart is banging against my chest. "Why not?"

He licks his lips, his hand flexing over mine. "Because I want to."

"But I –"

"Because I want to push your dress up and look at your panties. Because I know you're creaming them right now and I want to see. I want to look at that wet spot and picture you creaming every night for me, up in your bedroom. And if I do that, if I imagine you, then I'm going to lose whatever sanity I have left. You got that? So you're going to protect her."

"Roman –"

He lets go of my hands and buries his fingers in my wet hair.

He presses his forehead over mine as he says in a guttural voice, "No, listen to me, you're going to protect her. From *me*. You're going to hold onto your dress and you're going to guard your pussy. You're not going to let me push your dress up no matter what I do, what I say. You're not going to let me see her. Tell me you understand."

"But –"

"Tell me you understand, Fae."

It's the Fae that does it.

It's the way he says it like a plea.

Like he's the one who's begging now.

He's the one who's good and I'm the one who's bad and tormenting him. And I never *ever* want to do that. I've pushed him enough tonight, so I look into his animal eyes that look almost anguished. "If I say yes, will you kiss me then?"

His jaw clenches and he tugs on my hair. "Fuck yes."

I smile slightly and fist my dress even more tightly. "Okay. I'll hold on to my dress. I won't let you push it up. I won't let you see her. No matter what you say."

A relieved sigh escapes him then. As big a sigh as the wind around us.

And then he kisses me as he promised.

Chapter 9

Something bad is going to happen. On the field, I mean.

I don't know how I know it but I do.

It's a feeling that's been plaguing me ever since last night and somehow has been exacerbated since the championship game started.

So I finally figured out how to attend the game and my own show.

I got to the auditorium way earlier than they asked us to and got ready for my dance before I ran all the way across the school – because my auditorium and his soccer field are on opposite sides of campus from each other – to attend the game with Tempest.

But anyway, here I am, decked out in an ice blue tutu and a white leotard and full-on make-up to look like a fairy, watching the game that's about to be done in like, ten minutes.

Our team only needs one more goal in order to win and things are looking good. Oh, and if Reed makes this goal, then he'll not only win the championship but also their contest.

Once and for all.

He's in the lead right now and he needs this last goal to seal his victory over my brother.

But I feel like something bad is going to happen.

If I'm being honest though, there's no reason for me to be feeling like this.

No reason at all. Everything is fine actually.

Everything is more than fine.

Because he kissed me. Last night.

He kissed me for a long, *long* time.

For a little while there I thought he'd never stop.

I thought *I'd* never stop.

Because when his mouth was on me, drugging me with his warm, wet kisses, I realized that I'd wanted this for so long. I'd wanted this every time he looked at me and every time he said something dirty and made me blush. I'd wanted this every time he brought me cupcakes and gave me a ride in his Mustang.

So yeah, for a little while there, he became my entire world.

Reed Roman Jackson and his mouth and his Mustang with foggy windows.

His Mustang in which I came.

Well, I came on his lap. Twice.

Because he wasn't happy with just once and wouldn't stop kissing me or rocking me in his lap. And like the ballerina I am, I danced and writhed as much as he wanted me to.

After two though, I told him to stop, as he predicted days and days ago, and for which I'd practiced like a good girl.

But instead of reminding me that all my practice failed, his gray eyes simply turned all soft and liquid and he kissed me on my sweaty forehead, making me burrow into his chest.

God.

I never ever imagined that he could be so… tender and sweet and just everything.

Anyway, after that I gave him his present.

The one I had in my backpack.

It's something that I've been working on for the past several weeks.

A sweater.

"Because you're always cold," I told him, because he always is.

That's why he wears his hoodies practically all the time.

"And because white's your favorite color, and look." I pointed to the black intarsia that I'd done on the front. "It's a mustang. An actual mustang, not the car. Oh and it was my very first intarsia project. It came out nice, right?"

I'd seen the pattern in a knitting book months ago – before I really knew him – and it'd reminded me of him.

So when I decided to knit for him, I went and dug the magazine up and well, I stabbed myself in the fingers with the needles a million times before I got the design right.

Reed didn't say anything. Not for a long time as he stared down at the sweater I made for him and I had to ask, "You don't like it?" I started pulling it away from his grip, which was surprisingly tight. "It's okay. Don't worry about it. I'm gonna make you another one and –"

"I like it," he said in a hoarse whisper, speaking over me.

And then he pulled me to him and pressed his mouth on my forehead.

He didn't kiss me there again though, no.

He just… breathed with an open mouth for a few moments like he couldn't get enough air and I let him.

That was all.

That was all that happened last night.

We kissed, he made me come, I gave him his present and then he drove me back to school just in time for Con to pick me up from the parking lot.

I haven't seen him since.

Which is understandable given the fact that his big game is currently underway, and I've been busy with my own practice for the show.

Maybe that's why I'm feeling uneasy.

Because of the championship game.

Because I know how important it is to him and to Ledger. Oh, and it's also the last game of their high school career.

Not to mention their last game together.

It should make me happy that they won't butt heads anymore — they're both going to different colleges on soccer scholarships — and this contest, no matter who wins, will finally be over.

But strangely I'm uneasy.

Ledger's in possession of the ball and he's running across the field with it. Just when he reaches a point where he can take a shot and score the goal, the winning goal no less, Reed barges in.

He swipes the ball from Ledger and there ensues a struggle between the two star players of Bardstown High.

They both grapple for the ball, trying to score the goal, somehow dodging the players from the opposite team as well.

Not that I had any doubts that they wouldn't be able to.

Together, the Mustang and the Thorn can defeat every single team in the state and they have. They're that talented.

I'm not afraid that they'll lose the ball.

I'm afraid about something else.

Something that happens right in front of my eyes.

While struggling to get the ball, they're both pushing at each other.

Until Ledger stops.

He comes to a dead halt because Reed has said something.

I see his lips move – the lips that I kissed last night in the rain and then in his Mustang, the lips that have made me smile and blush over the past months – and I see Ledger freezing over.

To the point where Reed finally steals the ball from my brother and scores the goal.

Sealing both the championship and his victory over my brother.

As the whole stadium erupts in cheers and laughter and happiness, I sit in my spot tense and shocked, afraid.

So afraid.

My eyes are glued to two of the most important people in my life.

He is that, isn't he?

Somehow Reed Roman Jackson, *my* Roman, has become one of the most important people in my life and I don't want to keep him a secret.

This is another thing that I've been feeling ever since last night.

Along with this premonition, I've been wanting to tell my brothers about him. Make them understand that he's not as bad as they all think he is.

But like yesterday at practice when they fought, Reed is in no mood to be good.

Even though he's gotten the thing that he wanted, the title of reigning champion, his mood is so black and so bitter that even I can feel it from here.

Even I can feel his fury.

And the only thing that matches Reed's fury and his agitated breaths as he glares at my brother while the Mustang camp of the team pats him on the back, is Ledger.

He matches Reed's black mood.

In fact, he's surpassed it.

And it's nothing new, see.

Reed has always been the one to provoke my brother and my brother has always been the one to give in to it.

So this scene shouldn't be too alarming, but it is for so many reasons, and when Ledger closes the distance between them, I can't sit still.

And neither can Tempest, who's also been glued to her spot through all the happiness and enthusiasm around us. Together, we manage to grapple through the thick, happy crowd and bound down the stairs to get to the front.

So we can see what's happening.

So we can see if our brothers are okay.

God, please let them be okay.

Please.

I'm chanting it in my head all through the journey that should've only been a few seconds but takes an age due to the excited and exiting crowd.

When we do reach our destination, I exhale a relieved breath.

But it only lasts for a few seconds.

Because the moment we get to the front and have a clear view of the field, somehow, *someway*, he sees me.

His eyes fall on me through the incoming crowd, through all the chaos, and I don't know what I see in the depths of them.

I don't understand the intense emotion reflected in them and it scares me even more.

It scares me that as he runs his eyes over my body it feels like the last time. Like he'll never see me again after this.

Like this is goodbye.

Before I can do anything about it, jump the fence and run to him or something like that, my brother turns to look at me too.

And as soon as *his* eyes fall on me, that dark brown that I've known for as long as I've lived and that has never ever looked at me with anything less than affection even when we've fought, I take a step back.

My knees tremble.

There's such hatred in them.

Such thick and pervasive betrayal that I don't know how to breathe.

I don't know how to live on to the next moment, and then he turns back around and before I can even blink, he punches Reed in the face.

That punch is all it takes.

It makes the already wild crowd go wilder and crazier and a riot breaks out.

On the field, in the bleachers and like yesterday at practice, everyone is on everyone. Only this is much, much bigger in scale and much more horrifying.

So much so that I think I'll get crushed under it.

Under the mad crowd and the insanity.

Somehow I don't though because Tempest grabs my hand and pulls me away. She drags me through the crowd, dodging people and keeping a firm grip on my hand.

I'm thankful for it.

Because if it wasn't for her, I'd be on the ground. My legs wouldn't hold me under the weight of my brother's gaze.

Under the weight of *his* gaze too.

The guy I'm in love with.

I'm in love with him, aren't I?

I love Reed and *God*, I don't know what just happened and I...

Finally, I can breathe because we're out at the entrance now. It's not as if the crowd has thinned out but the space is more open and air is easier to get.

I see security flooding onto the field, where the fight is still going on.

I can't see Ledger or Reed and I turn to Tempest, with a pounding heart. "I need to go find them."

"Wait, what about your show?" she asks, still holding on to my arm.

Oh.

My show.

That's about to start in less than ten minutes and they must be wondering where I went.

"I don't... I need to find out what happened. I need to... I need to go."

I let go of her hand and enter the field.

I start running toward the huddle, which is slowly getting controlled by security and teachers and coaches.

But I don't make it too far because I see someone I recognize.

Conrad.

My oldest brother.

He's somehow emerged from the huddle and is now marching toward me.

In fact, he's almost here and he looks furious. I'm used to him looking all intimidating and large but when he wears a suit with a tie — which he only does for championship games — he appears even scarier.

But I can't let that deter me.

I need to know what happened. What Reed said and why Ledger looked at me like he hated me.

When Con reaches me, I immediately break out with my questions. "What happened? I..." I glance to the crowd. "Is Ledger okay? Is... What happened, Con?"

My oldest brother grinds his jaw as he looks down at me, and even though his navy blue eyes don't hold the same hatred, my heart shrivels even more.

"Con, what happened? Please tell me. I –"

My brother grabs my arm then and starts dragging me away from the commotion.

I look back but still can't see Ledger or Reed or get any indication if they're going to be okay.

"What are you doing?" I ask my brother as I turn back around. "What... Con."

He comes to a halt in a relatively quiet and isolated spot along the bleachers, his face all tight and bunched. "You've been lying to us. You've been lying to Ledger."

"What?"

He stares at me for a beat before shaking his head. "All this time, we trusted you. I trusted you. I gave you everything you asked for. Every freedom, every comfort. And you've been lying. All those late practice hours." He shakes his head again. "I thought you were smarter than this, Callie. I thought my sister was..."

His jaw tics as he plows his hand through his hair and I watch him, watch my brother's face, drenched in disappointment.

I watch his face tighten with anger and betrayal.

Betrayal that I caused. That he somehow found out about.

God, he found out about it.

He somehow *knows*.

And with trembling lips, I have to ask, "How did you..."

"The boy you were lying for all this time, he was bragging about you on the field."

I'll brag about how pretty their sister looked the next day...

That's why Ledger looked so betrayed, didn't he?

That's why there was so much hatred in his eyes when he looked at me.

No, no, no.

He wouldn't do that. He promised me.

He promised.

He wouldn't break his promise like this.

He *wouldn't.*

I somehow pull myself together and say, "There has to be a reason. There has to be an explanation."

"Explanation."

I flinch at Con's angry voice but still, I grab his arm and plead with him, "Con, he's not like that. He's not. I know you hate him. I know Ledger hates him too but he's not all bad. He's not. You don't know him like I do. You don't…" I gather my scattered breaths again. "I was going to tell you, I promise. I was. I just… I'm sorry that I lied. I'm so sorry. But Con, there has to be an explanation for this. If I could just –"

"Enough," he snaps, making me shut my mouth and let go of his arm. Then he pulls in a deep breath, as if to calm himself. "We'll talk about this later, you understand? Go back to your show right now. You've got a show, remember?"

"I don't care about the show, Con. I need to see if Ledger's okay and I need to talk –"

"All you need to do is go back to the show. You need to go dance and we'll talk about this later, got it?" he orders. "Straight to your show, Callie. You're done wasting your time on him."

Chapter 10

I watch him from across the space.

He's sitting on an overcrowded couch with a bunch of his friends. There are girls in the mix, of course. But he's not paying attention to any of them.

In fact, all his attention is on his bottle.

The same one as yesterday. The liquor that looks like water, vodka.

Even though he's focusing on the alcohol, I'm still jealous of all the girls around him. I'm still jealous that they're trying to get his attention like they always do.

I want his attention.

I just don't know how to get it.

I'm too afraid to walk up to him.

I'm too afraid to ask him.

I'm too afraid...

Come on, Callie. Do it.

That's what you came here for, right?

Right.

That's why I abandoned my show and came to this place.

This place outside of my town where this strange party is happening and Reed is in attendance.

After Con told me to go back to the show, Tempest found me again. She dragged me away from the crowd and took me to a quiet place, away from the stadium.

Away from all the people, from all the violence.

Even she knew I couldn't dance like this.

She stayed with me as I cried and shook.

As my whole body was wracked with waves and waves of chills.

She stayed with me as I ran through a thousand different scenarios in my head. As I went over what I saw and what Con told me and what I know.

What I know in my heart about Reed.

About my Roman.

I'm not sure how long I stayed like that, huddled into myself with Tempest rubbing my back and my arms.

All I know is that when I could gather my strength, I asked her to find him.

I asked her to take me to him.

And despite vehemently disagreeing with it at first and saying that I needed to go home and take care of myself, she brought me here.

She said that she saw it on social media. Someone had tagged Reed on Instagram, saying that he was at a party outside of Bardstown.

So that's where I am, at a party, watching the guy I'm in love with chugging down vodka, surrounded by a drunk crowd.

I try to make myself move.

I try to make myself call out his name, wave at him, do something to catch his attention. But I'm just frozen in my spot, too scared to move.

A second later though, I don't have to.

Because as always, he senses me.

He looks up from the bottle and his eyes land on me instantly and they start to glow.

His wolf eyes.

They sparkle as he stands up from the couch and starts walking toward me, leaving everything behind.

The crowd parts for him as he approaches me, his gaze growing heavier and more intense with every step he takes.

The moment he reaches me and stops, I realize that he's wearing all black.

I don't know why that's important.

I don't know why I'm thinking about his black t-shirt paired with dark jeans. I don't know why I find his black leather jacket intimidating and dangerous, but I do.

I'm thinking about how all this darkness makes his vampire skin come alive.

How his bruises, old and new, come alive as well.

How he's too beautiful for words.

Too otherworldly. Too gorgeous.

He looks down at me with a strange kind of tenderness as he takes in my costume, my make-up that's ruined now, and my blonde hair twisted into a bun, which again is ruined, strands hanging around my face in tatters.

But the way his eyes melt at the sight of me makes me think that I'm the most beautiful girl he's ever seen.

It makes me think that *I'm* too beautiful for words. Too otherworldly. Too gorgeous.

"Fae," he whispers roughly, drunkenly. "You're here."

"Roman –"

"You look like a fairy," he says over me, bringing his hand up and tracing a finger down my cheek.

My mouth parts at his touch and the world disappears.

And I think, *you look like a villain.*

That's what he looks like, isn't it?

Dressed in black and dark bruises, the guy I'm in love with looks like a villain.

"Are you drunk?" I ask instead.

He looks down at the bottle in his hand. "A little."

I swallow painfully. Thickly.

Fearfully.

"I won," he says then, his busted lips stretching up in a smile.

A smile that looks so misplaced, so boyish and adorable on his sharp, villainous face.

"You –"

"I fucking won the game, Fae. I won. I'm the goddamn champion. Did you see?"

My eyes sting as I nod.

"You did, huh? I was pretty badass out there." Chuckling, he takes a sip of his vodka. "More than your fucking brother."

"What –"

"Hey, what about your show?" he asks, speaking over me again. "Fuck, did I miss it?"

"I don't care about the show. I –"

"If after all that practice, I missed your first-class, fantastic show, then I'm an asshole. I'm a motherfucking asshole. You should be mad at me. Here." He waves his free hand. "Hit me. Slap me in the face, Fae. Slap me in the fucking face –"

"No, Roman, listen to me." I speak over him, putting an end to his drunken rambling. "What happened?"

He appears perplexed. "When?"

I shake my head. "On the field. What happened?" I swallow again. "God, look at you. You're all banged up. What happened, Roman?"

He chuckles. "You should see the other guy."

"What did you say to him?"

"What did I say to whom?"

I fist my hands for a second, trying to keep my wits about me. Then, "Roman, please, okay? Can you focus for a second? Just... please. What did you say to my brother? What did you say to Ledger? Why did he... Why did he punch you? Why did you guys fight?"

I'm not sure if he's getting the gravity of the situation because his reaction is pretty casual.

His reaction is to squint his eyes slightly and shrug. "Ah, that. The fight."

"What happened, Roman?"

He takes a gulp of his vodka, swallowing loudly. "Yeah, I might have mentioned something."

My heart thuds. "W-what?"

He shrugs again. "I might've said something about me giving you a ride in my Mustang. About you loving it and fogging up my windows." A frown. "Not in those words though. I was dirtier than that but you know what I mean."

"Y-you what?"

Reed sighs then. "Look, I just wanted to piss him off, all right. He was gonna score. I had to do something. It was the championship game. My last chance to win."

"Your last chance to win."

"Yeah, I just wanted to win." He bends down slightly. "But if it makes you feel any better, I only won by two goals. Your brother was a worthy opponent. You should tell him that tonight. Tell him I said that. Tell him Reed said that he's good. A real pain in my ass with how good he is. But you know, the best man won. Tell him to not cry too much in his pillow."

There's a pain in my chest. A massive, gigantic pain, but I power through.

I power through because this isn't real, right?

This isn't him.

This isn't how he behaves.

He's never this drunk. He's never this… cruel.

He's had plenty of opportunities to *be* cruel.

He's had plenty of opportunities to be a player, a heartbreaker, to be all those things that they call him, but he's never taken them.

No, this isn't him.

He's never broken a promise to me and I refuse to believe that he did now.

Even though I saw it with my own eyes. Even though I saw it in my brothers' eyes, both Conrad's and Ledger's.

"What are you doing?" I burst out, desperately. "Why are you acting this way?

He thinks about it for a second. "I'm not acting."

"You promised," I remind him. "You made that pact with Ledger, remember? The pact that you were so crazy about. You promised you wouldn't tell. You promised you wouldn't use me against Ledger. You promised me that the first time I danced for you. You had tons of opportunities to do that but you never did and –"

"Right. I lied."

"What?"

He drinks from his bottle again. "I lied. I made it all up."

"You lied."

"Yeah. I kinda do that." He shrugs again. "One of my many bad habits but I try to love myself for who I am. I think self-acceptance is a very intriguing concept. It basically –"

I grab his t-shirt in my fists and snap, "Stop."

Finally, I think I've jerked him awake.

Finally, I think he's seeing me, hearing me.

So I tell him, "This isn't you. This isn't how you behave. I know it. I know. People are wrong about you. They think you're selfish and you're a jerk and you're bad. But you're not. You love your sister. You take care of her. You take care of *me*. You're not cruel. You're not. You protected me, Roman. Last night. I thought about it."

I nod and fist his t-shirt even tighter. "I did. I thought about why you didn't... have sex with me. It didn't occur to me until after you dropped me off at the school parking lot. You were protecting me, weren't you? You wanted to protect my innocence. That's why you told me to hold on to my dress. That's why you didn't even *ask* me to take care of you. You didn't and –"

Reed grabs onto my fists on his t-shirt and the muscles in his stomach contract as he growls, "This is starting to really piss me off now. I was having a good day, all right? I won. Yeah, I also got beaten up for it by your wonderful brother, who packs a really mean punch by the way. But it's fine. I don't care. I'm the champion. I've been waiting for this day ever since your brother stole the title last season. So yeah, I was having a brilliant fucking day and I would really like to get back to it. So I'm going to make this really easy for you.

"These past few weeks have been good. Fun. I mean, I still don't like twirling but I can see why dudes do it. And I'm not sure if I'm going to be walking into that cupcake store again. It's too pink for me. But I have to say that it's been interesting. Given the fact that the only reason it all started was because you're the Thorn Princess. But you're really fucking ruining it right now."

"What did you just s-say?"

"Look, it was a clear-cut way to mess with him. It's not as if I was thinking about it. It's not as if I was plotting ways to seduce my rival's little sister. But then you walked into my party looking all sweet and innocent. I tried to stay away, trust me. I even made that stupid fucking pact. But then you were so interested in me. I mean, why wouldn't you be? Every girl is, but I would have had to be stupid not to take it. I would have had to be too stupid not to take you. Especially when it was too easy to reel you in. Too easy to take you for a ride, make you do things. You practically stood on the edge of a cliff for me. All I had to do was give you a push. All I had to do was make you fall."

All he had to do was give me a push.

He's right.

I stood on the edge for him. My arms wide open, wearing a white dress.

And all he had to do was nudge me a little.

All he had to do was make me fall.

"You did all this so you could mess with Ledger," I whisper as numbness spreads through my veins.

His jaw clenches. "I did all this for soccer."

"So you could beat him."

"So I could beat him."

I repeat his words from a long time ago. "Because winning is everything."

"Yeah." His eyes flick back and forth between mine. "Besides, I showed you a good time, didn't I? So no hard feelings."

"No hard feelings."

"In fact, you should be thanking me."

I dig my fists into his torso. "I should be *thanking* you."

"Yes. For the fact that I made sure there was minimal damage."

"What minimal damage?"

Reed lowers his voice then, staring at me with flashing eyes. "I didn't fuck you, did I? I could've. But I didn't, and trust me, that was hard. It's not every day a guy gets a lap dance from a horny ballerina. I've had my fair share of cheerleaders and I know how bendy they can be. I know how bendy *you* could be. I've seen you dance.

"And some guys don't like virgins. They say they're too much work. You can't fuck them how you want to. But I'm not one of those guys. I like them. I like training them. I like breaking them in. I like when they bite their lip and make those hurting noises. I like when they push you away like it's too much for them. But you rub them in the right place and they cling to you like you're their entire world. I like that. I liked how you clung to me and how when you came, you looked like you couldn't believe it. You looked like nothing had ever been that good. And I could've rocked your world last night. Even more than I did. But I didn't. I let you go. So yeah, minimal damage."

"Why? Why did you let me go?"

"Consider this my good deed. Of the month." He thinks about it. "Year. I let you escape my evil clutches unscathed. Your brothers should thank me. It was torturous." He looks me up and down. "It still is. And if you don't want me to pick you up and carry you to my Mustang and drive you back to those woods and give you a *real* reason to spin and bend over like the pretty blonde ballerina you are, you should really let me go, Fae."

I do.

I let him go.

I step back from him.

Not because of what he said he'd do if I didn't.

But because of Fae.

Because he called me by the name he gave me.

A fake name.

A name that I held dear to my heart like a fool.

I clung to it at night. I put it under my pillow like a wish.

A name that made me feel like a real fairy.

His fairy.

"You're an asshole," I breathe out and almost cringe.

He said all these things to me and this is what I say to him?

This is *all* that I say to him?

This is the extent of my wrath?

"Now you know," he drawls.

"I can't believe I…" I trail off because I don't know what to say. I don't know what to think. What to feel…

I wrap my arms around my waist and bite my lip before trying again. "So stupid…" I shake my head, unseeing. "I can't believe I've been so stupid. I… God, I've been so foolish. I thought you… I fell in l –"

"You're not going to say the L word, are you?" he says, cutting me off.

I draw back, as if he has struck me.

"Well, you were," he murmurs and all I can do is stare at him silently.

All I can do is stare at the guy who's standing in front of me in dark clothes, not one ounce of softness on him, staring back at me with emotionless wolf eyes as he says, "Let me tell you something about guys like me. Guys like me, we like to play. We like to break hearts. Just because we can. Just because it's fun. You don't *fall* for guys like me. You don't pin your dreams and hopes on guys like me. You don't lie for them. You don't sneak around for them. You don't knit them sweaters. You called me a villain, remember? That's what I am. I like breaking hearts. I like breaking lovestruck dreams. I like feeding on the innocent love of innocent girls like you. What I don't like is for that girl to stand in front of me and cry about it. I thought I told you that the only thing I love is my Mustang. I thought you understood. I thought you were smarter than that. I thought your brothers taught you everything."

Smarter than that.

That's what Con said to me, didn't he?

He said that I was smarter.

He said that he trusted me.

And I lied to him.

I lied to all of them. To him, to Ledger.

Especially to Ledger.

The brother I have betrayed the most. I don't even know how he is. I haven't even seen him since the fight.

Because I came here.

Because I came running here to see the guy who lied to me.

Who lied and used me.

For soccer.

Who played with me and broke my heart because he wanted to win at a game.

I shake my head again, my vision getting blurred. "Yeah, I thought that too. I thought my brothers taught me everything. But apparently, they didn't. Apparently, I'm just a stupid girl who fell for a villain."

His features are tight now, stark and gorgeous and heartbreaking. "Well, consider this your first lesson in love and growing up."

Yeah, my first lesson in heartbreak.

"See you around, Fae."

With that he leaves.

As abruptly as he came into my life.

He walks back to that couch where the whole world is waiting for him with open arms. While mine is crumbling around me.

While my world is plagued with earthquakes and landslides, his simply blooms and sparkles, teeming with a new life, a new adventure.

He's going to New York this fall, isn't he?

Foolishly, I thought that we'd still keep in touch. That we'd find a way to be together. I even thought about spending the last month of school… being with him now that the championship game was over. Hanging out with him in the hallways, in the courtyard. Listening to music in his Mustang.

Yeah, I thought that.

In the deepest recess of my mind, I did think about life after the soccer rivalry comes to an end and after he leaves Bardstown High.

But as I found out tonight, I'm stupid.

And in love. With a villain.

With a guy who likes to break hearts.

***

I don't remember walking out of that party.

I don't remember finding Tempest out in the driveway either.

All I remember is that I'm here.

I'm outside, under the starry night and my best friend has a hold of my arm. She's trying to get my attention. She's asking me something, I know that.

But I'm too distracted.

I'm too focused on something that I saw as soon as I came outside.

In fact, it's the first thing I remember seeing: a flash of white.

A bright, sparkly white.

Brighter than the moon even.

A white Mustang.

His white Mustang.

The only thing he loves.

That's what he just said.

He said that the only thing he loves is his Mustang, and then all the numbness, all the fog that had surrounded me ever since he told me the truth, his truth, vanishes.

I turn to Tempest. "I-I need the keys to his car."

"What? Why?"

"I just... I need..."

Tempest grabs my shoulders and makes me look at her. "What happened, Callie? What did he do? What'd he say to you?"

I look at her, into her gray eyes, so much like her brother's. "I love him."

Sympathy overcomes her features. "I know."

"He used me."

"What?"

I have to wait for this pain in my chest to pass before I can speak. "H-he said he used me. Against Ledger. He did it all to mess with him. So he could win at soccer."

Her eyes are wide. "Oh God."

"I don't... I don't know how to stop this."

"Stop what?"

"This pain," I whisper. "I don't know how to make it stop hurting."

She hugs me then. "Oh, Callie. I'm so sorry. I'm..." She moves away from me. "Listen, Callie, my brother, I love him, okay? I love him to pieces, but he has a major self-destructive streak. He can be... toxic and –"

"Will you bring his keys to me?" I ask, cutting her off.

"Keys to his Mustang?"

"The thing he loves the most."

She studies me for a few seconds before nodding with determination. "Yeah. I will. Just wait here."

And I do.

And she does too.

She does bring me the keys after a few seconds and I don't ask her how she did it. How she swiped her brother's keys.

All I do is get inside his car and despite my many protests, Tempest gets inside too. All I do is start his car and drive away.

I'm sixteen now so I can get my driver's license.

In fact, Con was going to take me for my test next weekend and he's been teaching me for the past few months. Ledger has been teaching me too.

Him too.

He's the one who taught me to drive stick. He's the one who taught me that in his Mustang.

So this isn't the first time I'm driving this car.

Although this is the first time I'm driving it to this place.

I've been to this place before. With my brothers and a couple of times with my friends.

Never with him though.

I regret that.

It would've been poetic. Me driving to a place in his stolen car that we used to visit together.

But it's not.

It's tragic and catastrophic and awful.

Just like our Shakespearean names.

It didn't help, did it?

Changing them, calling each other by made up names. Rivalry and hatred still fucking won and it's so awful that I'm cursing and I don't even mind.

It's so awful that when I get there, to my destination, the lake, I stop the car.

I turn to Tempest. "I'm going to do something awful."

"I know," she says.

I flex my fingers on the wheel. "Aren't you going to stop me? He's your brother."

Tempest throws me a sad smile. "He's my brother, yes, and that's why I know that he must've done something really horrible for you to do this. I know what my brother is capable of, Callie. I know he broke your heart. I know he didn't just break your heart, he smashed it. Didn't he?"

A tear streaks down my cheek as I nod.

"Well, then I was right. You wouldn't do this otherwise."

That's all the encouragement I need.

I turn back and look at the lake, all shimmering and silvery under the moon, surrounded by trees. A slope leads down to it, a perfect slope for what I have in mind.

I start the car and pull at the gear. I put it in neutral and say to Tempest, "Get out now."

She does and I'm right behind her.

And then, standing on the forest floor, my ballet flats crunching the leaves and tears streaming down my face, I watch the love of his life sliding toward the lake at a steady pace.

Before it hits the water.

Before the water slowly engulfs it, swallows it down, eats it up like he ate up my heart.

Just when it looks like I'll never see it again, something goes off inside of me. Another earthquake. Another explosion, and I start to run toward the lake.

I start to dash toward it but Tempest stops me.

She grabs my arm and pulls me back. "Callie, no. Let it go."

"No, I can't... I..."

"Hey, it's okay. It's fine. Let it go."

"I have to... I have to save his car. I have to..."

"Callie, you can't go in there, okay? You can't."

"But I have to save it." It's going down and down, the bright white disappearing into the darkness. "I have to... He loves it and I... I can't hurt him like this. I can't hurt him..."

"Hey, hey, Callie. Look at me." She turns me around and shakes me, makes me look at her. "It's just a car, okay? It's only a car."

"But he loves it," I tell her, tears streaming down my face.

"He'll get over it."

"I have to save it," I whisper.

"You don't."

"I have to save the thing he loves."

"No, not right now, okay?" She hugs me again. "Right now, you just need to save yourself."

And then I can't stop crying.

I can't stop sobbing as I cling to my friend.

I cling to her like she'll save me like I want to save his car.

But the truth is that no one can save me.

I'm already dying.

I've already fallen in love with a villain.

A
GORGEOUS
VILLAIN

USA TODAY BESTSELLING AUTHOR
SAFFRON A. KENT

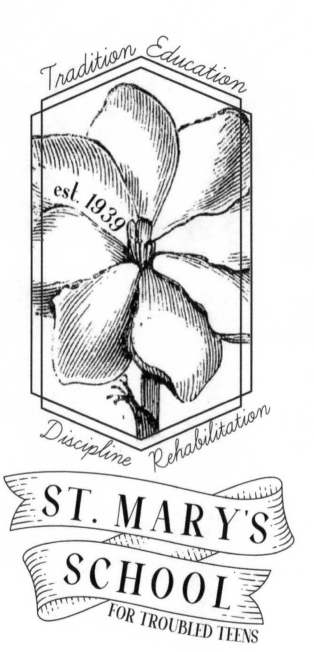

Tradition Education

est. 1939

Discipline Rehabilitation

ST. MARY'S
SCHOOL
FOR TROUBLED TEENS

Heart (n.):

A muscular organ with four chambers that beats in a rhythm

Broken Heart (n.):

A heart with cracked chambers that still beats but every beat is ar-
hythmic and hence, painful

Chapter 1

Part I

The Haunted Hero & The Broken Ballerina
Present
St. Mary's School for Troubled Teenagers

In the middle of the woods in the town of St. Mary's, there is a school.

It's a school only for girls.

Actually, it's a school only for bad girls.

Girls who break rules.

Who cut classes or steal and totally do not respect authority.

Some of them are violent and have anger issues.

Like punching a teacher in the face because they asked to see your homework and they kinda asked loudly. Which was not appreciated because you were hungover from all the alcohol you'd consumed the night before, illegally, and at a party that you should never have been at in the first place.

There's a girl here who did that.

People tend to stay away from her because she likes to break things.

I like her though. She's been good to me.

But anyway, not all the girls are this violent. Some girls are tamer.

Like, there's a girl here whose only crime was to steal a credit card because she saw a really cute dress at a store and she wanted to buy it. And she knew that if she asked her mom, her mom would say no. Because for some reason, her mom has this crazy idea in her head that her daughter is a spendthrift and hence should not be allowed to shop without parental guidance.

So yeah.

We're the bad girls and we've been sent here for reformation.

Because this school is a reform school and it's called St. Mary's School for Troubled Teenagers.

It was established years and years ago. Probably when dinosaurs roamed the earth.

Okay, fine.

That's an exaggeration.

It was established in 1939. All dinosaurs were long extinct by then, but still.

Anyway, if you stumble upon the website of this place or happen to pick up a glossy mustard-colored brochure at the principal's office, you will see that this prestigious place has a history of excellent education and iron-clad discipline.

More than that, it has a history of producing some very well-behaved and socially adjusted girls who go on to do great things in their lives.

As opposed to the not-so-great things that they did which landed them here.

I, for one, love this place.

I love the fact that I live here now. That I've been living here for the past two years, ever since my sophomore year.

I love the rules. I love the restrictions.

I love that there's a set time for everything.

Like, when to wake up, when to take a shower – every morning between 6 and 7AM. When to do your laundry – there's a laundry room located in the basement of the dorm building and you go wash your clothes on a schedule so it doesn't get overcrowded. When to do your homework or eat dinner or relax. And finally, when to go to bed: lights out at 9:30 every night.

They even tell you when you can or can't leave campus.

You need a special little pink permission slip signed by a teacher – sometimes they can be white, but I always cheer up when I get the pink ones.

Oh, and in order to receive those signed permission slips, you need to have enough good girl points, more commonly referred to – by teachers – as privileges.

And who keeps track of your privileges? The guidance counselor assigned to you, whom you meet with every week and who has a thick file of all your sins and occasional good deeds.

There's a girl here who hasn't gotten a permission slip to go out in a year now, not even for Thanksgiving or Christmas. Because she keeps showing up late to her classes and rumor has it that she's failing math and chemistry, hence her privileges have been revoked.

See? How wonderfully strict and suffocating.

On top of that, I absolutely adore the stern-faced teachers who hardly ever smile. But that's okay because they only want good things for you.

I adore the cinderblock buildings and cement pathways and iron bars on the windows.

Oh, and the big tall gates in the front that are made of iron and are painted black? They are to die for.

Not only are they architecturally sound and capable of keeping all of us inside, they also boast the motto of St. Mary's School at the top in large, wrought iron letters: Tradition. Education. Discipline. Rehabilitation.

Such a prison-like feel.

Who wouldn't love that?

Who wouldn't love the bench that I'm sitting on, all hard and of course made of concrete, out in the courtyard, which is also made of concrete I might add.

From here I can see the whole school: the buildings, the pathways and the iron gates keeping us caged and safe. The soccer fields. The woods in the back, just beyond the brick fence.

It's a perfect spot to sit in, on a dreary, gray fall afternoon, to remind me this is my life now.

My life that I love.

Love.

Love, love, love.

So. Much. Love.

This is not working, Callie.

This is so totally not working.

Okay, no. Wait. This can work. This can totally work.

Um, what else do I love about this place? What else, what else? What...

"Oh my God, are you listening?"

A high voice pierces my fog and I blink.

A face comes into focus. It's pale and pretty with blue eyes and thick bangs. And glasses.

Poe Austen Blyton, or just Poe, my friend. One of my best friends at St. Mary's, who makes living here, at this stupid reform school, bearable.

See?

Here's a thing I love!

"I love you," I tell her.

She draws back. "What?"

I grin. "I do, Poe. I love you. Don't ever think otherwise."

Then I turn to another girl who's sitting right to opposite me, Bronwyn Littleton, my roommate and also one of my best friends.

I motion with my chin and declare, "And you. I love you, Wyn. You're my favorite."

Wyn is an artist so she usually — by that I mean all the time — carries a sketchpad. She is the calmest person I've ever encountered in my life. Looking at her, her light-colored eyes, her long, brown braid and perfectly innocent face, you'd be so surprised that she is at a reform school.

Her sketchpad is the reason she's here, actually, or rather the fact that she loves to draw.

Her parents are rich, high-class types who don't want their daughter to waste her life on something like art and have always been on her case to give it up. So one day she'd had enough and in retaliation, she painted graffiti on her dad's car. And well, her dad sent her here as a punishment.

She looks up from her sketchpad and stares at me. "Uh, thank you. I appreciate that. I think."

"You're welcome," I say before turning to the third and final member of our group, Salem Salinger.

She's new at the school; she just started when we all came back from the summer for our senior year. She has huge curls and golden-brown eyes and she's here because she stole some money and was running away but got caught.

By whom, you might ask?

By her guardian, who also happens to be the very scary principal of this reform school.

Yeah, poor Salem.

She chose to mess with the wrong person and well, now she's here and I think I love her too. Even though I only met her for the first time when school started a week ago.

So I tell her, "And you. Don't think I forgot you, Salem. I love you too."

Her nose scrunches slightly. "I wasn't thinking that. Although I was thinking that this is a little weird."

Poe throws her arms at her. "Thank you. Yes. This is weird." She turns to me. "What's going on with you?"

"Nothing." I smile and sigh, trying to ignore the fact that this is our lunch hour and we specifically finished our very dismal-tasting lunch early so we could come out here and catch the sun, which was all bright and shining when we were inside.

The sun that suddenly disappeared the moment we stepped out of the cafeteria building, and by the time we got to this very hard and uncomfortable bench — as uncomfortable as our classroom desks — it was like there was never any sunshine whatsoever.

Wyn leans forward slightly. "Is it the First Week Blues?"

Okay, so we all have a term: First Week Blues.

It's a term coined by Poe back in our sophomore year, when it was just the two of us. Wyn came later, in our junior year, and as I said, Salem was sent here for her senior year.

Anyway, it basically means that we all go through a short period of feeling low and blue when we've just come back from our summer vacation.

Because we go from months of being free to being caged and restricted.

"No, these aren't First Week Blues," I reply to Wyn. "Because A, this isn't the first week anymore. This is the second. And B, why would I be sad when there's so much to be happy about?"

"Like what?" Poe asks.

"Like..." I look around.

After a deluge of them pouring out of the cafeteria, only a few girls remain outside. They all went back once they saw there was no sun to be had.

But then, inside is even more depressing, with beige lockers and walls.

So here we are, and on my sweep through the area, my eyes land on another thing that I love and had forgotten about.

Flowers.

Gardenias, to be exact. Tons of them, mixed in with daisies and roses and hemlock.

"Aha." I perk up because I like flowers. "Like flowers. Look! And the fact that we get to work on them this weekend."

Every Saturday, as a part of reformation and teamwork, all girls do a little bit of gardening. We mainly grow gardenias, the school symbol, because it represents purity and innocence.

It also represents secret love, which I'm pretty sure no teachers know about and it's sort of like a running joke between all the girls here.

Poe sticks her tongue out. "Ugh. I hate flowers."

I give her a look. "Everyone likes flowers, Poe."

"I like roses," Wyn adds.

"I think gardenias are cool," Salem pitches in. "What about you, Callie?"

Daisies.

I love daisies. I have dresses with daisies printed on them.

Or I had dresses with daisies printed on them.

I left them all in Bardstown the day I came here because I hate them now.

I hate daisies. I hate those dresses. I hate…

No, Callie. Now is not the time.

"I, uh —"

Poe saves me from answering — thank God — when she shakes her head and bursts out, "Can we get back to me, please? I was talking about something before Callie decided to go all crazy on us and declare her undying devotion."

I sit up straight, thankful for the distraction. "Right. Okay. I was totally listening though."

"Really? What was I saying then?"

"Uh…" I drum my fingers on the table. "You were saying that —"

"I'll save you the trouble. She was saying what she's always saying," Wyn says.

Poe turns to her. "What am I always saying?"

"How much you hate your guardian," she answers. "Because he sent you here. Because you wouldn't stop setting his clothes on fire and poisoning his food."

"I never poisoned his food." Poe points a finger at Wyn. "Never."

"So how did he end up in the hospital then?" Wyn asks.

"One time. That happened one time," Poe clarifies. "And it wasn't because I had poisoned his food. It was because I made him a peanut butter and jelly sandwich. Completely innocent. I did him a kindness. I was kind, people."

"He's allergic to peanuts, Poe."

"Yes! And I found that out later. When his tongue was swelling up." Poe throws her hands in the air, exasperated. "Why won't anyone believe me?"

Wyn looks at me then and winks, a small smile playing at her lips.

Oh, she's bad.

And I'm bad too so I wink back and chirp, "Because you're diabolical. And you're always talking about how much you wanna kill him and that you wouldn't mind if they sent you to prison for it either."

It's true.

Poe has vowed to kill her guardian and I'm pretty sure with her evil, troublemaking mind, she can do it and never get caught.

Poe, however, glares at the both of us. "I wouldn't. Just so you know. Even though I don't think that orange is the new black and I don't think I'm gonna look good in it, I'd still do it. I'd still stab his chest with my six-inch Prada heels – you know, the ones with suede that I really love – and I'd watch him bleed out and then when he's all dead and buried, I'd dance on his grave. Mark my words."

I purse my lips so I don't laugh out loud at her murderous expression, crazy eyes and flushed cheeks.

Somehow I manage to say, all serious-like, "But you hate dancing, Poe."

Poe is about to snap at me when Wyn interjects again. "Yeah, Poe, you hate dancing. You say your boobs hit your face when you jump around too much."

I grin at Wyn and she grins back.

Again Poe is about to snap but again, she gets waylaid. This time by Salem.

"They're excellent boobs though," she says, raising her hand and jumping into the conversation while looking at Poe's chest.

I look at Poe's boobs and Salem is right. Her boobs are excellent.

Poe has a naturally curvy body, big boobs, slim waist and wide hips, sort of like those eighties pin-up girls, and yes, I'm definitely jealous of her.

"Yeah, they're excellent," I agree, nodding and looking at my own tiny ones.

"Right? I mean, I'd kill for boobs like that," Salem says enviously.

Salem and I, we're the same body type, small and athletic. Courtesy of her being a soccer player.

I have to say that even though I grew up around soccer, I've never really been friends with a female soccer player.

"As much as I like you guys talking about my boobs, because let's face it, they are excellent," Poe says, pointing to them, "I have bigger problems right now."

Getting serious, Salem bites her lip. "Sorry."

I get serious too. "Yeah, sorry. Tell us what's wrong."

Wyn puts down her sketchbook, meaning she's paying attention, and all three of us lean toward Poe, eager to hear her story.

She blows out a breath, making her thick dark bangs flutter. "I can't go out this weekend. Miller took away my outing privileges. Again."

"What? Why?" I ask, outraged.

"I don't know, something I did last year. Maybe because I put a rat in her office."

Yeah, that.

Poe snuck a rat into her guidance counselor Miss Miller's office last year.

I have no idea where she got the rat from — probably on one of her rare outings — and how she managed to hide it from all of us. Until Miller screamed in the middle of a very peaceful school day and ran out of her room.

"Well, that was last year though. Can't she let it go?" Wyn asks.

"No." Poe mimics Miller's nasally voice, "'Because as you know the school policy is that all grievances get carried over to the next semester. So I'm going to have to revoke your outing privileges until midterms.' Fucking bitch."

"Ugh, I hate her." I shake my head.

"I can't believe I have the same guidance counselor," Salem laments.

I totally feel her pain.

Poe and Salem share the same guidance counselor and I swear Miller is Satan. My guidance counselor is pretty mellow on the other hand — another thing that I can admit that I like.

Poe bangs her fist on the table. "See? That's why I hate him."

None of us need her to elaborate who he is. Her guardian.

"This is why," she continues. "All of this is happening because of him. Everything wrong in my life is because of him. Everything. That stupid, tweed-coat-with-elbow-patches-wearing, unfashionable, old... man."

Wyn, Salem and me, we look at each other and press our lips to stop from laughing out loud.

"Old man." I nod.

"Unfashionable too," Wyn says.

"Yeah, let's not forget unfashionable," Salem instructs us. "And elbow patches."

I nod for emphasis before saying, "How dare he? Tweed coats, oh my God! The man should die."

Poe narrows her eyes before throwing her empty water bottle at me. "You guys are the worst."

And we burst out laughing.

Which somehow turns into the highlight of my day so far.

Sitting on these hard benches, under the gray sky, laughing

with the friends I've made at this reform school, I forget why I'm here in the first place.

I forget that I don't have any freedom now.

That I'm caged inside these brick fences and iron gates.

That I've been caged here for two years now.

Because one night when I was sixteen, my heart broke.

It broke so badly that I died.

I died from the pain, and when I came back to life, I went from being good girl Callie to a heartbroken girl.

A girl who, in the throes of her pain and her hurt, did something that she never could've imagined doing.

A girl who did it all in the name of love.

I became a girl who was supposed to land in jail for it — for the thing I did, the crime I committed — but somehow was sent here.

As a mercy.

Away from everything that I've ever known: my town, my home, my four older and overprotective brothers.

I forget all of that and just laugh.

Which makes Poe growl. "Fine, whatever. Laugh it up. The only choice I have now is to live my best life. Tomorrow night." She lowers her voice then. "When we sneak out."

Tomorrow.

Tomorrow is Friday.

Fridays are special.

On Fridays, we sneak out, all four of us.

And if tomorrow is Friday, then today is Thursday.

And Thursdays are special too.

For me.

Chapter 2

It's a little before midnight and everyone has gone to sleep.

Especially my roommate, Wyn.

Which works out great for me.

Because as I said, Thursdays are pretty special and I have somewhere to be.

So slowly, I climb out of my bed and go to my dresser. I open it and grab my pre-packed bag and creep out of my room.

Out in the darkened hallway now, I close the door behind me and look from left to right. The coast seems to be clear so I walk down the narrow hallway, which is flanked by beige doors and walls that have bulletin boards and motivational posters hung on them.

My feet are quick but quiet, matching the silence this time of night.

Well, except for the low drone of the television up front in the reception area.

There's a twenty-four-hour warden – they change shifts – to keep an eye on things and I've chosen Thursday in particular to sneak out because I know Miss Alvarez likes her late-night shows way more than she likes watching over the bad girls, and after two years of sneaking out, I'm an expert.

I know all the twists and turns of this hallway. I know how long it will take me to reach my destination if I walk at a certain speed. Twenty-five seconds.

It'll take me twenty-five seconds to go where I want to go.

I've timed it.

And sure enough, twenty-five seconds later I'm there.

At the exit.

Which is located in the back of the building.

It's a metal door with a trick handle. You have to jiggle it and push at it just so to spring it open; it's something that none other than Poe discovered the first year she was here with me.

The metal door thuds open and I step out into the September night, which is slightly chilly but nothing I can't handle.

I wedge a rock between the door and the jamb before I take off running through the concrete pathways and cut through the grass clearing toward the campus brick fence. Propping my feet on the gaps, I climb and cross over to the other side.

When I get down, I start running again.

From here I have about ten minutes to make it to the St. Mary's bus stop, which will take me where I want to go. I run through the woods that line the back of our campus and reach the bus stop just as the bus is pulling in.

The inside is empty except for a woman who's sleeping in the fourth row. It's slightly scary, traveling in an empty bus at midnight, but I have no other choice, do I?

I show the driver my bus pass — I bought it over the summer with my own money, thank you very much — and then I'm off again.

It takes about thirty minutes to reach my destination.

Back to my own town, Bardstown.

My heart always flutters when we cross that line, from St. Mary's to Bardstown, the town I grew up in and the town I adore.

The town in which I fell in love for the first time.

The town in which I fell from grace.

When the bus pulls in at my stop, I thank the driver and get off.

So far things have been okay, slightly risky but nothing illegal.

This next part that I have to do is sort of a felony.

I mean, it's not as bad as say, stealing someone's car and drowning it in the lake — which I have a little experience in — but it's still pretty bad.

Because as I said, I have no other choice, do I?

I pull out a pin from my hair and jam it into the lock on the door, twisting it in a precise motion. When the door clicks open — which I knew it would, I enter.

Into the Blue Madonna, my old ballet studio.

The place where I spent years and years training to be a ballerina.

Until they kicked me out.

Honestly though, kicked out is a harsh term.

They didn't kick me out, per se. They gave me a choice to leave and I took it.

By they I mean my teacher, Miss Petrova, who once upon a time was super proud of me and my talent.

She looked very sad when she said, "Parents are worried, Callie. They think you'd be a bad influence on their kids. I'm really sorry. You're one of my star students but girls are pulling out because they don't feel safe around you and I don't know what to do. I'm at a loss here."

So I told her that I'd leave.

See? She gave me a choice and I took it.

I left.

Because the girls — some of whom I'd danced with for years – and the parents didn't feel safe around me. Because of what I did.

Because of what my broken heart made me do two years ago.

I don't want to dwell on what I did and what happened after and how I came to be at St. Mary's instead of being sent to juvie.

The time will come for me to remember.

But for now, I'm here to dance and I will.

I'm here to fulfill my dream, the only dream I've had since I was five years old. Of going to Juilliard and dancing for the New York City Ballet Company one day.

When I left the Blue Madonna, my dream of Juilliard was sort of hanging in the balance. Miss Petrova's a Juilliard alumna and she was going to give me a great recommendation letter when the time came. And getting in there is so difficult and competitive that I needed that letter.

But after everything, I didn't think she'd give that to me and so I stopped thinking about it. I'd stopped expecting to end up at Juilliard. In fact, I'd started to look into other dance programs, like the one they have here at Bardstown Community College.

But then over the last summer, something changed.

Something sprung back to life.

I wanted that dream again. I wanted to at least try to have that dream.

So I decided to make an audition video for Juilliard after all. The applications for next fall are due by November and I'm doing it. I'm going for it.

That's why I'm here. To try.

I shed my dress in the bathroom to change into my leotard and my practice tights that I brought with me in my bag and get ready to practice.

The main practice area has polished hardwood floors and mirrors running along one wall, plus a steel barre for barre exercises. I sit on the floor to tie up my pointe shoes before I begin.

I do the warm-up exercises, stretching my legs, flexing my toes. I go through arm and leg positions one by one, checking my posture in the mirror, correcting the arch of my spine and the line of my shoulders.

When I'm done, I grab the CD that I want from the collection and put on the song that I've been working on all summer.

Well, I've been working on this song for the past two years actually.

It's the same one that I was going to perform at Bardstown High that night.

The one where I had to wear the wings because I was a fairy who falls in love with a human who betrays me in the end.

It's the song that I never got to do.

It's the song that I want to remember, however.

I want to remember the pain, the misery. The tears I've cried.

I want to remember my heartbreak.

So I never make the same mistake again.

And so I wear the wings; these ones are borrowed from the storage closet. They are cheap and made of fake silk as opposed to my furry, custom-made, heavy wings.

But it doesn't matter.

I'm not a fairy. I never was.

I don't need pretty wings. I can make do with these fake ones and as soon as I have them in place over my shoulders, I start the music and close my eyes.

I let myself remember now.

I let the beats drop into my body, my stomach and chest. I let them drop into my arms and my legs.

When I've become sufficiently heavy with memories and light with the violins, I raise my arms and take my first spin.

After that everything becomes easy.

Everything becomes natural.

Like I was born to do this song.

Like I was born to fall in love one day and have my heart broken. Like I was born to be the girl who dances on those broken pieces of her heart.

I jump and leap and spin and turn without my conscious volition.

By the time the song ends and I fall to the floor on my knees, my feet are throbbing and my cheeks are wet from my tears.

Oh yeah, that happens.

I cry.

I cry every time I let myself remember. I cry every time I dance to this song.

It's okay though. I'm used to the tears.

But I should stop now.

I'm here to dance, not waste whatever precious time I have on crying and…

Wait.

I feel something.

Something on the back of my neck that makes me jerk my head up and look out the tall window.

There's nothing there except the view of a quiet, dark street, with a lamppost pouring down yellow light and a lone bus stop.

But.

But it felt like…

It felt like I was being watched. Like someone was watching me.

Like he…

At the thought, I spring to my feet. I run to the back door, the door through which I got in, and go outside. It opens into a narrow brick alley and I round the corner to get to the front.

To get to the spot directly outside the window of the practice room.

Of course there's nothing here.

Of course.

But for some reason, my body is buzzing.

My legs feel restless, excited. My chest is filled with a rush.

A rush, an eagerness that I used to feel two years ago.

Back when... when he watched me.

When he'd come to the school auditorium and sit in the third row.

When he wanted me to dance for him and he couldn't take his eyes off me when I did.

Back when I was his fairy.

I lie. That's what I do...

I shake my head when his voice, his words — some of the last ones that he spoke — flit through my brain, my fake wings brushing against my back.

I'm being silly.

No one's here.

Sighing, I go back and I'm about to enter the building to finish practicing when I hear a thud, a boot hitting the pavement, and I spin around once again to look.

Okay, I did not imagine that, did I?

I did not imagine that sound.

Someone is here, and when a different possibility occurs to me, my heart leaps to my throat in fright.

What if there's an intruder?

An actual villain.

Not that he's any less of a villain, but still. What if there's some guy here, a thug, a thief. What if they've come to steal something from the Blue Madonna?

Oh heck no.

I'm never letting that happen. Never ever.

This is my favorite place in the world and I already feel guilty for breaking and entering. I already feel guilty for taking advantage of the fact that my ex-teacher doesn't have an updated alarm system and is super bad with security and technology.

I'm not going to let any harm befall this place.

So I fist my hands at my sides and widen my stance as I look around, glare around actually.

"Hello? Is anyone there?"

Seriously, Callie?

Such a stupid question.

Of course someone's there. I heard a sound, and if someone is wanting to do me or this place any harm, he's not going to tell me.

So stepping closer to the door, I try a different approach. "Okay, don't tell me. It's fine. I'm not an idiot. I know you're there. I heard you."

I narrow my eyes as I keep searching the darkness for the intruder but come up with nothing.

"Yeah, that's very mature and scary. Not talking." I shake my head and take another step closer to the door. "But the thing is, you made a mistake. You picked the wrong girl to mess with. I don't scare easily. Oh, and I know how to punch." I nod as I keep looking around and moving closer to the door. "Yeah, I can do some real damage if I want to, buddy. And maybe right now you're thinking, hey, this girl is tiny. She can't hurt me. But know this, I have four brothers. Four. And they're all tall and burly and muscular. They're all athletes, actually. Ever heard of the Thorne brothers? Yeah? I'm their sister."

I'm super-duper close to the door now as I continue, "So if you think you can overpower me, remember that my brothers will come after you. I will make sure that they come after you. I will make sure that they hunt you down and make you pay, you got that? So either show yourself or leave. Right now!"

I sort of flinch at the end but whatever.

That should get the message across that I'm not to be messed with.

Also, I'm one step away from the door and getting inside so if there ever was a time to dare him, this is it. So I wait for like three seconds before I jump inside and close the door with a bang.

And then I'm packing up.

I'm getting out of here.

The next bus should be here any minute so I change into my dress and close up. I run out through the front door and as soon as I cross the street to get to the bus stop, the bus is pulling in.

When we take off, I look out the window.

I look at the studio, the dark road that still stands empty.

I look at it and look at it, even as it grows smaller and smaller, and my breaths somehow both quicken and slow down. And my body is filled with both relief and a strange disappointment.

But then I see something.

A flash of white.

Bright as the moon.

Sparkling as a neon sign.

White. His color.

My mouth falls open and I press my nose to the window.

But whatever I saw, a flash, a burst, is so far away and getting further by the second.

Before I can confirm anything, we take a turn and the road disappears.

***

It's Friday.

Which means we're sneaking out, my friends and I.

That's the only thing I'm focusing on.

The only thing.

The other things — thing — is totally out of my mind. Because there's just no point thinking about it, you know? Because what happened last night — what I thought happened last night — never really happened.

It never did.

I only thought that it happened. I only thought that I saw something. A flash of white.

When in reality, I saw nothing.

In reality, I snuck out to dance, and in the process saved the Blue Madonna from an intruder.

I mean, if there was an intruder.

Maybe that was my imagination too, but who knows?

So yeah, I'm not going to think about what I felt last night or what I thought I saw. I'm only going to focus on tonight, on the fact that I'm sneaking out with my friends to go dancing and it's going to be amazing.

Every Friday — like Thursday, Miss Alvarez is on duty — we get low-key dressed up and sneak out to this bar called Ballad of the Bards to go dancing.

It's in Bardstown and one of the bartenders, Will, is Conrad's friend.

He lets us in as long as we don't drink any actual liquor since we're all underage. He's also nice enough to keep our weekly sojourns a secret.

Apart from Blue Madonna, it's one of my favorite places in Bardstown.

Even though it's located in kind of a shady part of town and the neon sign over the door flickers and goes on and off, I always get a cozy feeling from this place.

Not to mention, I love their music.

So Ballad of the Bards, like any other dance bar, is famous for its music. But their choices are unconventional. Instead of playing dance beats, they play sad music.

They put on songs about lost lovers and broken hearts, with deep violins and heavy, thick bass.

Maybe it's the fact that I'm one of them now, one of the brokenhearted, but I love it.

I love the melancholy. I love the misery. I love the fact that I can slow dance to this music and if I spill a few tears, no one questions it.

Because that's what you do when you hear a sad love song. You cry.

It's like crying in the rain.

And I cannot wait to get inside and lose myself in them.

I cannot wait to remember.

But as it turns out I'm not gonna need music to remember the mistake I made two years ago.

Because the reason that I made those mistakes... is here.

The reason why I did what I did and why I ended up at St. Mary's is right here.

He is here.

And I see him as soon as I enter the bar.

Actually, he's all I see. He's the only thing I see and the sight of him forces me to halt.

The sight of Reed Roman Jackson.

After two years.

After two long, long years, it forces me to stop. It forces the earth to stop too.

At least for me.

For me, the earth has stopped spinning and all the people on it have stopped existing. For me, the music is no more and the stars have gone out.

Because he's here.

Somehow.

How is he here?

Standing in the middle of the bar, he's taller than everyone.

He's broader than everyone too. And he has a spotlight on him.

Or maybe that's just his marble-like, vampire skin. That glows.

That still glows.

That still absorbs all the light in the space, leaving nothing for the rest of us.

Not even the choice of looking somewhere else.

He is like gravity, see.

If he's in the room, you can't help but stare at him. You can't help but revolve around him.

Even now, people are doing that.

People are revolving around him, giving him all their attention.

He's surrounded by a bunch of guys, and a couple of girls who are hanging onto his arms, and God, it feels like two years ago.

It feels like I'm standing in the corridor of my old school, Bardstown High, and I'm watching him work his dark magic on a girl.

I'm watching him appear both aloof and interested.

As he drives her crazy with desire. So much so that she raises her hand to brush her fingers along the ends of his hair.

I'm watching him and watching him and my lips part as I exhale a breath.

What is he doing here? Where did he come from?

Why is he still so beautiful?

The heartbreaker of Bardstown High. The Wild Mustang.

The gorgeous villain.

The guy who broke my heart. And whose car I stole and drowned in the lake for revenge.

Who a second later looks away from the girl, his gaze landing on me.

Just like that.

Just like always.

As if he knew I was standing here, in this exact spot. As if he knew that I was watching him.

And so after two long years, on a random Friday night, standing in my favorite bar in Bardstown, I see him.

I see the guy I haven't seen in two years.

The guy I never wanted to see after what he did to me.

Chapter 3

The last time I saw Reed Roman Jackson, it was my last day of school, my freshman year.

I was walking over to the parking lot at the end of the day, to get to my brother, Ledger's, truck so we could go home, when I saw him in his car.

Well, not his car.

His Mustang, from what I'd heard, was in the shop after what I did to it.

I didn't know what he was doing there because I was under the impression that he'd left for the day. That was why I was taking that route, where I knew he usually parked his car.

But now that I'd seen him, I didn't know what to do.

I was frozen in my spot. Unable to move. Unable to look away.

Maybe because he was alone and I hadn't seen him alone since that night when everything happened.

Since that night, he'd always been with a group of people. He'd always been busy and surrounded, unaware of my existence.

That day though, he was alone.

He had his eyes closed and he was sitting in the car with the music on and the windows down. I was too far away to know what he was listening to but I remember wondering if it was one of our songs.

Songs that I danced to for him.

It was silly of me to think that, to even entertain that thought after everything.

But standing there, I couldn't stop the rush of memories.

The rush of those moments when he'd drive me around in his Mustang and take me to the woods. When he'd put on music, sit on the hood of his car and watch me dance.

And the rush was so strong that my legs moved on their own.

My legs wanted to go to him.

I wanted to go to him.

And apologize.

Yeah, I wanted to apologize. How silly. For destroying his Mustang.

The only thing that he loved.

Then I wanted to hit him. I wanted to hit him and punch him and demand to know why he did what he did.

Why did he break my heart? Why was he so cruel?

Why did he betray me for a sport, for soccer?

Why wouldn't this hurt go away?

Why, why, why?

I wanted to ask him all that.

But before I could go to him, a group of his friends descended on him, taking away the opportunity, and I ran away. Thank God for that.

I took a detour to get to Ledger's truck and that was that.

That was the last time I saw him; he never showed up to his graduation and I never saw him around town.

That was the last time I saw the guy who broke my heart and

whose car I stole in order to get back at him.

And who pressed charges against me and wanted me to go to jail for it.

For doing that. For stealing his car.

But never mind that right now.

I have bigger problems.

Problems like he's here.

What is he doing here?

What the fuck is he doing here?

Great, Callie. Just great.

One sight of him and I'm cursing again.

One sight of him and my whole world is off-kilter.

My whole world is shaken.

Shouldn't he be in New York City? Living the life of a soccer star, being fought over by agents and recruits? And what about college? Doesn't he go to college?

It's September! People go to classes in September!

I take a gulp of my whiskey, trying to calm myself down.

I can't believe I'm drinking, whiskey no less.

I'm not much of a drinker and I hate whiskey.

But I needed something.

Something strong.

Something punchy, and whiskey is the only strong stuff I know; I have four brothers whose drink of choice is whiskey.

As soon as I saw Reed and he saw me, I took off and made a beeline for the bar because I needed alcohol and also because I needed to get away from my friends.

Who had also seen him and were asking all kinds of questions.

I never told them anything, see.

About what happened in the past. About how I ended up here.

I mean, except for the fact that I stole a car from a guy named

Reed Jackson and drowned it in the lake.

They don't know that he was Roman to me once.

They don't know that I loved him and that he broke my heart. And that I was supposed to end up in a juvenile detention center instead of at a girl's reform school.

And neither do they know that I sneak out every week on Thursdays to practice ballet, to chase my dream.

Not that they would object. In fact, I think they'd be super supportive about it.

But all of this is so ingrained in my past, so ingrained in him that I never had the courage to tell them.

And now suddenly, he's here and oh my God, I can't handle this.

I can't.

That asshole.

That fucking asshole. That fucking asshole bastard. That motherfucking…

A long shadow falls on me then.

A black shadow.

I'm standing outside the bar, propped up against the brick wall, drinking my whiskey. I couldn't stand to be in the same room as him. I couldn't stand to dance.

Not where he could watch.

So I stole my whiskey from Will and ran outside to calm myself.

But of course he's here as well.

Of course he's chased me down. Like he used to two years ago.

Nothing has changed.

Nothing.

And he's walking toward me.

His boots are thudding on the ground and I feel those thuds in my chest. I feel them in my heart. Like he's stomping on it with every step that he takes.

And all I can do is stand here, stuck to this spot, letting him do that.

Letting him stomp on my heart with those boots.

Black with a shiny metallic buckle on the side.

When he stops, I'm somewhat surprised to see that there isn't any blood on the ground, rivering from under his killer boots. The boots that just crushed and broke my heart all over again.

Okay.

Okay, I need to relax.

I need to calm down.

I need to take a deep breath and I need to look away from his boots.

I need to look at him. So that I appear strong and calm.

Even so, I can't.

I can't look at him. Not yet.

So I look at other things.

Things over his shoulders, his leather-jacket-wearing shoulders.

The jacket that I'm seeing after two years and it takes my breath away for a second.

Because he was wearing it that night.

The night he told me the truth for the first time. The night he told me that everything else up until that point had been a lie.

I've had dreams about that jacket in which he breaks my heart over and over again.

I almost wish he was wearing his hoodie.

His sweet-smelling, soft and cozy, white hoodie. The thing that takes some edge off his sharpness.

But a second later, I'm not even thinking about his hoodie.

I'm thinking about something else. Because my eyes fall on a different bright white thing.

His Mustang.

His baby.

Oh, it's back.

His baby is back and she looks good.

She looks exactly like she did before I tried to destroy her.

And oh my God, I'm so relieved that I can't help but say, "Your baby looks good."

I said that, didn't I?

I did, yeah, and I would be embarrassed about how breathless I sound about a car but this could be good.

In the sense that I said the first words now and all the break-up movies that I've seen — not that we had a break-up because we never had a relationship to begin with — always teach you to say the first words.

To get control of the situation.

To sound breezy.

"She does."

Two words.

Two words spoken in his smooth, deep voice after two years.

And the momentary upper hand I thought I'd gotten vanishes.

It just goes away and I start trembling.

And then I have to look at him because I can't not.

I can't not look at him and so I swivel my gaze and after two years I get to see him.

I get to see him from this close.

I get to see his stubble that makes me wonder if he hates it still. I get to see his thick eyelashes — I'd forgotten how thick they are, like a forest of dark curls. I get to see his plush, red mouth. The mouth that always sported a smirk and a cut or a bruise from getting into fights with my brother.

And his wolf eyes.

Gosh, his eyes.

Gunmetal gray and smoky and on me.

I was right.

Nothing has changed. Nothing.

He still has that same rugged beauty.

He still is so heartbreakingly gorgeous.

In fact, he's more gorgeous now, more tempting and dashing even. And I think it's his hair.

His rich, dark hair that's longer now.

It brushes the collar of his jacket and something about that makes my stomach clench.

Something about that makes me think of vintage movie heroes and villains with their leather jackets and long hair. With their devil-may-care attitude.

A cigar-smoking villain…

I shake my head and say, "Are you sure she's safe though? Your baby. In this neighborhood. People can be very dangerous."

People like me.

Not that I'd ever touch his Mustang again, but still. He doesn't know that and I'd like to keep it that way.

Although he doesn't seem to think that I'm much of a threat, because his ruby red lips stretch up and morph into his typical smirk. "Can they?"

That smirk makes my heart go boom, boom, boom before I find my voice and say, "Yeah."

"What do you think they'll do?"

Drown it in the lake again.

But I don't say it.

Because I don't want to drown it in the lake again and I don't want to joke about that.

But I do want to scare him a little so I tilt my head to the side and clench my fingers around the bottle. "I don't know, steal it? Again. Slash your tires. Steal your rims. Spray-paint your hood. Smash your windows. Douse the whole thing with liquor and burn it down once and for all."

His amusement only grows. "That's... quite a creative list."

"I'm creative."

"And definitely dangerous."

"Oh, you're in for such a surprise, trust me."

"Does it come with a little bow tied around it? Your surprise."

What?

What is he...

My whiskey-doused brain finally catches up when I notice where his wolf eyes are.

They are on my stomach, my waist, and I finally get what he's talking about.

My dress has a bow wrapped around the waist and in his usual style, he's commenting on it. Because that's what he does. He comments on my dresses.

And holy crap.

I realize something else too.

I'm wearing white, his favorite color.

And he's looking at it like it's his favorite thing ever. Especially that green bow and the lacy ruffled hem that's grazing my bare thighs.

"No, it comes with long nails and sharp teeth," I tell him with a sweet smile and a chirpy voice.

He lifts his eyes then. "Well then, I'll be over here, sitting on the edge of my seat, waiting to unwrap it."

Ugh.

Of course.

Of course he'd say that. Of course he'd twist my words and turn them into something dirty and seductive. Something that would make me blush and squirm.

And like the idiot I am, I am blushing.

What is wrong with me?

"As much as I'm enjoying talking to you," I say with my chin raised, "I don't have time for this. So let's do it."

He looks at me for a few beats before repeating my words flatly. "Let's do it."

I widen my stance, shift on my feet like a fighter, getting ready to throw punches. "Yeah. Let's do this thing so you can leave me alone."

The sooner he does what he came here to do – which if history is any indication, is probably to ruffle my feathers and make me uncomfortable with dirty innuendos – the sooner I can move on from this awful, terrible coincidence of seeing him again.

Because it is a coincidence, isn't it?

Him being here, at the same bar, at the same time.

Reed notices my stance and asks in a low voice, "Are you sure?"

"Yes. Come on. I'm ready."

"Okay." He nods, his eyes hooded. "Where do you want it?"

"What?"

"Yeah, where do you want it?" He gestures toward the wall that I'm standing against. "Here, up against the wall? Or in the back seat of my car." He doesn't give me the time to respond to his statement. "It's been two years, but I remember how much you seemed to love writhing on my leather seats. And if I'm being honest, I'd love to see that again. But lady's choice, of course."

"What... I..."

As I sputter out confused syllables, I understand his meaning. His stupid meaning.

He's talking about all the times I danced and writhed on his leather seats while he took me out on those rides. While he put on the music and I danced for him even when I was sitting down.

Because I loved dancing for him. Because I was an idiot.

I loved writhing on his lap too. That one time in the rain…

But I don't want to think about that right now.

Not in front of him.

"You're funny," I tell him and his wolf eyes sparkle with humor. "And delusional. If you think I'm letting you touch me ever again, you need your head examined."

"Is that so?"

"Yes." I grit my teeth at his condescending tone, at the tone that has the power to make me feel all young and naïve. "Because it's never happening. So say what you came here to say and leave."

He looks at me thoughtfully. "Hmm. I'm not so sure you want me to leave though. Because this feels like a dare, and you know how much I like those."

I know.

I do know.

He likes dares. He likes provocation. He likes to rile people up and ruffle their feathers like he used to do with Ledger on the field. When they played together back at Bardstown High. When they were rivals.

As I debate throwing this bottle at him, I say, "It's not a dare, it's reality. Touch me and lose your teeth. So you really need to leave now."

Instead, he takes a step toward me and I press myself into the wall even more.

"You're not making it easy though," he drawls. "Leaving."

"Get away from me or I'll punch you, okay? I'm not kidding."

Of course he thinks I'm kidding and does the opposite of what I'm asking him to do.

He takes another step toward me and I swear to God, it's such a big step that he's almost here. He's almost where I am and I have to hold my breath because I don't want to breathe the same air as him.

I don't want to find out if his scent, his delicious scent, has remained the same after two years or not.

"If you keep talking like that," he dips his face toward me, reminding me of how short I am compared to him, "I'll start getting ideas."

"What ideas?" I squeak, wondering how it is possible that I forgot the difference in our sizes.

When I lived for those differences back then.

I lived for how tall he was, how strong, how he could pick me up while I danced on my toes for him.

"That you're flirting with me," he says in a husky tone.

I ignore the pounding of my heart and the rush under my skin. "Oh my God, you are delusional."

"You know you don't have to try so hard with me," he goes on like I haven't spoken. "You want me to touch you, Fae, just say the word."

Fae.

I breathe out.

I blink.

I didn't want him to say that. Because I didn't want to find out.

I didn't want to find out if it sounds the same.

My name. The name that he gave me two years ago.

It does.

It sounds exactly like it did two years ago.

Intense and intimate. Like it belongs to me. Like I was made to be called that.

Blonde and tiny with the limbs of a dancer, his dancer.

His fairy.

But I was never his and that is not my name.

"Hey, Reed." I stare into his wolf eyes and throw him a false smile. "I know it's been two years and all, but my name is Calliope Thorne. People also call me Callie. And if I'm being honest, I'd rather you not call me anything at all. But asshole's choice, of course."

Those eyes of his become intense as he murmurs, "Calliope Juliet Thorne. I know what your name is, Fae. I also know what my name is. Do you?"

Yes.

Yes. Yes. Yes.

I do.

I do know his name.

I know his name like I know how to breathe.

Like I know how to cry in my pillow at night, biting down on it so I don't make a noise.

I know his name like I know how to hurt when I see someone wearing a white hoodie on the street. When I see a girl so in love with a guy that she only has eyes for him and no one else.

I know his name, yes.

Reed Roman Jackson.

My Roman.

Or so I thought.

"You said that our names made us Shakespearean, star-crossed lovers," he says, bringing me back to the moment. "A teenage tragedy. And I told you that they didn't. Because what did fucking Shakespeare know? To me, you'll always be Fae. And to you, I'll always be Roman."

I did say those things to him. I did tell him about our names and I did warn him to stay away from me.

It was a warning for me too.

If only I had listened to it myself.

If only I'd stayed away.

"I remember," I tell him, staring into the face of the villain I fell in love with. "I remember everything. I remember everything I said to you and everything you said to me. And that's why I know that we are a teenage tragedy. Because you made sure of that, didn't you? So get away from me because I wasn't kidding about you losing your teeth. Reed."

But again, instead of moving away he gets even closer, and I find out the answer to another question that I didn't want to know.

His scent.

It's still the same.

He still smells of wildflowers and woods. He still smells of open roads and freedom.

The freedom that I don't have anymore.

The freedom I lost the night I stole his Mustang and tried to destroy it.

The Mustang that he built himself.

He did, yes.

I didn't know that, see.

I had no idea that the thing I was destroying, the thing that he loved the most in the world, was also a thing that he had made himself.

Reed Roman Jackson, the richest boy at Bardstown High, in Bardstown, had built his Mustang with his own two hands.

I found that out later.

Much, much later.

After all the damage was done.

I don't even blame him for calling the cops on me. I never blamed him for calling them.

I've only ever blamed him for breaking my heart.

I only blame him now, for smelling the same even after two years.

And while I'm so busy smelling him and remembering the

past, he's doing something else. I don't realize that the reason he's so close to me is because he's stealing from me.

My whiskey bottle.

It is only after he's straightened up and moved back that I realize that my hand is empty and his is not.

That... asshole.

"Give it back," I order.

Staring at me, he puts the bottle to his mouth and takes a long gulp. As if to taunt me.

When he's done drinking my whiskey, his red lips glisten and his face sparkles like the moon that hangs low in the sky. "See you around, Fae."

And just like that he turns around and leaves.

I should be relieved.

I should be, I know.

This is what I wanted. I wanted him to leave me alone.

But I don't feel relief. Not at all.

I feel anger.

I feel so much fury right now. So much heat in my body that I can't contain it.

I can't contain this massive outrage, this massive wrath at what he said just now, the words that he used.

See you around, Fae.

The same words he said to me the night he smashed my heart to pieces. When he turned around and never looked back as I stood there, crying.

Before I know it, I've taken off after him.

I've started to charge at him like a crazy, wounded animal. I probably sound like one too, grunting and groaning, and in the back of my mind, I know I shouldn't be acting this way.

You're not a violent person, Callie. You don't do this.

But I guess I'm violent for him.

I'm a bad girl for Reed Roman Jackson.

He's at the back door, just about to enter the bar, and I'm about to crash into him until I don't.

Until he spins around at the last second, intercepts me and spins me around too, pinning me to the brick wall. And then I'm right back where I started, pressed against a wall, staring up at him.

Only this time things are worse because he's closer.

Much, much closer.

And he's touching me.

Oh God, he's touching me.

He has his hand on my stomach and he's using it to keep me in my spot. He's using it to trap me.

He's actually holding me hostage right now and oh my God, I lose it.

I completely lose it.

"Take your hand off me," I tell him, my legs jiggling. And when he doesn't comply immediately, I start to struggle. "Take your hand off me. Take your hand off me right now!"

Thankfully, he does.

He raises them in the air, my whiskey bottle clutched in one, and says, "If I wanted to touch you like that, I would've done it by now. So you can stop losing your shit any time now." He takes a sip of my whiskey again. "And while you're at it, stop attacking innocent people, yeah? Not sure if they covered it at St. Mary's but it's not exactly how responsible citizens conduct themselves in society."

"Oh, you think you're innocent?" I snap.

His liquor-laced lips twitch. "Well, between you and me, only one of us has been arrested. And only one of us is going to a reform school. So you tell me."

I fist my hands at his dig. I fist my hands and clench my teeth.

God, I hate him.

I hate him. I hate him. I hate him.

I hate the fact that he's bringing it up.

That I was arrested.

That he had me arrested.

But I'm not giving up so easily. "Aw, are you jealous, Reed? Don't worry. It'll happen to you too. It's only a matter of time, trust me."

He loves it, my answer.

I can see that.

He loves that I'm not giving up, that I'm fighting back.

The lines around his pretty lips loosen up. "Thank you for your vote of confidence, Fae. I really appreciate it. But until that day comes, I'd like to keep believing that I'm as fresh as a fucking daisy. Which is more than some people can say."

How bad can prison be really?

If I kill him, I mean.

If I charge at him once again and claw his eyes out.

His pretty wolf eyes.

"Give me back the whiskey," I demand again.

"I don't think so."

"It's mine. You stole it."

"You stole my car." He takes another swallow of it. "I think I'm allowed this."

"I will —"

"Since when do you drink whiskey, anyway?" he asks over me.

"Oh, I don't know. I met this asshole about two years ago, who recently came back into my life like the plague. Maybe since then."

His eyes narrow at my cursing and my heart starts thudding in my chest.

Thudding and booming and pounding.

Because of his obvious displeasure at my cursing.

Because he still thinks that he has the right. To feel any displeasure in the first place.

"Glad to see I still affect you like this."

"What are you even doing here by the way? What about your stupid soccer practice? Shouldn't you be utilizing every single second being the best soccer player ever? Winning is everything, isn't it? That's what you said."

He did.

And that's why he betrayed me. So he could win against Ledger.

Something flashes through his face at that, something inscrutable. "Why don't you let me worry about soccer?"

"You know —"

"And you've become quite the expert now though, haven't you?" he almost rasps and my heart pounds, pounds, pounds in my chest. "Cursing and drinking, breaking curfew to go to a bar."

"If you thought you were going to find a good girl, then I'm afraid you're going to be disappointed."

"Tell me something, because I'm extremely curious to know. Where did you learn that?"

"Learn what?"

"How to pick a lock."

"What?"

"Do they teach you that at St. Mary's? 'Breaking and Entering 101,' or is it called 'How to Pick a Lock in Ten Easy Ways.'" A lopsided smirk greets me as he takes another sip of my whiskey and continues, "That was some really impressive work last night, Fae."

Last night.

Right.

I forgot about that. I forgot that I did see him last night. It wasn't my imagination then.

But hold on a second.

"You saw me pick the lock?"

"Yeah, I saw you run through the woods too. Behind your school. I saw you get on an empty bus and then I saw you trying to threaten who you thought was an intruder."

Oh my God.

Oh my God.

He was there the whole time.

"Oh my God! Were you stalking me?" I squeak, outraged and violated and so freaking angry right now.

I'm not sure if it's my question that makes his cheekbones jut out in answering anger but his next words are brimming with fury. "I wasn't going to say anything but fuck it. What were you thinking?"

"What?"

"What the fuck were you thinking, Fae? You know how dangerous it is, don't you? Sneaking out like that."

"I —"

Again, he doesn't let me speak. "And then to threaten someone. Fucking dare someone who you think means to do you harm. When you're all alone. When you've got no back-up plan. What were you going to do? If he'd actually taken you up on your stupid little offer. Fucking ballet him to death?"

I take a step toward him, stabbing my finger. "Hey, I know how to punch, okay? You know that. I've got four brothers and —"

"Yeah, and I'm guessing they don't know about your nightly excursions, do they?"

"Keep my brothers out of it."

As soon as I blurt that out, I know I've made a mistake.

I know I've fallen into one of his invisible traps.

I know.

But the words are out there and he's heard them, and now his eyes are glowing.

His pretty wolf eyes are glowing with satisfaction and my racing heart both sinks and soars in my body at the same time.

"Are you asking me to keep a secret, Fae?" he asks, his voice low.

The next breath that I take comes out broken.

It comes out like a hiccup.

Like my breaths are all tangled up in him, in this villain who somehow has come back into my life like he never left.

"Don't you dare, Reed."

His eyes drop to my bright green ballet flats. "You know my price, don't you?"

Tingles rush up and down my legs and I curse them. I curse my limbs for getting excited.

For getting restless as if they're still sixteen and stupid.

"Again, you're insane. Because I'm never doing that. Never ever. I'll die before I dance for you."

The slant of his jaw becomes more pronounced, more angular, as he stares at me with a look that I don't understand.

But still makes me shiver.

"You're not sneaking out again," he commands.

"Excuse me?"

"You want me to keep it a secret, you're going to stay put. In your dorm room. Where you should be right now. But I'm going to let this slide." He gulps my whiskey again. "You promise me that and I'll take your secret to the grave."

I look at him, standing here in his dark clothes.

That leather jacket that I hate but that makes him look so beautiful, so tempting.

Such a heartbreaker.

A villain I should stay away from.

But I don't.

I walk toward him.

And I don't stop until I'm so close to him that I have to crane my neck to look into his treacherous eyes. "You think that I'm going to get scared like I did two years ago, don't you? You think I'm going to do your bidding. So I'm here to tell you something: I'm not. I'm not the same girl anymore. I'm not naïve or innocent or stupid. You know why? Because when I was almost sixteen, I met a villain in the woods. He was beautiful and gorgeous and like an idiot, I fell in love with him. I believed every word he said to me. I believed every touch and every smile and every look. Until I realized that everything out of his mouth was a lie and his hands were dirty. So I escaped. I got out of his evil clutches. Unscathed. And I can do it again. So you should really rethink your strategy about blackmailing me. Because I'm not afraid of cigar-smoking villains from a bad fifties movie, or even assholes like you."

With that, I make a move to leave.

But I don't get to go too far.

He grabs my arm and stops me. His fingers dig into my bare flesh, setting my entire body on fire, and I can't help but struggle against him again. But he tightens his grip as he sweeps his eyes all over my face. "You still dance like a fairy."

"Reed —"

"And you look like one too," he continues, his wolf eyes dropping to my lips. "A pretty blonde fairy with dark lipstick lips."

Lipstick lips.

I wear lipstick now.

I forgot about that too.

I forgot that I'm wearing one right now and now that he's staring at them, my lips, with so much intensity and focus, I can't think of anything else.

I can't help but say, "Heartbreak Juju."

His eyes lift. "What?"

"The lipstick. That's what it's called."

It's dark blue with very subtle shades of green.

When I found it at a store a year ago, I knew I had to have it.

I knew it was for me.

For the brokenhearted girl that I am now.

Something flashes in his eyes, something heavy and grave, and before he can say anything, I continue, "It's my favorite lipstick. It suits me. Don't you think?"

I'm not sure what I expected him to say to that.

But he does say something and he says it with that same heavy look in his pretty eyes that gets my heart racing. "It does."

Chapter 4

The Hero

The first time I saw Calliope Juliet Thorne was when she was six and I was nine.

Until then I'd only heard rumors.

I knew that people called her the Thorne Princess.

The little sister of the four Thorne brothers.

People said that she could melt the snow with her sweet smiles. She could melt people with her shining blue eyes. Especially her brothers.

Whose hearts she held in the palms of her hands.

When she danced, people watched. When she spun, people stopped moving. They said no one danced like her.

The first time I saw her, that's what she was doing.

Dancing on the playground, by the rusted swing set.

I don't remember a lot about that day but I do remember

watching her. No one had to tell me who she was. I already knew.

Because I couldn't stop. Watching her, I mean.

I couldn't look anywhere else when she leapt and jumped and spun on her toes.

And then I remember walking toward her.

I don't know what made me do that but one second I was standing still and the next, I'd started moving.

It was as if she was gravity.

A blue-eyed, blonde-haired force of nature.

And good thing too because somewhere in her spinning and leaping, she lost her balance. But I got there just in time to catch her.

I grabbed her arm, and this part I distinctly remember.

I distinctly remember leaving muddy fingerprints on her skin, on her dress.

I remember dirtying her up because I guess before I saw her, I was playing ball or something and my hands were all messed up. I remember wanting to snatch them away, to keep her all clean, and yet all I did was hold her harder.

And when she stared up at me with her big blue eyes and said 'thank you' in a voice that reminded me of the cotton candy that my sister liked, there was no chance that I was letting her go.

But I had to.

Because her brothers descended on me.

By then I was familiar with them. With Ledger Thorne specifically.

We went to different schools but I'd heard about him. I'd heard about his older brothers too, soccer legends all and so he had to be one as well.

I fucking hated them for it.

I fucking hated them for their glory, their talent.

For the fact that I'd always seen them together around town, with their oldest brother Conrad leading the charge. Watching out for his siblings.

I fucking hated that they had each other when my sister and I had no one, not even decent parents.

And strangely in that moment, I hated them for leaving their sister alone and unattended.

For not watching over her, for almost letting her fall so that I had to swoop in and save her.

But whatever.

They were all there now and they'd pushed me away so they could take care of her and they could all go fuck themselves.

I didn't even know why I'd saved her in the first place.

Why I cared enough to save her.

Their sister was their responsibility, not mine.

Angry at myself, I walked away and I kept walking even when I heard her say in that sweet, cotton candy voice, But he saved me…

Again, whatever.

I don't think she remembers that day. A random kid from the playground saving her from falling.

Why would she?

I don't even know why I remember it, let alone why I'm thinking about it right now.

Maybe because I just saw her after two years at that shitty bar.

Maybe because I'd forgotten how small she is.

How short and fragile.

How easy to pick up and carry away.

Most of all I think I'd forgotten how she looked when she danced. How enchanting, hypnotizing.

Enthralling.

Like a true fairy.

They didn't lie, did they? All those people who talked about her when she was little.

No one dances like her.

And she does hold her brothers' hearts in her hands.

Because I used that two years ago. The fact that they all love her to death and will do anything for her.

I didn't set out to do that though.

Just to be clear.

I didn't set out to play with her heart and then break it.

I can be cruel and heartless, but using her wasn't my plan.

In fact, I stayed away from her.

I stayed away even when she showed up at my party in the woods two years ago, looking all innocent and lost. As if stepping out of a dream. I even followed the pact, the stupid fucking pact, that I'd made with her brother later.

We'd decided that we wouldn't bring each other's sisters into our rivalry and I agreed.

I agreed even when she made it really hard to stay away from her. I agreed even when she dangled herself in front of me at every turn, looking like a perfect opportunity.

Looking like a shiny trophy.

But.

The thing to understand is that I needed to win that day. I needed to be the reigning champion of Bardstown High.

I needed that title.

I hadn't won the previous year. That jackass, Ledger, won by one measly goal and stole the title from me. Just like he stole the captainship.

The captainship that belonged to me.

But Conrad Thorne, our coach and Ledger's brother, didn't like my playing style. He thought I was reckless and selfish and didn't think about the team.

Well, I fucking carried that team. Who cared if I thought about them or not?

So yeah, I needed that win.

I needed it because I knew it would upset my father. It would upset him greatly, and let's just say it's my life's mission to upset my old man.

I'm a generous son that way.

I'd decided that I would serve that win to my father on a silver platter and that's what I did.

Again, just to make it clear, I waited until the last moment. To use her, I mean.

I waited until I had no other choice. I waited until Ledger had the ball and he was about to score. And there was no other way to steal the ball — and in turn the win — except using his sister against him.

Besides, as I told her that night, I did her a favor.

Yeah, I remember what I told her that night. Even though I was massively drunk, I remember.

I also remember that she was knitting me sweaters, for God's sake. She was lying to her brothers to be with me. She was getting way too involved. And it needed to be stopped.

I'm not the kind of guy who dates or does relationships, and I'd already told her that, didn't I?

But she didn't listen, apparently, and I had to take matters into my own hands.

But none of that matters anymore: the championship win, the stupid rivalry, the fact that I broke her heart for it all. Because I ended up at the same place.

I ended up where I never wanted to be. In Bardstown.

Inside my father's study, back in our house.

It's been two years since I've been inside this room. Two years since I've seen these leather couches; these polished hardwood floors and the wall-to-wall mahogany bookcase with all the shiny books that my dad never reads, since he's not into books or education.

He's into money. And according to my dad, good education doesn't always mean good money.

Look at him for example, he's a high school dropout who helped his dad start a construction company when he was only eighteen. That went on to become this multi-million-dollar empire that he presides over today.

But anyway, I haven't been inside this room for a long time and I'd forgotten how suffocating this space is. How it feels like something is wrapped around my throat, a phantom noose of some sort, and my father's evil fingers are tightening it and tightening it.

Until I can't breathe.

Yeah, I've never been able to breathe around my father.

But that's not the problem right now, my suffocation.

The problem is that there's this woman, standing just inside my father's study, who's currently running her left hand down my arm.

She has long, blood red nails.

That she probably pays a lot for. For the upkeep, I mean.

My father would want nothing less.

Nothing less than pretty manicured nails to scratch his old, shriveled-up balls.

The fact that I can think about my father in those terms without throwing up all over these hardwood floors is a testament to how far I've come.

I think I also deserve credit for not throwing up on her shoes. What's her name again? Cindy, Sydney? Stephanie?

I don't know. She's new here. I think.

All my father's secretaries look the same to me. They're always young and pretty and blonde. They're always very eager to please.

Him and also me for some reason.

To that effect, this new one smiles at me, her lips as red as her nails. "Good night, Mr. Jackson."

"Reed," I push out somehow. "Just Reed."

Her smile widens as she looks up at me. "Reed."

All right, that was a bad idea I think. Asking her to call me by my name. It makes me want to throw up even more. But then I hate to be called by my father's name so really it's a toss-up.

"Were you on your way out?" I ask her in my most polite voice.

She must be; it's definitely not normal office hours and I almost crashed into her as soon as I entered my father's study.

Smiling, she peers at me through her lashes. "Yes. I was leaving. I was just... helping your dad with something."

"I bet you were," I murmur. "What a hard-working employee you are."

"I try my best."

"I don't doubt it."

Her smile knows no bounds, and then something occurs to me. Something extremely disturbing given the fact that she's still touching me.

"Are you a lefty?" I ask.

She looks slightly taken aback by my question but whatever. If she refuses to take her hand off me, then I need to know.

She glances down at her fingers on my arm. "Uh, yeah. Why?"

Fantastic.

I was afraid of that.

I was afraid that her hand might've touched other things — things like those shriveled-up balls that I was talking about — before it touched me.

Aaand there you go. The bile is up to my teeth now.

"You look like one," I reply, clearing my throat. "Well, allow me to get out of your way and let you leave."

I step to the side and thankfully her hand falls away.

She gives me a heated look before nodding. "I'll see you to-morrow."

Yeah, not a fucking chance in hell.

The moment I see her at the office tomorrow, I'm turning around and walking out of the building.

But just to fuck with her, I throw her a slight smirk and rasp, "Can't wait."

Her eyes light up and she practically prances out the door.

Poor... Sabrina?

Okay, I give up.

Poor whatever the fuck her name is, is going to learn real fast that I don't pick up my father's discarded ones. It's the principle of the thing and the fact that my dick doesn't work for women like that.

No offense to the women.

All offense here goes to the man who brought me into this world and who constantly cheats on my mother. And who a second later says, "She likes you."

I've been watching her leave, but at his voice, I turn around and there he is.

My lovely father.

All the way across this huge room, sitting on his throne. Or his chair that looks like a throne.

It's been here for as long as I can remember. Upholstered in polished brown leather, it has a high wide back. It makes him look larger than life. It makes him look like the king of the world, or at least Bardstown.

He specifically had it made for himself, actually.

I think he saw it on TV, this throne-like chair, and he wanted it so much that he had it custom built.

That's my father; he wants things.

He wants money. He wants power. He wants women. He wants an ugly-ass chair that he saw on TV because he thinks it makes him look rich and powerful.

He is those things, yes. But he also loves to show off.

He loves to shove it in your face, how rich and powerful he can be.

"How tragic for her then that I don't," I reply, remaining by the door.

"Don't be so hasty in your judgement, son. Stephanie's new but she has her uses."

Ah, Stephanie, and she is new.

I hum. "Good for Stephanie. But I think I'd find her more useful if she wasn't fucking my father."

At this my dad laughs.

He has a booming laugh, loud and echoing, and just like that it becomes a real struggle, a real fucking struggle, to not feel that noose tightening around my neck.

When he's done laughing at me, he says, "Such prudishness. Still. I thought time would make you more receptive. But you continue to surprise me."

Yeah, because this isn't the first time my father has suggested that it's okay for me to — how do I put it? — avail myself of his conquests. He's definitely availed himself of mine in the past and so I stopped bringing girls from school over.

For all his greediness, my father can be a very generous man. He's happy to share things with me, his one and only son. His wealth, his power, this company that he's built from the ground up.

"Yes, I'm an enigma." I sigh and brace myself. "Is there a particular reason you wanted to see me tonight?"

As I was heading out of the bar, I got a text from my dad,

asking me to come see him in his study.

I've had plenty of summons like these over the years and they never end well. So I'm not particularly looking forward to this conversation. But I don't have a lot of choice in the matter like I did before.

Like I did up until two years ago.

Up until then, I'd blow him off. I wouldn't answer his texts, wouldn't pick up his calls. I'd be purposely difficult to get a hold of. It used to be easy too. I used to have soccer practice, parties, friends, school and all those things.

I would actually take pleasure in avoiding him. I'd take pleasure in showing him the finger, doing things he hated just to spite him.

But now not so much.

Now I don't have very many excuses.

Such as soccer.

Yeah, I don't have soccer anymore, and I'm not going to get into the whole thing as to why. Because the reason doesn't matter. Suffice it to say that I don't play and neither do I go to college.

Not that that's been a hardship, not going to college.

Like my father, I never liked education. I was only going to classes to have minimum grades so I could play and piss off my dad. Since I'm not playing, I'm not going to waste my time on homework and assignments.

"Just wanted to check in on my son," he replies almost gleefully. "Welcome him back from New York. I have to say I missed you."

Yeah, of course.

He wanted to check in on me. He wanted to rub it in my face that he can check in on me and that one call from him, one measly text, and I'd come running.

As I said, my father wants everything.

Such as my complete and utter obedience. Complete control over me.

"And I have to say that I can't say the same," I quip.

Chuckling, he settles back in his ugly-ass chair. "I've always liked your sense of humor. I'm sure it'll come in handy as you adjust to the new workplace. I'm looking forward to having you here. And the fun starts tomorrow, huh? The big party in your honor on transferring from the New York office to here. The future CEO of the company. This is all going to be yours one day."

Right.

So I work for my dad. The thing I never wanted to do. I have been working with him at his company, Jackson Builders, for the past two years now. I was in New York up until now, handling things up there because that's where I was needed. My father's words, not mine.

But now he's called me back and I'm supposed to obey him.

And I have.

I'm back, aren't I?

Even though I'm sure that this big move back was just a way for him to show his power over me.

"Anything else?" I ask, wanting to get out of this suffocating, four-hundred-square-foot and yet claustrophobic office as soon as I can.

But he won't let me go so easily.

He knows how much I hate it here and he'll make me take it.

He's going to make me suffer.

"Yes." On his desk, there's a file that he slides toward me. "I've got a job for you. Your first job here in Bardstown."

A job, of course.

A violent sort of energy flashes through my body at his words.

It's nothing new though, this violence in me. It's been brewing for the past two years, ever since I started working for him. Ever since he forced me to work for him and made me his lapdog.

"And what does this job entail?" I ask.

"The usual. There's a piece of land that I want. But the owner is being difficult."

"So, we're going to make things more difficult for him, then?"

"Of course." My father smiles. "We're going to increase the pressure until he cracks."

It's not a miracle that my father owns everything in this town and it's not all hard, honest work either. He likes to bend the rules, fuck with people and their lives as long as he gets what he wants.

Like screwing with their bank accounts so they can't pay their mortgage. And when they can't, the bank gets involved. That's when my father steps up and offers to pay off the debt in exchange for the land.

I have first-hand knowledge about that.

About his business dealings.

About how he fucks with someone's life. That's how he got me actually. By fucking up someone else's life.

I go over to the desk and pick up the file. I recognize the name on it, Henderson. He owns a bookstore in town, I think.

I went to school with Mr. Henderson's son, Martin Henderson. He was a good kid.

I know it's not going to make a difference but still, like an idiot, I speak up, "I went to school with his kid."

My father chuckles. "So?"

"So you want me to destroy someone I know."

So far I've only fucked with people I haven't known. I try not to think about it too much. But this is new. This is fucking new and I know I won't be able to stop thinking about it.

"For business only."

"Yeah because that makes everything so much easier, isn't it?"

This time I've amused him so much that his chuckle turns into laughter and I fist my hands and tighten my muscles again.

Damn it.

His laughter really strangles me to death.

"You're so easily offended, aren't you?" he says once his laughter is under control. "Yes. It does."

"Why can't someone else handle it?"

"Because I want you to handle it."

"I think I'm going to have to pass."

That pisses him off, my refusal.

"Are you sure you want to say no to me?" he asks. "You know how upset I get when I hear that word."

"Apparently not enough to have a heart attack or something."

His nostrils flare and all the charm and all the ease that he portrays to his investors at his parties slips even further. He goes from being a posh businessman to just a man from the wrong side of the tracks who managed to own everything that he ever set his eyes on, either by hook or crook.

"You remember what happened last time when you said no to me, don't you?"

I do.

I do remember it.

"Yeah, last time when I said no to you, you blackmailed me into working for you."

His eyes narrow. "And whose fault is that? I let you run around, do whatever the fuck you wanted while growing up. You wanted to be a little shithead who hated his daddy, fine. But you don't fuck with me when I ask you nicely. I asked you to quit soccer, forget about the championship game, that fucking scholarship — like you even needed a scholarship when your father's loaded — and come work for me. But you didn't listen. So I had to show you who was boss."

"And you're the boss, aren't you? Always."

"Yes. Because I always win," he declares, his features morphing into something harsh, villainous. "I always get what I want. So instead of being an ungrateful son of a bitch, try showing some gratitude that I'm leaving you this company. That I'm going to teach you how to fucking run it, because I'm not letting you ruin my life's work. And I'm not leaving it in the hands of someone as incompetent as you."

Yeah, that's been the whole saga.

My father and his company. How he built it and how he wants me to run it. How he won't let me escape it. How he'll do anything to force me to take the reins.

Although in his defense, he did ask me nicely.

In my senior year, he asked me to not apply for a soccer scholarship. Repeatedly. He asked me to quit the team. Repeatedly. And when I didn't listen, because I was such a shithead who hated his daddy, he gave me an ultimatum the night before the championship game.

He told me that if I showed up to play the next day, he'd make my life very difficult. He would hate that, but he'd do it.

Not only that, he even showed up at the game. Maybe to intimidate me I think.

So to fuck with him, I made sure that I won. Right in front of his eyes.

And well, he delivered on the promise.

He did make my life difficult. So I really have no reason to be angry or frustrated because I brought this upon myself.

But I am angry and frustrated.

I am fucking furious, not because he fucked with me, but because in the process of fucking with me, he fucked with someone else too.

He fucked with her.

The girl whose heart I broke and who stole my Mustang.

***

Tempest calls me as soon as I get into the car after my disastrous meeting with my dad. I'm about to head to the hotel I'm staying at, because I can't stand staying at this house, but I go alert.

"Pest, you okay? W —"

She doesn't let me speak. "Did you go?"

"What?"

"Did you?" she demands.

I look at the time on the dashboard.

It's after 2AM and she sounds wide awake. She sounds like she never went to sleep. "What the — Are you okay? Where are you?"

"Okay, first of all, I'm fine. I'm in my dorm room of course, watching Netflix. You don't have to sound so freaked out and go into your Big Brother Mode. And second of all, did you go or not?"

I sigh and sit back.

Her calls in the middle of the night aren't a rarity. Plus to be fair, her calls don't always mean bad news.

Sometimes my sister just calls because she can't sleep.

Because she just saw a movie or a show that she really wants to talk about and she chooses me because apparently, I'm her BFF. I think it's best friend forever or something fucked up like that.

But I'm also her brother, her big brother.

So obviously, I'm going to freak the fuck out if I get a call from her at an odd time.

"Pest, what have I told you about calling in the middle of the night? When it's not an emergency."

She mumbles, "You said to not do it."

"Yes. And why is that?"

"Because it freaks you out."

"Correct. So what do we do when we get the urge to call Reed? Just for the fuck of it."

She sighs sharply. "We stop ourselves and we try to go to sleep."

"Good."

"Fuck you, Reed. You don't have to be such an asshole. And just so you know, this is an emergency."

My lips twitch as I rest my elbow on the window and put my head back against the seat. "What is it?"

"Did you go or not?"

"Did I go where?"

"You know where. Did you go to the bar or not, Reed?"

"No."

She gasps. "You're lying. You're lying to me. To your own sister."

I close my eyes and bang my head against the seat a few times. "How the fuck do you know I'm lying?"

"Because I saw your picture," she explains. "One of your stupid girlfriends posted a picture of you on her Insta. With location. Ballad of the Bards. You can't outrun social media, bro."

Fucking Insta.

It's how half the time my sister knows what I'm up to. I usually tell people to keep it on the down low. That I don't want the whole world to know what I'm doing. But apparently, it's a big ask.

"Well if you already know, then why are you asking?" I say to Pest.

"Because I was giving you a chance to tell me everything on your own."

"There's nothing —"

"Did you see her?" she asks excitedly and I clench my jaw. "Tell me you saw her. Please. I know she was there. She goes every Friday."

Yeah, she does.

Turns out, she climbs over the fence to go to this shady bar in a shady part of town with her friends.

Every Friday.

When Pest first told me about it, a couple of years ago, I wanted to drive down from New York. I wanted to scale that fence myself,
find her in her dorm room and shake some sense into her.

I've even thought about ratting her out to her brothers.

A million times, actually.

Because what the hell is she thinking? Sneaking out to a bar in
the middle of the night. Dancing with drunks. Who I've always been
pretty sure watch her.

They watch her when she spins. When she rolls her hips and
writhes her body. When she laughs.

Like she was doing tonight.

And I was right.

They were watching her. They were leering at her. A couple of
them even dared to dance with her. I took care of that though. One
look from across the distance and they skittered away like bugs.

Fucking pussies.

So I have thought about it, putting a stop to it and keeping her
safe and in her dorm room where she belongs. But then Pest stopped
me.

My sister reminded me that she's there, at St. Mary's, because
of me. Her freedom was taken away after how I broke her heart so I
really don't have any say in the matter, in what she does or doesn't do.

But fuck that.

Fuck that to fucking hell because this is about her safety. This
is about her well-being. And she doesn't just sneak out once a week.
She does it twice.

Twice, for God's sake.

At least, she did this week.

If I hadn't been driving around last night, unable to go to sleep because I was back in this hellhole town, I never would've known.

It was pure coincidence.

Me coming upon her as she emerged from the woods. She was so engrossed in her own world that she didn't even notice me, a car with glaring headlights down the road, and Jesus Christ, what the hell was she thinking?

That's why I went.

That is the only reason why I went to that bar tonight, to give her a piece of my mind.

And because she was fucking crying at her studio and I… I just… needed to see her after that. But that's it.

My fists are clenched as I clip into the phone, "I saw her."

"And?"

"And what?"

Tempest sighs. "Oh my God, Reed. Talking to you is like pulling teeth."

"Well, then there you go. You shouldn't."

"As if." I bet she's rolling her eyes. "I'm not letting you go so easily. This is the first time you've seen her in two years. Two years, Reed. I've been telling you and telling you to go back and see her. Or just talk to her, but you wouldn't. So of course I'm gonna ask questions. And if you want me to leave you alone, you could just answer them and be done with it."

She's right. That's the best course of action here.

"Fine. Ask your fucking questions."

She squeals into the phone and I have to pull it away and wait for her to just fucking talk as I shake my head.

"Okay, so did you talk to her?" she asks excitedly.

I clench my jaw for a second before replying, "Yes."

"What did you talk about?"

"Global warming."

She sighs again but she isn't deterred. "Okay, fine. Don't tell me. Just tell me this: were you mean to her?"

"I'm never mean."

"Oh my God." She gasps again; my sister is dramatic. "You were, weren't you? Why, Reed? You're supposed to be nice to her. You know that she's miserable in that place. You know that."

I clutch the phone tightly. "Well, she wouldn't be in that place if she hadn't stolen my car."

And if my father hadn't fucked with her because of it.

"She stole your car because you were being a dick to her."

"I was being honest."

"Yes, and in the process you broke her heart. She was in love with you, Reed."

There's a pain in my chest.

Like someone has kicked it, my ribs, on purpose.

Like Ledger, her brother, has kicked my chest and punched my stomach because I broke her heart.

"And how is that my problem?" I snap into the phone, trying to ride through the burning pain. "I never asked her to fall in love with me. But she did, stupidly."

I don't do love. I don't even know what love is.

All I know is that I have a father who may or may not be a fucking psychopath, whom I'd like to strangle with my bare hands one day. I don't have space for anything else in my life other than that.

"Falling in love with you is not stupid," Pest says.

I pinch the bridge of my nose as I sigh. "Yeah, let's make a rule okay, Pest? When we talk to Reed, we don't use the L word."

I purposefully use the tone that I know she'll hate. That's the only way to get her to shut up. But again she isn't deterred. "I'm not going to shut up, just so you know. I know you want me to but I'm not going to. I'm going to keep talking and I'm going to tell you that yes, you can be rude and very insensitive sometimes. For example, right now. And you can be controlling and you think you know everything but you're not that bad, Reed. You think you are but you're not. Look what you did for her. How you saved her —"

I cut her off right there. "Is there anything else?"

I'm ready to end this conversation but she doesn't let me go. "Are you really never going to tell her?"

"Pest," I warn.

"Seriously, Reed? You're never going to tell her what you did for her. How you got her out of that whole stupid juvie situation with D —"

"Keep talking and I'll hang up," I cut her off.

Her sigh is long and loud. "Fine. Fine. Whatever. I won't say a word. Except."

"Except what?"

"Except to tell you that I love you," she says sweetly.

I'm suspicious. "You love me."

"Yes," she chirps. "And I think you're the best brother in this whole world. Even though you broke my best friend's heart."

Despite everything, my chest warms, but I do have to ask, "What do you want?"

"Nothing." She's outraged. "I just… I know how much you hate seeing Dad and now you're back there. So I don't wanna fight with you."

I swallow.

The only good thing about the past two years is that I was in New York, close to Pest. So if she wanted me, I could go to her immediately. I could be there for her.

But now I'm here and it fucking sucks.

"I'm fine," I tell her.

"You always say that. But I know. I know you hate Dad."

"As I said, Pest, I'm fine. You don't have to worry about me," I say because she doesn't have to.

She's my little sister. I'm supposed to take care of her, not the other way around.

"But I do," she replies. "You're my brother. Actually, you're not only my brother, you're my everything. You're my person, Reed. And you've been there for me like no one else has. Not Mom, who doesn't really have the energy for anything other than Dad. And definitely not Dad and —"

"That's because he's an asshole."

I don't really care how he treats me. How he uses me or manipulates me or fucks with me. How he wants to control me. I don't even care about the fact that my mother doesn't have the time or energy for me.

I don't need their time or love or affection or whatever the fuck kids get from their parents.

But Pest is sensitive. She needs them. It hurts her that Mom doesn't care about her and that Dad has no use for her. All she's really got is me.

The guy who knows nothing about love or how to be sensitive and shit.

But I made a promise when we were kids. When she'd come to me, crying and upset, that Mom wouldn't play with her or that Dad wouldn't see her science project, that I'd be there for her.

I'll protect her, and that's one promise I intend to keep.

"Yes, he is," she says, breaking into my thoughts. "But I don't need him. Because you take care of me. You're my hero."

"I am, huh?"

"Absolutely."

"Well, then you should listen to me and stop calling me in the middle of the night for no fucking reason."

She growls. "You're an asshole, you know that?"

I chuckle. "Go to sleep, Pest."

"Okay, fine, I will, but first you have to promise me something."

"What?"

"You'll say sorry to her. When you see her."

Pain in my chest flares up again and I tell her, "I'm not seeing her."

"You are," she tells me. "Because I'm going to tell you exactly where she's going to be tomorrow."

"I don't want to know."

She ignores me. "And you're going to apologize to her for being such a dick tonight. Promise me. And you're going to apologize to her for what happened two years ago. I know you want to."

I grit my teeth. "I don't."

"You do too," she protests. "Because that's why you spent the better part of last two years drunk and oblivious. So much so that you worried me."

I did – for a little while there – and I will never forgive myself for that.

As I said, she's my little sister. I'm supposed to take care of her and not the other way around.

Even so, I tighten my muscles. I absolutely refuse to give in to her, to my sister's demands. It's exactly what she does when she wants me to do something for her.

"Reed? Promise me," she prods.

I clench my eyes shut. "Fine."

Looks like I'm seeing her again tomorrow.

Even though I made another promise to myself that I never would.

Chapter 5

It's Saturday.

Meaning, today we get to go out. Legally, with permission, without having to sneak out.

Well, only me and Wyn.

Poe can't go because her privileges were recently revoked by one Mrs. Miller, her guidance counselor. And Salem can't go either because she's new and she needs a certain amount of good girl points before she can earn the privilege for a day outing.

Their plan is to spend their precious free but still imprisoned time at the library because we have a big trigonometry assignment, which I've already done. I've been telling them to do it for days now but they haven't listened. So now they'll suffer.

Our day passes are good for six hours or up to five o'clock in the evening, whichever comes first.

And I don't want to waste even a single second of that on the wrong side of the iron gates. So Wyn and me are off as soon as we can, catching the same bus that I do Thursday nights. Although this time of day, it's full of people, most of them St. Mary's girls.

Our first stop is what used to be my most favorite place in the world. These days I don't like going there but I do anyway because it's important: Buttery Blossoms.

"You sure you don't want it?" Wyn asks, referring to the cupcake she's currently eating, scooping out the silky chocolate frosting with her little plastic spoon and offering it to me.

Of course I want it.

It's a cupcake, for God's sake. And a Peanut Butter Blossom at that.

But I can't have it.

And it's not because I'm a ballerina who needs to follow a strict diet.

Or at least, it's not only because of that.

It's also because I'm a stupid girl who fell for a villain.

So I don't get to have any; it's my punishment.

I shake my head, digging into my stupid fruit cup. "Nope."

Wyn frowns and puts it in her mouth, licking the spoon. "Are you sure? Because this is very good."

I hate her.

"I know." I narrow my eyes at her. "I work here over the summer, remember?"

I do.

Again, because I'm a stupid, brokenhearted girl who needs to remember.

Who needs to remember all the ways she was stupid in the past so she doesn't fall stupid again.

Wyn takes another bite of her frosting. "Yeah, I don't know how you can work here and still not eat this. This is so good, Callie."

If she says it one more time, one more, I won't be responsible for what I do.

As it is, it's so hard to sit here and watch her eat my favorite thing in the world and not have any myself.

As hard as it is to see new knitting patterns in those online magazines and on Pinterest and not getting my knitting needles out and getting down to business.

Because once upon a time, I not only fell for a villain, I made him a cozy sweater too.

So all of this is my punishment.

No cupcakes even though I force myself to work in a cupcake shop and no knitting even though I make myself browse through those magazines all the time.

"Wyn, if you don't stop oohing and ahhing over this cupcake, I'm going to…"

I trail off then.

Because something absurd happens.

Something out of this world. Something that I never even imagined would happen.

Something like him appearing out of nowhere at our table and sitting down — actually, literally — across from me.

He's sitting across from me, at our table.

At Buttery Blossoms.

And he's staring at me with his pretty gray eyes all intense and piercing.

What?

"What?" I say out loud. "What are you —"

He turns away from me and focuses on Wyn. "Hi."

Her eyes pop wide at his voice. I don't blame her. It's deep and smooth, rich.

Like the chocolate frosting that she's been consuming.

"Hi," she says in what I think is her breathy voice.

"I'm Reed," he introduces himself and offers her his hand.

I watch that hand, stuck out in the air, with long, graceful fingers. With broad, masculine knuckles, and I don't…

What is he doing here?

Wyn has no choice but to offer hers and shake his hand. "I know."

He wraps his fingers around her palm and gives it a squeeze.

That I somehow feel in my own hand.

His grip. His strength.

And for some reason, I want him to let go of her hand.

I want him not to touch her and it's so absurd, this thought, that I shut it down immediately.

"So you've heard about me," he drawls in that voice again.

But this time, he also brings out his sexy, charming smirk and I grit my teeth.

Wyn swallows. "Yes. And your Mustang. The fact that you love it. And like, it's your most prized possession."

"Well, you know everything about me then." He squeezes her hand again and I fist mine in my lap. "And I don't even know your name."

"It's Wyn," she blurts out, kind of dazed by his attentiveness. "I mean, Bronwyn. But people call me Wyn."

"Bronwyn," he repeats. "That's a pretty name."

"Thanks," she replies, blushing and tucking a strand of her hair behind her ears.

Finally, Reed lets her go. "So Wyn, I'd like to ask you something."

"Uh, sure."

"I'd like to talk to your friend here and I'd like to do it alone. So you wouldn't mind giving us a minute, would you?"

She glances at me, unsure. "I'm not…"

He smiles at her again, that jerk, his wolf eyes all hypnotizing and beautiful. "I promise to keep her safe."

Yeah, says the villain.

I decide to jump in then. "No."

I even bang my hand on the table and they both look at me.

Wyn is slightly startled, but Reed is all relaxed and casual.

Out of the two, I only have eyes for one of them though.

The villain who's just promised to keep me safe. Who I really, really hate to admit looks gorgeous right now.

Even more gorgeous than he did last night.

At night, Reed looks like a gorgeous, otherworldly creature.

In the daylight though, he looks untouchable. His vampire skin appears indestructible.

Like even the sun can't touch him or his moon-kissed skin.

Like even the ball of fire up in the sky pales in comparison to the glow in his animal eyes.

And he's wearing my most favorite thing in the world: his white hoodie.

All soft and cozy and so familiar that I feel something lodge in my throat.

Lodge and hurt.

Even so, I manage to sound stern as I say, "She's not going anywhere. But you're leaving. Because I don't wanna talk to you."

Obviously, he settles himself at our table even more.

I should've known.

This is what he used to do back at Bardstown High, when I'd tell him to go away. Either from the auditorium or the dusty closets that he was so fond of locking me in.

Right now, he slides down the booth seat — pretty pink leather —and widens his thighs. His boots inch forward on the floor and almost touch my black Mary Janes.

Resting his hands on the white table, he says, "That works out then. Because I don't want you to talk. I just want you to listen."

I sigh sharply. "What are you even doing here? I thought this store was too pink for you."

That's another one of the things he said to me that night. And shadows move across his features, making me think that he remembers.

He remembers all the things he said to me that night.

All the awful, terrible, true things.

"It is." He threads his fingers together. "But as I said, I'd like to talk to you. And I'd rather not talk when we have company —"

"She's not going anywhere," I tell him, cutting him off. "Whatever you wanna say to me, you can do it in front of her."

I don't know why I'm so adamant about that.

I don't know why I need Wyn here but I do. I do need her to be here.

I need one thing to go my way. One thing.

Because ever since I saw him at the bar last night, I've been praying and wishing and hoping.

I've been praying that I don't see him again. That I never see him.

That last night turns out to be a coincidence.

Because I'm still reeling.

I'm still reeling from the fact that I saw him after two years.

That I heard his voice and smelled his scent.

I'm still reeling from the fact that even now he stares at me like he did back at Bardstown High. That even though I had decided that I wouldn't dance, I did — just to show him that his presence didn't affect me — and he tracked my every move like I belonged to him.

So I want my friend with me, period.

"If you insist," he agrees as he sweeps his eyes all over my face, my body — or whatever he can see of it — without saying anything else.

I narrow my eyes at him. "Well, what is it?"

He lifts his eyes and a hint of a smirk appears on his full lips. "Nice skirt, by the way."

My fisted hands in my lap unfurl and rub against the fabric at his words.

Another perk of going to St. Mary's.

It follows you everywhere.

Like a scarlet — or rather mustard — letter.

Meaning even though we get to go out and be free for a few hours, we're not really.

Because we're only supposed to wear our school uniform: white blouse, mustard-colored skirt and knee high socks with black Mary Janes.

Unless it's visitation week and you're accompanied by a parent or a guardian.

So everyone you come across on your outing knows who you are. They know that you're from St. Mary's, the all-girls reform school in the woods.

"Is this what you wanted to talk about?" I ask.

"I especially like the color," he goes on as if he didn't hear me, his eyes on my skirt, the little portion of it that's hanging off the side of the seat. "Mustard, is it?"

I jerk the fabric toward me, hiding it away from his predator eyes. "Of course you think that. You're deranged."

He doesn't mind the insult though. "Actually, I like the whole get up. That ribbon in your hair. Your knee highs. Those schoolgirl flats."

This time, his eyes travel down to rest on my legs.

And I feel my skin heat up.

So much so that I have to curl my toes inside my flats and jerk my legs away from his eyes as well.

Especially because Wyn is here.

She's watching our exchange with wide, fascinated eyes, and now I'm regretting letting her stay. So I go to rectify that but he doesn't let me.

Looking back at my face, he speaks before I can. "I have to admit. I've dreamed about this."

"Dreamed about what?"

"About you," he almost rasps. "In your St. Mary's skirt. In fact, I had one yesterday. Would you like to know what it was about?"

"No," I snap, fisting my skirt, squirming in my seat.

As if I'd ever believe that he dreamed about me.

As if I ever crossed his mind in the last two years.

He's only saying these things to make me uncomfortable and I'm this close to standing up and walking out.

But then he begins to talk and I can't move.

Because he leans forward and pins me in my place with his heated gaze. "So in my dream, you have this skirt on. It's short and pleated and so fucking you, all good girl and innocent. It flutters around your thighs every time you move and it drives me so fucking crazy, watching you walk in that thing, watching you smile and look at me with your big blue eyes, that I ask you to dance for me. I ask you to jump and leap and spin on your toes, and you do it. But it's not enough. I'm fucking greedy. So I tell you to spin faster. And you do that too. You do it so beautifully, so gloriously, like you were made to do this. Like you were put on this earth just to dance for me whenever I want, wherever I want. So I start to feel guilty."

Don't ask.

Do not ask, Callie.

"Guilty about what?"

"About the fact that I'm tricking you and you've got no clue."

"Tricking me how?"

His lips twitch with a secret knowledge that I don't have yet.

But his eyes are all grave and intense as he replies, "The only reason I asked you to spin on your toes for me is because I wanted that skirt of yours to flip up. I wanted that skirt of yours to spin with you. Because I wanted to see. I finally wanted to get a peek of what's under your pleated, good girl skirt."

By the time he finishes with his story, my legs are all sweaty and sticking to the seat.

My thighs are clenched as well.

They're all tight and tingly and restless and...

"I think I should go."

A soft voice breaks my fog.

It's Wyn.

Who's been sitting here all this time — at my insistence, no less — and who heard everything. Every single word. Every single dirty word.

Crap.

How did I forget about her?

How did I forget that my friend was sitting right here?

From the looks of it though, he didn't.

He didn't forget that she was here.

In fact at Wyn's words, his mouth tips into a tiny smile as he drawls, "Yeah, I think so too."

And then without moving his eyes away from me, he stands up and makes way for her to do just that.

As she's leaving, Wyn presses her lips together — no doubt to keep her smile or laughter or whatever at bay — and mouths good luck before disappearing.

As soon as Reed sits back down, I snap, "You did that on purpose. You said all those... dirty things in front of her on purpose."

He looks at me calmly and picks up his coffee mug, which I didn't even notice he had up until now.

He takes a sip of it as if he has all the time in the world, before putting it down and deigning to speak. "I gave you a choice. But you kept insisting."

I growl, wrapping my fingers around my half-drunk lemonade and thinking about throwing it in his face.

But I won't.

I've already displayed a lot of violence ever since he came back into my life. Which was not even twenty-four hours ago.

"How did you even know I was going to be here?"

As soon as I say it, that question — how he knew — becomes big.

It becomes the question of the hour. Of the day. Of the week even.

How did he know I was going to be at Buttery Blossoms to-day? And what about Ballad of the Bards? How did he know I was going to be there last night?

I look at him with parted lips. "Are you stalking me? Are you really stalking me? Like, really, really."

For some reason, my heart starts to pound.

My fingers slip and tremble around the glass and I can't catch my breath.

I wouldn't put it past him.

If he can lock me up in closets, he can stalk me too.

He cocks his head to the side, still calm as ever, as he asks, "Why, does it make your little ballerina heart spin in your chest? Knowing that I've been keeping tabs on you."

No.

Absolutely not.

It doesn't make my heart spin in my chest. It shouldn't.

I'm not that girl anymore. I don't like to be locked up or chased after.

I don't.

I'm smarter.

"No," I tell him, trying to sound all authoritative.

"Maybe it makes you tingle a little bit to find out that even after two years, the first thing I do when I come back to town is to hunt you down and watch your every move."

"It makes me feel violated."

He watches me a beat.

Then, "Relax. Stalking isn't an interest of mine. I hear it's something crazy ex-girlfriends do. Or girls who fall in love with you even after having been warned. No, wait. I think they steal cars." He throws me a mock boyish look as he sips his coffee again. "My bad."

I clutch my glass tightly. "Are you —"

But he continues, "Anyway, you have a bad habit of writing really long emails to my sister. And my sister has a bad habit of blurting it all out."

"Tempest?"

"The one and only."

I frown, trying to put all the pieces together. "She told you I was gonna be here?"

"A word of advice: if you want to keep secrets from me, don't tell them to my sister."

Tempest.

My best friend from my old life and the sweet little sister of the guy I fell in love with.

I did tell Tempest where I was going to be, yes.

I usually do.

We pretty much email each other every other day.

After the whole car-stealing debacle and him pressing charges against me and me almost landing in juvie, I thought I'd lose Tempest's friendship as well.

Even though she helped me and stole his keys, she's still his sister and so I thought she'd inevitably take his side.

But she never abandoned me.

She still came over to my house whenever she was in town; I wasn't ready to go to her house though. She still visited me, hung out with me.

In fact, she was the one who got me through that last month of school, after the championship game and my dance that I didn't get to do, and the whole horrible summer before I came to St. Mary's.

We still see each other.

Although not as often as I'd like because of all the stupid outing rules of reform school, but I love her. Not today though.

Today I want to strangle her.

Because I thought we had a pact.

Like our brothers, we made a pact too after everything happened.

A pact of no brothers.

Meaning our brothers would have no place in our friendship.

We wouldn't talk about them. We wouldn't mention them. It would be like we had no brothers.

Although one thing never made sense to me.

I knew why I was making the pact, but I'm not sure why she did.

Why she never wanted to hear about Ledger, whom I know that she liked two years ago, and I never asked; she respected my space and so I respected hers.

So I don't know why she'd rat my whole schedule out to her brother.

But anyway, right now I need to deal with him and ignore the slight sinking in my chest.

The absurd sinking.

That feels like disappointment.

Because he wasn't really stalking me as I'd assumed.

See? Absurd.

"So she sent you here?" I ask, confused, my mind going two years back.

To that closet when he came to give me his sister's birthday invitation. The day he gave me his name, Fae.

"No," he says with an irritated frown. "No one sends me anywhere. But she does think that I should apologize."

"For what?"

"She had a long list."

I look at him for a beat. "I'm sure she did. But apology not accepted."

"You should probably wait for me to apologize before you say that." I open my mouth to say something but he goes on. "That's not why I'm here. I'm here to ask you something."

I draw back slightly. "What?"

His jaw moves back and forth in annoyance before saying, "Do you sneak out to Blue Madonna every week?"

"That's none of your business."

He studies my features for a few moments before sighing sharply. "I'm going to be honest with you, I didn't want to see you again. It wasn't my plan when I came back to this fuckhole town. But now I'm assuming you sneak out every week to go to your ballet studio. Like you do to go to that shitty bar with your friends. Is that correct?"

"It's not a shitty bar," I say, offended.

That frown on his forehead grows. "You're joking."

"I'm not. It's a great bar."

"It's a dance bar, Fae. The only dance bar where when they put on the music, instead of dancing, you want to kill yourself."

I ignore the flutter in my chest at Fae and say, "You only think that because you have crappy taste in music."

It's a lie. He doesn't.

I like his taste in music.

It's usually a mix of vintage rock bands and modern hip hop, and well, it's not a secret that I love it. He knows that too; I've danced to it quite a lot, haven't I?

So before he can make a comment about it — dirty, of course — I continue, "And their whiskey is excellent too, don't you think? It's so excellent that people steal it just to have a sip."

"If you think that then you should probably just stick to your lemonade and leave the hard liquor to the grown-ups," he says, tipping his chin to my half-drunk glass of lemonade, not taking my bait.

"You're such a —"

"The point is," he speaks over me, "that I'm willing to give you a ride to your ballet studio."

"I'm sorry?"

"Just so you can stop being stupidly reckless and taking the bus at midnight. Where at worst, you could be kidnapped and murdered and at best, robbed and raped."

I have no words right now.

I don't.

He's insane.

"You're insane," I tell him.

"And you're lucky." He sips his coffee coolly. "That I'm willing to drive you around on your foolish errands."

"Foolish errands?"

"Yes."

My fingers claw at the lemonade glass as I say, "The reason I have to run those foolish errands is because I'm stuck at St. Mary's. And in case you forgot, it's a reform school. Meaning they don't have a ballet teacher. Because apparently, ballet doesn't rank so high when it comes to restoration and reformation of teenage criminals."

"Well now you know, don't you?" he says with a harsh jaw. "Next time you'll think twice before stealing someone's car with the intent of destroying it. Almost wrecking your future in the process."

I bite the inside of my cheek at his words. I bite it so hard that I think I taste copper.

I taste the broken pieces of my heart, my foolishness.

My recklessness.

And I gulp it all down with a hard swallow. "Yeah, you're right. I will. I will think twice about it. At least then I won't be stuck in a cage, trying to chase my dream. Trying to break into the one place that was supposed to get me there but they kicked me out instead and —"

"What?"

I flinch at his severe tone. "What?"

"They kicked you out."

"Yes."

"Why?"

I frown at his ticking, angry jaw. "Because I stole your car."

"So?"

"So... apparently you steal one car and the world suddenly thinks that you're running a grand theft auto ring," I tell him as I grow increasingly confused again.

What is it to him if I got kicked out?

"They said that to you?" he asks then, his voice all low and his features tight.

"I..." I shake my head. "What does it matter what they said to me?"

"What about Juilliard?"

"Again, none of your business. Besides, it's done. It happened two years ago."

"Yeah," he snaps, his fingers digging into his coffee mug. "And

I'm wondering how the fuck did I not know about this until now?"

My mouth falls open then.

I do realize that this might be the first time he's hearing of it.

It's not as if I told Tempest about it, about being kicked out and my Juilliard plans. I was too embarrassed to tell her. So I get that if his sister didn't know, he didn't know either. I mean, how else would he have come to know?

But that tone? How the fuck did he not know?

Who does he think he is?

I lean forward. "You didn't know, Reed, because I didn't tell you. Because it's none of your business. Because when you so completely broke my heart and betrayed my trust, I decided that I wasn't going to treat you like my whole world and share things with you."

That jaw of his, clean-shaven this morning and angular as ever, keeps ticking as he stares at me with heated eyes. "Blue Madonna, right?"

I open my mouth to answer him and then close it before saying, "I don't know what's going on with you. I don't know why you think that you can tell me what to do like you did last night or why you think I should share my life story with you. But it's getting really old and I want you to stop, okay? Oh, and I don't need a ride from you."

"You're taking it regardless."

I scoff. "What makes you think that I'm going to get inside your car and let you drive me around after everything?"

His nostrils flare. "If I'm willing to let you anywhere near my car, you better get inside it, Fae. And you better smile your good girl smile and say thank you in your sweet voice to show me your gratitude no matter where I decide to drive you. After everything."

"And if I don't?"

He smiles then.

A humorless, cold smile as his animal eyes flash. "See, the

thing is that I know where you live. I've been to your house, remember? And as much as I'll hate going back there and talking to your brothers, I'll still do it. For you. I'm sure they'd be very interested to know what you've been up to. Behind their backs. Besides I did it once, remember? At the championship game no less. So I could win. I can do it again."

My heart is thundering in my chest. "You're blackmailing me again."

He shrugs, his massive shoulders swelling up and down. "I'm giving you a choice."

He's a villain, isn't he?

How did I not see this before? How did I not see his true colors?

How did I ever — God, ever — fall in love with him?

But it's okay.

It's fine.

As I told him last night, I'm not the same girl. I'm not going to do his bidding. When he tells me to jump, I'm not going to ask him how high.

Time to show him that.

So I take a deep breath and smile. "Fine. I'll go with you."

He watches me. "You will."

"Yes." I nod, still smiling. "I mean, I don't like it because I freaking hate you and I wish I never met you. But you're right. There's no need for me to be reckless and stupid when I can be smart. So if you're offering me a ride, I'll take it."

Reed is suspicious.

He studies my features, and I school them to look serene and calm.

Which is hard, but somehow I manage to do it.

When he's satisfied, he sighs and throws out a short nod. "Good." Then he murmurs almost to himself, as he sips his coffee,

"Because I didn't bring your brother that deal just to have you snatched up by another villain because of your stupidity."

Deal?

Mention of it throws me slightly and I almost slip up.

But again, somehow I manage to keep smiling as I tighten my grip around the lemonade and wait for my chance.

I get it when he looks away from me and puts the mug down on the table.

I spring up from my seat then and before I can second-guess it, I dump my lemonade on his lap. And before he can have any sort of reaction to that, I stomp on his foot.

The one that was super close to me when he decided to settle in and crash my brunch.

"You can pay the bill, asshole," I snap.

I think he chuckles. I'm not really sure because my focus is on the next part of my plan: running and getting the heck out of there.

Wyn, who's been sitting at a table by the door, looks at me with shocked eyes.

"Run, run, run," I tell her and she jumps up from her seat and does what I asked her to.

Together, we push open the door and burst out of there.

My heart is beating in my ears. My body is full of adrenaline and I don't know where I'm going.

I don't know where I'm taking Wyn, but she doesn't question me. She keeps running beside me even as people watch us zoom down the sidewalk, in our mustard-colored skirts and our flying braids.

We keep running until I come upon an alley, far enough away from Buttery Blossoms, and take a turn into it. Coming to a halt, we both prop ourselves against the brick wall, panting.

I'm not sure how much time has passed until Wyn asks, "What happened?"

I roll my head against the wall to look at her. "I dumped my lemonade on his lap."

Wyn's eyes go wide before a chuckle bursts out of her. "You did not!"

I chuckle too, unable to believe that I did that. "Then I stomped on his foot."

At this, she explodes in a loud laugh. "Oh my God."

I laugh too before I ask, "Do you think I hurt him?"

She laughs again. "Probably."

Frowning and looking up at the gray sky, I say, "I don't know why I care."

She sighs beside me. "He broke your heart, didn't he?"

I swallow, blinking my eyes. "Yes."

"Well then, he deserved it."

At her fierce tone, I look back at her. "He pressed charges against me."

"What?"

I nod, looking up at the sky again, the color of his eyes. "I mean, I did steal his car and tried to destroy it. And it was his most prized possession. He built it himself."

"He did?"

"Yeah. I didn't know it at the time." I swallow again as something painful presses against my throat. "At the time, all I wanted to do was hurt him the way he hurt me and… stealing his car seemed like the best idea. Destroying something that he loved like he destroyed me. I don't fault him for wanting to see me punished for it. I just…"

"What?" Wyn asks with concern in her eyes.

I sniffle, realizing that I've started to cry.

God, what an idiot.

Ashamed, I clench my eyes shut and fist my hands as I whisper, "I just wish that he had fought for me like he did for his car, you know? I just wish that I was important. To him."

I wish that I was more than a stupid girl to him who fell in love and stole his car. I wish I was...

All my thoughts pause when I remember what he said just now.

I didn't bring your brother that deal...

That deal.

What deal?

Chapter 6

Tempest was the one who told me.

That Reed had built his car himself.

She didn't want to though.

She didn't give me this piece of information for the longest time. Because she thought I had so much to deal with already. My heartbreak, rumors at school about the Thorne Princess falling for the Wild Mustang, her brothers' enemy.

Everything happened publicly that night, didn't it?

We fought at a party. I stole his car from that party. I didn't show up for my own dance show.

I even got arrested; not publicly, but still.

So everyone at school knew everything and they all thought I was love-crazy. That whole month, they watched me like I was going to blow up any second.

But anyway.

One weekend while Tempest was hanging out at my place, it slipped out of her mouth. She said something about Reed working on his car and it snowballed from there.

I kept hounding her until she finally spilled the beans.

She told me that Reed loves cars.

He's something of a car aficionado.

Not only that, but he worked at a garage out of town called Auto Alpha. No one knew about this, so I was supposed to keep it a secret, and that was where he got interested in cars and built his Mustang from parts.

I remember being so shocked. Speechless.

I was with him for months and I had no clue.

I had no clue that he'd built his own car, let alone worked at a garage. According to Tempest, he worked because he wanted to get away from their dad and also to stick it to him, even if secretly.

I also remember feeling a twist in my chest.

A sharp pinch.

Reed and his dad.

Even though I had no right to feel anything for him anymore and I shouldn't even have felt the need to, I still couldn't help myself from wanting to go to him.

Wanting to apologize about the car. About his dad.

Wanting to just… talk to him.

But it was so silly, wasn't it?

He would never open up to me about his dad, and well, what would I have said to him anyway? It was better to keep my distance and so that's what I did.

That was the last time Tempest and I talked about her brother, because that's when we made the pact and so we never broached the subject.

I never sought out any information about Reed.

Never Googled him. Never stalked him on social media.

I buried him.

Somewhere deep inside of me. Somewhere only I could reach

him when I wanted to remember and torture myself over my mistakes.

Until now.

Until today.

Because I need to know. I need to know what deal he made with my brother. What was he talking about?

Since today's Saturday, it's phone day at St. Mary's.

Every week like clockwork my oldest brother, Conrad, calls me at 7PM. He calls me and then conferences the rest of my brothers in: Stellan, Shepard and Ledger.

Every week I eagerly wait for their call. I usually arrive at the phone room way before the time and hang out in the hallway until Miss Fletcher, the one usually manning the phones, calls for me. And when she does I run to grab it.

I run so I can talk to my brothers.

Whom I love to pieces.

Whom I only get to talk to once a week. Because of my stupidity.

Because of what I did, the crime that I committed and because of what I put them through.

You know, when I stole his car and drove it into the lake, I wasn't thinking. Or rather, I was only thinking about the pain in my chest and the blow of his betrayal. Of all the lies he had told me.

I never once thought about what it would do to my brothers.

How it would upset them. How it would make trouble for them, having a thief for a sister.

Besides, I wasn't the only one who got betrayed that night, was I? They got betrayed too. By me.

I was lying to them. I was lying to Ledger, the brother that I was closest to, and hanging out with his enemy. And then I went ahead and became a criminal as well.

I still can't erase all the guilt of my sins. I still can't get rid of this shame.

Even though they forgave me. They did.

God, did they.

Stellan was probably the first one, my rational brother. He got Shepard on board and Shep got Ledger. The brother whom I'd betrayed the most.

I still don't know how he found it in his heart to forgive me, but he did.

I guess he was angrier at his enemy than at me. Whom he actually beat up after everything happened. I only know because Reed came to school that Monday with bruises all over his face.

Anyway, that whole summer, along with Tempest, my brothers helped with my grief too. They all had their plans — Ledger and Shep were set to go on a road trip with their friends; Stellan had a summer job in the city — but they all canceled everything and hung out with me.

I guess that's why my guilt is so huge even now.

Because they're all so wonderful and amazing. They still treat me as their baby sister before I betrayed them.

Except Conrad.

He was mad at the time. Madder than all three of my other brothers. More disappointed too. He could barely stand to be in the same room as me.

He still feels the same.

And so when he calls, he's the one who talks the least. Which wouldn't be too atypical because my oldest brother doesn't talk a lot to begin with, but his silence these days is laced with disappointment and anger at me.

I know that. I can feel it.

But still, I need to know.

I need to know what deal Reed was talking about back at Buttery Blossoms this morning and in order to do that, I'm breaking the norm.

Instead of waiting for Con's call, I'm calling him. I need to get him alone to talk about this.

Unlike many girls at St. Mary's, I do have the privilege of making my own phone calls. It's one of those difficult privileges to have that I've earned after a lot of good girl behavior and excellent grades.

And tonight, I'm going to use it.

I'm in the phone room, inside a mustard-colored booth, with the black headset of a rotary phone pressed to my ear. I've already dialed the number and my brother picks up after the first ring.

From the tone of his voice, it sounds like Conrad must've jumped to answer the phone. "Callie?"

"Yes. Hi, I —"

He doesn't let me speak. "Are you okay?"

Oh!

Crap.

He probably thinks that something is wrong with me. That's why I'm calling instead of waiting for him to call.

I grab the receiver with the other hand as well, as I reply, "Yes, I am. I just —"

"Are you hurt?"

"No, not at all. I'm not hurt. Everything is fine, Con. I just —"

"Then what the hell is going on? Did you do something?"

"What?"

"What the fuck did you do, Callie?" he booms into the phone.

I flinch. "Nothing. I did nothing. Why would you assume that I did something?"

His voice is sharp as ever when he replies, "You're calling me out of the blue, ten minutes before I'm supposed to call you. What else would I think?"

Right.

I get it. I understand his point.

It's not as if he's wrong to think that.

I did screw up once, and well, I did it in such a massive way that only once was enough.

Swallowing, I say, "I didn't do anything, Con, and I'm sorry I worried you. I just... I wanted to ask you something."

"What?"

I wince slightly at his curt tone.

Okay, do it.

Ask him.

Ask the question, Callie.

"When I was... when everything happened and they arrested me. And they told us that there'd be a hearing and they'd most probably send me to a juvenile detention center. How come... why didn't they? Why did they reduce my charges so I only ended up at St. Mary's?"

They did.

They reduced the charges against me.

The cops came to the house the very next day in the afternoon and since I was a minor, Conrad had to go into the station with me. Even though I'd told him everything — I confessed about lying and falling in love and then stealing his car the night before — it still came as a shock.

It still jarred my brothers that I was being taken into custody and the charges against me were such that I could actually end up in a juvenile detention center.

At least the cop who took me in was nice. He used to be Con's friend from Bardstown High and he kept reassuring us that even though things looked bleak just then, we could hire a lawyer who could turn this all around.

And then I remember Con stepping out of the room.

I remember hearing his loud, booming voice, demanding to talk to someone in charge, someone with a fucking brain who knew this charge was bullshit, and that he would get a lawyer and sue every single one of them including that son of a bitch who pressed charges against me.

I also remember crying in the interrogation room before Con came back in and said that it was settled.

That they were reducing my charges and that I was free to go now. But as my punishment, I'd have to attend St. Mary's come that fall.

When I asked him what happened, he said that it was none of my concern and that he'd taken care of everything because the charges were bullshit to begin with.

That was all.

That was all he said and I was too embarrassed, too scared to ask anything else, to be anything else other than relieved, so I never ever broached the question again.

I was just grateful that I wasn't going to juvie. I was grateful that I had a brother who loved me enough — even though I embarrassed him so brutally — to have my back like that.

Is it any wonder then, that he's still mad at me?

"Why?" my brother asks curtly, pulling me out of my thoughts, pulling me out of those few hours that were the scariest of my life.

"Because I need to know," I say with almost a strangled voice. "Because I... I need to know what you did, Con. H-how you took care of it. I'm sorry I never asked before. I was too scared. Too embarrassed to ask you. But I should have. I should have been a good sister like you were a good brother. I should've asked what you went through to... to get me off. What you did to get me free."

Or almost free.

He's silent for a few seconds.

And my heart is thudding in my chest. My heart that's broken and beaten and so painful to live with is pounding and pounding as I wait for my brother to say something.

Anything.

As I hear his words over and over.

I didn't bring your brother that deal...

"Nothing," Conrad clips.

"What?"

"I did nothing."

"I don't understand."

His exhale is sharp and short. "I didn't have to do anything. It was him."

The way my brother says him, I don't have to ask who he's talking about. His tone is all harsh and clipped and self-explanatory.

"W-what do you mean?" I ask.

"It means that I was all ready to go to court and fight this thing. I was all ready to hire a lawyer and teach that rich prick a lesson. But he called me and he said that he'd gotten all the charges reduced and all you had to do was attend St. Mary's. I was opposed to it. I didn't like it. I didn't like his fucking face. And I told him that. I told him that I'd go to court and fight his bullshit charge. And that fucking punk reminded me that even if I did go to court, I would never win. Because the Jacksons own the town. They own the police, the judges, the lawyers. And so this was the only way. And when I told him that I was going to break his fucking face for what he did to you, he was generous enough to say that I was welcome to it. Only I'd have to take a fucking number because Ledger wanted to get there first."

Conrad has never ever spoken so many words together, in one conversation.

And the fact that he did it now convinces me that he still has a lot of anger inside of him. At me, at him.

At his old star player.

Con has always hated the rivalry between Ledger and Reed. But he's especially hated Reed for being reckless and selfish on the field.

But I don't get it.

Why have me arrested in the first place and then have the charges reduced? Just like that.

"W-why would he bring you the deal when he was the one who pressed charges?"

A moment passes.

Then two, and I'm about to prod him because I can't take it anymore, but Conrad breaks his silence. "It wasn't him."

"What?"

"It was his father."

"His father?"

"Yes."

"B-but they said Mr. Jackson and…"

"He's not the only Mr. Jackson, is he?"

He isn't, no.

He's not the only Mr. Jackson.

But for the life of me it never ever occurred to me that his dad would be involved. The man I'd never even seen. Not once in all the times that I'd been to their house.

He was always either away for business or at the office.

I saw their mom once though.

She was on the balcony, looking so small and beautiful with her blonde hair fluttering in the wind. I guess Tempest and Reed both get their dark hair from their father.

The man who had me arrested for stealing his son's car.

"So you… knew this the whole time?"

"Yes."

Oh my God.

I press a hand on my stomach and lean against the booth.

All this time, I thought it was him.

Because it was his car, the thing that he loved the most. So it made sense that he'd want to punish me for stealing it. And strangely, those charges hurt me even more.

Because he cared about his car more than he ever cared about me. Which I knew already but still.

He didn't though.

He didn't.

He had the charges reduced. He… he brought my brother the deal.

I can barely draw a proper breath or form a coherent thought in my head. But still, I make myself ask my brother, "Why didn't you tell me?"

"Why do you think?"

"You knew that I thought it was him. You knew that. Why didn't you tell me if you knew?" I ask, tears welling up in my eyes.

"Because you're naïve, Callie," he snaps, his voice making me flinch, and my tears fall harder. "Because I didn't want you to paint him as a hero who swooped in to save you after everything that he did. Because I wanted to protect you. Because I wanted you to be smart. I wanted you to move on and live your life and think about your future. I didn't want you to waste your life over a guy like him. A guy you almost destroyed your life for. A guy who broke your heart and made you cry."

God, I wish I could hide myself somewhere. I wish I could stop this shame from spreading out over my body. I wish I could stop these tears.

But more than that, I wish I could hug him.

I wish I was back home with him so I could tell him how sorry I am for everything that I put him through.

My brother who brought me up. Who's more like a father figure to me — to all of us — than my brother.

As it is, all I can do is whisper, "I'm not going to waste my life over him, Con. I've learned my lesson."

But maybe that's not enough to convince him because he speaks in a rough, heartfelt whisper. "Do you remember what I told you, Callie? Two years ago, I told you that Reed Jackson is an asshole. I told you that he isn't the guy for you and I still mean that. I don't know why he had those charges reduced. I don't know if it was his conscience or if he was playing a game and I don't care. I don't fucking care, you hear me? Because if he ever so much as looks at you again, ever, I'm going to take him apart. I'm going to break every single bone in his body and I'm going to take my time with it. Do you understand that, Callie? Stay away from him."

***

It's Thursday and I sneak out a little earlier than I usually do.

It could be slightly riskier, since Wyn hasn't really gone to sleep yet. But it's not, because she knows everything now. About the Blue Madonna, my ballet dreams.

Him.

I told her.

After last Saturday at Buttery Blossoms where Reed showed up, I had to. And now I'm wondering why I didn't talk to her sooner. Because she totally believes in me, in my ballet dream, in Juilliard.

She also thinks that there's more to him than I think. Because I also told her what Con revealed on the phone call.

How the guy who I thought had me arrested was actually the one who got me off on a reduced charge.

He saved me.

Isn't that surreal? Isn't that… what I always thought of him?

Back at Bardstown High, I always thought that he had more to him than what he showed the world.

But I was wrong.

I was so wrong that when I learned the truth, look what I did.

Look what I became.

My brother is right. He might have saved me — for whatever reason — but I know better now. I'm smarter and I'm not listening to Wyn.

I'm staying away from him.

That's why I left earlier than usual and got on a different bus. It was just as empty but whatever.

That isn't the point.

The point is that I need to stay away from him. And he has no business telling me what to do.

Hopefully my whole violent display at Buttery Blossoms managed to make it clear that I don't want anything to do with him.

But apparently not.

Apparently it's too much to ask, because he's here.

At my silent, empty ballet studio, Blue Madonna.

I see him in the mirror.

All the way across the room, he is standing behind me, propped up against the white wall. He has his arms folded across his chest and from the looks of it, he's been here a long time and he'll be here even longer than that.

Because he appears so… engrossed, so absorbed in the moment.

In me.

In my bowed body.

I'm on my knees, see.

With my fake, feather-light wings slung across my back, I'm

on the floor and my body is bent in an arc, and he's watching that arc, tracking it with his wolf eyes.

My shoulder blades, the slope of my spine, the line of my neck, all the way up to my tight, blonde bun.

And he's so enamored that he doesn't even know that I've spotted him.

Not until I unfold myself and stand up.

Only then do his eyes snap up and clash with mine. And what a clash it is.

I feel the impact of it right in my chest, right where my wounded heart lives, and I spin around to face him.

"You're here." I state the obvious. "Again."

I knew he'd come.

Even though I was hoping that what happened at the cupcake shop might give him the message, I knew he'd follow me like he used to two years ago.

He's a predator, isn't he? A villain, and I'm the lost girl at midnight.

That is exactly why I chose to make my point that he can't control me like he did before by getting here the way I wanted.

Reed doesn't answer right away.

He's watching a drop of sweat sliding down my throat, and when it disappears under the neck of my leotard, only then does he lift his eyes and say, "Because you ran from me the other day. Again."

His usual statement said in a dangerous tone jacks up my breaths. It makes me hypersensitive. So much so that I feel that drop he was watching slide further down my body, reaching between my breasts.

But I try to focus on what he's saying.

"I had to. You were being an asshole," I tell him.

"And you were quite the picture of politeness yourself."

I fist my sweaty hands at his accusation. "Well, you made me angry."

"So you dumped your lemonade on me."

My eyes go to his foot then, his right one that I stomped on. "And stomped on your foot."

He narrows his eyes slightly as he continues, "You also left me to pay your bill."

I wince.

I can't believe I did that.

I've never, not in my entire life, run out of a restaurant without paying the bill.

Not until him.

But then that's nothing new, is it?

I do things for him that I've never done. I feel things for him that I've never felt before.

He turns me into a different Callie. His Callie.

His Fae.

Swallowing, I dispel these useless thoughts. "Well, you broke my heart so I think I'm allowed that."

His eyes flash when I throw back his words from the bar. "You are."

"But even so, I can give you back your money. I have some cash in my bag."

I do, and I can pay him back.

His folded arms flex as he considers my offer. And they're so big and sculpted that I can see the hilly contours of them, his biceps, even through his hoodie.

His soft, cozy, warm hoodie.

Finally, he says, "Yeah, money is not what I'm interested in tonight."

Like always, his tone is what gets me. His tone that sounds all dangerous and villainous.

And something else that I'm trying not to think about, seductive.

I lick my lips. "Are you here for revenge then?"

He glances down at my lips for a second. "I haven't decided yet."

I don't think a threat that sounds like a threat, feels like a threat, should also make things move inside of my stomach.

Innocent things like butterflies and tingles.

Corrupt things like thick, heated desire.

"Before you decide either way," I begin. "I want to say something."

He arches an arrogant eyebrow. "I'm listening."

I want to purse my lips and narrow my eyes at his condescending tone, but I keep my features blank and say, "Even though you deserved it, it wasn't my intention to do those things. It wasn't my intention to dump my drink on you or stomp on your foot. Or even attack you like I did back at the bar. I'm not this violent person, despite all the evidence to the contrary. I don't do these things. I don't..."

I don't steal cars...

I don't say that but it's right there. On the tip of my tongue.

That and the question, why.

Why did he save me? Why did he have the charges reduced after how I tried to destroy something that he'd built?

As I said, he deserved it, but why?

Reed, on the other hand, has no hesitation in asking me that question.

"Then why did you?" His voice is thick and raspy. "Do those things."

I know he's asking me about these recent events and not what I did two years ago. Still, I answer him like he is. "Because... because you make me crazy. You make me angry. You make me do things that I never thought I'd do in a million years. You turn me into this…"

I trail off again and again he picks up the thread. "I turn you into what?"

Those innocent little things inside of me, those corrupt little things, all of them go haywire. They go crazy and chaotic as I whisper, "Bad. You turn me into a bad girl."

Fae.

Maybe that's the magic in him. That dark magic that makes girls do things for him.

That makes them go crazy for him, fall in love with him even though they know that he'll always end up breaking their hearts.

His gorgeous features are blank so I have no clue what he's thinking right now and it's not my business to figure it out either and so I keep going. "And that's why I think it's better if… if you stay away from me."

At this, he says something even though his features are still unreadable. "You want me to stay away from you."

I nod.

It's more of a jerk than a smooth motion. "Yes, I do. Aside from what I just said, my brothers will lose it. They will kill you for going near me. And —"

"I can handle them," he says. "Haven't I told you this before?"

I grit my teeth and purposefully stop my breaths.

I refuse to breathe.

Refuse to take air into my lungs and give life to my body, give beats to my heart.

All these years later, his cavalier attitude still gets me. His reckless, cavalier, daredevil attitude.

God, Callie. You idiot.

"Even so. I don't think we have anything to say to each other after what happened."

"You mean how you stupidly fell in love with me and I broke your little heart."

It shouldn't hurt this much.

What he just said.

The wound inside my chest shouldn't flare up and pulsate as if it's new, freshly inflicted. But it does.

Maybe because he said it without flinching.

Maybe because he can talk about breaking my heart as if it's so inconsequential that it doesn't even warrant a change of tone or a ripple in his features.

And maybe that's why my eyes sting. "Yes. So unless you're trying to use me again, I suggest you leave."

"I'm not trying to use you," he says, studying my face. "You don't have anything that I need."

I want to laugh at myself then.

I want to laugh at my own stupid self that his statement made me flinch. That the fact that I'm now useless to him makes something contract in my chest.

"Well then, there you go," I say with clenched fists. "I'm useless to you. So staying away shouldn't be so hard, right? I don't have anything you need and I don't want you around either. Besides, you don't even live here anymore, do you? You live in New York and I've heard it's amazing. I mean, my brothers are crazy about that city. I bet you have a wonderful life at college. I bet you have great friends. People must be crazy about your soccer skills and you must be the campus stud and soccer superstar or whatever. So what are you even doing here, wasting your time? Who cares what bus I take or how I get to my studio? I really think you should leave and resume your awesome life and —"

"That's different," he says, cutting me off.

"What?"

He motions with his jaw, his gaze dipping down to my lips. "Your lipstick."

My hand goes up and I touch my lips.

It's so bizarre that he noticed. So strange and unexpected, his observation and his interruption, that all I can do is say, "Uh, yeah."

His eyes come up. "So?"

"So what?"

"What's this one called?"

I lower my hand and automatically reply, as if I'm still in a fog, "Train Wreck Princess."

It's blue with subtle notes of green and is overall lighter than Heartbreak Juju, which I wore the night of the bar.

"Why, because you're a princess?"

"I'm —"

"But you're not, are you?"

You're a fairy...

His long-ago words flutter through my mind and probably in his mind too. Because his wolf eyes glint. They sparkle and so does his vampire skin.

And for a second, the studio vanishes, the polished hardwood floors, the barre, the mirrored wall, and all of that gets replaced by those woods.

The woods that we used to go to.

That lonely dark place where I used to dance for him.

Where I danced for him for the first time and he called me a fairy. Where...

"You're a fairy," he finishes his earlier spoken statement, his eyes grave and his lips tipping up.

I believed him.

Back then, I believed that I was a fairy.

Not anymore though.

Even though the wings at my back flutter and rustle against my spine as if coming alive now that he's here. "No, I'm not."

"You're fucking up your développé écarté devant," he says. "Isn't that what it is?"

I watch him a beat. "Yes."

"And you're supposed to hold it? For eight counts."

I remain speechless, motionless. He remembers.

He keeps going though. "And if you can't hold a position in ballet, it's supposed to be a big fucking crime."

How does he remember everything like I do?

When I always thought that all this time he's been living his glamorous life in New York, I probably never even crossed his mind.

He straightens up and moves away from the wall.

Keeping his eyes on me, he starts to walk. Toward me.

And when he does that, again all I can do is stand in my spot, all frozen and immobile. Like I used to two years ago, whenever he decided to prowl toward me.

I used to stand glued to my spot, my traitor legs refusing to move.

My traitor heart refusing to slow down, and I'm about to stop him. I'm about to tell him to not come anywhere close to me.

Because I don't know what's happening.

I don't know what he's doing.

I don't know how and why he remembers everything from two years ago. And neither do I know why he saved me.

But my wayward, confused thoughts break when I realize that he wasn't.

Coming near me, I mean.

He was going somewhere else.

He was going to the black stereo off to the side. And when

he reaches it, he bends down on his knees and starts fiddling with the buttons.

I finally string some words together as I watch him. "What are you doing?"

"Helping you with your routine."

"My routine."

When he's done with it, he comes back to his feet. "You want to go to Juilliard, don't you? Well, you're not going with the way you're dancing. Because it sucks."

I'm too shaken up to take offense.

Besides he is right.

It does suck. I can't, for the life of me, hold that pose. I can do développé à la seconde, which is folding your leg out to the side, but écarté devant is my weakness.

Even so, I don't need his help.

I don't need him to give me any more reminders of before. Of when he used to help me, make me better. I already remember those days plenty on my own.

I'm already plenty devastated and broken.

"I don't need your help."

"You're getting it nonetheless."

"You hate twirling, remember?"

"Maybe I've changed. Maybe now I'm ready to embrace my feminine side."

"You —"

"Unless you're afraid," he says, tilting his head to the side.

"Of what?"

"Of me." His eyes turn hooded. "Touching you."

I frown as my spine goes up. "Why would I be afraid of that?"

He shrugs, his shoulders that were already massive have now become even more muscled as they move. "I don't know. You tell me."

"I'm not afraid of you." I narrow my eyes at him. "Disgusted, yes. But afraid, no."

He hums thoughtfully. "Maybe you think that once I put my hands on you, you won't be able to control yourself."

"Control myself from what?"

His ruby red lips stretch up in a smirk. "From touching me back."

"You mean my fist touching your face?"

His smirk only grows as if I didn't say anything. "From wanting me. From falling for me again."

"You —"

"I mean, you did before, right? I twirled for you a little and you thought I was your knight in fucking armor." Then, "Wait, shining armor. That's what you called it, isn't it? You thought I was your knight in shining armor." He chuckles then, thick, syrupy condescension dripping from it. "I mean, there are silly teenage girls who fall in love at the drop of a hat and then there's you. You, who lives in a house made of cupcakes and whose dreams are full of pink glitter. And who thinks that every story is a love story where the prince is going to get down on his knees and offer you forever. And you both will ride off into the sunset. In his Mustang."

By the time he finishes, I'm flushed.

With anger.

My spine is the straightest that it's ever been and my chest is the heaviest. It feels like my bones have turned into iron and all I want to do is use them to hurt him.

To hurt him like he's hurt me.

Like he continues to hurt me.

But I won't.

I won't lower myself to his level. I know he's provoking me and I know he wants me to give in.

And I will.

But in a different way.

In a way that will prove him wrong. That will show him that I will never ever be that stupid again.

"Fine," I say, fisting and unfisting my hands at my side. "Let's do it. But only because you taught me that not every story is a love story and you're the villain everyone said you were."

He watches me a beat before he throws a curt nod and bends down, hitting play on the stereo.

The sound comes on, the buzzing static before the music fills the air.

This moment has the power to send me back to the past, to Bardstown High, to the auditorium. But I keep myself in the present. I keep myself grounded to Blue Madonna as I walk toward him to begin.

I try to erase my memory.

I try to develop amnesia.

Especially when as he sees me approaching, he widens his stance and dips his chin like he used to do two years ago.

Especially when the violins come in and I have to assume position, my arms straight up in the air and my calves stretched up, my weight supported on my toes.

Especially when I remember that when I danced for him, I felt perfect.

I felt beautiful.

I felt like a flawless ballerina, and when I take my first turn under his scrutiny, that feeling comes rushing back.

The feeling that I've been missing.

The feeling that I'm on fire. That the wings on my back can really fly me away and that I'm spinning so fast that my toes have left the ground and I can levitate.

The feeling that I'm really a fairy.

I haven't had this in two years.

Not since he went away.

But tonight it's back.

Tonight, I feel perfect. I feel beautiful and ethereal.

I feel like a fairy.

His fairy, as I dance around him.

As I twirl and leap and jump and lose myself in the music like I was made for it.

As he watches me with a certain kind of possession in his eyes, the same kind from two years ago.

I don't want to, though.

I don't want to feel perfect or on fire or ethereal.

I don't want to feel his.

But I do, and when the time comes for him to lift me and he puts his hands on my waist and gives me a boost after two long years, stars explode in my veins. The violins are so loud that they shatter the ceiling, the sky, and I throw my arms up in the air, my lungs swelling up with his scent of wildflowers and woods.

I'm so lost in it, in his grip, in the fact that my soft flesh gives so easily beneath his strong fingers, that it takes me a few seconds to realize that the music has stopped.

I don't even know where the time went.

I don't even know how it moved so fast and there's pin-drop silence now.

Except for our breaths, panting and heavy.

I lower my arms then and put them on his shoulders, looking down.

As always, his eyes are already on me, a gunmetal gray so intense and liquid that I could drown in it. I could drown in the deep lake of his wolf eyes.

And I should save myself.

I should look away.

I shouldn't admire his thick lashes, the strands of his dark brown hair that flutter over his forehead. The long strands that make me think that he needs a haircut.

I shouldn't flex my fingers on his shoulders and knead the muscles. I shouldn't marvel over how big they feel now, how strong and rock-like. Even more than before.

Like he's been pumping iron for the past two years, building himself muscle by muscle, tendon by tendon.

And why wouldn't he?

He's an athlete. A soccer player.

The best soccer player.

The one who won the championship two years ago. Who defeated my brother, the Angry Thorn, and became the reigning champion of Bardstown High, the Wild Mustang.

I bet people still remember him. They remember his victory. They remember his swagger, his style, his legend.

And if they remember him, they probably remember me too.

They probably remember what the Thorn Princess did in the name of love.

How she went crazy.

For him.

And God, I need to get away from him. I need to leave.

I need to save myself.

"I have to go," I whisper and hastily climb down his body.

Looking away, I step back from him and in my mind, I'm already putting things back, closing down the studio and catching the bus back to St. Mary's when he decides to break the silence.

"I'll drop you off."

Chapter 7

He's waiting for me by his Mustang.

He's leaning against it, his arms folded, one ankle crossed over the other.

When he told me that he'd drop me off, I didn't argue with him. I didn't want to prolong our time together and I didn't have the energy for it either. Giving in seemed like the best course of action.

Now though, not so much.

Because I can't stop this pain in my chest, this wild thunderous beating of my broken heart.

This is how he always waited for me.

Leaning against his car, his strong arms folded, his animal eyes — that I think can see even in the dark — pinned on whatever door that I'd come out of.

Usually his front door.

Because that was when he'd take me out on rides, when I visited Tempest over the weekends, and he'd bring me back safe and sound before my curfew.

And I'd run to him.

I'd rush down the cobblestone driveway to get to him, to go wherever he planned on taking me before ending up in the woods so I could dance for him.

Tonight though, I walk slowly.

I breathe slowly too. In and out.

But most of all, I don't look into his eyes. I don't stare back.

I keep my eyes on his black boots with metallic buckles even though I know that he doesn't have such qualms.

I know that he is staring at me.

I can feel it.

I can feel his eyes looking at me as I walk toward him, taking me in, my changed dress, my tight bun, my ballet flats.

But I power through it. I power through the short walk and when I'm close, I see that he unfolds his ankles and straightens up. And then he does something that knocks the breath out of me.

Like it used to before.

He walks around his car and opens the door for me.

He always did that, and two years ago I didn't know what to make of it.

I didn't know how to protect myself from his charms, from a villain with manners.

He'd stand there with the door open, his eyes tracking my every move as he'd wait for me to get in. So he could close the door after me as well.

And turns out I still don't know how to do that, how to protect myself.

Because when he opens the door for me tonight, my whole body trembles. My breaths come out faster and I have to dig my nails into my palms to make it all stop.

"Thank you," I say, finally looking at him, remembering my own manners.

His reaction to my thank you is not the same, however.

Before, he'd smirk or say something inappropriate or simply stare at me with bright intense eyes to make me blush.

Tonight, he does stare at me and his eyes do glow.

But he makes no comment. His stubbled jaw is harsh and his gorgeous features are tight.

Despite everything, I'm slightly disappointed, but I ignore it and get inside and then I have other thoughts. Other things to contend with besides his changed reaction.

Things like I'm inside his Mustang after two years. His Mustang.

Somewhere I never thought I'd be.

And those trembles intensify.

I shake as hard as his car does when he snaps the door shut after me.

Last time I was in this car, I drove it into the lake.

I was crying and shaking and in so much pain. And strangely it comes back to me that on that night, his Mustang smelled the same as it does tonight.

Wildflowers and woods.

And his seats, they feel the same too. The same plush smooth leather. The carpet even. Everything feels the same, cozy and warm and thrilling.

When Reed gets inside, I want to ask him about it.

I want to ask him how he managed that.

How he managed to put it all back together the same way as before.

He must be good then, right? Extremely good with cars if he could achieve this level of perfection. And I want to ask him.

I want to ask him why he never told me that he worked at a garage, that he has this amazing talent. So much so that he built this car with his own hands. Why he never shared those things with me, those little parts of himself.

Well, because he never loved you, Callie. You never meant anything to him.

Right. Of course.

There's nothing for me to say to him then and so I let him drive me back to St. Mary's in silence. Soon though, the ride comes to an end and we reach our destination.

He parks the car by the side of the road and I know that I should get out and leave. I should walk back through the woods and scale that fence to go back to my room.

But I can't.

Because there is something that I want to say to him. There is and I can't let it be.

I can't keep quiet anymore.

Not when I've been wanting to do this for the past two years.

I've been wanting to do this since the moment I saw his Mustang disappear into the lake.

"I'm sorry," I blurt out.

There's no indication at all that he heard me. He's staring straight through the windshield. I'm not sure what he's staring at though; it's all dark.

But I don't let that deter me.

I hug my bag to my chest and continue, "About your car."

Yes, I'm apologizing.

Because I'm a good person. I feel guilt. I feel regret. I'm not like him.

At this, there is some movement — the clenching of his jaw — that alerts me that he's more attuned to my words than he's letting on. I'm not sure if it's a good thing or bad, that clench, but as I said, I won't be deterred. "You hurt me that night. You broke my heart, and even though you deserved all my hatred and all my anger, you still do by the way, I never should have done what I did. I never should've stolen your car and driven it into the lake. I don't know what I was thinking. I wasn't thinking, I guess. I was… I was hurt and in pain and I just wanted to hurt you back. And your Mustang seemed like the best way to do that and —"

"I know."

I blink. "What?"

His jaw moves again, all tight and rigid. "I hurt you. So you wanted to hurt me back. I know that."

"I didn't know," I blurt out.

"Didn't know what?

"That you'd built your car." His grip goes tight on the wheel and before he can say anything, I speak. "I didn't know that. I knew you loved it but I didn't know that you'd built this car yourself. I didn't even know that you could do something like that, Reed. I had no idea. I had no idea that you worked in a garage and —"

"Who told you?" he cuts me off.

His jaw is ticking and I fist the fabric of my backpack because I know he's angry. Extremely angry.

His wolf eyes shine a different way when he's angered. They become all dark and dangerous, narrowed. His jaw becomes a true V, as if his agitated emotions have chiseled it down.

This is exactly what used to happen back on the soccer field, with Ledger. This is how all their fights would start, and I know from experience that I should back off now.

He wouldn't physically harm me, of course, but I shouldn't anger him further.

But I don't care. So I tell him, "Tempest."

"Tempest," he bites out.

"Yes, but you have to know that she didn't tell me this for the

longest time. And she wasn't going to. She was going to keep your secret. It was me. I forced it out of her. It's my fault. Not hers."

Reed watches me in the darkened interior of the car.

If there's a moon out tonight, it's hiding in this part of the
world. But even so, I know he can see me clearly. I, on the other hand,
am struggling.

I only see him in tight lines and shadows and when he moves
his jaw, I know he's going to speak. "Are you done?"

"No."

A ripple cuts through the still air and I'm forced to look into
his glowing eyes that are somehow both dark and bright at the same
time.

"Excuse me?"

I raise my chin. "I want to know how."

"How what?"

"How you saved me?"

At this, his reaction is so unexpected that I can't breathe for a
second.

Not to mention, so violent.

Those knuckles that were already jutting out almost tear
through his moon-kissed skin. He almost tears the wheel off with his
grip. And when he looks at me again, I flinch at the ferocity in his wolf
eyes.

"I saved you," he grits out.

I'm not sure what it is that I said that made him so angry, that
made his cheekbones even more pronounced, but I somehow manage
to respond. "I always thought it was you. I always thought that you
were the one who reported me, who pressed charges. I guess it was my
mistake. I just assumed it would be you. But it wasn't. You didn't press
any charges against me. You —"

"Get out."

I don't.

I won't.

I have to know. I have to know how.

How did he save me? What did he do?

"Con told me," I continue, hugging my backpack to my chest, pressing my back against the door, watching his angry frame. "Again, he didn't want to. He let me believe that it was you who did everything, but he told me the truth. That it wasn't you. In fact, you came to him with the deal. You made those charges go away. Reed, I need —"

"Get the fuck out of my car, Fae."

I shake my head. "And it was your d-dad, wasn't it? He pressed those charges against me. And I know you don't like to talk about him. But Reed, what did you do? You must've done something, right? To make him back off. To get me off the hook. What did you do, Reed?"

Maybe the why doesn't matter. Maybe his conscience did wake up, as Con said. Maybe he saved me to amuse himself, to do his good deed of the year.

Like he did two years ago. When he let me go, unscathed, from his clutches.

When he left me a virgin.

But I want to know how.

I want to know what he had to do.

Because it's his father.

The man he hates.

The man I've never even met but who wanted to see me punished for what I'd done to his son's car. Not that I blame him. I take full responsibility for my actions.

But I know, I know, there's more to the whole story and I need to know what.

"What did you do, Reed? What did you have to do to save me from your father?" I ask when he doesn't break the seething silence.

And it's as if that word — save — is some kind of a trigger for him, making ripples cut through the air again. His hands on the wheel vibrate. His entire frame vibrates.

His eyes were already dark, already angry, but now they become bottomless pits.

They become the eyes of a demon. The villain that he is.

Someone so heartless and cold that I almost breathe out in wintry vapors. And when he turns toward me completely, it takes all of my courage, all of my bravery, to stay put.

Not to shrink back. Not to run away.

That's when he grabs me.

Or rather, my backpack.

When his hand shoots out and fists it.

He uses it to bring me forward.

To bring me closer to him, to his icy heat and his chilly blazing eyes. "You can't take a hint, can you?"

"I just —"

"Why?"

"What?"

"Why do you want to know what I had to do?" His grip on the backpack tightens and he inches me forward again as he leans over me with narrowed eyes. "Why are you so curious, Fae?"

I swallow, afraid and trapped and God, thrilled. Thrilled to be so close to him. Something I don't want to be.

"Let me go," I tell him sternly.

"No," he says in a rough, edgy tone. "Not yet. Not until you tell me. Tell me if it's happening again."

"What's happening again?"

He runs those angry, somehow both heated and chilled eyes over my upturned face. He pauses at my lips. He studies the color of Train Wreck Princess, the lipstick I chose for tonight.

And my ballerina heart spins in my chest.

"Your heart," he murmurs as if he knows, and my eyes go wide. "The one that you gave me so stupidly and the one that I broke. Because I didn't want it. Is it starting to beat faster now?"

"What?"

"Yeah, now that you know it wasn't me. That it wasn't me who got you arrested for stealing my car. Is it starting to race and pound and spin? Is your heart coming back to life now, Fae? For me. For the guy who broke it in the first place. Are you going to tell your friends about me now? About how I saved you and got you free."

My own eyes narrow at him. "You're such an ass—"

"Yeah, you've said that before," he cuts me off, giving my backpack, giving me, a vicious shake. "A million times. I suggest you remember that. I suggest you remember who you're talking to. Who I am. What I did and what I'm capable of. It's none of your business what I did to save you. Because I didn't save you, did I? You're still trapped. You're still caught in a cage from which you have to sneak out to go dancing with your friends. You have to jump over that fence to chase your ballerina dreams.

"So let me explain to you in a way that your brain full of pink glitter and love stories will understand. When you go back to your dorm tonight, I want you to tell your friends a little story. I want you to tell them that when you were almost sixteen, you met a villain in the woods. He forced you to dance for him. He made you do things. He made you sneak out and lie to your brothers. He made you break all your good girl rules and turned you into a bad girl. And despite all that, you fell in love with him. Despite all the fucking warnings and all the cautionary tales, you fell in love with him. You gave him your heart and he broke it. He broke it into a million little pieces and you got so upset that you stole his car. You got arrested for him. For his love. You should tell them that. You should tell them that this car, his Mustang that you drove into the lake, he rebuilt it. He put all the pieces of it back together to remind himself that while he can fix his car, he can't do the same with your heart. He can't mend your broken heart. Because that's not his forte. He doesn't really care about hearts and love. So if you ever make the mistake of falling for him again, he'll take those broken pieces and fucking smash them. And he'll keep doing that until there's nothing left in your chest. Do you understand that?"

My lips are parted. "I —"

"Do you understand that, Fae?"

I wince. "Yes."

He studies my face in darkness, my trembling lips, my wide eyes, my up-tilted neck. "Good. I'm glad. Now I want you to stop running from me. You want to throw tantrums, be mad at me, hit me, dump your drinks on my fucking lap, you can. But when I say I'm going to give you a ride, your answer is going to be yes. Because it's about your fucking safety, all right? And you're going to wait for me, here, next week at midnight. If you don't, I will come after you. And you're going to let me help you. Because I broke your heart, yes. But I'm going to make sure that nothing happens to your dream."

Chapter 8

The Hero

I was five when I found out that my father was a villain.

Because he'd made my mother cry.

I saw them through the crack in their bedroom door. My dad was talking to my mom in a low voice. He was saying something to her that I couldn't hear but I could see the effect of it on her face. I could see that with every word he said, her features crumpled up.

It was a sight that scared me.

I don't remember ever seeing my mother like that.

And so when my dad left the room after a while, I ran to be with her. She was sitting on the bed, her shoulders hunched and her head bowed. I tried consoling her, asking her what was wrong, but she never told me.

All she said was that everything was fine.

I was five; of course I believed her.

But my mother was lying that day.

Because over the years, I watched. I watched it all with my own eyes, how my father broke her heart over and over. How he cheated on her, neglected her until he needed something from her. How his attentions were short and wandering.

So much so that one night I saw him fucking the nanny.

In his office chair no less, the one that he had custom made. And he was doing that when she was supposed to be taking care of my sister.

Back when Pest was little, there was a time when she used to have nightmares. Since her room was right across from mine, I'd always wake up when she did and I'd try to put her to sleep. It had gotten so bad that we had to see the doctors. And so Mom had specifically hired a nanny to take care of Pest at night.

But when I woke up that night, I went to her room and found the nanny gone.

I shushed my sister and put her back to sleep before I went in search of her.

The fucking nanny.

I was only eight but I was raging. I was furious that she wasn't there to take care of my sister. And then, I heard noises coming out of my dad's study and there she was. The nanny.

Instead of taking care of my sister, she was taking care of my father. I had her fired the following day; I planted Mom's jewelry in her room and made it look like she'd stolen it.

But that's not the point.

The point is that my father is a douchebag and by the time I was eight, I'd decided something.

I decided that I hated him.

That I loathed him for making my mother miserable. I loathed him for never giving any attention to my sister. And I loathed him because even then he thought he could control me.

So when I was eight, I decided to do everything in my power not to. Not to be controlled by him. Or not to be his devoted little son.

If he wanted to show me off to his business partners when I was a kid, the future CEO of the company, or show me the ropes of how it's all done, I made sure to make myself scarce. I made sure to stay busy, stay lost in the town, stay drunk at the party he'd thrown where he wanted to show me off.

If he hated that I was wasting my time on soccer and that my coaches thought that I had some real talent, I made sure to play harder. I made sure to run away to that soccer summer camp he hadn't wanted me to go to. If he asked me to quit the team, I decided to get a fucking scholarship.

I decided to go pro, get a million-dollar contract and throw it in his face.

Not that I could do it now because you know, I don't play anymore, but it was a nice little wish to have, that kept me going while I was growing up.

So my father and I, we're at war.

We've been at war ever since I was a kid.

Every war has collateral damage, doesn't it, though?

The collateral damage of ours is her.

The girl I saw spinning on the playground when I was nine. The little blonde ballerina. The one who dances like a fairy and who stole my car when I broke her heart to hurt me.

She didn't know what she was getting herself into. At the time I didn't know either. I was high on my win, on the fact that I'd done the exact opposite of what my father wanted, of what my father had asked the previous night.

Yeah, I broke her innocent little heart in the process. But what do you expect of a villain anyway?

Not to mention, I defied him in style.

I won.

But somehow my father got wind of it, that a girl had stolen my car. Or maybe he was keeping better tabs on me than I'd arrogantly expected. And since he'd had it with me and my tantrums, he took advantage of the situation.

He used her to get what he wanted.

We Jackson men are real bastards, aren't we?

I used her to win at soccer so I could piss off my father and he used her to get to me.

"Nice song."

My thoughts break at the rough, gravelly voice and I pull myself from under the '68 Chevy that I'm working on. It's a sweet ride, or at least has the potential to be.

Right now it's a dump though.

Salvaged from a yard, it's all rusted and banged up. Needs a new engine, new tires, new paint job. It's got alignment issues when you drive and the sound of it starting is like an animal being tortured.

But I've got plans for it.

Especially for that engine. I'm going to build it from scratch, rebore the cylinders, put in new pistons. It's going to be fucking sexy when it's done and it's going to purr like a kitten.

And Pete knows that. The guy who just interrupted me.

That's why he gave me the job even though I don't work with him anymore. He knows I can make it run and look like a million bucks.

I press a few buttons on my phone and lower the volume of the song I've been playing. "Hey, what time is it?"

"Time for you to go home."

I chuckle and get up and put away the wrench as I shoot back, "Which means it's past your bedtime, isn't it, old man?"

Pete is old, yeah.

He's probably north of sixty and you can see every inch of that age on his ruddy face and his white beard. Pair that with a beer belly and the red and white checkered shirt that he's wearing right now, Pete is a regular Santa Claus.

I met him when I was thirteen.

Back then I only knew him as the guy who was giving my dad trouble.

Since my dad has a habit of wanting things and acquiring things, Pete's garage called Auto Alpha in Wuthering Garden, one of the towns that neighbors Bardstown, was in his sights. Pete was and is known, among other things, for restoring vintage cars and selling them for a fuck-ton of money.

My dad offered Pete a lot of sweet deals to give it up to Jackson Builders. My dad was going to turn it into a car showroom or something. Despite my dad's intimidation tactics, a lot of them illegal, Pete never budged and my dad had to back off.

I guess Pete was the only man I ever saw who stood up to my dad.

Pete laughs at my comeback and offers me a beer. "So this song. Is it about her?"

Leaning against the Chevy, I was about to take a sip of the beer but I stop. "What?"

Pete has no problem sipping his beer though. He has no problem smirking either. "You've had it on repeat since you showed up at the shop."

I showed up at the shop only an hour ago so I don't know what he's bitching about.

I knew I wouldn't be able to sleep tonight.

Especially because of where I'm coming from. Dropping her off at St. Mary's after her midnight practice.

"And?"

He shrugs. "It's got a ballerina in it. She's a ballerina. I put two and two together."

It's the song that I made her dance to, that first time. And yes, it has a ballerina in it.

But so what?

It doesn't mean anything.

I stare at him a beat before going ahead and taking a long gulp of the beer. "Your beer's shitty."

He laughs again, this time harder than before. "And you're an asshole."

Back when I came to see him for the first time, we struck up a weird friendship.

He was a lonely old man whose wife had just died and I was a punk kid who came to look at the guy who stood up to my father. I respected his rebellion.

Plus something about his garage, located off an isolated turn in the highway, surrounded by woods and cliffs, seemed like an awesome place to hang out. An awesome place to get away from my own house, my father, the town where he owned everything.

So I'd come here every chance I got.

Pete taught me everything I know about cars. He let me build my own car even.

Actually, I didn't know it was going to be mine at the time.

It was the first car I worked on, my Mustang, and when it was done, Pete just gave it to me.

I refused; I told him that I could get a hundred cars like that. I could pay, could buy it from him; on top of my father's wealth, my mother's father had me and Pest set up with a trust fund that my own father can't touch so money has never been a problem for the Jackson kids. I was only building the car because it was another way to piss off my father. Well, secretly.

For some reason, I never wanted to throw this in his face. I threw soccer in his face plenty but I couldn't do it with my time with Pete. Maybe because I'd never met anyone like Pete, strong, proud, decent, and I'd never enjoyed anything — not even soccer — as much as I enjoyed working on cars.

Anyway, Pete told me to shut the fuck up, keep my trust fund money, take the car and start working on earning my own money for a change.

So I did.

I worked here all through high school. I earned my own money, which I started to spend instead of spending my dad's money; another way to defy him. And slowly, this garage, Pete, working on cars, building them, became soothing to me. Relaxing. Since my mornings were busy with school, soccer, fucking around with friends, I'd come here at night.

I've never been much of a sleeper anyway and working here took away my stress.

"What are you doing up so late?" I ask him.

"Couldn't sleep."

"Going through the photo albums again?"

"Yeah." He throws me a small but fond smile. "She was fucking beautiful."

I chuckle; I can't help it.

Pete is a lovestruck fool and he's completely gone for his wife, Mimi. She died of a heart attack years ago and now he's left behind, looking at her photos every night, missing her, telling everyone tales of their love story.

I don't believe in love or whatever.

But I guess if I had to, I'd say that Pete's probably got it.

"So are you going to tell me or not?" he asks.

Damn it.

"Tell you what?"

"You've been down here a few times now. More than a few times. And you're here tonight. Should I regret giving you the keys?"

"Maybe I'm here because I've moved back now."

When I lived in New York, I'd usually see Pete once or twice a month.

I'd drive down to Wuthering Garden from New York City and try to spend a weekend or something, working in his shop and generally helping him. He's allergic to computers so I'd help him with his accounts and stuff.

But over the past few days, ever since I moved back, I've been here thrice.

He raises his eyebrows, not believing me. "Is that really why you're here? Because you've moved back."

Something angry moves in my chest and I clutch the bottle tightly. "They kicked her out."

"Who?"

"Her ballet studio," I reply, taking a long, angry gulp of the beer. "Blue fucking Madonna."

You know what, I was right. This beer is shitty.

It's doing nothing to calm me, relax my suddenly tightened muscles.

"What the fuck? Why?"

"Because of what she did."

What she did.

That's the whole problem, isn't it?

She stole my car and now she's paying for it. She's paying for it even when it wasn't her fault.

That angry thing inside my chest hisses.

Pete watches me for a few beats. "Are you going to do something about it?"

He knows all about that night.

I'm not the sharing type, but if I was going to share what happened that night with anyone, it was going to be Pete. Maybe because he knows about my dad. He knows what a piece of shit he is, and so when my father pressed those charges against her to manipulate me, I told Pete.

"I already did. If they want to stay open in Bardstown, in my town, they better make it up to her." I take another gulp and can't help but add, "She sneaks out every week. To go practice. She takes that shitty bus. All alone."

"Well, I don't think you've got a say in that."

I frown. "I know. So I've been told."

Why does everyone keep telling me that? That I don't have a say in what she does or doesn't do.

I know already, all right?

I fucking know and it fucking bugs me.

It makes me furious that I can't do anything about this whole situation. It makes me furious that she was going to end up at juvie. And so I gave my father everything he wanted in exchange for him reducing those charges. And even with reduced charges, she ended up caged.

It makes me fucking furious that my father probably doesn't even remember her name, the girl whose life he played with in order to get to me.

I thought at least at St. Mary's, she wouldn't be shut up in a detention center, among criminals.

She would have friends. She could see her brothers.

Yes, she wouldn't be able to dance like she did before. But Tempest assured me — this I had to ask her — that she was still dancing. She still had plans of going to Juilliard when she graduates.

But for that fucking ballet studio to kick her out like that, for them to reject her as if she wasn't the best student they ever had, the best fucking ballerina to ever come out of that shithole.

It makes me want to tear that place apart.

It makes me want to burn it down.

"She's going there to teach herself," I continue, my chest tight. "She's doing it all alone."

"And are you going to do something about that?" Pete asks.

"Yeah," I say fiercely.

I'm going to help her make that audition video. I'm going to help her get into Juilliard because she belongs there. Because I'm not going to let anything else be taken from her because of what happened two years ago.

Before I remember what she did last week at that cupcake shop and again tonight, when she made me chase her down. I can't help but chuckle slightly.

My fierce Fae.

I like that.

I like that she's trying to stick it to me. That she's trying to put me in my place. Like she did when she stole my car.

Not gonna lie though, I didn't expect her to do that. Not my good girl Fae. But again I liked it.

I liked that she was trying to hurt me.

After everything, she has all the right.

"Well, trying to at least. She isn't making it easy," I continue.

Pete chuckles too. "Giving you a hard time, huh?"

"She dumped her drink in my lap," I tell him and he hoots with laughter. "I didn't have extra pants, all right? It was fucking embarrassing."

That kills him.

That completely kills him and he's wiping tears by the end of his laughter. "Remember what I told you? Back when she stole your car. She sounds like my Mimi. She put me through hell."

"She put you through hell because you're an asshole too."

Grinning, he points his bottle at me. "You're gonna have your hands full, boy."

"Yeah, I'm not trying to put my hands anywhere near her, so."

"Good luck trying to keep that promise," Pete tells me.

"Fuck you."

Don't get me wrong, I'd like to put my hands on her. In fact, I'd like that very, very much. I'm a guy, aren't I? And an asshole at that.

She does it for me. She always has. Her tight ballerina body and those big blue eyes and that good girl braid.

And now with her feistiness she's fucking irresistible.

But I won't.

Because it's better that way.

I've fucked up her life enough already. My father has fucked up her life enough. She didn't deserve to get caught up in the war between my father and me.

She didn't deserve to be used by the both of us and become collateral damage.

That's why I stayed away from Bardstown for the past two years. That's why despite my sister's constant nagging, I never talked about her, asked about her, showed any interest in her.

Because for all my hatred for my father, I'm no better than him.

That's why I'd promised myself that I'd never see her again.

I broke that promise though. Another promise I've broken when it comes to her.

But I'm not putting my hands on her.

Once this audition video is done, I'll be gone. It's not much, what I'm doing, but this is all I can do.

And then it will be just my father and I, and this war. And I swear to God, I'll find a way to beat him, to get out of his clutches.

To win once and for all.

But for now, she's caged because of me, isn't she? So I'm caged with her too.

Chapter 9

Every Thursday at midnight, he waits for me by the side of the road.

He drives me to the Blue Madonna and helps me practice. He helps me with my stretches and warm-ups. With my lifts and turns.

He watches me dance like he did two years ago.

With bright, intense eyes. With an eager, excited body that turns every time I do, that spins when I spin to keep me in sight.

But I don't dance for him.

I don't.

I promised myself that I wouldn't. And so I don't.

I'm only letting him drive me to my studio and help me with my routine because it's smart.

In the sense that my routine really sucked and the deadline to submit the audition video is approaching fast. And I need all the help that I can get. I'm not jeopardizing my dream because of him again.

If he wants to help me — for whatever reason — I'll take it.

Although it's surreal.

So freaking surreal that he's back in my life.

And I see him every week.

But I'm trying not to dwell on those things. I'm trying not to dwell on the fact that what I thought to be true for two years, turned out to be a lie.

It turned out that he saved me. From his father, no less.

I'm trying not to think about it, about what he must've done to make that happen.

Because he's right.

I'm not really free, am I?

I'm still caged. I'm still sneaking out. My dream is still hanging in the balance.

It's difficult though. To not wonder about things.

Especially when one day, I get an email from my old ballet teacher, and I mention it to Reed while he drives me to the studio that very night.

"So," I say, glancing over at him. "I got a very interesting email today. Would you like to hear about it, Reed?"

"Do I have a choice, Fae?" he asks mockingly, without looking away from the road.

I narrow my eyes at him and I know he can't see it but his lips twitch in amusement anyway.

"It was from my old ballet teacher," I tell him and his fingers tighten on the wheel. "Apparently, she's super guilty about kicking me out. She apologized about it. And in order to make up for her mistake, she will give me a recommendation letter. Not only that, she also put me in touch with one of the faculty members at Juilliard who also happens to be on the admissions committee. Juilliard, Reed. My dream school. Out of the blue, Miss Petrova decides to help me out because she thinks it might help me with my application. Out of the blue. Two years later. Can you believe that? How interesting, isn't it?"

Reed shrugs all casually. "It is interesting."

"Right?"

"Yeah, it's interesting how you find completely uninteresting things, interesting."

I fist my hands in my lap. "You did this."

"Did what?"

"You made her do this, didn't you? You forced her to send that email."

"I wouldn't call it force," he replies, still keeping his eyes on the road.

I turn toward him then. "Oh my God, you did. Did you blackmail her, Reed?"

At this, he glances over at me, his wolf eyes all cool and pretty. "What do you think I am, Fae? A villain."

"Yes. And you do that. You blackmail people. You lie to them. You use them. That's what you do."

His jaw clenches for a long second before he says, "I didn't blackmail. I didn't have to. I asked her nicely and she agreed."

"But you —"

"Look, she had no right to kick you out, understand? What you do on your time is your fucking business. And besides, it was her loss. She lost the best ballerina she ever had or will ever have. So I just showed her the light."

And then I have to grit my teeth and curl my toes.

I have to keep sitting in his Mustang, all still, as if nothing happened, as if he didn't pay me a compliment and as if my stupid heart isn't spinning in my chest.

But then the next week he comes to pick me up, things get even worse.

Because there's something waiting for me in his Mustang.

A pale pink box with a pink satin ribbon around it.

I don't have to open the box to know what's inside of it.

I stare at it with my throat tight, holding on to the open door of his car. "I don't eat those."

From the corner of my eye, I see his chest move sharply. "Why's that?"

I swallow, glancing at him. "Because I don't. Because I'm a dancer and I need to watch my weight."

His own hand on the door flexes. "I can still carry you with one hand. So I think you're fine."

He can.

He can carry me with one hand and I try not to shift my gaze over to his arms. His sculpted biceps. His strong, graceful fingers.

He was built before, when he was the soccer god of Bardstown High, the Wild Mustang. But he's something else now. He's strength itself. It drips off his body like a thick syrup. It wafts off his body like a delicious scent.

"Do they still call you that?" I ask, because I can't stop myself. "The Wild Mustang."

"What?"

"At your college. Do your soccer groupies still call you that? By your nickname."

His gorgeous face is blank, inscrutable as he watches me. "Yes."

It shouldn't bother me.

It should not bother me at all.

He was always popular and a player. Why wouldn't he still be the same now?

Still though something contracts in my chest and I can't help but say, "You must be very popular then. Not that there was any doubt whatsoever. I mean, everyone knew you were going to go pro, be all famous and whatnot and —"

"Yeah, I'm a regular stud," he says, bites out almost, cutting me off. "Are you going to get in the car or not?"

"I'm not going to eat the cupcakes," I tell him again.

And he asks me, again, "Why?"

"Because I just told you. Because I'm watching my weight and because it was…"

Because it was our thing.

Because it was something that he brought me. And even though every time he did that, I told him not to bother because I was getting fat and yet, I waited for him to do just that.

To bring me Peanut Butter Blossoms.

I don't say that though. And I don't have to.

Because he gets it.

Because for some reason, he remembers everything about our time together. Even though it was inconsequential and insignificant to him.

Or rather, significant only in the sense that he used me to win against my brother.

With sharp features turned even sharper, he says, "Because I brought you cupcakes two years ago. To fool you. And you did get fooled. So now you're punishing yourself for falling into my trap. Because that's what you do, don't you?"

"I don't…" I trail off because I'm lying.

Of course I do that.

I punish myself so I can remember to never make the same mistakes again and I hate that he knows this about me.

"You do," he says, his wolf eyes narrowed. "You lied to your brothers about coming to my party that one time and you walked on eggshells around them for the rest of the week after that."

I did.

I did walk on eggshells after lying about going to his party, the one that started everything. Because I felt so guilty.

That for days after that, I tried to make up for it in a hundred different ways. By never being late coming back from school; by doing Ledger's laundry without him having to pester me about it; by cooking Con's favorite things and so on.

I purse my lips. "Yeah, I did. Because I hate lying. Especially to my brothers."

He watches me for a few moments, the muscle on his cheek pulsing before saying, "It was me. I fucked you over. I broke my promise to you. Deliberately. Because I wanted to win. I picked soccer over you. And then broke your heart. I'm the asshole here, understand? So if you want to punish someone, punish the villain in your story. Not yourself." His eyes rove over my face. "Being gullible is not a crime. Seeing good in people is not a crime either. Taking advantage of it is."

I watch him then.

Speechless.

I never thought of it that way. I never thought that I see good in people. I mean, I do, but I never made that connection. I never thought that that's what I was doing with Reed.

I was though, right?

I did see the good in him and he took advantage of that.

I trusted him and he broke my trust. And maybe he's right.

Maybe trusting people is not a crime, breaking that trust is.

He's the criminal. And I'm the crime he committed.

"Are you going to eat the fucking cupcake or not?" he pushes out when all I do is stare at him.

At this beautiful criminal, this gorgeous villain.

"Apologize," I blurt out and as soon as I say it, my spine goes up.

My resolve strengthens.

"What?"

"Apologize to me," I tell him. "Because you're right. I have been punishing myself. For the crimes that you committed. You're the asshole here, the villain. And so apologize. Say you were an asshole. To use me like that. To abuse my trust. To break my heart like that. I apologized for stealing your car even though you deserved it and now it's your turn. And apologize not because your sister wants you to but because you should."

His nostrils flare and I raise my chin.

I'm not budging from this spot until he apologizes to me.

His jaw tics for a few seconds and his grip on the door tightens before he loosens it and says, "I'm the asshole here. I used you, abused your trust and broke your heart. I shouldn't have done that. So yeah, I fucking apologize."

It wasn't exactly the heartfelt apology I was looking for but it's fine.

It's Reed.

He's rude and insensitive and an asshole like he just said. So I'll take it like I'm taking his help.

"Thank you."

"So am I forgiven then?"

I look at him for a few seconds before I shake my head. "No. Not really. I don't think anything you can do will ever make me forgive you."

He looks back at me for a few seconds too. "Good."

I feel a twinge in my heart and I swallow. "Fine."

"Now, are you going to get inside the fucking car or not?"

"I will." I throw him a regal nod. "And I will eat those cupcakes too. In your Mustang. Because I don't care about your stupid rule of not eating inside your car."

He does have that rule.

He told me that once and all the time we were together, I never broke it. But I'm going to break it now and he can't stop me.

"Fine." He throws me a short nod of his own. "You can eat

your fucking cupcake in my car."

So I finally get inside his car and open the box of cupcakes. When he closes the door, I hear him mutter, That rule was never for you anyway.

Again, I try not to dwell on those nearly silent words. I try not to let any warmth invade my chest.

But as I said, on nights like this, it becomes hard.

It becomes hard to ignore that for all his asshole ways, he did get me off the hook and he did apologize to me.

And one Thursday, a week later, it becomes almost impossible to ignore.

Because first, he comes to pick me up at midnight, wearing a suit.

A legit suit with a tie.

His jacket is off, but he's wearing a dress shirt that stretches really nicely over his chest, and a loosened tie.

For a few seconds I can only watch him with wide eyes. Because he looks so… dashing. So freaking handsome and gorgeous and worldly.

Like the rich, arrogant boy he is.

A man actually.

And the second thing happens when I get inside his Mustang and my eyes fall on some papers and files scattered on his backseat. It's not the files themselves that trip me up, it's the black logo on them, Jackson Builders.

His dad's company.

The company that Reed has sworn never to work at even though that's what his dad has always wanted for him.

That's what pushes me over the edge.

That file and his suit.

That's what makes me break the pact. The pact that I'd made

with Tempest of no brothers and no seeking out information about Reed.

About the last two years.

About what really happened and what he did to get me free.

***

He's waiting for me by his car.

Like he always does.

Leaning against it, his arms crossed over his chest, his ankles crossed as well.

I can see him through the woods, his tall form, his dark jeans.

Tonight there's no light in him, no softness. Nothing to sand down the beautiful, reckless edges.

Because tonight he's forgone his hoodie that he usually wears. He doesn't have his suit on either, which I only saw for the first time last Thursday, which made him look all old and mature and so experienced.

Tonight, he has that leather jacket on.

The one that I hate because he wore it when he broke my heart, looking so gorgeous while doing it.

I watch him in that without making my presence known.

I watch and notice and analyze him.

His hair is grown out even more in the past month. If he didn't need a haircut before, he definitely needs one now.

I look at his body.

His big shoulders, broad and strong. His lean, cut torso.

Then I move down to his thighs.

They bulge under his jeans when he shifts on his feet, showing me how powerful they are. His thighs, his calves.

I have to admit that I've always been so fascinated by them, by his legs. By his footwork.

I'm a ballerina, right?

I see footwork in my dreams. I've seen his footwork in my dreams too.

I've seen him stealing the ball, dribbling it across the field, sending it flying across the field so many, many times. Both in real life and in dreams.

I also have to admit that when I decided to never seek out any information about him, cut all the ties, I was sad that I'd never see him play.

I was sad that I'd never get to witness his breathtaking footwork, his majestic skills on the field.

I was sad.

I am sad tonight too.

Sad and miserable and so melancholic. So blue and gray.

As gray as the smoke coming out of his mouth. Because he's got a cigarette clenched between his teeth.

He hardly ever smokes, this villain. The one who blackmails and locks me up in closets and chases after me when I run. But if he's smoking tonight, then that means he's cold.

Even though the October weather isn't all that chilly. Not yet.

But I know him.

I know that he gets cold easily. That's why I made him that sweater. The night before everything happened.

The night he kissed me.

I wonder what he did with it. I wonder if he threw it away.

I don't have the courage to ask him though.

Besides, I'm going to need my courage for other things tonight.

So I walk toward him, coming out of my hiding place. My feet crunch on the leaves and the gravel, alerting him to my presence, and he looks up.

His gaze homing in on me as always.

His gaze roving all over me as always.

Like he has every right to do that. He has every right to watch me, take me in, take me apart, turn me inside out and cast me aside when he's done. And tonight, his wolf eyes are even hungrier.

Because I'm wearing his favorite color.

White.

An ivory dress with a lacy overlay and a zipper in the back. My flats are white too. With my blonde hair in a braid snaking down one side of my shoulder, I'm dressed up as his favorite meal.

All dewy-eyed and daisy fresh.

And when he pulls the cigarette out of his mouth to lick his lower lip, I feel like one too.

A meal.

"You're wearing white," he murmurs, and I fist my hands at my side.

"I am."

His forest-thick eyelashes flutter as he takes me in again. "Why?"

"Because I felt like it."

And because it's your favorite color...

I haven't worn white ever since I saw him at the bar. I've actually been going out of my way not to wear it. To wear something completely opposite of white every Thursday, black, blue, orange, anything other than white.

Just because it's his favorite color and because I didn't want to dress myself up in something he likes.

Not tonight though.

Tonight things are different.

The air is different too. The moon, the sky, these woods, everything.

"It suits you," he says, looking me over a third time. "Innocence."

I look at his jacket again and the cigarette clutched between his fingers. "And villainy suits you."

His lips tip up in a smirk and he takes another drag before letting it out. "Is that why you're standing all the way over there? Because I'm a cigarette-smoking villain and you're afraid to get closer?"

"I'm not afraid of you," I reply from where I stand by the tree, and his wolf eyes glow. His vampire skin sparkles as if in challenge. As if he can make me afraid if he wants to.

But that's the thing, I've never been afraid of him. And that turned out to be my doom in the end.

His doom too.

Isn't it?

"Are you cold?" I ask him then. "Because you smoke when you're cold."

He continues to watch me for a couple of seconds before he flicks his cigarette away and crushes it under his boots like it's a love-filled heart and he's bored of it. "You know me, don't you? Yes, I'm cold."

"Where's your hoodie?"

His eyes narrow. "I've got a jacket."

"I hate your jacket."

"You hate my jacket."

I nod. "Yes. Because this is the jacket you wore that night."

"What night?"

"The night of the game. The night you won that contest against Ledger." I shake my head then. "For the longest time I saw that jacket in my dreams. I saw it so many times. So many, many times that I thought bad things happen when you wear that jacket. I know it's a silly thought but I just —"

I stop talking when he straightens up from his car.

When he grabs his jacket and rolls his shoulders, his dense thick shoulders, and takes it off. He takes his jacket off as he stares at me, letting it fall on the ground.

Just like that.

"There. It's gone," he says, his jacket lying at his feet, his biceps corded and naked in his V-neck light-colored t-shirt. "Are you going to come here so we can go?"

"But you're cold."

"I'm fine."

With parted lips and a heart that won't stop pounding, I watch the veins on his wrists, on the back of his hand, thick and beautiful. I watch the arms that he uses to pick me up as I practice.

To help me.

I watch them and ask, "What about your practice?"

"What?"

I look at his face then. "It must be brutal now, right? At college level." His eyes narrow. "Ledger can barely come home these days. He's always at the gym, always on the field, practicing. He wants to be like Shep. Who got picked in the first round of the draft. You know that, right? That Shep got picked. Stellan would've been too but he never wanted to go pro. Not like you."

His chest is moving up and down, pushing at the fabric of his thin t-shirt. "Get in the car."

I shake my head, standing my ground. "So is it? Is it brutal? Is your coach riding you hard?"

"Get in the car."

"You'd easily be picked up in the first round too," I say and almost lose my courage but I have to keep going. "J-January, right?"

The next breath he takes pushes out the fabric so much that I think it's going to get torn apart. Reed is going to tear apart his t-shirt in one long breath and God, I can't stand it.

I can't stand his agitation. I can't stand what he did.

What he had to do.

To get me free.

"Are you fucking getting in the car or not?" he growls.

"No."

"What?"

I shake my head as my eyes sting. "I'm not going with you."

"You're not going with me."

I shake my head again. "No. Not until you tell me."

"Tell you what?"

"What you did," I say, fisting my dress. "Not until you tell me what you did to save me from your father."

As expected, the word save triggers him.

It makes him shift on his feet, assume a battle stance, as a thunderous expression crosses his features. "Are we back at that again?"

"Yes." I swallow. "Tell me. Tell me what you did, Reed."

He begins to walk toward me then.

Stride over to me.

And as always, I stay put. My legs won't move.

I watch him, his thighs, rippling, shifting under his jeans, dripping with power. I watch them in all their majestic beauty and my heart twists.

It wrenches and pulses and cries out for him.

When he reaches me, he backs me up.

He crowds me with his body and makes me walk backward, his shoes clashing with my flats, until my spine bumps into something. A tree, rough and edgy.

Like him.

He dips his face toward me, his shoulders hiding the world

from my eyes, and I crane my neck up, not wanting to see anything else in this moment anyway.

"What do you know?" he growls.

"Everything."

His jaw is hard. "Tempest."

"I made her," I tell him hastily. "I forced her to tell me. I saw those files in your car last week. Jackson Builders. And so I called her and practically pried it out of her."

He bends down even more.

Putting his hand on the tree by the side of my neck, he lowers himself over me, his chest still heaving. "That's what you do, isn't it? You pry and pry and stick your nose in things that are none of your business."

My ballerina toes go up and I stretch myself as much as I can to bridge the gap between our heights. "But it is my business. Because you did it for me. To get me free."

"I told you —"

"You did, didn't you?" I cut him off because I'm not letting him deter me. "That game. That championship game, that was so important to you, that you needed to win. That was your last, wasn't it? That was your last game."

I'm watching his face. I'm watching all the angry, violent things pass through his features and yet I can tell that he's digging his fingers into the bark.

I can tell that he's almost clawing at it.

"That's what you did," I continue, my neck still tilted toward him. "That's what you had to do to get me free. You had to give up soccer. You don't live in New York either, do you? Because your dad asked you to come back. Because you work for him now, at his company. The place where you never wanted to end up at. But you did. Because of me. I stole your car and you had to give up soccer, something that you loved to —"

"I don't love soccer."

"What?"

"Fuck soccer."

"W-what do you mean?"

"I mean," he says, his teeth clenched, "I don't care about soccer. I never did."

I come down to earth then.

My toes can't hold my weight and so I have to come down on my heels and press my spine against the tree even more. "But that's... that's not true. All those years of rivalry. All those fights with Ledger because you wanted to be the best. You wanted to win. You betrayed me for it. You love soccer. You —"

His harsh chuckle stops me.

Harsh and brutal and full of something that feels like hate.

"I don't love anything," he says, his voice guttural, coarse. "When are you going to get this through your head? I don't fucking love anything. Soccer was just a way to fuck with him. My father. Soccer was just a way to show him that he can't control me. That I won't be the son he wants me to be. Because he's a fucking monster. He's a fucking psychopath. A shitty husband. A shitty father, and so I wanted to get back at him. So no, I don't love soccer. It hurt like a motherfucker to give it up and become my father's bitch, to let him win two years ago, but I don't love it. I don't love anything. I don't have space to love anything when I'm so full of hate."

His eyes are black by the time he finishes.

Demon-like.

Someone so full of hate that every soft, fragile thing inside of him is gone. Is swallowed by this darkness.

And God, it's even worse.

It was bad enough that he didn't love me, that he used me,

chose something else over me. But the fact that what he chose — soccer — is not even his love, I don't know what to do about that.

I don't know how to cope with that. I don't know how to cope with the fact that he has no space for love. Because all his spaces, all his corners are taken up by hate.

He may love his sister or a car but not much else.

I believe him now though.

As I look at his fire-breathing demon eyes and his flared nostrils, I do believe that he doesn't love anything. He's probably incapable of it.

His chest is not only heartless but it's barren and there's no chance of a heart ever growing in it.

That makes me so sad, so miserable. So blue.

Bluer than before.

That I strangely want to cry and hug him.

"You don't love anything," I whisper, wondering if maybe that's why he's always cold, because he's so full of hate.

His gorgeous features bunch up for a second. "No."

"That's —"

"You should be happy though, shouldn't you?"

"What?"

"You should be happy that that was my last game," he explains gutturally, a humorless smile twisting his mouth. "Soccer is why everything happened, didn't it? Soccer is why I betrayed you. I fought with your brothers. So you should be happy that I'm not playing anymore. You should be happy that my father got what he wanted. That I'm his lapdog now. You should be happy that I'm getting punished for breaking your heart. That the villain in your story is getting his due. All this time that you've been punishing yourself for falling for me, I was already getting put in my place."

I have to part my lips then.

I have to breathe through my mouth because my lungs are starving for air.

My body is starving for it too.

I'm starving and dying and writhing in pain.

Because the answer is no.

I'm not happy.

Maybe I should be. Maybe I should laugh and smile but all I want to do is cry.

All this time I thought so many things. I thought he was the one who got me arrested. I thought he was living his life in New York, being a soccer god, being worshipped by people, fulfilling his dreams, doing something he loves.

But as it turns out, he doesn't love the game that I thought he did and he was just as caged as me.

He is just as caged.

And for the life of me, I can't be happy. I can't find joy in his misery.

Maybe this is the curse of a brokenhearted girl.

The curse of falling for a villain.

If you love him once, you hurt for him forever.

I blink my eyes, realizing that they are wet as I whisper, "No. I'm not happy. I can't be. It doesn't matter what you've done to me. How much you've hurt me. Or how much I hate you. I can't be happy when you're suffering. I can't take pleasure in your misery."

His eyes turn even angrier then.

As if he hates the fact that I don't like his suffering. That even after everything, I can't revel in it.

"I may be a villain but you're just as stupid and naïve in this white dress as you were when you were almost sixteen," he rasps.

And before I know it, my hand shoots up and I slap him in the face.

My eyes go wide when I realize what I've done.

When I realize that he hardly blinked, hardly even moved his face but my palm is burning. It's stinging with the force of my slap, with the shock of it. With the violence.

This wildness he invokes in me so easily. This passion.

I thought that after knowing how caged and trapped he's been because of what I did, all this furious fire would go out. But apparently not.

So when he lowers his face even more and stares into my eyes, as if giving me the go-ahead, telling me to put him in his place, slap him once more, I do it.

I smack his face once more.

And a third time and a fourth and when that's not enough, I punch his chest. I beat at it with my fists and keep going until he grabs my wrists and pins them on the bark.

Not only that, he pins my entire body to the tree as he moves closer to me.

As his strong chest pushes against my arched one.

As his lean torso presses against my ribs.

"Does that make you happy now?" he asks, his jaw all tight.

No.

No, it doesn't.

Especially when I realize that I've become an animal tonight too. One who can see in the dark like him because I clearly notice my scratch marks on his face. My red fingerprints and where my nails have marked his skin.

"Oh my God, Reed. Y-you're hurt," I stammer, knowing my statement is stupid.

I wanted to hurt him and of course he is.

But I don't like it.

I don't like that I hurt him and that I'm still angry. But I don't know what else to be.

God, I'm so screwed up. So tied up in knots. All because of him.

He thinks so too, Reed.

Because he chuckles roughly. "Jesus Christ, Fae, you kill me. You fucking murder me with your goodness."

I'm ashamed to say that I shift on my feet at his tone, at the fondness in it. At the familiarity, and I struggle against his hold. "Let me go."

His ruby red lips twitch and his hooded eyes rove over my face and stop at my lips.

That I have to lick because he won't stop staring.

"What's this one?" he whispers.

I lick my lips again as a blush fans over my cheeks. "None of your business."

He looks up and there's amusement lurking in his gaze. "Are you trying to hide it? The name."

"No."

A full-fledged smirk overcomes his lips then. "Fae's getting shy, isn't she?"

"Stop…" I struggle against his hold again because my blush is burning my cheeks. "Let me go, Reed."

He flexes his grip around my hands and I try very hard — as I've been doing for the past few minutes —not to feel his grip, feel his skin, the pads of his fingers, the meat of his palm.

The fact that there's only a sliver of distance between our bodies.

"Not until you tell me."

I glare at him and he chuckles again.

"Fine," I say. "Sex and Candy."

It's green, dark and pretty, and when I wore it, it felt like the right choice, wearing something green. Because I felt green, all un-trained and inexperienced.

But now I don't think it's a good thing, feeling so out of depth in my white dress and dark green lipstick.

Especially when the mere name of my lipstick makes him grow heated.

Especially when I can feel that heat running through my own veins. Because I'm trapped now, between him and the tree, and he's got a hold of my arms as he stares down at me.

All hungry and intense.

"Sex," he drawls.

"And candy," I tell him to make a point.

"Because your lips taste like candy?"

"You'll never know, will you?"

His wolf eyes glow. "I already do, remember?"

Yes.

I do remember.

Although I don't want to. Although this is one memory I try not to bring up when I'm punishing myself for falling in love with him.

That night. The rain. His mouth. His Mustang with foggy windows.

"No," I whisper.

"Yeah, you do," he counters. "You remember everything. Like I do."

He does remember everything and now I know why.

Because like mine, his present is the product of his past too.

Our past.

Instead of fighting against it, the past and his tight grip, I let myself go loose then. "I remember." I let the floodgates open. I let this one memory douse me. "I remember that you let me go. You let me escape your clutches."

His eyes narrow for a second. "Unscathed."

Maybe it's madness. Insanity. Maybe Mercury is in retrograde tonight.

Because none of it feels wrong.

Remembering doesn't feel wrong. Remembering with him doesn't feel like wrong either. It doesn't feel like I'm about to drink a toxic potion labeled love.

"I didn't want you to," I tell him, which of course he knows but still.

His fingers around my wrist tighten as if to say that he won't make the same mistake again. He won't let me out of his evil clutches a second time.

"I know." His jaw tics as if remembering it. "Hardest fucking thing I've ever done in my life. Noblest fucking thing too."

"And also so atypical of you."

"Fuck yeah, I'm not a good guy."

"No, you're not. But that night you were." I breathe heavily. "For me."

Another tic of his jaw. "Yeah."

I bite my lip before saying, "It's strange, isn't it?"

"What?"

"That I become a bad girl for you and you become a good guy for me."

His lips twist with a humorless smile again. "Yeah. Although it wasn't really worth it."

"What wasn't?"

"Becoming a good guy."

I frown. "Why not?"

"Because it sucked. Being the good guy." His grip on my wrist shifts as he continues, "Especially when you have a monster boner in your pants refusing to let up. For days."

"For d-days?"

"Yeah, what the fuck did you think would happen, Fae? When you give me a lap dance and beg me to bang your brains out."

"I didn't beg," I protest and also lie.

Because I did.

He chuckles again because he knows I'm lying and continues, "And when my Mustang smelled like you."

"It did?"

"Yeah, for weeks after that. Even though you drowned it in the lake for your revenge. Even though I had to change the seats, I'd still smell you. I'd get a whiff of your candy smell and just like that I'd get a motherfucking boner the size of your pretty little arm in the middle of the day."

I press my lips then, to stop my laughter from spilling out.

This is not a laughing matter. None of this is, but I can't help it and he obviously notices, obviously, and growls, "You think this is funny, Fae?"

Dutifully, I shake my head. "No."

"If your brother knew I was taking a hit of his sister's scent every time I drove my car, he would've drowned it in the lake himself. He would've hunted me down and this time instead of using my body as a punching bag, he would've killed me."

"But you could've handled him, right?"

He gives me a lopsided smile. "Fuck yes."

"Now I'm happy," I blurt out.

"What?"

I swallow, debating whether I should tell him but already knowing that I will.

Already knowing that I've drunk the potion now and it's making me crazy. So much so that I arch my spine and move against him. His hard body shudders and I revel in it.

I revel that I made him do that.

"That you suffered," I say.

"Yeah?"

"Yes. When I was crying in my pillow at night and in classes and during lunch and practically all the time, I'm glad you were suffering too. I'm glad that when you were haunting me, I was haunting you too."

Maybe that's what I want.

I want to haunt him, his dreams, his thoughts, his empty chest like he's haunted me.

Maybe I want to be his demon like he is mine.

A demon that needs to be exorcized.

Maybe I want to be his Fae in all the ways he is my Roman, even though I don't want him to be.

"You want to hear all the ways you've haunted me, Fae? All the little ways you've crept up on me over the past two years?"

I nod. "Yes."

"Let me tell you about that then," he says, finally letting my hands go, and so I touch him back.

While he puts his hands on the tree, making a cage of bones and muscles, I put mine on his waist. I touch him, his strength, his heat even though he's always cold on the inside, after two long years and my eyelids flutter.

My fingers jerk with life.

"Let me tell you about that night, when I saw you sneaking out to your studio. I'd just driven down from New York after a long fucking day in that shithole office to go to another shithole office and I was tired as fuck. But I couldn't sleep. So I decided to drive around, and there were a million places I could've gone to but I chose that highway for a reason. I chose to cross over from Bardstown to St. Mary's for a fucking reason. I chose it for you."

He licks his lips, shifting his body against mine, and I'm so hypnotized by his words, by him, that I shift too. "Because I knew that's where you lived. I knew that beyond that brick fence, you might be sleeping in one of those cinderblock buildings. But you weren't, were you? You were sneaking out. After everything that I did — not that I did a lot — but after how I wanted to keep you safe, you were running around town at midnight. It pissed me the fuck off, Fae, I'm not gonna lie. It made me furious. It made me want to pick you up off the road, put you in my Mustang and drive you to an isolated, unknown place just to put the fear of God in you. Just to teach you all the dangers lurking in the night."

He is the danger.

Him.

I've always known. I've just not cared and even now, a current goes through me at his furious words.

I fist his t-shirt, his muscles rippling under my knuckles. "But I've been doing it for two years now. It's perfectly safe, Reed, and —"

"I know," he says with clenched teeth, cutting me off. "I fucking know. Why do you think I showed up at that shitty bar the next night? My sister didn't just tell me about your fucking cupcake shop and she doesn't just tell you things either. She tells me things too, and for the past two years, she hasn't shut up about you. Every time she talks to you, every time she sees you, she can't stop talking about you. And I pretend that she's bugging the fuck out of me. I stomp and I kick things and I tell her to shut the fuck up. All the while hoping that she won't."

My breaths are all jumbled now.

I'm breathing so fast that they're stumbling, falling all over each other. "I-I didn't... I didn't think you'd... I didn't know."

I did haunt him then. I did.

He lowers himself even more then, pushes his chest into mine.

"Yeah, you didn't. You didn't know that even now, my Mustang smells like you. Even now when I get inside it, the first breath I take is you."

Before I can say anything to that, he does something so… primitive and primal that all I can do is let him.

He smells me.

With his hands still planted on the tree by my head, he dips his face and takes a whiff off my forehead. But that's not all. He grazes the side of my face with his nose as he smells me there too.

And he growls.

Like he really is an animal, a predator, and I bite my lip really, really hard.

So hard that I think I taste blood.

But it's okay.

It's fine because everything else inside me is bleeding too. Everything else inside me is bleeding lust.

Thick and tangy and coppery and so, so syrupy and delicious.

"Geranium," he rasps against my skin. "Yeah?"

"Yes."

He nuzzles his nose on my jaw. "And sugar."

"Uh-huh."

"Rare body oil."

I tilt my head back even more, giving him access to my neck, to my scent as I hold on to him like he'll save my life, when in reality, he's the one drowning me.

He's drowning me in desire, and wordlessly I nod as he rubs his nose on the column of my throat.

"Because you like them. Still."

"Still."

He looks up at me then, bowed over me with his strong, big body. "You wanna know how you haunt me, Fae? This is how." He shows it to me again by taking a whiff of my skin and I arch into him.

"This is what you do to me. This is what you did to me two years ago. You made me an addict, a junkie who's looking for his next fix. Who's been looking for it all this time. Because two years ago, I had a taste of a drug. I had a taste of my Fae and she's been in my system ever since. She's been running in my veins, my bloodstream and I've got no way to purge her. I've got no way to get rid of her. And I've got no way to get more of her either. So I'm stuck. I'm stuck with this need. This ache. I'm stuck with you. I'm nothing but haunted, Fae. I'm nothing but this ache. I'm nothing but pain."

I look into his bright eyes, bright with haunting, bright with pain as he said and I whisper, "Me too."

He licks his lips. "What?"

"I'm pain too."

Like him I'm nothing but pain. I'm nothing but haunted. I'm nothing but his.

Still.

After all this time, I'm still his. And I don't want to be.

I don't want to be his.

Somehow I already know what he's going to say next.

"You remember what I told you?" he asks. "That night."

I dig my nails into his hips. "Hold on to my dress."

"Yeah." He licks his lips again as if he's already tasting me on them. "Can you do that for me again? Can you hold on to your dress for me? Don't let me see her."

Can I?

Can I hide from him again? Can I hide what's between my legs from him again?

I did that once.

I listened to him. I obeyed him. And look where we are now.

I let him protect me, my body, but he didn't protect my heart.

He broke it instead and I've been in pain ever since. He's been in pain too.

We've both been haunted and caged in so many ways because of what happened, what we did to each other. It's time we end this.

It's time we break away from each other for good and move on. And somehow I already know what we have to do in order to do that.

I know what I have to do also.

In all my madness and desperation and my veins filled with that toxic potion that I drank because it was labeled love, I shake my head. "No."

"What?"

"I won't hold on to my dress for you. Because you don't have to protect me anymore," I say, looking into his eyes. "B-because I was… I was with someone else."

Chapter 10

Love made me do it.

That's what I'm going to say to myself years later when I think of this night.

When I think of what I just said to him.

Love and a broken heart. That's what made me say it.

I can't believe I did though. I can't believe I said that and I can't believe he heard it.

Not only that, he understood it too.

Because as soon as I told him, his breathing got wild.

His chest expanded and swelled under his t-shirt and his shoulders became massive and even broader. And now he's crowding me even more, eating up all the air, all the space around me with his enhanced, heavily breathing body.

"What'd you just say?"

Even though I'm trembling now and the night has gone darker because of how changed, how angry Reed has become after my confession, I forge ahead, my voice calm.

Because that's the only way.

That's the only way this will end.

"There was someone else. After you."

He shifts on his feet, his torso rubbing against mine, his chest scraping against mine too.

I'm surrounded by him. Surrounded and trapped and at his mercy.

"What someone else?" he growls.

"A guy that I met."

"Where?"

"At the bar."

"The shitty bar that you go to."

"Y-yes. Toby."

He breathes out sharply at the name, his chest contracting, his stomach hollowing out. As if in revulsion. In protest.

"What about Toby?"

I'm still fisting his shirt at the hips but now I open my palms and splay them over his hard muscles. I try to absorb all his anger, his violence in my skin.

Because I know he's going to get even angrier. When I tell him everything.

"I met him one night. Back when I started at St. Mary's. Back then everything was… difficult. Everything hurt. Everything made me feel lonely and… You… I was still so mad at you. My anger was so fresh and…"

"And?"

God, I know this will hurt him.

I know it.

I know how possessive he can be. How dominating and authoritative. Even when he has no right to be any of those things with me.

Not anymore.

But I remind myself that this is the only way.

"And I wanted to forget you. I wanted to forget everything about you. I wanted to forget that I ever met you. That I fell in love with you. So I…"

His biceps are vibrating now.

I can feel them disturbing the still air. Still and somehow charged too.

Smelling of wildflowers and woods and geranium and sugar. And lust.

Smelling of us and our desire.

"You what?" he bites out, his eyes blazing with anger.

His features are so tight that I raise my hand and cradle his jaw, his rough, stubbled jaw, as I hurt him with my words. "I… He was nice to me. And he had these laughing brown eyes and he was… kind. He was kind, Reed." I press my fingertips on his ticking jaw. "He was kind to me. He didn't make me angry like you do. And he didn't make me mad or blush or… or bad. Like you do. He didn't…"

He didn't do anything for me, to be honest.

He was nice and he asked me why I looked so sad. Why my eyes were puffy and why my lips looked like they never smiled. He asked me why I looked like a girl who was lost.

I never would've noticed him if not for Poe.

Back then I used to be sad all the time and even though Poe didn't know the reason she always stuck by me. It was her idea to sneak out and unwind. And I was too sad to care about getting caught so I went with her.

"What happened?" Reed asks, his words sounding like blades in the air.

"I… I let him… He kiss —"

"Don't," he snaps, cutting me off, almost pressing his forehead against mine, making me taste his command on my tongue, my trembling lips.

And that jaw that I'm touching now after two long years, I rub it.

I try to soothe away the tightness from it. I try to soothe him because I'm not finished. Because I have to keep going for the both of us.

"He didn't just…" I tell Reed. "He did… other things. He took me to this dark corner, away from everyone and I went with him and he —"

That's when his hands come off the tree and he puts them on me.

He wraps one around my throat and buries the other in my hair. He messes up my neat and tidy strands as his fingers latch onto my hair. He even squeezes my throat to get a good, possessive grip around it.

When he's satisfied with how he's trapped me and how my lips have parted at his dominating hold, he says, "Are you trying to hurt me?"

"No," I whisper.

"Is this your fucked-up way of giving me pain? Of teaching me a lesson for breaking your heart. For throwing away your love."

"No, Reed. Listen —"

"Then what the fuck are you doing?" he snaps so loudly that I flinch.

He grips my neck so tightly that I go up on my tiptoes to give him more access. To give him more of me to squeeze and grope and grab.

"I'm trying to tell you that you don't have to protect me anymore. That I'm not some innocent flower that you met in the woods two years ago. I'm not. I haven't been that girl in a long time, Reed, okay? You don't have to tell me to hold on to my dress or to keep my legs shut when you're around."

His thumb presses down on my pulse. "I don't, huh? I don't have to protect you. I can do whatever I want with you then?"

"Yes. That's what I'm saying. And where do you get off trying to protect me anyway? You're the guy who hurt me. You're the reason I'm like this. All broken." My hands creep up to his hair then and I grip his longish strands. I grip them and a breath puffs out of me because they feel the same as they did two years ago. Rich and soft and cozy, and tugging on them, I continue, "And I'm the reason you're haunted. And I want this to end."

"To end," he says roughly.

"Yes. I want this to end, Reed. I don't want to be broken anymore. I don't want you to be haunted. We need to move on. We need to forget about each other. We need to forget that we ever met." I look into his eyes that have turned even harsher now. "I need to forget that I ever met you. That I ever fell in love with you. I need to forget you, Reed. I want to. And I want this to be the last time."

"Last time what?"

"That we see each other. I don't want... I don't want you to come here anymore. To pick me up or to drive me around. I'm safe, Reed. So I don't want you to be my chauffeur anymore. Besides, the audition video is done. So I don't need you anymore."

It got done last week. So this is it.

This has to be.

"You don't need me anymore," he repeats.

"No." I shake my head, feeling all achy and sad. "So promise me."

"Promise you."

I nod, my neck in his grip, my head feeling heavy. "Promise me this is the last time. And maybe one day..."

"One day what?"

"One day I can meet someone and I can fall in love with him. I want to fall for someone. A different guy. A good guy. A guy who doesn't hurt me like you do."

The muscle on his cheek tics and tics. "You want to fall for someone?"

My heart sinks.

It goes all the way, down and down, to the bottom of my stomach. I don't even think that I can hear it anymore. I don't even think I feel it.

As if my heart is hiding.

It's running away from me at the thought of falling for someone else.

But my heart is stupid. It has always been.

"Yes," I whisper.

He goes still then. At my response.

As still as my own chest. Like his heart ran away too at the thought of me falling for someone else.

But that's not true, is it?

He doesn't have a heart to begin with. His chest is a wasteland where no heart, no flower will ever grow and I was foolish to ever think otherwise.

I still am.

Because his stillness makes me want to cry.

Makes me want to take back my words and fall at his feet. It makes me want to tell him that I will never ever fall for anyone else.

I can't.

Because two years ago, I loved him too much and sometimes I still feel that love.

I hate it.

I hate that I can feel it in my chest but I feel it nonetheless.

But then, that's why I've done this, right?

To not feel it anymore. To end it once and for all.

"So say it," Reed commands after a few seconds. "Say the words then."

I'm not surprised that he already knows what I'm going to say. It's the strangest thing that we can sense each other's thoughts like that but I'm not going to dwell on it.

I'm going to say it.

"I-I think we should..."

His grip flexes around my throat, in my hair. "We should what?"

"You should f-fuck me."

It took me what felt like forever to say it but it doesn't take him more than a fraction of a second to repeat it. "I should fuck you."

I jerk out a nod and swallow that I'm sure he can feel on his rough palm. "Yes."

"Because you're not an innocent flower anymore. I don't need to tell you to hold on to your dress. Or to hide your pussy from me."

I'd forgotten.

I'd forgotten how filthy his words can be. Or at least what they made me feel when he talked to me like that. How they affected me.

How they sent currents running through my body, my stomach, my limbs. How my skin would tremble and become coarse with goosebumps.

"Yes," I reply, swallowing again. "It didn't work the last time. Protecting me, my body. So I think we should d-do it."

"Do it."

"I think we should get each other out of our systems. Get closure. So we can move on. We can —"

"Yeah, you said that." He squeezes my throat again. "You already said how you wanted to fall for someone else."

"Reed —"

He cuts me off again. "So you want me to fuck you, fuck that thing between your legs, so you can offer it up to someone else. A good guy. A guy who doesn't hurt you like I do. Am I getting it right?"

At his angry words, jealous words, a great, mighty tremble rolls through my thighs, through the thing between my legs, and I have to press my thighs together to keep my balance.

But then, I shouldn't have worried about falling because he's got a good hold on me.

A possessive hold.

"I didn't mean it that way. I just meant that we have to end this and —"

"And you've already done it, haven't you?" he growls, his wolf eyes narrowed. "You've already offered it up to fucking Toby. Toby with his brown fucking eyes and his fucking kindness. He was kind to you. Isn't that what you said? Toby was kind to you and so you went wherever he took you. And when he asked you, you spread your legs for him, is that it?"

"Reed —"

"Toby tell you that though? That you have to fuck someone to get over someone else. He teach you that?"

I tug on his hair. "Reed, that's not —"

This time he cuts me off not with his words, but with his actions. His fingers shift and ripple around my body and he comes ever so much closer to me.

His mouth breathes fire over mine as he rasps, "Let's see then. Let's see what that motherfucker taught you."

Before I can respond to that, he puts his fire-breathing lips on mine.

For a second I'm so shocked, I'm so taken aback, that I freeze. I don't know what to do.

I don't know if I should move or breathe or what. And I guess he has the same problem because he doesn't do any of those things either.

He only presses his mouth on me.

But then slowly he breathes.

Slowly, he opens his mouth over mine and his sweet and smoky breath fans over my lips. And his life-giving air goes down into my lungs and slowly resurrects all the dead spaces inside of me.

Slowly, I come alive and I breathe too.

I not only breathe, I open my mouth and I gulp down all the air he gives me.

And when I'm all alive for the first time in two years, I kiss him.

I kiss the guy I fell in love with when I was almost sixteen, and the sky opens up.

Exactly like it did two years ago.

Two years ago, when Reed Roman Jackson kissed me for the first and only time, the sky broke into pieces and scattered around us in raindrops. The same thing is happening right now and it's a shock to my body.

It's a shock to his body too but he doesn't take his mouth off like he did that time, and I thank God for that. I wasn't about to give him up. I can't. Not yet.

And it looks like he doesn't want to give me up either.

He doesn't want to let go of my mouth, so he keeps kissing me.

Although the rest of the things, he does them exactly as before.

Last time, he picked me up from the ground and cradled the back of my head. He made me take shelter in his big body before he carried me to his Mustang to protect me from the rain.

This time too he does all of that.

He picks me up and my thighs go around his waist. He cradles the back of my head but only to press our mouths closer and I wind my arms around his neck only so I can let him.

Still kissing, he takes me over to his Mustang.

And God, I'm going to start crying.

I'm going to start sobbing because he's still doing it, isn't he?

He's still protecting me.

After all the things I said to him just now. After how I've angered him and hurt him and invoked his jealousy and violence, he's still taking care of me, and my heart squeezes in my chest.

My heart cries for him. For this guy who has a penchant for acting like a hero when he's the villain.

Why does he do this though?

Why does he make me hurt for him? And Jesus Christ why does he taste so good?

Why does he taste like something I want to eat and consume and drink for the rest of my life?

Because he does and I missed it.

I missed his taste.

You'd think that a guy like him would taste spicy and tangy, but no. He tastes like my favorite dessert.

He tastes like cupcakes.

He tastes sweet and sugary and rich. So addictive, so toxic for my broken ballerina heart.

So injurious.

But fuck it.

Fuck it because I'm going to taste him tonight and I'm going to curse and open my mouth over his so he can taste me as well.

So he can taste me as much as he likes.

I let him eat me, eat my mouth. Bite at it, nip and lick and suck. Everything that he wants to do to me as he carries me to shelter in the pouring rain.

And with the grace of the athlete that he is, he opens the door and bends down to deposit me inside his car. And yes, we have to break apart for that to happen but the separation only lasts like two seconds before he's inside the car too and like the last time, I hurry over to straddle his lap.

And then we're back at it.

He's back at kissing me, grabbing my jaw to deepen the angle, and I'm back at kissing him too as I fist his hair, rub my fingers over his stubble that feels so smooth to touch but irritates the life out of him.

I don't know how long we go on kissing each other. I don't know how long he sucks on my lower lip or how long I claw at his t-shirt but somewhere during all of that, something has happened.

Something vital and important that hadn't happened two years ago and I feel it in my thighs.

I feel his hands on my thighs. Both of them.

His fingers are gripping me, my flesh, and they're so forceful, so dominating that it makes me whimper and gasp in his mouth.

Our lips break apart and we pant.

With a heaving chest, I glance down between us.

I see his soaked t-shirt that sticks to his contoured muscles and raindrops decorating his arms. But more than that I see myself.

I see why it was such a shock to have his hands on my thighs.

Because my dress — as soaked as his t-shirt — is all messed up.

My ivory dress with a lacy overlay that I wore for him tonight, that was hiding me away from the world, from his animal eyes, has ridden up.

All the way up to the tops of my thighs.

And he can see what he couldn't. Back then.

He can see my panties.

A peek of them at least. A very tiny peek of my cream-colored lacy panties, and he's right there.

His hands with knobby knuckles and long fingers and moon-kissed skin are right there. At the seam of my panties. So much so that if he decides to stretch out his fingers more, he'll touch it.

He'll touch me. My core, and even though it's covered, I don't think it's much protection from him.

I snap my eyes up to his face then and blurt out, "Reed, I need —"

He doesn't let me talk though.

He gropes at my thighs forcefully, making me gasp again and fist his damp shirt on his shoulders.

"No," he growls, sitting back in the seat, sprawled and wet and sexy. "You don't get to talk anymore. Time for talking is over. It's time for something else, isn't it?"

I swallow, staring at his features, all tight and leached of color. "Reed —"

"It's time for you to show me what he taught you." He squeezes my thighs again. "Show me all the new skills you've learned from him."

I shake my head, squirming in his lap. "This is not about that, Reed. You —"

He lets go of my thigh then and brings one of his hands to grab my face, cutting me off. Pressing his fingers on my cheek, he asks, "Did he teach you new moves, Fae, huh? New tricks. Did he teach my Fae, my pure, daisy fresh Fae, all the new shiny tricks? Is she going to dance dirty for me now, huh?"

"Reed."

"Because she knows everything now, doesn't she?" He shifts up from the seat, his muscles taut and angry. "Thanks to one fucking Toby. Who I'm going to end by the way. I'm going to find him and I'm going to tear him limb from limb for taking what was mine. What belonged to me."

I grab his face too then, my eyes stinging, my body burning

with his jealousy. With the heat radiating out of him. Out of his vampire skin and his black, villainous eyes. "It didn't belong to you, okay? It didn't. Please, Reed. This is about us. This is —"

He rises from the seat like a coiled animal then, ready to strike, to bite, to leave teeth marks all over my skin and poison my veins with his venom and my stupid heart rejoices at that. That he's leaving something in my body that will stay with me and it doesn't even care that it's poison and that it will kill me slowly.

"There's no us though, is there?" he growls, the words ripping out of his chest. "That's the whole point. There will never be an us. Isn't that why you want me to do this?"

At his word 'this,' that hand of his on my thighs moves and his thumb touches the seam of my panties.

For the very first time, and I jump.

I rock in his lap, and staring at me with anger, with lust, he presses that digit into my pussy. In the valley between my lips, making me moan.

"Isn't it, Fae?" he rasps, watching me. "Isn't that why you want me to fuck you, here." He presses his thumb again, his fingers on my face moving too, capturing my jaw and squeezing. "Answer me. Isn't that why you want me to stick my dick in your not-so-innocent hole? So it all ends tonight."

My lips part and I nod. "Yes."

"Good." He pushes his thumb into my core again and somehow finds that exact spot, that bundle of nerves, that makes me whimper and dance on his lap. "So you'll answer me. You'll answer me when I ask you. Did he make you cry?"

"What?"

"Did you cry for him, Fae? When he fucked you."

I shake my head. "N-no."

"Good. That's good too," he says roughly, his fingers squeezing my face again. "Because only I get to make you cry, you understand? Only me. Say it."

"Only you."

"Yeah. Me. Only I get to hurt you. I get to make you mad and pink and angry. Only I get to make you dance on my lap. Don't I?"

And he does. When he flicks at my clit again, rubbing the fabric of my panties over it.

"Yes."

"Why? Tell me why I get to do that."

"B-because only you are my villain."

"Fuck yeah, I am. And you're my Fae. Mine."

I claw at his shoulders, at his neck. "I'm not. I don't want to be."

"You've pissed me off, Fae," he snaps, his body vibrating against me, his thumb on my clit so urgent and pushy and so freaking maddening. "You've pissed me the fuck off and now you're going to pay for it. You understand what I'm saying to you? I'm going to make you pay for it. I'm going to make you cry."

His words make me moan. Or maybe it's his hands, his thumb on my clit that hasn't quit torturing me.

It could be his eyes too, all dark and aroused and violent and beautiful.

I don't know what's making me feel this way. This angsty and lustful and frustrated and eager. All at the same time.

All I know is that I want more of him, more of this even though I shouldn't want to.

"You know how I'm going to do that? How I'm going to make you cry for me, Fae?"

"H-how?"

"With my dick," he rasps. "With my big fucking dick. Tell me how big my dick is."

I can't tell him anything right now but I try.

I try my hardest. "As big as... my arm."

"Fuck yeah. My dick is as big as your pretty arm and when I stick it in here." His thumb makes me see stars at here. "When I pound your fairy pussy with it, it's going to feel like the first time. It's going to feel like the first dick you've ever had. The first monster dick that was ever crammed into your tiny snatch and you're going to forget all about your Toby."

"I —"

"When I fuck you, Fae, it will hurt you but it will feel like magic. And you'll love it. You'll love hurting for my dick. You'll love crying for it. And when you meet that good guy you're so dying to meet, when he fucks you, your pussy will still hurt for my cock. She'll still cry for it."

By the time he finishes, I want all his words to come true. All his lies to become my truth, and this feeling only intensifies when he takes his hands off my body and goes to unzip his jeans. When he pulls his t-shirt up slightly to reveal his cut abs and pushes his jeans down and gets out his dick and I swear to God I want to savor the moment.

I want to look at it, at his cock, at his stomach, his bare skin. I want to memorize everything.

It's the last time, see. The first and the last.

But I don't get to do any of that.

Because before I can even blink, he's pushed my panties aside, exposing me, and then he's there. At my hole.

The head of his cock is there and, still holding my panties, he raises his hips and pushes in.

He rams his way into my core and all my thoughts vanish. They leach out of my mouth in long groans and gasps as my mouth falls open and my spine arches up against the front seat of his Mustang.

And my hands.

They claw into his forearms, drawing blood. Because I've never felt this before. I've never felt this kind of pain.

It explodes in my stomach and coats my eyes with thick tears.

Tears for him.

Exactly what he wanted.

And even in this pain, my broken heart smiles. My stupid broken heart smiles and spins inside my chest, knowing that I gave him what he wanted.

After hurting him so much, lying to him so much tonight.

Because yeah, I was lying.

Or rather, I let him make assumptions.

Because I haven't done this before. No one's been inside my body before tonight.

Before him.

I did meet a Toby, yes. I did kiss him, but that was it. I couldn't mislead him when I was still hung up on someone else. I couldn't kiss him because I wasn't kissing him, I was kissing the guy who broke my heart.

The guy who's taken my virginity tonight without even knowing.

He never would've done this otherwise. I know that.

His protectiveness would've stopped him and I wanted this to end.

He's so strange, this villain.

Whose hips are raised and whose body is taut and bowed under me and who's breathing into my neck, puffing out warm breaths.

Who's lodged so deep inside of me that I can feel him throbbing. I can feel him pulsing as I try to draw breath. As I try to dull my own throbbing.

My own pulsating, beating core that is wracked with pain.

And I think just like I can feel him, feel his dick beating inside me like a heart, he can feel my channel pulse around his rod as well.

He lifts his head and looks up at me. His lips are wet and parted like mine and his eyes are drugged and shimmering as he looks into my wet ones.

His jaw clenches at my tears and I know, despite everything he said, despite all his anger and jealousy, he's brimming with regret.

And he proves me right when he carefully, oh so carefully, reaches up and wipes off a lone tear that had fallen down my cheek without me even knowing. He not only wipes my tear but he also wraps his big, strong arms around me and hugs me to his chest.

He hugs me so tightly that I can't stop my tears. I can't stop myself from crying for him as I burrow my face in his neck.

I feel him open his mouth on my forehead and breathe out in a puff as he shushes me. "Hey, it's okay. It's okay. I'll make it better, okay?"

I nod, rubbing my nose in his wet t-shirt.

He rubs his lips on my skin, rubs his arms on my spine, all the while making soothing noises, all the while whispering, "I'm sorry. I'm sorry. I got… I got carried away. I got so angry. I shouldn't have —"

"No, it's going away," I whisper back, looking up at him and meeting his molten eyes.

His thick frown ripples. "Yeah?"

"Yes. Just kiss me."

He studies my face for a beat, maybe to see if I mean my words, and when he's satisfied, he gives me what I want.

He kisses me.

In the exact opposite way of how he entered my body, breached my virgin hole.

He kisses me softly and tenderly and wetly. And hungrily too.

And I shiver in his arms, suddenly all achy.

All restless and hungry, just like him, and I'm the one who

makes the next move then. I'm the one who shifts on his lap because I want more. Because I want him, and of course he senses that.

He gets that my pain is slowly receding and to help me along, he brings his fingers back to my clit. He rubs it in slow circles, all the while kissing me as he moves under me as well.

He starts with slow, gentle pumps, languid and lazy. They heat up my blood and my skin. They fog up the windows with my gasps and moans.

They make my pussy leak too.

She cries for him like he told me she would and eases the way for his cock.

Suddenly his pumps have become shorter. His thrusts have become faster and so freaking good that I push back against him.

I moan into his mouth, fist his hair and twist my hips, rock them in time with his pounding cock.

I can feel the air growing hot, growing musky and thick. I can feel his abdomen bunching up and tightening under me, feel the muscles of his thighs.

I can even hear them slapping against my butt as he kisses me and plays with my clit.

And the fact that we're moving so fast, that I'm humping him and he's giving it to me, is causing his Mustang to shake, to move as well, puts me on the edge.

It actually pushes me over the edge.

The shaking car, the foggy windows, the rain, his kisses and him.

And I come.

My pussy convulses around his cock and a feeling the likes of which I've never experienced washes over me. I arch my back and throw back my neck as I grab hold of the roof and moan so loudly.

Even in this mindless moment, I know what it is.

I know what this feeling is as I rock my hips in his lap. It's relief.

It's more than relief. It's euphoria.

It's the feeling of being in his arms as I burst, after two long years, and I whisper, "God, Reed."

The moment I say his name proves to be his tipping point.

That proves to be the push he needed to jump off the cliff and he comes as well.

But instead of being all relieved like I was, he grows even more alert. He jerks away from me. He even pushes me up and over him so he can whip his dick out.

As soon as he does, I feel lashes of his warm cum on my trembling pussy and my thighs. I feel his entire body shuddering and trembling around me and I hug him like he hugged me when I needed his warmth.

I hug him tightly.

I hug him goodbye as he finishes what he started two years ago.

And he kisses me. On the forehead, tenderly, gently as he comes down from his high.

Like he also did two years ago.

Chapter 11

The Hero

There's blood on my thighs. On my dick.

Dried and brownish.

Only a few small spots, nothing big. Nothing that would draw my eyes to them.

But I'm looking at them now.

Back at my hotel room, as I step into the shower, I'm looking at these spots as the water washes them away. As the water swallows the dark red color. As it goes down the drain.

For a second I don't get it.

I don't fucking get it.

But then I know.

Like a jolt to my system, I fucking know. I fucking remember.

Her impossible tightness, the struggle to get in, her shocked breaths and jerks. Her tears.

That burned my skin when they fell on me.

She lied.

She lied to me tonight. She lied.

And that burning, that pain I'd felt when she cried because of me, because I'd physically hurt her with my callousness, comes back.

A severe, massive pain. The likes of which I've never experienced before.

And I'm quite adept at dealing with it.

It comes with the territory of being an athlete. You spend most of your life hurting, nursing one injury after another. Icing, bandaging, elevating, walking it off.

Just because I don't play soccer anymore doesn't mean I've forgotten.

But there's not just pain, there's anger too, and I've never felt this kind of an anger before either.

Anger at my own fucking self for not figuring it out sooner, for not figuring it out in the moment, and I'm quite an expert in handling anger as well.

Asshole father, remember?

I wasn't lying to her when I told her that yes, it hurt like a mother when he asked me to give up soccer in exchange for her freedom and come work for him. It made me angry too, furious, that I was so close to winning, so close to showing him once and for all that he wouldn't control me.

But it didn't make me as angry as I was when I found out my father'd got his evil clutches into her.

And it didn't make me as angry as I am right now.

As angry as I get when I think of something else.

I didn't have a condom on me.

She pissed me the fuck off, made my blood burn with jealousy and I wasn't thinking straight, all right?

I wasn't thinking about anything other than getting inside of her body, erasing that goddamn son of a bitch, and it didn't occur to me that I was bare. Not until I was already inside of her. Not until I was already coming and I pulled out.

I know I pulled out. I fucking know that but…

But what if that wasn't enough?

What if…

Jesus Christ.

The whole drive back from St. Mary's, I kept thinking that that was it. That tonight would be the last time. That I'd give her what she wanted. It didn't even make sense, me going there. The video is done.

If she wants to fall for someone, she can fucking fall for someone.

And she better pray that I don't ever find out who he is.

Because if I do, I will murder him. I will kill him just for breathing the same air as her.

That's what I do in my thoughts. When I picture her with someone. When I torture myself with the possibility that she might've moved on. That she's giving her sweet smiles to someone else. That she's fucking dancing for someone else.

But fuck it all now.

Fuck what she wants.

If she wanted me to stay away, she shouldn't have lied. She shouldn't have angered me, made me furious enough to hurt her like that. To make her bleed over my dick, my thighs.

To not only hurt her but to get inside her all bare, all thoughtless.

So fuck what she wants.

I'm seeing her again.

Chapter 12

There's something wrong with me.

For the first few days I try to deny it.

I try to deny that I'm sad. I try to deny that I cry in my pillow at night. That I can't sleep or focus. And that I'm just bone tired.

I try to deny that all of this is because it's over.

Because I've had closure now and because I'll never see him again.

Because it's crazy.

That I'm sad about that. That I'm sad about never seeing him when I didn't want to see him in the first place. When it upset me so much that I saw him at the bar and that he was back in my life.

When I asked for him to promise me.

I asked him for closure. I told him that I wanted this to end, that I wanted to forget him.

But somehow, despite everything, this closure thing has become the most painful experience of my life.

Even more painful than a broken heart.

So much so that it's hard to even get out of bed and go to

classes. It's hard to muster up the energy to sneak out to Ballad of the Bards when Friday comes.

My friends think I'm acting strange but I deny it to them too.

Besides, my friends have their own problems.

Especially my one friend.

Salem Salinger, and her problem has a name: Arrow Carlisle, our new soccer coach.

Yes, we have soccer here at St. Mary's.

It's more or less a team-building exercise that every student has to participate in. We get a choice to pick from a couple of sports. We play those sports as a team and learn how to live in a society.

Anyway.

With his dirty blond hair and blue eyes, that guy is a sun god. All the girls at St. Mary's are crazy for him and his good looks. He started at the school right around the time Salem did and it's been pretty apparent that she's crushing really hard on our new coach.

She hasn't said anything about it to anyone but I can tell; I have boy problems too, after all.

I'm not interested in soccer at all but even I know who Arrow Carlisle is.

According to my brothers, he's one of the best pro soccer players in the country, the star of the L.A. Galaxy team. He was the reason why Galaxy won the championship trophy last year and they were on track to win again this year.

Until Arrow got injured and was told to sit out a few games as a precaution.

He's here to recuperate, and meanwhile, he's coaching our sort of lame soccer team as a favor to his mom.

Who also happens to be the principal of this reform school and Salem's guardian who sent her here in the first place.

As I said, problems.

Salem has a lot of them.

And so instead of worrying my friends, I decide to go out with Wyn when the weekend arrives. Just to prove to them and to myself that things are okay.

That closure is a good thing and I got exactly what I wanted.

Freedom from him.

Only it backfires when I see him at Buttery Blossoms.

With a girl.

To be fair, that girl — Teresa — works there and I know her. She's pretty easy-going and fun. And hence super popular with the patrons. And from the looks of it, she's super popular with him too.

Because he seems very engrossed in what she's saying.

Which is probably why he can't see me.

Again, to be fair, I'm not inside the shop yet. I'm across the street from it and I was about to cross when I saw him, his dark head and his white hoodie.

That shines when the rays of the sun fall on him.

I'm never going to see that hoodie again, am I? I'm never going to touch it or feel it. I'm never going to touch his hair, smell his scent.

I'm never going to taste him or feel him.

Or dance for him.

No one's ever going to watch me dance like he does, like I really am a perfect ballerina.

No one's ever going to call me Fae...

Despite explaining this to myself for the thousandth time, a great wave of sadness grips me. It grips my heart and my body starts trembling. I tell Wyn that I can't walk. I tell her that I need to get out of here.

To her credit, she doesn't ask. She simply goes with me.

God, I love her and I hate that I'm making her skip out on her favorite brunch place. But I can't. I can't go when he's in there. With a girl.

When he's moved on.

This is him moving on, isn't it?

So it worked then, what we did. What I made him do. All my lies and misdirection worked and he's done with me. He's fucked me out of his system and as I've been saying, it's a good thing.

I just don't know why I feel so angry.

Why I want to go in there and punch him in the face. Why I want to cry and sob and curl into a ball.

So for the next couple of weeks, I try my hardest to get rid of this anger, this pain, this sadness. I try to distract myself and stay busy.

Busy, busy, busy.

With classes, with homework, with school activities, with gardening and counseling sessions. Days are easier to pass because there's always something to do and I have my girls.

But nights are harder.

I have a solution for that as well though. Wyn's stories.

When I can't sleep, I ask Wyn to tell me stories. Especially that one story that I love.

It's about a man she met one night.

The one she calls her dream man.

We don't know who he is. All we know is that a year ago when Wyn came here for the first time, that summer, she met a man. She says he was older than us, like in his late twenties or something. And somehow, crazily enough, that man became the reason why she came here to St. Mary's.

She hasn't shared this with anyone else except me; she's too shy, but I love hearing about this mystery man and making up theories about him.

With moonlight streaming through the barred windows and lying on my side on the bed to face her, I ask her one night, "Tell me about his eyes."

In the same position from her bed, she bites her lip and says in her soft voice, "Um, okay. So his eyes are blue. Like yours. But I think a little darker. Like navy, maybe."

"And his hair?"

"Dark from what I could see. It was night, way past my curfew. But sometimes I think there might be some light strands in there, I don't know. Maybe dirty blond."

"Like Coach Carlisle's?" I ask, referring to Salem's crush.

Wyn sighs. "Oh yeah, that would be awesome." She puts her hands under her cheek and continues, "And well, he came out of nowhere. Like one second I was alone and the next, he was there. I was sitting on the sidewalk, crying because I'd had a fight with my dad and suddenly there was this huge man and his shadow covering me. And I got really scared but then he talked."

I grin. "And what did he say?"

She smiles as well. "He asked me if I was okay and I told him that I was. And I thought that he would leave after that, anyone would have, but he didn't. He stayed and I still can't believe he stayed. And he didn't even try anything with me, you know? He just sat on the other side of the road, opposite to me, and told me that he had a sister my age and that if I wanted to, I could talk to him. And I did. I told him about my dad and how he was forcing me to go to law school instead of art school and all that, you know? And then he said something."

I love this part. "What?"

She looks at me and I know her eyes must be shining right about now. "He said that I'm a dreamer. And that I should keep dreaming and I should do what my dreams tell me to do. Because it's important. For some reason, I felt like he didn't, you know? He didn't do what his dreams told him to do, so..." She sighs. "So yeah, that's what he told me."

"And so you drew graffiti on your dad's car. Because he told you to follow your dreams?"

She chuckles. "Yeah, and all over the siding on the house. But also because he called me Bronwyn."

I laugh. "And you let that happen, Wyn?! Come on."

She laughs as well. "I know. How could I, right? I told him not to, actually. I told him that people call me Wyn but he didn't listen. He walked me back to my house — I could barely look at him all through that walk — and as he was leaving, he said, 'Good luck, Bronwyn.' And I just stood there because I never thought I'd like it. I never thought I'd like someone calling me by my name. Bronwyn."

"But you did like it."

"Yeah." She nods, her voice all dreamy now. "Because he said it. In that voice that somehow reminds me of summer days and cotton sheets, cut grass. Deep and lazy like Sunday mornings."

"You should've asked him his name, Wyn," I almost whine because I want to know his name myself.

She releases a mournful sigh. "I know. I'm an idiot. I told you I could barely look at him. He was just so…"

"Sexy?"

"Yeah," she agrees. "And big and masculine."

I hum. "Maybe one day you'll run into him somewhere. You can ask him then."

Wyn gives me a look. "Yeah, because life is just that amazing."

I want it to be.

For my dreamer, artistic friend at least.

I want her to see her dream man again. I want her to ask him his name, talk to him, tell him all the things she's been feeling ever since she saw him that one night.

And I want him to fall in love with her. I want him to be a good guy. A guy who will care for her heart, for her feelings. A guy who won't make her cry.

"He was a good guy, wasn't he?" I ask Wyn after a while.

"I'd like to think so. He made me feel alive though. For those ten minutes he was with me."

"I love that for you," I say, feeling an overwhelming love for her as I blink away my own tears.

Wyn watches me for a few moments before she hesitantly asks, "What happened, Callie?"

"Nothing."

"Something happened, didn't it? With him." She frowns. "Has he done something? Has he hurt you again?"

I swallow down a thick wave of emotions. "No. He didn't hurt me. Well, not more than he already has."

This time around, he didn't do anything I didn't ask him to. This time around, he didn't do anything that I didn't make him do.

You want to fall for someone else?

I do. I still do.

It hadn't occurred to me until that night, until I said the words. But I do want to fall for someone else. Someone other than him. Someone like Toby.

Someone who's at least capable of loving. Unlike him.

"So then what happened? Why have you been so sad?"

Sad.

Yeah, I've been that.

I don't know how to stop being sad at the thought of falling for someone else.

"It's just…" I bite my lip. "He gave up soccer and he's working for his dad. That's how he got me off the hook."

"What?"

"Yeah."

"But Callie, that's like…"

"I know."

"Huge."

I sniffle. "Yeah."

"Are you sure he's not in l–"

I cut her off. "Yeah, I'm sure. This is what he does. He did all those sweet things before and I fell for them and…" I shake my head. "I can't. Not again, Wyn. I can't forget what he did. I can't forget how he broke my heart. No matter how hard I try and… It's just my stupid broken heart that still…"

Beats for him.

I can see Wyn is blinking too and I know she's doing it to keep her tears at bay. "Hearts are stupid, aren't they? Foolish little dreamers."

I chuckle sadly. "Yeah."

"So your heart wants him then."

I bite my lip again. Harder this time. Much harder, so I can stop the thundering in my chest. This wave of ache and need.

"I'm not listening to it," I tell her. "I listened to my heart once and it didn't turn out so well."

Wyn nods. Then, "And what about the other stuff?"

"What?"

"You know, you've been sick a lot. And you haven't been to your studio."

Oh. That.

When I said there's something wrong with me, I meant that there's something wrong with me on multiple levels.

Levels like my stomach is acting weird this week. I'm either ragingly hungry or I'm throwing up or feeling nauseated. Especially around my favorite things, coffee and bacon. The bacon thing really saddens me because I don't get to eat it that often anyway because of my stupid diet. So I savor it whenever I eat it, but I can't even do that anymore.

I do fantastic with arugula or kale. Even lettuce.

Things that I've had to eat because of my diet but have never really liked in the past.

So I don't know what's happening there. It actually snuck up on me a few days ago.

Not to mention, I've been so tired, bone tired lately. So much so that ballet and practice and exercises are the last thing on my mind, which is fine because I already sent in my Juilliard application but still. I can barely drag myself out of bed in the morning and stay awake in classes after lunch.

I feel like my body is swollen and heavy and I just want to sleep till the end of time.

"Maybe I'll go next week," I say and smile reassuringly.

Hopefully I'll be better next week, won't I?

I have to be.

This can't go on forever. Especially when this is what I want. Especially when it's been three weeks since that night.

But hours later, long after Wyn has gone to sleep, I'm still awake.

I'm tossing and turning, so hot and so uncomfortable in my skin that I decide to sneak out. Coincidentally, it's a Thursday and so a perfect night for sneaking out.

I'm not going to the studio though because I don't have the energy or any will to dance, but I need some fresh air. So I creep out of the room, scale the fence and wander into the woods.

I walk aimlessly, my feet kicking up the leaves, crunching them, my fingers grazing the rough bark, the branches, trying to get rid of this nausea that has suddenly crept up.

I even walk over to the tree. The tree.

Just by the side of the road. Where he kissed me.

I'm an idiot for doing that. I know.

But I just wanted to see it. I just wanted to touch it.

As soon as I do though, I snatch my hand back, disgusted with myself, and walk away, ready to go back to my dorm room, when I hear something.

Tires screeching. Bang of a car door shutting.

Footsteps.

Loud and thumping.

I can hear the crunch of the leaves. I can feel the force of the heels stomping the ground right in my chest.

Strangely, I know it's him.

I already know it so I dive for the tree just by my side and hide behind it. I hunch my shoulders and try to shrink my body, try to make myself smaller because I don't want him to see me.

I don't.

What is he doing here? Why has he come?

He's looking for me, isn't he?

He's come to find me when he promised. He promised he wouldn't.

Yet he's here on a Thursday at midnight.

God, Reed.

I ignore my fluttering heart. I ignore that it soars in my chest, that a rush goes through me. At the fact that he's here.

I slowly look over my shoulder from where I'm hiding. I dig my nails into the bark when I see that he's striding down the path that I take to and from the fence. He's going to that spot, the spot from which we sneak out.

I showed him that spot the other night.

That night.

He actually carried me to that spot. After. In the rain.

Like I was his doll or something.

And I held on to him like I'd never let go. I burrowed my nose in the side of his neck, in the triangle of his throat, trying to fill my lungs with his scent for the last time.

He kept smelling me too, pressing his hot mouth on my forehead, breathing me in and breathing out.

I want to do that right now.

Jump into his arms so he carries me. Rub my nose in his hoodie, smell him, have him smell me.

Kiss me.

But I stay put as my stomach churns.

As I watch Reed march over to the fence, that I can only partially see through the trees.

As I feel dizzy.

Pressing my spine to the tree to keep my balance, I put a hand on my stomach and God, it feels so warm.

I don't remember my belly ever being so heated.

Why is it so hot?

But I don't have the time to think about it right now because he's come to a stop. Right at the spot in the fence where I asked him to let me down and where he watched me scale it and leave him to go back to my dorm.

Like he was really my Romeo and I was really his Juliet, sneaking back to my room.

In this moment, my Romeo is watching the fence, running his hands through his hair. His shoulders and back are shifting with what I think are agitated breaths and his stance is wide, battle-ready. As if he's going to tear the fence apart, take it down brick by brick, demolish it, all with those hands that are messing up his overly-long hair.

My belly lurches and churns and bile rises up my throat.

And oh my God, I think I'm gonna throw up.

I think...

Reed turns around then and looks in my direction, or rather

where I'm hiding.

And quickly, I duck even more behind the tree.

I clench my eyes shut, put a hand on my mouth to muffle the sounds of my breaths. The hand that's on my stomach, I press it even more as if I'm trying to stop whatever the heck is going on inside my body.

Whatever the heck makes me want to throw up right now and all the time, and that repels bacon and coffee and that makes me...

Wait a second.

Just wait a freaking second.

I'm throwing up all the time. I'm tired and I'm depressed and I smell everything and everything makes me nauseous.

And I can't remember the last time I had my period and wasn't I supposed to get a period a few days ago?

But maybe that's fine. Maybe I'm just a little late.

It doesn't mean anything, right?

My stomach churns and roars and I can feel him running his eyes frantically over the area. I can feel him looking for me, hunting for me, and it's getting harder and harder to stop this chaos in my stomach.

Oh God.

Please, Reed. Please, please, please.

I'm not sure what I'm pleading for. Am I pleading for him to leave or to find me or to tell me that whatever I'm thinking, whatever I've discovered about my body is false?

Maybe I want him to tell me that it's not right.

That it can't be.

There needs to be some other explanation. That it can't be what my body has been trying to tell me for the past few days.

But he doesn't do any of that.

He doesn't find me and tell me that it's all going to be okay, no.

He leaves.

Just as he'd come, out of the blue, almost jogging up to the fence, he walks away from it. I hear him leave. I hear his footsteps thumping and retreating.

Until I can't hear them anymore.

Until I open my eyes and fall down to my knees.

Then I throw up on the ground, my heart rebelling over letting him go and my body rebelling over what we did three weeks ago.

Chapter 13

He's the first thing I see as soon as I enter Ballad of the Bards. I'm not shocked to see him though.

It's Friday and he knows where I go on Fridays.

Even though I haven't been here in three weeks, ever since that night. And I would've skipped tonight as well but I've already worried my friends a lot and I couldn't skip without telling them something, everything, I don't know.

But I can't.

I can't tell them anything. Not yet.

Not until I figure things out myself. So when they asked, I said yes and I did it with a huge smile on my face to make it look convincing.

But anyway, he knows where to go to find me.

The shock comes from the fact that he wants to find me in the first place. That he wanted to find me last night as well when I hid from him.

When I figured out that...

That I am. I know I am.

My body has been trying to tell me this for days now and I've ignored it. I can't ignore it now.

So I know.

I've known it for about twenty-four hours now.

I've known it ever since last night when I threw up in the woods. I knew it when I got back to my room and first hugged my pillow to my body because I was so scared — I still am — and then cried in it.

I knew all through breakfast this morning, through trigonometry, geography, history, biology. I knew it when I went to see my guidance counselor and she asked me how my week had been and I told her it was fine. Everything was the same.

Even though it was a lie.

Because everything is not fine. Everything is not the same.

I don't think it will ever be the same after what I've known for the last twenty-four hours.

And now he's here.

He's standing at the same spot that he was back when I first saw him after two years. But unlike the last time, he doesn't have people around him.

He's alone and it looks like he's been waiting for me. It looks like he's been watching the door.

My heart tries to race at the thought.

At him watching the door, waiting for me to show up. But I harden it.

I make it stop.

Because he shouldn't be waiting for me. He shouldn't be watching the door for me.

And I shouldn't want him to.

I do everything in my power to stop my heart from wrecking my ribs, from leaping out of my chest at the sight of him. And I think

I'm successful. I think.

But I forgot one thing. Or rather, didn't take that thing into account.

I didn't take into account the fact that instead of it all ending that night, something began.

Something took root and I feel it in my body now, and even though I've managed to calm down my heart, I can't calm it down.

The flutters in my abdomen.

A quickening, something pulsing to life, and it's only getting worse the more I stare into his wolf eyes.

And I have to put a hand on my belly.

My skin feels just as warm and heated as it did last night.

As soon as I do that though, I know I've made a mistake.

Because God, his animal eyes — they really never miss any-thing — drop down to my belly. And his arched cheekbones flood with a flush as if he can feel that warmth himself.

When his lips part slightly as if on an exhale, I snatch my hand off.

His eyes snap up and my own pop wide at the look in them.

All angry and dark. Possessive. Filled with knowledge, some-how.

Of what's inside of me.

But it can't be, right?

He can't know. It took me days to figure it out myself, granted I was distracted but still. He can't figure it out by just looking at my hand on my stomach.

Right?

But he starts to move toward me. He starts to bulldoze his way through the crowd to get to me and I don't know what else to do except run.

Again.

Because this wasn't the plan, okay?

This wasn't how I wanted to tell him. Did I want to tell him?

I don't know.

I only just found out myself. I haven't even had the time to process it all. And second of all, we were supposed to be free of each other.

I was supposed to be free of him. I was supposed to forget him and move on.

But this is the opposite of all that.

So blindly, I turn left and push my way through people. I push my way through their sour breaths, the smell of liquor, the heavy violins in the air. All of which is making me slightly dizzy and nauseated.

But somehow I manage not to fall to the ground or throw up.

I somehow make it to the back and turn into a hallway. Somehow, I find the door that I'm looking for — an office that all employees use. The reason I come to this bar and the reason I know Will, the bartender, is because my brother Conrad used to work here and I used to accompany him when I was little.

I've spent a lot of time in that office and I know for a fact that it's cozy and has soundproof walls. Although back then, I never ever thought that I'd come to find refuge here, in Con's old office, in this condition.

If he knew...

Don't think about that now, Callie.

Don't.

I finally get inside the office but when I go to close the door, something is blocking it.

Or someone.

Him.

The tall broad body of the guy I was running away from.

He has his large hand on the door, pressing against it, stopping it from closing.

He was right on my heels, wasn't he?

When I look into his eyes, all molten and heated, still sporting that dark light of possession, I get my answer. That yes, he was. He was right at my heels, chasing me.

Slowly, I back away from him and slowly and authoritatively, he enters.

His cheeks still have their slightly flushed look and his jaw, stubbled as always at night, is clamped shut as he watches me.

I back away from him. "What are you doing here?"

Without taking his eyes off me, he closes the door behind him and locks it shut. "Chasing after you. As always."

My heart thunders in my chest.

It's not because he locked the door just now. No, that doesn't surprise me anymore.

It's his familiar answer.

That he came here for me. Like he went to the woods last night.

That he was chasing after me.

I shake my head to dispel these stupid, useless thoughts as I keep backing away. "Well, you should stop. You promised, Reed. You promised that we wouldn't see each other again."

"I didn't."

"What?"

His eyes pierce into mine. "You wanted me to promise but I didn't."

I stare back at him, studying his features, which look gorgeous. As gorgeous as ever. Even though his hair's grown out and his strands are messy, all disheveled, probably courtesy of his fingers. Even though there's a certain kind of strain on his features. A certain kind of tiredness and something so akin to regret.

And I realize that he's right.

He never promised.

I wanted him to but he didn't.

So I guess he didn't break it then, the promise. Because he never made it in the first place.

When he notices the realization on my features, his jaw becomes even tighter, his fingers fisting at his sides. "I know I'm a bastard. I know I've lied to you. I've broken promises before. But I'm never going to make a promise to you that I won't keep. Not anymore. And that's a promise."

I finally reach the end of this office.

It's not a very large space to begin with and from what I can see from the corner of my eye, it looks the same. A large wooden desk by the door, a dark leather couch adjacent to it and a dresser right opposite the desk.

Which I touch with my spine and come to a halt, my lips parting.

At his promise.

At the look in his eyes, stark and intense, that makes me want to believe him.

I swallow, pressing my hands on the dresser behind me. "So then why are you here? What do you want?"

My eyes go wide when I say those words.

Those words from our past: What do you want?

Whenever I said those words to him, they ended up changing my life. They ended up being my doom and I can't believe that I've said them now.

Even my body knows it.

The thing inside my body knows it and I feel flutters in my belly. Vicious, brutal. Fierce.

As soon as I say these words, Reed steps away from the door.

He starts to walk toward me. "You."

Even though I knew he was going to say that, I fist my hands and press my spine into the dresser even more. "Me what?"

"To tell me the truth."

"What?"

As I said before, this isn't a big space and so he reaches me in a few long steps. And when he delivers his next statement, he's right here, leaning down over me, his wolf eyes all fiery. "Because this time it's not me, it's you. Who lied."

"Lied about what?"

Bending down even more, he puts both his hands on the dresser behind me and I feel a shake at my back. "About Toby."

My breaths hiccup then.

Toby.

Right.

I've been so engrossed in everything over the past weeks that it never even occurred to me that he might've figured it out. That he might've somehow found out that I was in fact a virgin.

That he was the one who took it, my virginity, like he wanted to.

"How do you…"

"How do I know?"

"Yes."

"Because I saw it."

"Saw what?"

Another shake at my back. "Your blood. On my dick."

My thighs clench. "My b-blood."

The vein on the side of his neck pops out and pulses. "You bled, didn't you?"

I claw my fingers on the dresser. "Yes."

I did.

I hadn't noticed it until I got back to the dorm. There were red spots on my cream panties, the hem of my ivory dress. On my thighs too, super high, just by my core, and God, I saved it.

I saved the dress.

Like some lovesick fool, I put it in the back of my drawer, never to be looked at but never to be thrown away either.

Reed's face blanches for a second at my answer and I almost put my hands on him. I almost soothe the tight lines but I stop myself at the last second.

I stop myself from touching him. Even though my fingers are starving.

"I made you bleed," he says roughly. "I hurt you. You made me hurt you with your lies."

"You didn't hurt me," I blurt out.

He scoffs. "I felt you, Fae. I felt how tight you were. I've been jerking off to it. Like an asshole, I've been blowing my load all over my bedsheets for three goddamn weeks to how tight you were. How I made you cry with my first stroke."

"I —"

"Because you did, didn't you? You cried. So yeah, I hurt you. I hurt her. I hurt your fairy pussy that hasn't had anything inside her. Has she?"

"No."

"No," he rasps, his eyes flicking over my features. "Not a single thing, huh?"

I swallow again, blush burning my cheeks. "My fingers. Sometimes. And a t-tampon."

I don't know why I say it.

Why I tell him that, but I couldn't not.

With the way he's watching me. With the way he's depending on my answer like that, hanging on it.

At my reply, an additional vein on his temple makes its appearance and pulses. "A tampon. So you made me feed my fat dick to a pussy that's only known a tampon. You know my cock is fat and big, don't you? You felt it."

I curl my toes inside my flats as a phantom throb starts up between my thighs. "Yes."

"And you lied to a guy like that. You lied to me." He grinds his jaw. "You pissed me the fuck off with your made-up stories and —"

"I wasn't making up stories," I tell him, craning my neck up. "Toby was real. He did kiss —"

"Shut up," he snaps. "Shut the fuck up right now, Fae. You don't want to finish that sentence. You don't want to finish it when it's been killing me."

"Killing you?"

"Yeah, it's been killing me that I hurt you and I didn't even get to make it better."

"But you did make it better, remember? You hugged me and you —"

"Not like that."

"Then how?"

I feel him shake the dresser again, the biggest shake yet I think. I notice his chest heaving, expanding under his t-shirt, those veins pulsing, beating like the heart he doesn't have as he says, "It's killing me that I made her cry and I didn't get to lick her tears off. I didn't get to soothe her with my tongue. She must've been all sore and puffy. Swollen and red. After the way I abused her. After the way I beat her up with my cock and I didn't even get to suck that soreness away. I didn't even get to make nice with her with my mouth. I didn't even get to tell her that my dick, the thing that hurt her, he's a horny bastard. He wants to hurt her again and again. He wants to use her up but I won't let him. I won't. Not until I take away her pain. Not until I kiss it all better. It's killing me, Fae."

I was wrong.

The shake that I feel when he finishes is the biggest one yet and I lose the battle with myself.

I touch him.

I touch the furious lines of his features, rub my thumbs over his arched cheekbones and the hollows of his face. I even touch him with my body, crash my softness against his harsh surfaces, his hard and heated muscles.

He shudders and I can't stop the undeniable relief that floods through my veins at getting to touch him when I thought that I never would.

Going up on my tiptoes, I tell him, "It's okay, Reed. I swear I was fine. I swear —"

"Was she though?" he asks, cutting me off. "Was she all red and puffy?"

That throb in my core grows and becomes a current, strong and thrumming. "A little. But —"

"Was she swollen too? All bruised up."

"Reed —"

"Was she?"

"Yes."

"How long?"

I press my hand on his face even harder, press my body into his as I answer, "A couple of days. I couldn't..."

"You couldn't what?"

"I couldn't sit in class," I whisper.

His nostrils flare and his jaw jerks under my palm. "You couldn't —"

"But it was fine. I promise. I went to the nurse and I got medication."

"You got medication."

I nod. "For the pain, and so it was fine."

I did.

I kept throbbing between my legs so I went to the nurse and told them I had a headache. Which wasn't that far from the truth anyway. Every part of my body was hurting back then.

I didn't mind the soreness between my legs though.

During all those miserable days, that soreness was the one thing I didn't wish away. And now that it's gone, I wish it back.

I want it to come back, that fullness, that delicious stretch, that hurt, so he can make it better. Because for all my hate and anger at him, I can't see him like this.

I can't see him regret our night, what we did, what I wanted to happen.

"I took care of myself, see?" I continue, looking into his eyes, reassuring him. "I told you. You don't have to protect me all the time. It's not your job."

Anger ripples through his features then.

As if like 'save,' the word 'protect' is his trigger as well. As if he hates that he doesn't get to do that for me.

"Not my job," he pushes out before glancing down.

At my belly, and I suck in a breath.

I pull my hands away from him. I pull myself away and go back down on the floor.

He lifts his eyes and I have to press my spine against the dresser again. Because that possessive light is back. It's dark and bright and hot and it makes flutters move inside my belly.

It makes me think that he knows.

He knows.

"For the last three weeks, I've been trying to track you down," he says, his gaze coming back up. "I've been waiting by the side of the road. I even went to your fucking fence, wanting to scale it. I've been going to your favorite places. To your pink cupcake shop, and I talked to the most boring people I've ever met in my entire life. Just so I can ask them about you. Because —"

And then I have to ask him, how can I not, "What boring people?"

"I don't know. Some waitress."

"Teresa," I breathe out.

"What?"

"Her name is Teresa. The waitress you were talking to."

His eyes narrow. "How the fuck do you know?"

"Because I was there," I confess, lowering my eyes. "I saw you. I thought you'd moved on or something. And when I saw you with her, I —"

"You ran."

I look up at him through my lashes, at the anger in his expression, and nod. "And I know about the fence too. I-I was there last night. I hid behind a tree." He grinds his jaw as I go on. "I didn't want to see you. After… you know."

His jaw tics for a few seconds. "Yeah, I do know. Good thing though I found you here. Because I'm done fucking around. I'm done being played with. Because if I hadn't found you here, this time when I went to your fence, I was about to climb up. I was about to hunt down your dorm room. And make no mistake, I would've found you. I would've woken up your whole fucking school to find you. I would've broken into your dorm and carried you out of there on my shoulders, you understand? Because I'm running out of patience now and we've got things to talk about."

I know.

I know.

I know we do.

But he has to understand that I don't know how. I don't know how to tell him that...

I take a few fearful breaths as my stomach churns. Bile rises up my throat but I somehow manage to whisper a lone word. "I'm..."

Before I trail off.

Before I have to swallow and breathe out.

I can't say it. I can't. I can't.

I...

And he breathes out too.

As he studies my face, as he probably studies the fear on my features.

He grinds his jaw again before exhaling a resigned breath and filling the silence. "First, I want you to know that I'm clean. Do you understand what I'm saying to you?"

It takes me a few seconds to really get his meaning.

When I do, my cheeks get even more heated because I didn't think of that.

In everything, I didn't think of that at all.

"Yes," I whisper.

A grave look enters his eyes. "I mean it. I'm clean. I haven't had sex in a long time. I wasn't lying when I said..."

"You said what?"

Another tic of his jaw. "When I said you haunt me. I'm not gonna lie, I've tried. But I..." He shakes his head. "I couldn't. Mostly because I spent a lot of time in the past two years, either drunk or angry. At the shitty job, at my fucking father. So yeah."

My heart twists at the shitty job.

The thing he has to do because he made a deal with his dad. For me.

God, what a sad, awful pair we make.

"So you... d-didn't?" I whisper, the only thing I can do at his big revelation.

He swallows. "No."

Oh God.

He didn't.

He couldn't. Like me and I...

"I –"

He doesn't let me speak though. "If I wasn't clean, if I didn't know that I was clean, I never would've fucked you raw. Nothing you could've said to make me do that. To put you at risk like that. I want you to know that."

I nod. "I know. I know you wouldn't have."

I absolutely do know.

I know his crazy protectiveness. His crazy need to keep me safe.

Which has been the biggest irony of my life ever since I met him.

Ever since he made me dance for him in the woods.

The villain I fell in love with somehow acts like a hero.

And maybe that's why it didn't occur to me. That he'd put me in jeopardy like that.

As soon as I realize this, I realize something else too.

I realize that he pulled out in the end.

I mean, I knew that. I remember that. I felt him come outside of my body but I hadn't grasped the real importance of it. The true importance of him pulling out.

It was smart, yes, but more than that, he did it to protect me.

He did it to keep me safe.

Even after I asked him not to, he protected me that night in so many ways.

As if he knows what I'm thinking about, he says, "Not that it did much good, did it?"

Before he glances down again and my belly feels warm at his comment.

Heated and alive.

"Reed," I say, and he looks up.

Thank God.

I don't want him looking at my belly.

Not right now.

Not yet.

"You know what else happened that night, don't you?" he asks, studying me. "Besides me taking your virginity."

The quickening in my belly grows.

It grows to epic proportions and I feel this absolute stark need to touch it.

To cradle my flat belly.

Just because he's watching it.

Just because he's waiting for me to say something. When I don't, he asks, "Is there something you want to tell me?"

My chest starts to heave and the craving to touch my belly reaches the sky.

The answer to his question almost bursts out of my mouth and shocks me. I didn't think that this would be my answer. I swear I didn't.

I didn't think my answer would be yes.

Yes, yes, yes.

There is something that I want to tell him.

There is.

For all my running and hiding and denying, I never thought that when he asked me point blank, when he looked at me with those possessive eyes, the urge to tell him would be this strong. That I would have to stop myself from saying it.

That I would have to tighten my body and clench my teeth to keep this thing a secret.

But I have to.

"I'm on the pill," I blurt out.

I'm not.

I tried once, for my bad periods. But it messed me up so much, my hormones and made me throw up so badly that I had to get off it.

"Yeah?"

I jerk out a nod. "Yes."

He licks his lips. "That's an excellent lie, Fae. And it would work on me, if I hadn't bought you dozens of your fucking cupcakes when you get your periods. Because those are the only things that make you feel better. Because you can't even take a pill for it, can you?"

Oh God.

I didn't... I didn't think of that. I'd forgotten that he knows me so well, that he has seen me on my periods and I can't tell him.

Not yet.

I have so many things to figure out. So many things to think about.

All I've figured out so far is that somehow that night wasn't the end. No matter how much I wanted it to be.

That's all.

And I need to think.

I need space. I need...

"One week."

His words break my frantic thoughts. "What?"

Reed's eyes circle my features, study my wide eyes and trembling lips before he takes his arms off the dresser. Before he lets the abused furniture go and opens the muscular cage that he was trapping me in.

He steps back and my sweaty palms slip on the dresser.

"You have a week," he explains, all tall and unapproachable now.

"For what?"

"To come to me and tell me. And this time, Fae, you can't run. You can't hide. Because I need to know." He glances down at my belly again for a second before looking up. "I have to."

With that, he leaves and I sag in relief.

I take my first full breath and all the tightness leaves my body because I have time. He gave it to me.

To figure things out first.

Chapter 14

My mother was eighteen when she had my brother Conrad.

She was a senior in high school and absolutely in love with my dad. When they found out she was pregnant, my mother dropped out and my dad got a job at a local construction company.

I think that company was owned by the Jacksons. Because everything in Bardstown is owned by them.

But anyway, they both dropped out and got married. My mom got a job as a waitress in a local diner and they both promised that they would do everything that they could to love their child and give him a good life.

And then slowly over the years, they had more kids.

With more kids came more jobs, more responsibilities.

Until they had me.

I was an accident. They planned on stopping after Ledger. And I think the fact that I was unplanned — the second unplanned baby after Conrad — made my father decide that he'd had enough.

And so he left.

I've never seen my dad. All I know is that his name was Jeffrey

Thorne and he had golden brown hair and blue eyes. Conrad and me, we take after him. The rest of my brothers take after Mom, dark hair and brown eyes.

I guess when I was little, since no other father figure was ever around and since Con has always been there for me, I thought he was my dad. I think I even used to call him that, Daddy. I don't remember doing any of this but my brothers tell me.

And then Con told me the truth one day when I was old enough to know it; by then my mom had already died.

He told me about our dad leaving right after I was born.

When I asked him if it was me who made him go, he hugged me and he said that no, it wasn't me. That Dad was going to leave anyway. When I asked him if he was going to leave too, he looked me in the eyes, the color of his slightly darker than mine, and said that nothing on this earth would ever make him leave me, nothing at all.

So I guess I never really wondered about my dad because I had Con and the rest of my brothers.

But I have wondered about my mom, Cora.

Over the years, I have dug out her old recipe books, her old clothes that my brothers never threw away. She was the one who always baked and who always knitted sweaters and mittens. I found tons of her knitting books in our attic.

I have wondered about how it would feel to have a mother.

In my head it feels like the most fun ever.

Someone to talk to, someone to gossip with, someone to giggle with. Someone to watch all the chick flicks with, eat ice cream with, talk boy troubles with.

It feels like heaven.

And hell at the same time, because I'll never ever get to experience it.

I'm wondering about my mother now.

I've been wondering about her for the past few days. I've been wondering what she would tell me, how she would react. If she'd be disappointed in me.

That I'm following in her footsteps.

Or if she'd be supportive. If she'd lend a hand and guide me. If she'd be there for me.

Like my friends have. Wyn and Salem and Poe.

I told them. I had to.

I mean, they would've figured it out on their own. I've been throwing up a lot more this week than I was the previous week. And right now, as of this moment, I hate all kinds of meat.

I hate its smell. I hate when I accidentally see it on someone's plate in the cafeteria. I hate when someone even says bacon cheese-burger.

So yes, I've been throwing up.

And not only in the mornings. At nights too.

The only good thing is that miraculously, somehow I make it through classes and so no one else, other than my girls, knows what is up.

I thought they would judge me when I told them. I thought they'd call me an idiot. If not that, then at least a cliché. A high school, small town statistic.

Because I've called myself that. A million times since I found out last Thursday in the woods.

I've called myself names.

I've called myself a stupid, idiot slut who couldn't keep her legs closed for her almost ex-boyfriend. A stupid, idiot slut who didn't think about condoms.

Who couldn't move on and now her life is ruined.

In my most emotional and irrational moments — which have been a lot in the past week — I've cursed at him. I've hated him for ever coming into my life, for making me fall in love with him, for being so difficult to forget, so difficult to hate and so easy to love.

I've thought about not telling him too.

I've thought about keeping it a secret.

Just to spite him. Just to make him suffer. Just because he hurt me two years ago and just because I don't want anything to do with him.

I don't know. I'm irrational.

And pregnant.

I am pregnant.

Pregnant, pregnant, pregnant.

At eighteen.

I'm freaking pregnant.

It's a word that never ever gets out of my head now. I keep saying it to myself and I keep touching my belly.

I keep thinking about what I'll do.

How can I ever turn this around? What good can ever come out of this?

I'm ruined, aren't I?

My life is ruined.

But then two days ago I woke up and my mind was clear.

It was so clear that I decided something.

I decided that I could call myself names and cry about what happened. I could call it a mistake and curse at the fates. I could punish myself like I've always done. Or I could wipe my tears and take charge.

I could make a plan. I could be strong like my mom was and do what needs to be done.

Besides, punishing myself in the past has never worked, has it? Something that he taught me himself.

So I'm not going to do it again, and this time I have someone else to think about other than myself.

So I've been reading up at the library.

Apparently, they have pregnancy books. Like actual pregnancy books, not biology stuff. I wonder who thought to add those to the catalog, at a girl's reform school no less.

But anyway, I've been reading and I've been making lists.

Because I read somewhere that you should make a list when you're anxious. And I'm anxious. Books say that anxiety is a common symptom of being pregnant.

So I can't eat meat. I'm throwing up day and night. I'm anxious and emotional. And I cry a lot too.

But it's okay.

It's fine.

I've got a plan.

It's not a perfect plan, but this is all I have.

My girls seem to like the plan, but they hate parts of it.

"I really think you should reconsider," says Wyn in a hushed voice because we're at the library. "I really think there has to be another way."

"It's fine," I tell her, trying to calm her down. "It's going to be okay."

Wyn doesn't listen. "Remember what Salem was saying the other day? She could talk to Principal Carlisle for you. I bet if Salem talked to her, we could find a way. I mean, I don't think Salem's her favorite person right now but still."

Wyn's talking on Salem's behalf because Salem's not here right now.

She's taking a few days off.

Because remember the problems that she had? Or rather the problem: Arrow Carlisle.

Yeah, that problem blew up last weekend and resulted in what I think — and both Poe and Wyn agree — has to be the biggest ever scandal at St. Mary's School for Troubled Teenagers.

Well, until they all find out about me.

That I'm pregnant.

But anyway, that's the bad news, the scandal. The good news is that I think — and again both Poe and Wyn agree — that the soccer god, Arrow, might be crushing on her as well.

I mean, we're not sure because he hasn't said anything — because he's a guy and he's stupid — but I'm really crossing my fingers that he soon will.

"Okay, fuck talking to people," says Poe loudly before she remembers where we are. Then with a lower voice, "We could try to keep it a secret for a while. I mean, you're not gonna start showing until your seventh month or something anyway. By then it will be too late."

I can't believe she said that.

Especially when we have all these pregnancy books open at the table in front of us.

I look around to make sure no one is listening in before telling my dear friend, "It's the fifth month. You start showing in your fifth." I point to the book. "It says so right here: 'you're glowing and you're showing.' Which if my math is right is going to come around in March."

Then before they can all start arguing again, I shut it down. I tell them that this is the only way.

But I have to do the hardest thing first.

I have to tell my brothers. Tomorrow when I go visit them.

That I'm pregnant with the baby of the guy they all hate.

Because I only have one week before I have to tell him, and this time I'm not going to run.

I'm going to face it all head-on.

***

I think I'm going to throw up.

In the middle of the dining table. At our house.

Because my brother Conrad has ordered all my favorite things. From my favorite restaurant no less.

Bacon and chicken. And mac and cheese.

There's so much mac and cheese, and until I found it on the table, I didn't know that it was one of my triggers. And now I'm going to ruin it all, all the effort he's put in for me.

But it's more than that.

It's more than food.

It's the fact that my other brother is here. The one I had no idea was going to be home this weekend and the one I'm dreading telling this piece of information that I have the most.

Ledger.

In fact he was the one who came to pick me up at school, completely shocking me. And then he whipped out a large pink box from Buttery Blossoms with enough cupcakes for my friends and I threw my arms around him and started sobbing, shocking him in return.

But anyway, here we are now, sitting at the table, eating dinner.

Well, they're eating dinner and I'm just staring at it or at the soft blue wall that has all our photos, from childhood to high school.

Actually, now that I notice, the baby photos are only mine.

Me in a tiny tutu and ribbons; me with my mom at the park; me eating cupcakes with a six-year-old Ledger; me smiling toothily at the camera while sitting on a teenage Con's shoulders; me smiling toothily at the camera again while teenage Shepard and Stellan kiss my fat baby cheeks.

And then there are pictures of me through the years, all grown up, and I realize that this is my life. In pictures.

This wall contains my entire life as I've known it.

With my brothers.

I'm the centerpiece and I never noticed this before.

I never noticed how cherished I am.

I mean, I have, but this is something else.

This is tangible proof and tears well up in my eyes and I'm about to burst out crying but I'm stopped by Con's statement.

"You're not eating."

He's looking at my plate with a frown and I blurt out, "I'm eating."

He looks up at my false answer. "Is there something wrong?"

Yes.

"No. Of course not."

"I ordered your favorites."

"I know," I tell him, nodding as I fist my hands in my lap. "And they are. They've always been. As you know. So thank you."

"So what's the problem?" he asks and my heart starts to beat faster.

My stomach churns and I feel the bile rising up my throat.

This isn't the first time Con has ordered me my favorite foods when I've come for a visit. He might be angry at me for the things I've done in the past, but he's also my brother. My biggest protector. The only father figure I've ever known, and he takes care of me despite everything.

It always makes me feel guilty that despite making his life harder, he still looks out for me.

And my guilt is even stronger tonight. My dread too.

Because I have to tell him.

I know it's going to piss him off. It's going to make him angrier at me than he already is. Maybe he'll think I'm stupid like I was two years ago.

But I can't not tell him.

Last time, I kept everything a secret, making it feel like even more of a betrayal. All the lies that I'd told. All the sneaking around that I'd done.

Even though they've all forgiven me — except Conrad — even Ledger, for falling in love with the very guy they'd told me not to, I know that this time it might be much harder.

This time they might not forgive me at all.

But still, I have to tell them, and maybe I should just get this over with. "Uh, it's —"

"Wait," Ledger says from the other side of me. "Are you on your weird diet again?"

"What?"

Ledger sits back then, shaking his head. "Holy shit, you're on your weird diet again."

"Are you?" Con asks me.

My heart jumps at his question as I swivel my gaze toward him. "Am I what?"

Pregnant.

"On one of your crazy diets," he asks.

Oh. Right.

I swallow thickly. "No, I don't do that anymore." Con looks like he doesn't believe me and so I insist, "I promise. I don't." Then, I turn to Ledger. "I don't, I swear."

Ledger stares at me for a beat before his lips twitch and a chuckle breaks out of him.

I eye him suspiciously. "Are you thinking about... that?"

That chuckle becomes a laugh and he has to put down his fork because suddenly, he's doubling over with it.

I stab my fork at him. "It's not funny, Ledge."

He only laughs harder. "Oh fucking Christ..."

"Stop it!"

He doesn't. "I can't get his face out of my head." He snorts. "He fucking pissed his pants."

I press my lips together to stop myself from laughing even though I know I shouldn't.

I shouldn't laugh at him or his face as Ledger said.

Him being my other goofy brother, Shepard.

But it is funny.

So fine, there was this one time when I was on a juice fast and I baked cookies for Shep and Stellan because they were visiting for the weekend. I wanted to do something nice for them, but now I know that I never should've done that because I was on a diet and was cranky.

And the aroma of them. The taste of chewy cookies and melted chocolate, gah.

I resisted all evening.

I resisted when Ledger told me that I should at least have one. When he waved it under my nose, jerk, to get me to break. I resisted when Shep made all those moaning noises and Stellan told me sternly to just eat the fucking cookie instead of going through with the crazy diet.

But the good, determined girl that I am, I resisted.

Until everyone went to sleep.

I crept down to the kitchen because it was getting harder and harder to fall asleep and I had ballet class in the morning. I thought that one cookie wouldn't hurt.

But it turned out someone was already there and as soon as I saw a silhouette, without really thinking about it, I picked up the first thing I saw, a kitchen cleaner, and started screaming and spraying.

Freaking the bejesus out of who I thought was an intruder.

It was only Shep though.

And I'd somehow sprayed him in the eyes and also on the

cookie that was half hanging from his mouth. That he had to spit out because he was screaming too. And with all the screaming and shouting, the rest of them woke up and ugh.

It was a whole chaotic thing.

"I think you should call him and apologize again," Ledger says, laughing. "He's never going to live that down. He's been tainted for life. Because his sister tried to kill him for eating cookies."

And then I can't stop my own laughter because it was funny, and I guess Ledger is right.

I have scarred Shepard for life.

Now every time he comes around and I make him cookies, they all call him the Cookie Monster.

But my laughter is short-lived because amidst all the snorting and snickering, I hear another deep chuckle.

It's Con's.

And I completely freeze.

It's been so long since I've heard it and it fills me with such great joy that I really don't know what to do. Ledger doesn't have this problem though because he keeps laughing and sputtering, "Remember what he said, 'If this gets out, I'll murder all four of you in your fucking sleep.'"

Con chuckles again. "Yeah. I'd like to see him try."

Ledger stabs a finger at him. "Hey, I could take you. Come on." He raises his arms and flexes his biceps then. "Look at these babies, huh."

Con gives him a bored look. "I could snap you like a twig."

"Ha! You wish, big bro."

"Just eat your dinner."

"You wanna meet me outside?" Ledger challenges. "Come on, let's go. Let's end this here and now and see who's the strongest." He waves at me then. "Come on, Calls, you can be our witness as I wipe the floor with our big brother and begin my supremacy."

I burst out crying then.

I know it's a crazy reaction to my brothers bantering with each other but I can't help myself. Usually my brothers goof around, especially Shep and Ledger, but it's been years since I saw Conrad joining them.

And I know it's because of me.

Because of what I did and how I disappointed my oldest brother.

Maybe I don't have to tell him, I think wildly.

Maybe Poe was right. Maybe I don't have to tell anyone anything, not until it's too late.

"Callie, what's wrong?" Conrad asks, sitting up in his chair, a thick frown between his brows.

Ledger goes alert too. "Hey, Calls, what's up? What —"

Sniffling, I wipe off my tears. "N-nothing. I just… I just miss you guys so much. And I don't get to see you a lot so… yeah, I'm just being silly."

Ledger relaxes. "Oh well, Con's got some big news on that very front."

I sniffle again. "What?"

Ledger gestures at Con and I look at him. Con puts down his fork and straightens up. "They offered me a job. At St. Mary's."

"What?"

"As their new soccer coach."

"Soccer coach?"

Con nods. "I know they have a temporary coach now, Arrow Carlisle. But they want someone permanent because he's leaving to play for his team and they approached me."

I know he's leaving.

It was part of that big scandal with Salem but I… They approached my brother?

"I said yes," he continues. "I thought it was…" He looks slightly uncomfortable right now. "The past two years haven't been great and I thought it would be a good move for the future. Me being there. We could see each other. More. Before you go to college next year."

He said yes.

My brother said yes. Because of me. Because he thought it would be good for us after the awful, awkward two years that we've had.

I don't know what's worse.

The fact that he's ready to end the awkwardness and look to the future or the fact that he's going to take a job at the school that's going to expel me the second I reveal my secret to them. The school where my secret will spread like wildfire. Where they'll call me names. Where they'll gossip about me, tell each other stories about how much of a slut I am.

How stupid I am for getting pregnant in high school.

And my brother is going to be there.

In the midst of it all.

He'll have to face humiliation on a daily basis.

Because of me.

I can't let him.

I can't.

"I'm pregnant."

It comes out garbled.

Even I don't understand it. But I know they did. I know that because everything just… stops.

Everything suspends and freezes.

The clinking of silverware and the dishes. The rustle of feet on the floor. The shifting of their bodies in the chairs.

Their breaths.

My own breath.

"Who?"

That growl belongs to Ledger and I wince.

Even though he hasn't raised his voice. It's the tone. It's the knowledge in that tone.

He already knows who.

I press my hand on my stomach. "I —"

"Is it him? Is it that motherfucker?" he asks again in a low voice, and again I flinch.

I half expect Conrad to growl 'calm down' at Ledger but he doesn't. He's eerily quiet and I want to look at him and ask him to say something.

But Ledger has all my attention. "It is, isn't it? It's him."

"Ledger —"

"Oh Jesus Christ." He springs up from his seat and he does it so violently that his thighs smack against the table, shaking everything, the dishes, the spoons, the ketchup bottle, the water.

He doesn't notice it though. He's looking at me as he walks back.

As if in shock.

And then as if he can't look at me anymore, he spins around and plows his fingers through his hair.

"Ledge, listen to me, please."

He turns around at my voice. "Did he force himself on you? Did that asshole do this to you without your permission?"

My eyes go wide. "What? No." I shake my head. "No. Absolutely not. He didn't. I was —"

"Willing," he speaks over me with gritted teeth and flashing eyes. "You were willing. Is that what you're trying to say? To get fucked by him."

"Ledger," I breathe out.

"What?" he spits out. "You can do it. But I can't say it?"

I blink back tears. "It's not like that. Please, Ledger."

He shakes his head again. "I know he's back in town. And I know he isn't playing anymore. I heard that. I know he quit right after that fucking championship game that ruined everything. I don't know why though. But if history is any indication, I bet it has something to do with his dad, doesn't it?" He laughs, all ugly and angry. "Good. Fucking fantastic. He never deserved to play anyway. He never deserved to go anywhere near a field. He doesn't love the game like we do. He doesn't respect it. So yeah, it's fucking fantastic that he isn't playing anymore. So what, did he use that on you? To get you to sleep with him, huh? Was this a pity fuck?"

Every word out of Ledger's mouth is like shrapnel.

It cuts and bites. And makes me want to tell him to stop.

To just stop.

I can't bear it. I can't bear to hear the hate in Ledger's voice.

"No, he did it to… to save me." I focus on Con then, who's sitting there with a blank, inscrutable expression. "The deal that he made so I didn't go to juvie. His dad wanted him to quit soccer in exchange for my freedom and he did it. He works for his dad now."

He got himself caged because he wanted to gain my freedom.

Then I turn to my other brother, the one who's breathing heavily, staring at me like he can't believe I made the same mistake again. "I know you're angry at him, Ledge, and I don't expect you to forget all the things that he's done to you in the past. But —"

"Have you forgotten?" He speaks over me again as if his rage won't be contained. "What he did to you. How broken up you were, how depressed. How we all had to see you sad. Do you know how difficult it was? Do you realize how fucking hard it was to see you pine over a guy who never cared about you? Who took you for a ride? Who only did what he did to get one over on me?"

I stand up from my seat then.

On shaking legs, I go to him and grab the sleeve of his t-shirt. "No. Absolutely not. I didn't forget. I can't, okay? That's the whole problem. I can't forget what he did and I can't forget him and God, Ledger, I'm so sorry. I'm sorry for putting you through all that. I never meant to fall in love with him. I never meant to betray you. Please, you have to believe me. You're my whole world. You guys are my whole world and I never meant to hurt you. I never meant for any of this to happen."

"But it did."

Swallowing thickly, I nod.

Ledger studies me for a few long seconds before he jerks his arm out of my grip and begins to walk away. He walks out of the dining room and marches down the hallway, and I call out after him, "Ledger, what are you doing?"

I run after him when he doesn't answer.

I find him at the front door, turning the knob and stepping out into the November night. I'm about to go stop him when I hear, "You're not having a baby."

Like before, everything stops.

My heartbeat. My breath.

I turn around to look at him. My oldest brother, who's spoken these words. Who's finally said something after I so tactlessly broke the news to him.

He stands in the living room, just by the leather couch, all tall and broad.

Commanding.

"What?" I whisper.

"You're not having this baby," he repeats.

"W-what does that mean?"

A harsh emotion passes through his features. "It means that

you're going to have an abortion."

I put a protective hand on my belly then. It's not even a conscious thought. "A-abortion."

Con eyes my hand on my belly and his chest moves with a sharp breath.

"I'm going to call Dr. Hartley tomorrow," he says, referring to our longstanding family doctor. "And see if he can recommend a clinic. Something discreet and reputable. I'll try to get an appointment, probably for this weekend. It will be hard but I need this taken care of as soon as possible."

"But I —"

"So you can go back to school Monday."

"But I don't want you to take care of it."

His thick brows draw up together and his voice goes even deeper. "Excuse me?"

Swallowing, I take my hand off my belly and fist my fingers at my sides.

I run through all the arguments and points that I'd listed in my notebook. All the reading I've done and all the information I've collected.

Deep breaths, Callie.

I can do this.

I can absolutely do this. I can make my case.

"I don't want you to take care of it, Con. I-I'm not getting an abortion," I tell him.

"Are you fucking joking?" Con thunders.

I flinch at his tone.

I want to hide at his tone. I want to just agree with him but I can't. I have to fight.

I have to.

I have to think of... her.

"I'm not terminating my baby, Con," I say, trying to hold on to my courage.

"Your baby."

"Yes." I raise my chin. "My baby."

When I was making all the decisions, I also decided that it's going to be a girl.

As I said, I don't remember anything about my mom except what my brothers have told me and it has always made me sad.

Not having a mom. Not having a friend in my mom.

So I'm going to have a friend in my baby girl.

Of course I know that you can't decide these things, but still. I'm going to have a baby girl and I'm going to take care of her. I'm going to love her and be there for her like I imagine my own mother being there for me before she died. And as soon as I decided that, there was no thought of terminating her.

There was no thought of killing my baby.

I've already lost my mother, I'm not going to lose my baby too.

"Your baby that you're having at eighteen fucking years old," he snaps in a raised voice.

This time I'm better able to handle it though.

I hardly flinch when I say, very calmly, "I'm Mom's age when she had you."

His response is to clench his jaw, grind his teeth as he stares at me angrily. But again I don't let it deter me.

I have to make my case.

"I know you think it's a mistake. I know that. I know you think that I can't do it. But I can. I know I'm young and it will be hard. I'm not saying it won't be. But if Mom could do it, I can do it too. In fact, I have a plan. I made a plan, Con."

I look around and find my green backpack sitting on the floor by the coffee table. "I have it in my bag. I have a list of all the things that I need to do before she gets here. First, I'll quit school. I know that's not ideal. I know that. But I need a job and I need to save up money right now. But I'm not giving up on my education. I'm not. I've decided to get my GED while I wait for her to be here, and once she gets a little bigger, I'll enroll in online classes or night classes. There are so many options these days, Con. It's not like before. I looked at so many brochures online and you can take out student loans. There are options for young mothers, see?

"And I know that..." This is slightly harder but I have to do it and so I forge on. "I know I have to quit ballet. I have to quit the dream of being a ballerina. But it's okay. I'll get a new dream. I'll get a new goal. I can do it. For myself and for her and —"

"Who's her?" he asks.

His voice has calmed down and I can't help but think that maybe I'm making headway. Maybe he gets it now. I'm not all prepared but at least I have a starting point, right?

I touch my belly again and smile hesitantly. "Her. I think it's a girl."

He stares at my midsection for a beat, expressionless. Then, "What job?"

"What?"

"What kind of a job are you going to get?"

"I was thinking my summer job. At Buttery Blossoms," I say. "I guess it won't be enough though. So I'll try to get a second job. Maybe nights or something. Or on the weekends."

"And where will you live? While you're out of school, working two jobs."

I swallow.

For this, I need him. I really need him and strangely, I'm so afraid to raise this point.

I shouldn't be though.

He's my brother. Of course he'll see the wisdom in it. But God, after the past couple of years that we've had and the way he's reacting right now, I don't know.

I don't know what he's going to say but I answer him nonetheless. "I was thinking here. With you. Until I save up enough to move into my own apartment."

"Here."

"Yes."

"No."

"I'm sorry?"

"You're not living here," he says again, declares almost. "And neither am I going to sit back and watch you destroy your life like this. That's why you're going to get an abortion. I'll take you to a clinic and you'll get it done and then we'll never speak of this again."

"I'm not getting an abortion, Con. I'm not," I repeat, this time in a louder voice, something I didn't think I was capable of tonight. "Mom didn't —"

"Mom is fucking dead," Con snaps, his anger so thick and palpable, his blue eyes are shooting fire. "She's gone and she isn't coming back. But I'm here and I'm telling you that you're getting an abortion and going back to that school to get your diploma. And then you're going to that community college to become the fucking ballerina that you've wanted to be since you were five years old. End of discussion."

I stare at him, speechless.

It's not that I begrudge him his anger. Not at all.

He's well within his rights to be mad at me. To be disappointed in me, but I don't know how to explain it to him that even though I never expected to get pregnant at eighteen and it wouldn't have been my first choice, I can't kill her.

I can't even call her a mistake because if I call her a mistake, then what about the rest of the world? The odds are stacked against her anyway and I have to do everything in my power to make it easier for her.

She's mine.

I can't undergo a cold procedure to flush her out of my body.

I'm already in love with her.

Conrad sighs then, deeply, heavily, as if trying to get himself under control as he begins, "She never finished high school, Mom. You know that, right? She dropped out. She never went to college. Never went anywhere outside of this town. Never did anything. She was born here and she fucking died here. And when she was alive, she worked three jobs. Three fucking jobs. But even that wasn't enough. She was always falling short, cutting corners. She couldn't afford day care. So I had to stay home whenever I could to babysit you guys.

"Do you think I liked that? Do you think I liked taking care of you? Wiping up spit and vomit? Cleaning up after you? Do you think a fourteen-year-old enjoys something like that? Instead of hanging out with my friends, chasing after girls, I was chasing after you. I was always chasing after my brothers and sister. When I went to college, on a soccer scholarship no less, I thought I was finally free. I thought I could live my own life now. But then she died. I wasn't even in college for a full month when I had to come back. To take care of you all. Do you think I never had dreams of my own? Do you think all my dreams are tied to yours?

"Mom made a mistake. A huge mistake by having me when she wasn't ready. And I had to pay for it. Me." He pounds his chest. "I have to pay for it for the rest of my life. Is that what you want for your baby? To pay for your stupid mistakes? And what about him? Do you think he'll help you?"

Him.

At the mention of him, the flutters in my belly go haywire.

I know — I read in the books — that you don't really feel the baby until your fourth month. But I don't care what the books say.

I can feel her now.

So strongly. So vividly.

She does this whenever he's mentioned. Like she knows him already.

"I always told you to stay away from him. Always. He's exactly like our father," Conrad says. "Selfish. Arrogant. Irresponsible. Mom kept thinking that he would change. He would make promises that he would. But I saw him for what he was. He was a fucking asshole who never kept his promises. Who lied and who cheated on her over and over. I never told you that, did I?"

Shocked, I shake my head and whisper, "No."

"Yeah, he'd cheat on her. He'd sleep around. Why? Because his freedom was taken away too soon. Because he didn't want responsibilities. So Mom had to bear them. So Mom had to work herself to the bone to provide for all of us. I was happy the day he decided to leave. We were better off without him. Mom was better off without him. She bloomed after he left. Because he was poison. Mom kept thinking that he was a hero but he turned out to be a villain. Like him. The asshole who didn't even protect you from all this."

He did.

He did protect me.

He's protected me in so many ways and hurt me in so many others but he did try to protect me from this.

It didn't work. But he did try.

"It doesn't matter anyway." Conrad releases a long sigh. "Because if Ledge doesn't kill him, I will. And I will make it painful. So you better pray that Ledge finishes the job and kills that asshole before I get my hands on him. But make no mistake, Callie, I won't let you ruin your life. I won't let you ruin your dreams. I couldn't protect you before but I'm going to protect you now."

Chapter 15

The Hero

"Jackson!"

I hear my name shouted like a vile curse from behind me and I stop walking.

I knew he'd come for me.

I got a couple of texts from my old high school buddies that Ledger has been asking about me, about where to find me. They didn't tell me why but I could figure it out.

I could figure out that they knew.

That she'd told them.

I knew she was home this weekend. Pest told me because I asked. Because I'm done pretending that I don't want to keep tabs on her.

Especially now.

And so I've been waiting for him, for Ledger, to come for me.

Like I was two years ago.

When I broke his little sister's heart and him and his friends jumped me in the woods, the ones where she danced for me for the first time. Took him two days to come get me back then.

I'm glad he's working faster now.

Turning around, I fist my hands at my sides as I watch Ledger stride through the parking lot. I just got done at the office, poring over this new construction project in the town of St. Mary's, a strip mall.

It's exactly as boring as it sounds but I don't care.

I don't fucking care that I have to work at this company. That now I might have to keep doing it for the rest of my life.

Before, I used to think I might get out one day.

When she's graduated from St. Mary's and she's at Juilliard, too far away for my father to touch, I might think about winning this war.

But now I don't care about getting out.

I'll work here, if I have to. For the rest of my life. If that's what it takes to keep my father happy and out of my life.

I have other concerns now.

Other goals. Other wars that I need to win, like protecting people.

Keeping them safe and untouched at all costs.

At any fucking cost.

When her brother reaches me, I nod at him. "Ledger."

His chest is moving up and down in agitation. I can hear his furious breaths.

He's always been a hothead. Not a good quality in a soccer player, but extremely helpful when you want to screw with someone. And I have. Screwed with him. A lot.

Just because I could. Just because it was fun.

Just because I was at war with my father and I wanted to win and Ledger was in my way. He's more collateral damage. So I don't blame him when, instead of using his words, he uses his fist on me.

I even see it coming.

I see his shoulders twitch and tighten, his right arm shifting back a little before he swings it and lays one precisely on my jaw.

Fuck.

He's gotten stronger, hasn't he?

The pain explodes in my jaw and I ricochet back, almost stumbling. But somehow, I don't go down. I manage to stay upright, and that pisses me the fuck off.

This is all he's got?

After what I did to his sister.

So when I finally straighten up, crack my neck and tap my pulsating jaw to get ready, I decide to up the ante. "Well, good to see you too, Ledge."

My casual response enrages him more, as I knew it would. And so the next time he comes at me, he does it harder. So much so that I go back a couple of steps, my jaw on fire.

Yet I don't go down.

Yet I straighten back up and face him, his wrathful eyes, his furious face as he bites out, "You fucking asshole."

What the fuck is he doing?

He's embarrassing himself. He's embarrassing me.

I need him to do better than that.

"Yeah, same to you." I jerk my chin at him. "Not that I don't enjoy our witty repartee but care to enlighten me on why we're meeting like this? Feels like old times."

The vessel on his temple seems to be on the verge of exploding. "You're fucking kidding me, right?"

I pretend to think about it. "Not really, no. If I was, you'd be laughing. Trust me. I've got a killer sense of humor."

Another punch.

Now we're getting somewhere.

"You know, we could go back and forth like this," I tell him, panting, wiping the blood off my chin, "or you could just tell me what the fuck your problem is. So I can properly thank you for this special treatment."

That does it, I think.

That gets him going and he stares at me like I'm the lowest of the low. "Yeah. Yeah, let me tell you what you did. Let me tell you exactly what you did, you motherfucker."

With that, he launches himself at me.

His fists come crashing down, his bones connecting with mine, over and over and over.

And I take it all.

I welcome it all. I welcome his wrath, his fury, his anger.

I welcome his disgust at me.

It finally matches mine.

It finally rivals my crime. What I did to her.

And yet it's not enough. Not for him or for me.

So he keeps going.

He keeps punching me, hitting me, and I keep taking it and stumbling back and when I think he's finally beaten me down enough that I'm going to lose my footing, my back connects with something.

My Mustang.

My fucking Mustang saves me from going down.

And Ledger grabs my collar, pulling at it and smashing my back against the metal. "Did that jog your memory, huh? You remember what you did now?"

I'm panting; every muscle in my body throbs and pulses. My fucking legs are trembling and yet I'm still standing. It pisses me the fuck off.

"I think…" I breathe out, tasting blood. "I'm gonna need a little more."

He shakes me again, making my bones jar, and I groan.

"You fucking asshole, you ruined her life. You ruined her life. You realize that, don't you? You realize what you did to my sister."

I do, yeah.

I do realize it. I realize that I've ruined her now. I've destroyed her.

I speak through the pain in my chest, in my body. "You really don't wanna know… what I did to your sister."

As expected, he pushes me into the car again.

"You're a fucking piece of shit, aren't you?" He tightens his grip on the collar of my dress shirt. "I should kill you for what you did to her."

"You should."

"But if I killed you tonight, then you wouldn't be able to see."

I spit out blood. "Yeah? See what?"

He chuckles then, his fingers tightening. "What I'm going to do to your sister." Another chuckle. "She's a firecracker, isn't she? Tempest."

I don't know where I get the energy, the strength to move my hands, let alone grab his collar. I don't know where I get the strength to shake off his hold and fucking maneuver him so I have his back against my Mustang now.

All I know is that if he says my sister's name again, I'm going to rearrange his face in a way that he's not going to like.

"Don't talk about my sister," I growl, my body screaming in pain.

"Yeah?" he bites out. "Pisses you the fuck off, doesn't it? And I haven't even done anything yet. To her."

"You want to kill me, Ledger, you better stop talking. Because if you rile me up enough, it's going to be you who dies tonight."

He laughs, sharp and hollow. "Yeah, I don't think so."

And then, I feel the sharpest, fieriest pain that I've ever felt in my life. So much so that I finally stumble back and my body goes down.

I finally fall on my knees, my vision going blurry for a few seconds.

Because Ledger has kicked my ankle. My right ankle, which has weakened from years of playing soccer. And since he's played with me, used my weakness against me on the field due to our rivalry, he knows about that.

Like I know that his left knee bothers him more than the right because of an old injury he had back in our junior year.

"Watch your back, Jackson," he says, moving away from the car and laying a last punch on my jaw that makes me go completely down on my back. "You don't want to mess with people who know your weaknesses. Years of soccer should've taught you that."

He leaves then.

While I stay on the ground, my entire body on fire, chuckling at the pain, watching the night sky.

***

In a white dress and a flimsy green cardigan, she stares at something.

Through the window of her darkened studio.

She doesn't know that there's a Mustang parked a block over and I'm sitting in it. And that I'm watching her. I've been watching ever since she scared the fuck out of me when she appeared out of nowhere, walking down the street.

In fact, I don't think she knows anything that's happening

around her.

And with every second that passes, my anger mounts.

What the fuck is she thinking?

What the fuck is she doing here in the middle of the night?

Where in the fucking fuck are her brothers now? Especially now when they know that she needs to take better care of herself. Especially now that they know how I fucked her over.

Again.

Only this time I've done it worse.

And so this is pissing me the fuck off.

That she's out here alone.

But more than that, it's making my chest tight, my lungs contract as I watch her stand there, looking at her dream through the glass.

I've been watching it too.

That dream.

For the past week, I've either been working on my Chevy at Auto Alpha for long hours — Pete thinks I've gone crazy but he doesn't interfere because he knows what I did — or I've been driving here to this street, watching her dark studio.

Just so I can imagine her, dancing, spinning on her toes inside that building.

Like a fairy.

Like she was born to do.

She moves then.

She walks away from her studio and I can't get air inside my body. I choke on the pain as she stops a few paces down. In front of another ballet studio: Baby Blues.

A sister branch of Blue Madonna, where they teach ballet to little girls.

It was the studio she went to before switching over to Blue Madonna, I know. I've seen her through the glass window countless times.

She's pressing her hands on that same window now, as if she can see something. As if she can see, she can imagine, picture her — our...

"Fuck," I mutter quietly as my sternum almost caves in on me, and climb out of the car.

I snap the door shut, the sound of it echoing in the night and finally alerting her that someone's here.

She spins around, her eyes finding me.

I stride toward her and I see her shoulders sag in relief. I even see a small, trembling smile on her lips and I think I've lost my mind, that pain is making me hallucinate.

But at least I have enough sense left that I know it's real when she stumbles on her feet. And I hasten my steps to get to her, catch her, before she falls.

I wind one arm around her tiny waist and the other behind her knees and pick her up.

"Reed," she gasps, her blue eyes wide. "Thanks."

I clench my jaw. "What are you doing out here?"

She frowns and clutches my t-shirt. "I'm taking a walk."

"You can barely stand."

"I can too." She sticks her bottom lip out. "If you put me down, I can show you."

"I'm not fucking putting you down."

She rests her head on my shoulder, peeking up at me through her eyelashes. "You know, you curse too much, Reed."

"That's the least of my crimes."

She sighs. "I know."

I squeeze her body in response and it feels much too thin.

She's small to begin with, tiny bird-like bones, but I know that she's lost weight. I can feel it.

I can see it too.

I can see that she's ruined. Completely and irrevocably.

Her cheeks are sunken and there are deep circles under her eyes. Eyes that are red and swollen. From all the crying, I assume.

This is me.

I've done this.

She raises her hand and lightly grazes her fingers over a bruise, studying me as I've been studying her. "Ledger did this, didn't he?"

"Doesn't matter."

"You look completely destroyed."

I have to chuckle at this. Harsh and angry.

At the fact that she's been thinking the same thing as me.

"It's fine," I tell her again and begin to walk.

"That's what you used to say. Two years ago."

"Yeah, things haven't changed much since then. I'm still the same asshole. Besides, this isn't anything that I didn't deserve, so."

Her eyes fill with tears and I squeeze her against my body again, her tears enflaming my pain, making my injuries throb.

"I told them," she confesses. "I only wanted to tell Con but Ledge was home too. I didn't know that he was going to be there. And Con, he wants me to get an a-abortion and —"

"Doesn't. Matter," I snap out again.

Abortion.

My body recoils at the word and I almost fall down on my knees. The only reason I manage to stay upright is because I've got her in my arms and I'll be fucking damned if I'm dropping her.

Fucking abortion.

I want to do something drastic, fuck up this world because of how much I hate that word, but it's not my decision to make, is it? It's not my motherfucking decision.

I can feel her blinking up at me, all drowsy. "Where are you taking me?"

"To my car."

"The one I stole?"

"Yes. The one you stole."

"How did you get it back to how it was before?"

"What?"

"The car," she explains. "It feels like before."

"I worked on it all summer. Back then."

"All summer?"

"Yeah."

She hums. "I didn't mean to do it. To steal your car."

I squeeze her again. "You've already said that."

"Why were you so mean to me? You said all those things that night. I can never forget them."

"Because I wanted you to hate me," I say against the tightness in my throat.

"Why?"

"Because I broke my promise to you."

She has an adorable frown on her forehead. "Oh. Well, I did. I do. Hate you. And that's why I'd never tell you."

"Never tell me what?"

"That you're a genius."

"A genius."

She hums again. "Yeah. A car genius. And a soccer genius. I hate how good you are with things." She gasps then. "Maybe you should do it for a living. Build cars. And get out of your awful job."

"Just go to sleep."

She doesn't. She rubs her cheek against my neck, making her geranium and sugar scent explode over my senses. "I'm going to miss it."

"Miss what?"

"Spinning on my toes."

Not yet, I tell myself, I can't fall on my ass while I have her in my arms.

I squeeze her featherlight body again – I can't seem to stop – almost plaster her to me, and somehow she likes that.

She likes my brutal grip and sighs happily, her eyes closed. But she won't stop talking. She won't stop making my body hurt with her words. "But it's okay. I don't care about ballet anymore. I don't even care about Juilliard. I care about other things now. Her…"

"Go. To sleep," I growl.

And she does.

Fucking finally.

When I deposit her in the car and buckle her in, my eyes drop down to her flat stomach. I stare at it for a few beats, feeling my heart thunder in my chest.

Before lifting my eyes up to her peacefully sleeping face.

I promised her the other day at the bar that I'll never make a promise to her that I won't keep. And so I repeat the promise I'd made a week ago — as soon as I saw her touch her stomach — now.

I promise that I'm done hurting her.

I'm done ruining her.

From now on, along with protecting her from the rest of the world, from my fucking father and his evil clutches, I'll protect her from me.

I'll protect them both.

Chapter 16

Part II

The Lonely Boy & The Girl in Love

This isn't my home.

I know this as soon as I open my eyes and take in the space around me.

Grayish-white walls, hardwood floors. A giant window taking up the entire wall to my left.

Even the height of the bed, when I climb out of it, is wrong. It's too high, the mattress too thick and fluffy.

But the thing that gets my heart going the most is the scent.

It's a scent I know.

It's a scent that's deeply and achingly familiar to me, but there's also something different about it. Something so soothing that my stomach that roils in the morning is strangely calm.

I'm not sure what this soothing aroma is but I'm thankful for it.

I'm thankful and I'm frantic as I leave the room, dash out of it really, my bare feet slapping on the hardwood floor.

I have no idea what this place is or where I'm going as I almost run down the hallway that's flanked with white doors, but I know who it might belong to.

I know who brought me here.

Him.

He did, didn't he?

Instead of taking me back home, he brought me to this strange place that for some reason doesn't feel as strange as it should.

It's his scent, I think, and all the white.

Last night I wasn't thinking clearly.

I was hurt and sad and afraid. It was like someone was sitting on my chest, suffocating me. So I snuck out of the house to get some fresh air.

I wasn't expecting to walk for so long or to end up at Blue Madonna. I wasn't expecting to see him there either. I wasn't expecting to be brought here.

When I come out of the hallway into the living space filled with soft blue-colored couches and cozy rugs and see him sitting at the marble kitchen counter, bent over something, I don't expect to feel a painful twisting in my heart.

A deep angst in my gut.

Ledger did a number on him.

Last night I was so out of it, I barely noticed the extent of the damage he had done. But under the bright kitchen lights, I can see it all.

The red-purple bruises, dark and angry and so painful looking. Both his eyes are red and swollen. His lip is cut. His jaw is bruised up and I can't be sure but I think his nose is dented.

Maybe I gasp or make a distressing noise at the pain that he must've felt last night, must still be feeling, because he looks up and his wolf eyes connect with mine.

All those conflicting feelings that I always experience when he's around make my knees weak, but I pace myself and start with the most obvious thing. "This isn't my home."

Instead of answering me, those wolf eyes of his take me in and for the first time I realize what a wreck I must look right now.

My dress is all wrinkled. I probably have sleep lines on my face, or at least my features must be swollen with it, with sleep. My hair feels all messed up, flowing down my back, my braid coming untied during the night.

"You sleep well?" he asks.

"What is this place?" I ask, looking around. "What am I doing here?"

He pushes something away, a book, I notice, and straightens up. "It's a vacation home."

"What vacation home?"

"A place where people go to take a vacation."

"Is it yours?"

"For now."

I'm confused. "What —"

"You never answered my question," he cuts me off. "Did you sleep well?"

"What? That's not even the point. The point is —"

"The point is that you were tired. You could barely stand up. I had to carry you to my Mustang. So I'm asking you how are you feeling when you shouldn't have been out at midnight in the first place."

God.

Him and his stupid protectiveness.

I fist my hands in frustration but then release a sigh and answer just to get this over with so we can get to the point. "I'm fine. Thank you. I shouldn't be here. I should be back home. I should be with my brothers."

"And I'll take you there."

Frantic, I walk closer to him. "You'll take me there. Are you insane?"

"Not the last time I checked," he answers casually, every single bruise on his face standing out against his vampire skin.

"Oh my God," I breathe out. "You are insane. Do you know what will happen when my brothers see that I'm missing? They'll freak out. They'll lose their minds, and then you'll roll in, in your Mustang, dropping me off, and they'll think that you kidnapped me or something." I shake my head and look over his shoulders and out the kitchen window. "No, you will not take me home. You need to put me in a cab right now. It's still dark out so maybe they don't know that I'm gone yet, okay? Call me a cab."

"No."

"What?" I throw my hands up in exasperation. "Do you not see how this is going to look? They'll call the cops on you, Reed, and I'm not even kidding right now."

"I know all the cops."

"Fine." I fold my arms across my chest. "Then they'll kill you themselves. Ledger already did half the job, didn't he?"

"He did, and they're welcome to try."

Agitated, I unfold my arms and fist my fingers. "What are you doing? I need to get back home, Reed. Conrad would be so worried and furious and —"

"He has nothing to do with this."

Finally, Reed's voice is raised. His tone is tight and angry, matching the occasion.

Suddenly I remember what I told him last night. About abortion. Up until now I didn't, but as I stare into his intense eyes, his tight mouth, I remember.

"Does he?" he asks with clenched teeth.

I swallow. "No."

"Good. We're on the same page then."

"But —"

"Your one week is up."

The calmness in my belly vanishes. It's not the nausea that plagues me every morning though. It's the flutters. The heat. The life inside of it.

It's like she's waking up.

Even though she isn't more than a few cells, occupying the littlest of spaces, I still feel her waking up and I take a deep breath. "I know."

His jaw clenches then, as he stares at me and slowly stands up, his bar stool screeching against the floor. Again slowly, he puts his hands on the island, his fingers splayed out, his veins standing taut. As if he's using the island to keep his balance.

As if his body is trembling as badly as mine.

"Tell me," he says in a low voice, the muscles of his shoulders stark in his white t-shirt. "Give me the words."

I wanted to tell him a week ago when he asked me at the bar. But I'm glad I didn't because I had nothing figured out then. I have a plan now and he's a very important part of it.

And so I've thought about him a lot.

I've thought about what's going to happen between me and him, between us.

But like he said that night, there's no us.

There will never be.

That's why everything happened and that's why we're here. So

I've decided that I'll give him a choice. And he's going to decide what he wants.

I cradle my stomach and watch his chest move with a breath as I whisper, "I'm pregnant."

At first, he doesn't do anything except remain still. Making me think that his breath has frozen. Even his blood has stopped flowing.

But then his lips part and he exhales.

His chest moves again and his hands, glued to the island, shake slightly.

"Pregnant," he repeats.

I press my belly. "Yes. With your baby."

He drops his eyes to my abdomen, making my fingers feel a sudden heat, making me think that he wanted to do it, to stare at my belly, for the longest time. But he was stopping himself for some reason.

"With my baby."

This time when he repeats my words, his voice has whittled down to a whisper. His bruised, beat-up features have whittled down to the most minimalist of expressions.

And I'm not really sure what he's thinking, but like I did with Con last night, I have to stay strong. I have to keep marching on and say all the things that I want to say. "And I'm keeping it."

He looks up. "You're keeping it."

"Yes." I raise my chin and widen my stance as I continue, "I'm keeping her. I'm not getting an abortion. I can't get an abortion. I just can't. I can't even bring myself to say the words without wanting to throw up, so, I can't do it. But I understand if you're not okay with that. I understand. I mean, what guy wants to be a dad at twenty-one? Not to mention, our situation is even more complicated. We have issues. You have issues with love. I have issues with you. And every time we come together, all we ever seem to do is make things even more complicated and hurt each other. And I wanted that to end. We were supposed to come to an end that night. Instead now we're tied... for life.

"So I understand if you don't want any part of this. I understand if you think this is a mistake. But she's not a mistake for me. I want her. I'm keeping her and I don't expect anything from you. I can do this on my own and I will. I have a plan and —"

"What's the plan?"

This is the second time someone has asked me about it, and even though I'm still reeling from Conrad's anger and rejection, I tell Reed. Because I will keep telling anyone who asks. I will keep repeating it until the whole world knows that I'm going to fight for her.

I keep my chin lifted and my battle stance grounded as I say, "I'm planning on quitting school. I'll talk to the principal this Monday, move out and get a job. I was planning to live with Con but I think I'm gonna get my own place now, something cheap, and save up. Of course, Juilliard is no longer an option and that's fine. I know I have other talents. I can figure things out for myself. But I'm not getting rid of her."

The silence that follows feels excruciating.

Maybe because I've been talking a lot. I've said too many words and now the quiet is unbearable.

Especially when the only thing that's filling it is my panting, heaving breath.

"Her."

Even though he's only said one word after my deluge of them, flutters move and swirl in my belly, and for the second time since last night, I say, "It's a girl."

I detect another shake of his arms. "Y-you already..." he swallows, "know..."

It's the shake in his voice that gives me some indication. Some clue as to what he wants. Because I've never ever, in all the time that I've known him, seen him this unsure, this shaken and taken aback.

But I'm afraid to hope.

I'm afraid.

"No, I don't. I can't… it's too early. But I want it to be." Before I can stop myself, I ask, with stupid hope in my voice, "Do you have a problem with that?"

He slowly shakes his head. "No."

I exhale a breath. "You don't?"

"No." He licks his lips as he keeps staring at me. "I'd like a girl."

My eyes circle wide. "You w-would?"

"Yeah, a tiny ballerina in a pink tutu with blonde pigtails. I'd like that."

He'd like that.

He said that, right?

He said, he'd like that. He'd like a girl with blonde pigtails and a pink tutu and Jesus Christ, I think I can breathe. Relief bursts through my veins and my body sags. "Well, she could… she could have dark hair."

Like you.

Like her…

Like her daddy's.

I think he hears my unspoken words because his lethal, animal eyes melt. "No, she's going to have blonde hair."

Like you. Like her mommy's.

He doesn't say it either but I hear it. He's not done talking though and these next words he says fiercely. "And she's not a mistake. It doesn't matter how she… she came into existence. But she's not a fucking mistake."

His words, intense and spoken with so much heat, shock me.

They leave me speechless for a few seconds and all I can do is blink at him.

But then I notice something.

On the island, where he's still standing bent over.

A book, and as I stare at it, my words burst forth. "You're reading a book."

He straightens up abruptly. "And?"

I ignore his defensive tone. "I've never seen you read a book before. Not even in school. But…" I'm still staring at it when it occurs to me. "It's a pregnancy book." I snap my eyes to him. "You're reading a pregnancy book."

His cheekbones are flushed and he rubs the back of his neck, frowning. "It's not exactly noteworthy."

He even picks up the book from the counter and puts it in the drawer, as if he's embarrassed at being caught. And I can't… I can't help but think it is.

It is noteworthy and it is crazy and gosh, adorable that he's so embarrassed. And so unlike him.

And I can't help but ask, "You've been preparing, haven't you? You've been reading up. For the past week. Like me."

He stares at me a few moments, his jaw tight before he replies, "Yes."

Yes.

He has. He's been preparing like me.

Even though I'd been running from him, even though I hadn't told him myself, he was getting himself ready. He was reading up on things like me.

"What if I had told you…" I pause to calm down my racing breaths. "What if I'd said that I didn't… I didn't want her."

His eyes pierce into mine. "Then I'd have…" Now he pauses and I know that it is for the same reason as me, to calm down his heaving chest. "I'd have taken care of it. If that's what you wanted."

I know he would have.

I can see it on his face. In the determined look of his eyes. I also know that he wouldn't have liked it; that's also apparent on his face, but he would've let me make the decision.

Up until this point, up until he said it, I hadn't known that it was important to me.

This freedom of choice.

As important as it is that he wants her too. He really wants her. He doesn't think she's a mistake, and suddenly, everything sinks in.

Everything settles in my bones, the relief, that I feel dizzy.

I feel it so much that I stumble.

But he doesn't let me fall.

Like last night, he's there to catch me. He's there to put his hands on my waist to steady me. Not only that, he also picks me up and puts me down on the island.

"Are you okay? Are you… are you going to be sick?" he asks, his warm hands holding me tightly, keeping me grounded.

Without really thinking about it, I move closer to the warmth. I latch onto it with my fingers, grabbing onto his forearm and trying to breathe.

And I get a whiff of that scent again.

That scent which calms down my stomach, and I whisper, "What is that?"

"What?"

"T-that scent. It…" I swallow and dig my nails in his forearms. "It makes me…"

"Makes you what?" he asks, a thick frown between his brows. "What the fuck is going on, Fae? You want me to —"

I steal his words by fisting his t-shirt and pulling him close. I bury my nose in his chest and breathe him in, moaning, "Oh God."

He cradles the back of my head, his chest swelling and contracting against my burrowed-in face. "What —"

I cut him off again, this time with words though. "What is that scent?"

His fingers flex on my waist. "What scent?"

I look up at him. "That scent. Coming from you. Your t-shirt. It makes me feel better. I know it's not your regular scent."

"What's my regular scent?"

I nuzzle my nose in his hard, heated chest first before replying, "Wildflowers and woods."

He's offended, his chest vibrating with his words. "I smell like flowers."

"Uh-huh."

"Bullshit."

I can't believe I want to laugh when my body is rebelling against me, even though his scent and his heat have helped a little, but I do. I also want to tease him a little bit more so biting my lip, I tell him, "You do. It's like super sweet and —"

"Yeah, let's not talk about it."

"What, boys can smell like flowers."

"Your brothers tell you that?"

"They can also twirl, Reed," I tell him primly.

He squeezes me slightly, his eyes liquid. "Thanks for all the information, Fae."

"You're welcome." I nod, my lips trembling with an oncoming smile. "Oh, and it's okay for them to taste like cupcakes. Like you do."

I let my lips go then and grin. I chuckle even. But it only lasts a second, a microsecond actually.

When I realize what I just said.

I realize that I mentioned his taste and now it has come alive in my mouth. On my tongue.

It's crazy because I've only ever tasted him twice. How is it that I remember it so well? How is it that even now I want it, I want to feel it, eat it, inhale it like I'm inhaling his scent.

But that's not even the thing to worry about here. The fact that I've said something that I shouldn't have and now I can't get his phantom taste out of my mouth or I can't stop looking at his slightly parted ruby red lips.

The thing to worry about is that he's heard me.

And he's gone still.

Like a stone. A rock. A towering mountain with hard heated muscles and a battered gladiator face.

"I didn't…" I trail off because I was going to lie.

I was going to say that I didn't mean it, but I did. I did mean it because he does taste like cupcakes, sweet and toxic for my dancer's body.

Before I can say something else however, his jaw moves, still bruised and stubbled from last night, and his fingers clutch at me tightly for a second before they let go.

Before he moves away.

And in that process, I realize how close he was to me.

How my legs were spread so shamelessly, like they were on that night, and how my dress had inched up to the tops of my thighs. And how, how, it feels when his coarse jeans rub against my smooth skin.

How it takes my breath away.

When he's standing at a distance, I snap my thighs closed and lower my dress, a blush burning my cheeks.

This is not the time to think about that. It's never going to happen again.

I don't want it to happen again.

Reed's wolf eyes flash before he says, "It's my fabric softener."

"What?"

"The scent. I'll stock up on it."

"Oh." I grab the edge of the island and press my thighs together, feeling cold and bereft without his heat. "Thanks."

"What else?"

My heart thunders then.

Not that it stopped, really. It has been thundering ever since I found myself in this strange yet cozy house. Ever since I told him, and ever since he told me that he wants her.

But this is something else.

This is even more savage, this thundering.

It comes from his question. What it means and the look in his eyes when he asked it.

It's the same look that he has when he watches me dance. The intensity, the eagerness, the way his big body goes taut as a string.

He wants to know. Things about me.

He wants to know what I've been going through these past days. Doesn't he?

"Uh, I just get dizzy sometimes," I say hesitantly and I'm proven correct when his eyes flare with curiosity. "And I throw up a lot."

At this he frowns though. "What's a lot?"

I tuck my wayward hair behind my ears. "Like in the mornings. And also at night."

"Fucking morning sickness," he mutters angrily.

I can't believe he knows that.

I mean, morning sickness is the most common symptom of pregnancy and he has been reading books but I just… it's surreal.

So surreal that this is happening.

That I'm pregnant. With his baby.

And he wants to be a part of this. Not only that, I'm talking to him about my morning sickness. In all my planning, I never planned this.

I never planned that I would want to tell him. That I'd be talking to him like a girl who's pregnant by a guy she loves and so she wants to share every little detail, every little complaint, every tiny change that she's experiencing.

And I definitely never ever planned that he'd want to know, that he'd get upset over these changes and look so helpless standing there with his fists clenched and his angry frown. Like he's really a guy who loves that girl back and he wants to do everything that he can to make things easier for her.

And like always when he gets upset about something, I want to put him at ease. "But it's fine. I mean, saltines help. Also tea. Ginger tea if I can find it in the cafeteria."

"I've got saltines," he bursts out. "I don't have ginger tea though. But I'm going —"

"It's okay," I cut him off, assuring him. "Just tea helps too."

"What else?" he asks again.

I bring my hands on my lap and wring them as I share. "I hate meat now. Can't stand it. And coffee."

"Not fucking Peanut Butter Blossoms though."

"No, not Peanut Butter Blossoms. Not so far at least."

"Good."

"And I cry a lot these days."

"What's a lot?" he asks again with the same concern and anger on my behalf.

"I don't know. A lot. The other day Poe, one of my friends at school, stole peanut butter for me from the kitchen and I was so overwhelmed by it that I started crying."

His lips twitch. "And what else?"

"And then my other friend, Wyn, she drew a picture of me and a cute little baby and gave it to me during English lit and I literally started sobbing. In the middle of class. My teacher had to send me away."

His frown comes back then. "Who's —"

"And I feel her." I speak over him because if history is any indication, he might do the same thing he did with my ballet teacher, give her a piece of his mind or blackmail her.

"What?"

"I mean, all the books say that I really can't feel her right now because she's only a collection of cells but I don't care. I do."

His gaze drops down to my flat stomach before he says, "Books can go fuck themselves."

"You really shouldn't curse, Reed."

His wolf eyes flash again. "Cursing is the least of my crimes, remember?"

I swallow when he flicks his eyes over my face, my whole body actually. Looking me from top to bottom, getting my heartbeats up.

When he comes back to my face, the intense look in his eyes makes me clench my thighs together and ask, "Are we really doing this?"

"Fuck yeah."

I bite my lip. "It's going to be difficult."

"I'm not afraid of difficult."

I remember what Con said about our dad and the words slip out before I can stop them. "It's a lot of responsibility."

"I know."

"You might not…"

"I might not what?"

I swallow again, crossing my dangling ankles, curling my toes. "You might not be able to have… fun and stuff. Like you used to."

His eyes narrow. "Yeah, I don't have fun anymore, remember? Not since I met this blonde ballerina and made her dance for me."

You haunt me, Fae…

His raspy voice from that night floats across my brain and I suck in my belly. And the fact that he tried but he hasn't been with anyone in the past two years.

Don't think about that, Callie.

"My brothers –"

"I'm going to handle your fucking brothers."

And then I blurt something else out and surprise him once again. "Where's your bathroom?"

The sudden change of subject throws him. "Is it –"

I slide off the island and come down to my feet. "No, I'm fine."

"Then what…"

I approach him and crane my neck up. "Because I need to know."

He's confused again and I realize that I haven't ever seen him so out of his depth before. "Uh, down the hallway. Third door on the left."

Smiling up at him, I grab his wrist, shocking him further. Shocking myself too.

I tug on his arm and maybe it's the shock of things but he goes easily.

He comes with me where I take him as I walk down the hallway to the third door on the left. When I open it, Reed hits the switch and floods the most beautiful bathroom that I've ever seen with light. It's all glass and white marble, polished and wintry, and yet when I step inside with bare feet, the floor is warm and cozy.

Sort of like him, isn't it?

My gorgeous villain.

I let go of his hand and open the bathroom cabinet and thank God, what I want is right there.

The first aid kit.

I bring it out and set it on the marble sink and open the tap to hot water, adjusting the temperature of it.

"What are you doing?" he asks from behind me.

I look at him in the mirror, standing tall under the overhead light, looking beautiful even with the nasty bruises. "Something that I thought I'd never do again."

"Yeah, what?"

"Cleaning your wounds."

His wolf eyes sparkle with memories. That time when I was so eager to clean his wounds that I locked him inside the storage closet of the auditorium.

I never thought that I'd tend to him again. I never thought I'd want to.

But here I am.

"It's fine."

I knew he'd say that. "I know. It always is."

"So —"

"And I know that my brother is fine too."

"What?"

When the water is to my liking, I turn around and walk up to him. "You didn't fight back, did you? When Ledger came for you last night."

"Why don't you ask him?"

"I'm asking you."

"He's fine. I spared him."

"Like you did two years ago," I say, studying his damaged face. "When he came for you for breaking my heart."

The harsh lines of his face become harsher. "It wasn't anything I didn't deserve."

"I know that too," I whisper, swallowing. "But you didn't deserve this."

He scoffs. "I —"

"Because if you deserve to be punished for her." I press my hand on my belly and as always, he glances down. "I deserve to be punished too. You didn't do this alone."

His chest contracts and I hear him breathe out. "I'm not interested in talking about who did what. And as I said, I'm fine."

I feel the flutters under my palm. "And as I said, I know. But I'm doing this for later."

"For later?"

"Yeah. It's still dark out so maybe my brothers don't know I'm missing. Not yet. And I also know that no matter how many times I tell you, you won't put me in a cab. You'll bring me back yourself. Because for some reason, you're weirdly protective of me."

He shifts on his feet. "What's the point?"

"The point is that when you do bring me back yourself, they'll only beat you up again. This time for kidnapping me. So I want to clean your wounds before you get new ones."

Reed studies my face and probably sees the determination in it. Because I'm not budging.

If we're pointing fingers about who did what then I should be the one to blame. It was my spur of the moment plan. I wanted to move on so badly that I misled him. So if we're blaming someone, it should be me.

But we're not.

Because he's right.

It doesn't matter how she came into existence and it doesn't matter that this is going to be so difficult. Because she's not a mistake, and I'm not going to blame or point fingers when I have her to think about now.

When we have her.

He says gruffly, "Fine."

With that, he goes to the closed toilet seat and sits down on it and my breaths scatter for a second. I know why he did that. I know why he took a seat.

Because of the stark differences in our heights.

Because last time when I did this I had to get up on a stepstool to tend to his wounds.

So he's made it easier for me without me having to tell him first. He's even got his hands resting on his thighs, his veins all taut and thick under his moon-kissed skin. Like he's ready now and he won't stop me if I want to clean his cuts and scrapes.

And so I go to do that.

I walk up to him as he sits there like a king.

No, like a criminal. A thug. A villain.

All bruised up and battered and I'm the girl he's chosen to tend to him tonight. The girl who'll take care of him.

I clean them up as I try to control my breathing, my heart-beats. As I try to control this rush, this warmth in my chest at the onslaught of memories and the fact that he's being so... good.

So docile.

For me.

But his eyes tell another story. His eyes are thrumming with currents, with pulses that makes me think of our one night together.

Don't, Callie. Please.

When I'm done and I go to put everything back into the cab-inet, I notice something.

Something I hadn't before: colorful little boxes stacked on the top shelf.

With trembling hands, I take one out — a hot pink one — and face him. "Why do you have these?"

He's standing now, his face still battered but at least he's got bandages and his cuts are clean. He looks at what I have in my hand and replies, swallowing, "Because you probably didn't have a chance to get these. Not in the dorms. Not yet."

He's right.

I haven't had a chance. "I was going to go get one this week-end while I was home. But you…" I glance back at the cabinet. "You bought like a ton."

Just like when we were talking about the book, his cheekbones sport a slight flush. "I didn't know which one would be best."

I know what he means. Because there are so many. I Googled them at school.

Rapid detection. First response. Early detection. Digital countdown, whatever that means. And I was so dreading it.

I was so dreading going to the pharmacy all alone and getting myself a pregnancy test. I was dreading walking down the aisle, stand-ing there and picking out the best one among hundreds.

And then I was dreading taking the test. All alone.

But I don't have to now, do I?

I don't have to buy the test all alone. I don't have to take the test all alone either.

Because he already bought me one and he's here.

I blink as I feel tears filling my eyes again.

God, I have to stop this. I get emotional about everything, on the littlest things.

But then, this is not little, is it?

Nothing that has happened here today is little.

Because somehow there's an us.

"Thank you," I whisper, hugging it to my chest, hugging it right where my heart is spinning.

He watches me for a few seconds and then throws out a short nod. "I'll wait outside."

With that he leaves.

And I do the very first thing a girl does when she finds out she's pregnant: take a pregnancy test.

Chapter 17

The door is thrown open as soon as we get there.

The door to my house, I mean.

We live in a decent neighborhood, not too rich and not too poor, where all the houses pretty much look the same. All the front yards look the same too, mostly with slightly overgrown shrubs and messier grass — people don't have a lot of time to tend to their gardens or the money to hire regular help so they do the best that they can — and more often than not cracked cement driveways.

It belonged to my mother. I've lived here all my life. All my brothers have lived here all their lives too.

And despite being a house full of rowdy boys, who have been parentless for the last fourteen years, this is the first time a noise of this level has erupted out of our house.

An explosion, followed by the brother who's closest to me in age marching out of the house, bounding down the stairs before I've even gotten out of Reed's Mustang.

The sky is slowly lighting up and dawn is breaking.

After taking the pregnancy test, which basically confirmed

that I'm pregnant — that dark pink line was really hard to miss — I was ready to leave. I was ready to race back home because I knew my brothers would be up and I knew they would've somehow figured out that I wasn't home.

I knew that they wouldn't have been able to sleep all night after the news I gave them and they would be worried sick.

But as it turned out, Reed's scent could only hold off my morning sickness for so long. Because as soon as Reed pocketed the test — he's keeping it, and when I told him that was gross, he simply looked at me and said that he didn't care — my nausea won the battle.

I spent the next hour alternately heaving and dry heaving in his toilet bowl.

While he was right by my side, holding my hair back and God, he wouldn't go away.

No matter how many times I told him to.

Although I will admit that I didn't want him to leave. I liked being held by him. I liked that he was rubbing my back and making soothing noises.

I know I should guard myself better.

I should care about not getting too close to him now that we're doing this together.

But my nauseated self, my scared self from the past week ever since I found out that I'm pregnant, liked his nearness, his support, his strength. And the fact that he didn't let me leave that cozy house without having some tea and saltines. The fact that he cared.

But now we're here, in front of my house, and the reality is setting in.

The reality that Reed is not the guy for me and I can't trust him again. But I'm pregnant with his baby.

And that my brothers hate him for a reason.

My belly flutters with nerves, with her, and I jump out of the car before it's even completely parked to go intercept Ledger before he gets to Reed.

Reed, on the other hand, is completely relaxed, or was relaxed until I made the crazy dash out of his Mustang. Now he's glaring at me as he emerges.

But before he can say anything, which from the looks of it he was going to, my brother reaches him and grabs the neck of his hoodie.

"I should've killed you last night," Ledger growls, shaking Reed and pushing him into his Mustang, making the car shake.

"You should've," Reed breathes out, his mouth tight with fresh pain and the pain from the already-inflicted wounds. "But then no one would've been around to do your job last night."

"What the fuck is that supposed to mean?"

"It means what the fuck were you doing, letting your sister run around town in the middle of the night last night?" Reed snaps, grabbing Ledger's fisted hands on his hoodie. "Do you have any idea what kind of condition I found her in? She could barely stand."

"I'm going to —"

"Stop, Ledger. Let him go," I speak over my brother as soon as I reach them.

I even grab Ledger's arm and try to tug it away and Reed snaps, "Get the fuck back, Fae."

I don't.

I can't.

Everything is happening so fast. Everything is just spinning out of control and we haven't even been here for more than five seconds and I need it to stop.

I need them to stop fighting.

So I keep tugging on Ledger's extremely strong arm, which hardly budges. "Ledge, please. I don't want you guys to fight right now. Can we please just talk?"

My brother looks at me then, his dark eyes made even darker with fury. "You spent the night with him?"

"Ledge, please."

"Did you?"

"Yes," I reply. "No. I mean, it wasn't my intention, Ledge. I was just —"

"Yeah, got it," he snaps and jerks out of my hold so easily.

As easily as he did last night.

But maybe last night I was more in control of my faculties, which is a surprise given how nervous I was. Right now though, I've been rendered so weak from my morning sickness and my absolute dread that I stumble back, dizzy and suddenly so faint.

I think I'm going to fall or throw up or both, but then I feel a strong arm going around me and my body clashes with his.

I know it's him.

I know he's here to catch me again.

The guy who broke my heart once.

And an absurd thought flashes in my mind that he'll always be here to catch me. When I fall.

Pulling in his calming scent, I grab his hoodie at the chest and blink up at him. "Thank you."

His brows are drawn together and under the orange sky of dawn, his bruises look on fire. "I told you to stay back."

"But I was —"

"Calls, fuck. You okay?" Ledger says, concern evident in his voice and on his face as he comes to stand beside me.

I'm about to answer him but Reed snaps, his arm going all tight and possessive around me. "Get away from her."

Ledger's chest pushes out on a sharp breath. "She's my sister, asshole."

"And if you hurt her again, you're really going to regret not killing me last night."

"Yeah, you're one to talk. After what you did."

"Please. Stop," I burst out. "Both of you. Just stop."

They do stop.

But I'm not sure if I'm the one responsible for making it all happen, because that's when my oldest brother emerges from the front door and climbs down the porch stairs, his presence and his voice commanding.

"Ledger, that's enough for now."

Ledger's jaw clenches in protest and anger. But he does obey Con and stand back.

However, he doesn't stay quiet. "It was him. He took her last night."

I move away from Reed then as I speak out. "He didn't take me. He didn't." I feel Reed move beside me and I know he's going to say something but I don't give him a chance. "It was me. I went out last night after you guys went to sleep. I just needed some fresh air."

Con has finally reached us now.

We're still standing on the sidewalk and my oldest brother takes in the scene with his inscrutable dark blue eyes.

Ledger is standing with his legs far apart, in a battle stance, his fists clenched at his sides, his eyes screaming murder at Reed. And Reed is standing much the same way, only his face is all messed up.

I can't help but think that Con has seen this scene play out a hundred times on the soccer field. Reed and Ledger, his two star players, facing off against each other.

"Are you okay, Callie?" Con asks me and my heart squeezes at the concern on my brother's face.

"Yes, I am. Con —"

"You brought her home," Con says, his gaze moving away from me and stopping on Reed, his tone measured and controlled.

"She shouldn't have been out that late."

Con throws him a short nod. "I agree."

"She looked distraught," Reed continues. "She had no idea what was going on around her."

Con's face goes tight. "It's on me. I might've been a little harsh."

"Yes. You were," Reed tells him and my brother's eyes harden for a second.

Again I jump in, addressing Con, trying to keep whatever peace I can. "You weren't."

Con's eyes settle on me and he grinds his jaw.

I see regret on his face and my heart squeezes with so much love for him. So much adoration and respect and also regret at bringing this upon him.

At hurting him again.

I approach my brother with all the love in my heart.

I come to stand in front of him and say, "You were not harsh, Con. You're my brother. You were worried about me and I gave you the worst news in the world. I get that." I swallow, blinking back tears. "I get that I hurt you. I keep hurting you and I'm so sorry for that. I don't know what else to say. I don't know how to make it up to you and maybe you'll never look at me the same way as you did before. Before everything, and I don't blame you."

I turn to Ledger then.

He's at last looked away from Reed and even though his stance is still the same, wide and battle ready, his eyes are liquid. His features are rippling with pain and I want to go hug him.

But maybe he'll reject me now after what I've done and I don't think I can take it.

So I keep standing in my spot as I address Ledger, "I don't blame you for being angry and for hating me, Ledge. I actually wasn't even expecting you to forgive me the first time. But you did and I'll never forget that. You were there for me, that summer. You and Stellan and Shepard, and I'll always, always, love you for that. You guys are the best brothers a girl could ask for and so I'm going to be a good sister to you and tell you that you don't have to forgive me this time."

I turn to Con again. "You don't have to forgive me either. You can hate me, Con. It will hurt me but I'll take it. Because you never asked for this, for this kind of disappointment and burden from your sister." I swallow again. "You're the only father figure I've known and you mean more to me than you can ever imagine. You're not just my brother. You're the guy who brought me up. I wouldn't be here without you. You're my everything.

"And I wish that I could give you what you want, Con. But I can't." I cradle my belly. "I can't kill her. I'm sorry. I'm not capable of killing her. She's mine now and maybe she's only a bunch of cells right now and I don't even know for sure if she's a she but I can't. Please, Con. I'm sorry."

After I'm done, it feels like Con studies me for the longest time.

For the longest time, he doesn't say anything.

And as I said to him just now, it hurts.

It hurts that my brothers might never forgive me. That one decision, the most important decision that I've ever made, is going to tear us apart.

And it hurts even more when Conrad looks away from me and addresses Reed. "Are you aware that my sister wanted to go to Juilliard?"

Clenching my eyes shut, I bow my head.

"Yes," Reed says from behind me.

But he doesn't stay there.

He comes forward. He stands toe to toe with my brother, both tall and strong.

"She's wanted it ever since she was five," Con tells him. "I took her to all her dance classes. I attended all her recitals and shows. And then I watched her get kicked out of her ballet studio."

My eyes are on my brother but I know the lines around Reed's mouth have tightened. I can feel it.

"After me," Reed says in a low voice.

"After you," Conrad continues as he stares at Reed. "I also watched while she got arrested. I went with her to the police station. I watched while her future hung in the balance. But you know that part, don't you? You brought me the deal."

"It wasn't enough."

"No, it wasn't. She still had to go to that school. She still had to live in a dorm, follow all the stupid fucking rules. Because of what you did to her. How you used her and abused her trust. For a sport."

"I know."

Reed's voice has gone threadbare. It has become a series of gruff syllables and grunts and I fist my hands at my sides. Because for some reason I want to touch him.

I want to take his hand in mine and give it a squeeze.

But I won't.

I can't.

Definitely not in front of my brothers. I've betrayed them so many times. I can't keep making the same mistake.

"Now, Callie tells me that you gave up soccer for her. To get her freedom. That correct?"

Reed's bruised jaw tics for a moment or two before he replies, "Soccer was just a means to an end. And yeah, I gave that up. I'd do it again though."

I have to part my lips at that, along with digging my nails in my palms and curling my toes.

I have to breathe through my mouth as I watch Reed standing

up to Conrad like this.

For me.

"Means to an end," Con murmurs. "Something to do with your father, I presume."

"Yes."

"Your father is an asshole."

Reed throws Conrad a short nod. "Something we agree on."

Conrad nods too. "But I don't care about that, you understand?"

"I wouldn't expect you to."

"Good. Because I care about my sister."

Another short nod. "I know."

"Are you aware," Conrad says and shifts on his feet, "that she's going to quit school and get a job. An apartment. She's also thinking of quitting ballet. So apparently, you've ruined her life. You've broken her dream, a dream she's had since she was five."

"Not yet."

Conrad wasn't expecting this answer. I wasn't either.

"Care to explain that?"

I see Reed's chest undulating, his nostrils flaring as he shifts on his feet. "I know you hate me. I get that. I respect that. I respect how protective you are of your siblings. How you've always been protective of them. I'd watch you, you know. Back then. Back when I was a kid. I'd watch how you always walked a step behind them. How you'd always keep an eye on them when you were around town. How you sometimes rode the bus with them to drop them off at school. I watched you. And then you became my coach and I saw how protective you were of your players. Of the game. The integrity of the game, of the players. I both liked and hated that about you. Especially when it interfered with my agenda. When I wanted to do things my way. When I wanted to win. Not the game. I mean, yeah the game but it was more about sticking it to my asshole father than anything else.

"So if you want to take a swing at me right now, break my bones, rearrange my face for being selfish and reckless and exactly what you always thought I was, then you're welcome to it. But I want you to know one thing. I want you to know that I'm going to make sure her dreams are safe. I broke her heart once. But I'm not going to break her dreams too. I haven't done much in life for other people. I've always been too wrapped up in my own shit. Besides, the world can go to hell, I don't care. It's full of crap anyway. But you and I, we can both agree on one thing at least: Your sister is one good thing in this world and I screwed her over. But I'm not going to do that anymore. I'm not going to fuck her up more than I already have."

When I go to draw a breath, I taste salt on my lips.

I taste water. My tears. I taste my broken heart.

It doesn't taste broken though, not really. A broken heart tastes sour and bitter. This tastes sweet, like sugar.

Like cupcakes.

Like him.

And I would've analyzed it more, what this means, how my broken heart can change in taste, but the guy who's responsible for all of this isn't done yet.

He has more declarations to make. He has more ways to make me ache for him.

"And she's not quitting school. Not on my watch."

Chapter 18

It's Monday and I'm at St. Mary's.

It's not that Monday though.

The Monday that I thought I was going to talk to the principal and quit school. That Monday was going to be my last day at school, but it somehow became a normal Monday.

A Monday like any other.

Meaning, I didn't talk to the principal and I didn't quit school.

It's a week after that Monday and I'm still here.

I'm still going to St. Mary's. I'm still with my friends. Whom, to be very honest, I was going to miss the most. If I had quit.

It's the end of the day and all my girls are standing out in the courtyard at a special spot. The reason that we, or rather they have chosen this spot is because they want to look at the black metal gates that mark the entrance to the grounds.

Because they're all watching something through those bars.

Or someone.

"All right, so don't kill me," Salem begins, her eyes focused on that someone, "but your guy is really hot. Like really, really."

"He's not my guy. Also can I tell Arrow that you said that though?" I tease her.

Blushing, she elbows my arm. "Ha. Ha. Funny."

I chuckle.

So remember the scandal from a couple of weeks back that I said was the biggest scandal at St. Mary's? And how we were all hoping that Arrow would come around and declare his love for Salem?

He did.

Just a few days ago actually — I'm glad I was here when she told the story — and according to Salem, it was pretty epic. And it was.

The guy wrote her a poem.

I mean, of course it was epic, and now she's always blushing and smiling.

Like she's doing right now.

"Stop, he's not hot," Poe goes, swatting Salem's arm, her eyes fixed on that someone too.

"Are you kidding me?" Salem swats her arm back. "He totally is. Look at how that suit jacket fits him. It's like he's going to burst out of it at any moment. And if you focus really hard, you could actually see his abs through that shirt."

"That's why hot is a very tame word for him. Duh. Callie's guy is like…" She clicks her fingers as it occurs to her. "He's a DILF. He's a total DILF."

Smiling, Wyn nods. Her eyes are somehow away from her sketchbook for once. "That's our Poe. Always so classy."

"What, he's going to have a baby, isn't he? He's Callie's baby daddy. Of course he's a DILF."

"But do you really have to say that?" Wyn asks. "Do you really have to use that word?"

"Um, yes. I'm honoring him. I'm paying a compliment." She turns to me then. "Are you sure he doesn't have a brother?"

I shake my head at them. "Again, he's not my guy. He's not my anything."

"Oh right, of course. You just happen to be having a baby together." Poe rolls her eyes at me. "And he just happens to be waiting for you at the end of the day."

Now it's my turn to swat her arm. "And second, stop drooling over him."

Salem chuckles. "Not your guy. Suuuure."

Salem and Poe high five and Wyn laughs.

Even though I purse my lips at them, I don't blame them for admiring him.

He does look gorgeous. And you can see his abs through his shirt.

But the thing that gets me the most is his hair.

It's really grown out in the past couple of months. So instead of looking all civilized and tamed in the gray suit with white dress shirt, those long, unruly strands make him look the opposite.

They fall over his forehead and get tangled up in his starched collar and make him look like the reckless, wild beast that everyone used to call him at Bardstown High.

The Wild Mustang.

The one with wolf eyes and vampire skin.

The boy that every mom wants her daughter to stay away from. The boy that every dad wants to run off his porch when he comes calling for his baby girl.

Even though he's not playing anymore, he still embodies that nickname, and the reason he's here, standing outside of the black gates, leaning against his white Mustang, is because he's come for me.

He's come to pick me up after school. He's been coming to pick me up from school for the whole past week actually.

"I can't believe you're not living with me anymore," Wyn says from beside me, pulling my attention away from him.

Something gets stuck in my throat. "I know. I miss you. I miss all of you."

I'm pretty used to crying at everything — although this does call for tears — but all my girls have moisture in their eyes and in this moment, I'm so glad that I could stay.

That he made me stay in school.

Because I swear to God, I would've missed them like crazy.

Just the fact that I'm not living in the dorms with them anymore has me so upset.

Because I'm not.

I'm living somewhere else now.

The only girl in the history of St. Mary's who gets to live off campus.

It makes sense though, doesn't it? I am also the only girl who got pregnant in the history of St. Mary's while going to St. Mary's.

All courtesy of the guy who's waiting for me.

He made all of this happen.

While I was making plans, he was making plans of his own. I already knew that, but I didn't know how elaborate those plans would be. They put my plans to shame.

They involved pulling all the strings, throwing his Jackson weight around and keeping me in school. They also involved finding me a place to live and not letting me take a job because I need to focus on graduating and taking care of my health first.

And also ballet.

He's not letting me quit that either.

My dream.

Because he's already broken my heart, he won't break my dream too. He won't let anything happen to the dream I've had since I was five.

He said that to my brothers and I have to say that my brothers love this plan. All four of them.

Which would be surprising, given the fact that they all hate him, but it's not.

After the whole showdown on the curb and Reed's promise to Conrad, my brother invited him into our house and they spent that whole day listening to Reed's plans and hammering out details. Even Stellan and Shep came down from New York to chime in.

I always knew that Reed was exactly like my brothers in the protective department but it was never more apparent than it was when they were brainstorming ideas.

In our dining room.

In the same room where only the night before I'd broken the news to my brothers and I'd thought that my bond with them, that life as I'd known it, would be over.

In that room, I got something that I always wanted.

I always wanted them all to get along, my brothers and Reed. Back in Bardstown High that was all I thought about. I wanted them to put their vendetta and ego and differences aside, because deep down I knew that they could be friends.

But then everything happened and I buried that.

I shoved that hope under layers and layers of hurt and heartbreak.

I never thought that my crazy wish from two years ago would come true now. Especially now, when everything is even more chaotic.

But somehow it has and no, they're not friends. God no. But they're not fighting either, and that's enough for me.

All because he has a plan and he's promised to make it happen.

He's making it happen.

Anyway.

I say goodbye to my friends and take a deep breath. With my

green backpack over my shoulders, I begin my walk down the concrete pathway toward the black gates.

And his eyes land straight on me.

So far he's been staring down at his phone and appearing as if he was completely oblivious to his surroundings. But I know he's not.

I know this is what he does.

I've watched him do it for the past week.

In the afternoons, he arrives at the school and climbs out of his Mustang to wait for me. And then he focuses on his phone until I say my goodbyes to my friends and start to walk toward him.

As if he's giving me privacy.

He's letting me say my goodbyes in peace before I go to him.

And so as soon as I break away from the group, he looks up, his eyes clashing with mine.

They flare as he watches me walk toward him, leaving everything behind. The school, my friends. And he straightens and begins to walk toward me as well. Slowly, lazily, to match my small steps. As if timing our walk. Synchronizing it so he reaches the black gates the same time as I do.

It takes me a minute and a half to do that. I've timed it.

I timed it last week, last Monday, the first day he came to pick me up, and exactly ninety seconds later, I'm out the black gates and on the other side.

And he's standing in front of me.

"Hi," I say, looking up to him, my heart spinning, the flutters in my belly raging.

She knows he's here as well.

He doesn't say anything to that. Again, I knew he wouldn't.

Instead he looks me over.

He studies my face, my braided hair that's held together with a mustard-colored ribbon. He even eyes my uniform skirt, my Mary

Janes.

I try to stand tall and straight under his heavy scrutiny, under his sparkling wolf eyes.

The scrutiny that makes me feel like a young schoolgirl while he stands there in his grown-up business suit, making sure that I'm okay.

Because that's what he's doing. I know.

He's making sure that no harm has somehow befallen me in the six hours that I've been at school.

In the six hours since he last saw me.

Because he drops me off at school in the mornings as well.

"Everything go okay?" he asks, reaching out to take my backpack from me.

See? He was making sure I was okay. And he thinks I can't carry heavy things such as my backpack.

I nod, looking at his face. "Yeah."

The bruises that Ledger gave him don't look as angry but they're still there, pockmarking his features. Again making him look more criminal in his suit than civil.

I notice an old scrape pulsing angrily, just by his jaw. "What happened here?"

"What?"

I raise my hand and touch it, his jaw, and it clenches. "Here. It looks like you scraped your old cut."

Reed stares into my eyes for a second before replying gruffly, "I might've... scratched something."

"Your stubble," I conclude and he shrugs in acquiescence. "You need to be more careful, Reed. Your old cuts —"

"Any morning sickness?" he asks, cutting me off and stepping away from my touch, as if he's done with the topic of his cuts.

As if he's done letting me worry over him.

I lower my hand and fist my tingling fingers. "A little."

His features tighten up. "Were you able to eat something?"

"Salad."

He tells me what he thinks of it by exhaling sharply.

My morning sickness has gotten worse over the past few days and Reed hates it that I have to endure it during classes. My brothers hate it too and together, for an insane second, they thought that I should stop going to school altogether until it passes.

I put my foot down though. I put my foot down on some of their other plans too, but that's neither here nor there.

Anyway I told them that if they wanted me to not quit school and get a job then I'm doing this the right way. Meaning I'm going to classes and I'm doing my homework and keeping my grades up.

They had to relent.

But I think it was mostly because Conrad is now the soccer coach and he knew he was going to be here to keep an eye on me after Reed dropped me off.

"Someone say something to you?" he asks then and I fidget with my skirt slightly.

Yes.

"No," I lie to him.

He frowns. "You sure?"

Well, no.

Someone did say something to me. A group of someones. Girls from junior year I think. They didn't so much say something to me as at me.

It was during lunch.

I was getting my salad and they pointed at my tray and giggled and they may have mimed throwing up. Or something like that.

To be fair, I had thrown up only an hour before. I had to rush out of class in order to do that and the news spread like wildfire. As

I knew it would, about me getting sick, about me being the only girl living off campus.

About me being pregnant.

They all know now and they are all very scandalized. Again, as I knew they would be.

I knew that me being pregnant at eighteen would be a much bigger scandal than what happened with Salem. And it is. At least, I'm happy that some of the heat has been taken away from her. Because for a while there, they were all watching her.

They still do but now they watch me as well.

Our group has become the most rebellious of all.

We're the St. Mary's rebels.

In fact, my guidance counselor, who I always thought was my friend of sorts, requested that they switch me to a different counselor now that I'm pregnant.

I'm not going to lie. That did hurt, but it's okay.

It's not anything that I didn't expect.

So I'll live. But from the looks of it, he won't.

"Yes, I'm sure," I tell him. "Can —"

He looks over my shoulders. "Then what the fuck are they looking at?"

I know what he's talking about.

Like me and my girls, there were others watching him as well. They're still watching him and now me.

On his first day here, the whole school watched him pick me up after school. They stood outside the cinder block buildings, gathered in the courtyard and watched me walk up to him. Over the past week, a lot of people have lost interest but a lot of them haven't.

So they watch him.

They watch me walk up to him and they watch as he takes me away in his Mustang.

By now they know who he is.

There are several rumors about him and me, and of course one of them is that we're together. That he's my boyfriend and I'm having his baby.

I am having his baby but he's not my boyfriend.

He never wanted to be and he never will be.

"You," I reply.

"What?"

"Girls always look at you, remember?"

"I don't like it."

Surprised, I laugh. "Are you serious? You loved it. And you always watched them back. And –"

"I didn't."

"What?"

"Watch them."

"I…"

I forget what I was going to say because with the way he's watching me, it looks like… he's trying to say that he didn't watch them.

He watched me instead and that's absurd, isn't it?

He moves his eyes away and goes back to glaring at the girls over my shoulder. "If they want to watch, I'm –"

"Just ignore them. I do."

"You shouldn't have to," he growls.

"I swear it's okay."

He narrows his eyes for a second before taking a step toward the gate but I stop him.

Physically.

Well, maybe that gives the wrong impression. I can't physically stop him from anything. He's bigger than me, a lot bigger and stronger.

He's like a towering mountain, a building, and I'm like a bag of feathers to him.

I can't stop him, but I do.

I put a hand on his hard stomach and he comes to a halt, going all rigid.

He glances down at it, at my small, pale hand on his white shirt, before looking up at me. "Let me go."

I have to take a moment before answering him. "No."

He flexes his fingers on my backpack that he's holding. "Take your hand off, Fae."

And I swear to God, my heart spins so fast in my chest that I think it will break out. It will burst out of its cage made of bones like I burst out of mine, the cage of cinderblocks and black gates.

The one he sprung me out of.

The guy who's so much stronger than me but somehow is letting me control him like this.

Letting me make him do things.

Like he could. Make me do things I mean. Back then.

Back when I was in love with him.

Swallowing, I say, "No. You're not going in there."

His jaw clenches. "I am."

"No, you're not. We're leaving."

"Fae."

My own stomach clenches as I press a hand on his. "No. You're not going to fight with anyone, Reed. I won't let you. I told you that it's okay. They'll lose interest after a while. If they want to look at something, let them. I don't care. But you're not going in there and doing your thing."

"What's my thing?"

"Blackmailing people."

"This is going to be much easier than blackmail."

"Oh, that makes me feel so much better."

"That's the idea."

I sigh. "No. You're not going. Besides, aren't we late for our appointment?"

He stares at me, all belligerent and angry, and I stare back.

I'm not belligerent though, no.

I'm breathless.

My lips are parted and my heart is racing.

Because I don't know what to do anymore.

I thought I knew.

I thought that all I had to do was remember my mistakes from two years ago so I won't repeat them. I thought that if I remembered every little thing he did to me and that if I carried every little piece of my heart that he broke, I'd be safe.

I'd be safe from him.

But I don't think I'm safe anymore.

He backs off then. He obeys me and his muscles go lax under my fingers, like I've managed to tame this beast with just my touch.

"This isn't over." With that, he throws a last glance over my shoulders and commands, "Let's go."

***

The room's stark white and smells of bleach.

Which is to be expected, because it's an examination room.

We're at a private clinic.

For my first doctor's appointment.

Because in addition to taking a pregnancy test, there's another thing a girl does when she finds out she's pregnant. And like everything else so far, Reed has taken care of that too.

Even though the clinic is out of town — not in Bardstown but in the neighboring town of Wuthering Garden — Reed has assured my brothers and me that she's a good doctor and comes highly recommended.

As soon as we came in, a nurse in pink scrubs gave us a bunch of forms to fill out.

Which again Reed took care of.

He asked me questions when he didn't know the answers but mostly it was all him.

Then that same nurse ushered us into an examination room. She told us that a technician would be with us in a few minutes and that in the meantime I should change into a white gown. She also gave me a cup to pee in along with a thick Sharpie so I could write my initials on it, for the pregnancy test.

When I told her that I'd already done it, she smiled and told me that it was just standard procedure.

And now we're here.

I've peed in a cup and written down my name on it. I've changed into the yellow-ish gown and the technician has just entered the room.

Her name is Christina and she's all energetic and happy as she tells me that today she'll be doing my first ultrasound. She'll also do an internal pelvic exam, which is basically to quickly check my uterus, cervix and vagina and make sure that everything is okay. Not to mention, she'll do a pap smear, check my weight and blood pressure and things.

So basically an overall exam to make sure that me and the baby are healthy.

"All of these procedures are very basic and standard," she says, snapping on her gloves. "There might be some slight discomfort during the pelvic exam but it's nothing to worry about. If it becomes too uncomfortable, let me know, okay?"

Swallowing, I jerk out a nod. "Okay."

Once she's taken my weight and other vitals, she tells me to lie down on my back, with my butt slightly hanging off the edge of the table. She also tells me to put my legs into these archaic-looking metal contraptions called stirrups and relax.

Because this will be quick.

Nothing about it feels quick though.

Especially when she pulls up a stool where my legs are spread and I'm completely exposed under my gown.

I hadn't realized that I'd grabbed onto the edge of the exam table and all my breaths were tangled up somewhere down my throat and my lungs.

Until him.

Until he appears at my side.

So far he was standing on the opposite side of the room, leaning against the wall by the door. He kept his eyes on me during the weight check and everything.

As if keeping guard over me. As if Christina meant me some harm.

I don't know when he moved though.

But he's here now, at my side, and his long, graceful fingers wrap around my wrist, making me let go of the table. Making me grab onto him instead. And my fingers, they like that so much, so very, very much, that they latch on.

My fingers latch onto his and my breaths come easier.

The surging nausea in my stomach calms down too because he did what he said he'd do. He stocked up on his fabric softener and she likes that, the tiny bundle of cells in my stomach.

And the discomfort.

That vanishes as well because I'm looking at him. Into his eyes.

His molten gray, intense eyes.

I don't mind the stretch then, of the speculum that Christina has inserted inside me. I think I only wince once and squeeze his hand for like three seconds until I adjust to the pressure. In my head, I take that as a victory.

Not him though.

His fading bruises ripple and he snaps at Christina to be careful.

And even though I say sorry and tell her to keep going — which she does after looking slightly intimidated by Reed — and stare up at him and shake my head, I can't stop my ballerina heart from spinning.

I can't stop myself from going breathless again when his jaw clenches, making me aware that he doesn't like that. Me asking him to hold back.

A second later though, Christina's voice breaks our stare when she says, "And there's the tiny little thing. The baby."

At this, we both snap our eyes to the monitor so we can see her.

Or at least see something.

Because for the love of God, I can't.

I cannot see our baby.

And I tell her that and laughing, she points it out for me. The little dot that's supposed to be her. She also tells me that the due date is in July.

My stomach flutters and I know it's not her but still. I'm assuming that it is and I'll keep assuming until she does move inside of me.

But anyway, Reed sees her right away and I'm not going to lie, I hate him a little bit for that. That he could see her while I couldn't.

Although my ire melts away when he asks Christina to make four copies of it.

Of her.

And he does it while his fingers flex against mine.

Soon though, I have to let go of them, his fingers, because it's over. And Christina tells us that the doctor is waiting for us in her office.

Dr. May is a friendly woman in her fifties maybe who asks me all kinds of questions. She takes my complete family medical history and prescribes me prenatal vitamins. She hands me pamphlets that I can read and get myself informed about the upcoming changes in my body and tells me to call the office any time I feel the need to.

Then it's Reed's turn.

To ask questions.

And he has a lot of them. The very first one is what the fuck can we do about my morning sickness. And why the fuck won't it go away? And what the fuck we can do to give me a break from it?

All his exact words, not mine.

The doctor is patient, however. She says that we can't do much about it. Every woman's body is different and it sucks but I'm going to have to ride through it. And usually it clears up by the second trimester. However, if I really can't bear it, she can prescribe me some mild anti-emetics.

Honestly though, these things take a natural course and she doesn't think there's any cause for worry at this point. So I refuse the anti-emetics — despite Reed being all upset over it — and thank the doctor for all the help.

And then Reed drives me home.

My new home that I'll be living in for the foreseeable future.

It's not my old house where I wanted to live with Conrad.

This is another thing I put my foot down about.

Living separately, living on my own.

Because after everything that happened and what Conrad told me about him taking care of us while growing up, I wasn't going to burden him more. He's already taken care of me and my brothers, he deserves a break now. Especially now that he's got a new job. He doesn't deserve a pregnant sister living in his house.

So I told them I'd live in an apartment close to school and once I'm out of St. Mary's and have a job, I'll pay them back for everything.

But Reed refused.

He already had a plan for that too.

So I'm going to live in this house.

It's a house made of all glass, or mostly glass with tall windows taking up all the wall space, and it sits on top of a cliff in the town of Wuthering Garden.

It's the same house that Reed brought me to that night. When he found me on the street outside of the Blue Madonna. His vacation home, or a vacation home that's his for now.

I haven't been able to really crack who it belongs to other than the fact that it belongs to a friend of his and is located close enough to the clinic and my school.

It's gorgeous though.

Just like the guy who's driven me over from the clinic in his Mustang.

As soon as he comes to a stop, he climbs out and walks around the car to open the door for me. The first day I got out by myself and it pissed him off. So now I wait for him to do his thing.

It's not something he used to do two years ago though.

He'd get the door for me once when I was climbing in. I was free to climb out on my own after that.

Now he likes to help me with that as well. Just as he likes to help me with my backpack, which he's still carrying as he walks me to the front door.

He only gives it back to me when I'm at the door, exactly on the threshold, with the door unlocked, ready to go in.

I know what he's going to do now.

"You've got your phone with you?" he asks like he always does.

"Yes."

Last week he bought me a new cell phone. Cell phones and personal technology are prohibited at St. Mary's so I had to leave my old one, the one I had at Bardstown High, at home. I told him that I could still use the old one but he shot me an irritated look and bought me my current phone.

My brothers wanted to pay for half of it.

Reed gave them an irritated look as well but they glared at him back, so my brothers split the cost.

"And groceries and things are stocked?"

"They are."

I have groceries for days actually.

Because again, Reed bought me everything over the weekend and then my brothers showed up with groceries too. So I have two sets of every food item. After a lot of discussion, they have now come up with a rotating schedule as to who will bring me groceries what week. This was a much more heated discussion than the cell phone one because they'd found out that Reed had already hired a cook and a housekeeper to come every day.

"Good. I'll come by tomorrow to pick you up. Same time," he instructs. "Lock the door after me."

As usual.

He picks me up and he drops me off. He gives me instructions and then he leaves. Only to do it all over again the next day.

Because he doesn't live here with me.

He lives in a hotel. One of the most luxurious hotels in Wuthering Garden, only fifteen minutes away from me. He made that very clear when my brothers asked him about it.

When he told them he already had a house for me, Con's first question was where would Reed live. And he said that he'd be staying in a different place but close enough to get to me in record time if something happened.

As much as my brothers hate that I'm living alone now, they agree with this. They don't want Reed anywhere near me even though I'm having his baby and he's taking care of everything.

Before he can leave though, I ask, "Are you going back to the office?"

He's taken aback by my question, I guess because I usually let him go without comment. But not today.

Today I have to say something to him.

His eyes flicker with suspicion as he answers. "Yeah. Why?"

"Just curious." I shift on my feet. "So I was thinking something."

His suspicion only grows. "And what might that be?"

"What do you... do for fun?"

"What?"

Ugh.

Seriously? What am I asking him?

But now that I've said it, I forge ahead, "I-I mean, all I've seen you do this last week is go to the office and take care of me and... What do you do after this? Like hobbies and stuff. Do you work on cars, I mean... there must be something you do to relax."

It's been bothering me for days now.

The fact that this job is killing him and that he has to do it because of me. He should be doing what makes him happy.

Like cars maybe and...

"I don't have time to relax."

"But –"

"Just lock the door after I leave."

"Does he... know?" I ask him then with wide eyes.

"Does who know what?"

"That I'm pregnant. Your dad." I pause to swallow down my racing heartbeats. "Does he know that you're doing all this for me?"

The man who wanted to punish me for stealing his son's car. And rightfully so.

The man who forced Reed to give up soccer in exchange for my freedom.

I wonder if he knows and if he does, what must he be thinking about it. About the fact that I'm pregnant with his son's baby.

The flutters inside my stomach make an appearance and I can't help but put my hand on my belly. And when I do, his eyes inevitably focus on it.

There's a purple bruise on his right cheekbone that ripples at my question. It thrums just like the look in his gaze, all angry and determined. "You don't have to worry about my father. I've got it under control."

"But Reed —"

"I can handle my dad, all right? It's fine."

That's exactly it, isn't it?

That he keeps saying everything is fine. That he's taking care of everything.

And I'm letting him because I know how important this is for him.

I know that.

I feel that.

That's why he stood in front of Conrad and made him a promise. That's why he made all these plans. That's why he put so much thought into them, so much care and so much detail. He must've made hundreds of lists to be able to pull this off.

That's why I'm letting my brothers take care of everything too.

Because I know this is how they take control of the situation. This is how Conrad makes sure that nothing falls apart. This is how he copes with things. Like he did when Mom died and he had to take care of everything.

I know if I take this away from my brothers, this control, it will only make matters worse. I know if I take away his control too, it will only piss him off.

And I'm grateful, you know?

God, am I grateful.

Up until a couple of weeks ago, I thought everything would fall apart. I thought I'd be alone and an outcast. I was so scared. So, so scared.

But then he came and he saved everything.

I'm going to school. I have a place to live. I have a doctor. I don't even have to quit ballet. Not every girl is this lucky. I know. I'm the exception. I have a support system that most pregnant teenage girls only dream about.

And so I have to speak up.

I have to step in and stop Reed.

"I don't need all this, Reed," I insist, looking up at him. "I don't need a grand house and a cook and a private clinic. I know you want to be here and you want to make things easier for me and I'm not arguing about that. But all of this," I wave my hand at things, "it costs a lot of money, Reed. I know. I'm not an idiot. I don't need all this, okay? And so I don't want you working there just because of this. Because you have to provide for everything. You hate that company. You never wanted to work for your father. I know. But you had to because of me, because of what happened and what I did. So I'm not going to let you do something you hate.

"I mean, you're not letting me quit my dream. You even got me back into Blue Madonna. And I know soccer really wasn't your dream but you must have one, Reed. You must want something and I can't stand by and watch you do something you never wanted to do.

Besides, it's been two years. Can't your dad see that you hate it? Can't you explain it to him? I mean, he's your dad. He must want to see you happy. And if he's such an asshole that he doesn't care about anything else but himself then I can talk to him. I can apologize for everything I did. I can explain —"

He cuts me off when his arm shoots out and his fingers grab onto my bicep. They not only grab onto it, his fingers dig into the meat of my arm.

I feel them dimpling my flesh as he bends down over me, his eyes fraught with something that I can't place, that I haven't really seen on him. "You will never ever talk to my father."

"What?"

"Not ever. You won't even say his name, you understand?"

"Reed —"

"Do you understand, Fae?"

I nod before I can even think about it. "Yes."

His fingers still don't let up. In fact, he comes down at me even more. "My father has nothing to do with this. With you. He's not going to touch you. He's not going to even look at you. I won't let him. Not again. So you're going to put this thought out of your head and you're going to let me handle everything. Say yes if you understand that."

The violence in his words, the fierceness, makes me want to say yes. But more than that it's something else, something far needier than his ferocity.

Something that begs me to agree with him right now.

Like if I don't, it will destroy him.

"Yes."

He nails me with his gaze for a few seconds, as if checking whether my acquiescence is genuine or not. When he's satisfied with it, he straightens up, letting me go. "Now lock the door after I leave."

Chapter 19

Back at Bardstown High, I was fascinated with his legs.

His thighs.

The strength in them. The way his muscles bulged when he walked or ran. The way his strides were long and languid and authoritative, sexy.

I'm still fascinated by them, his legs.

But I'm more fascinated by his hands now. His fingers.

They are long and thick with rough, knobby, masculine knuckles. He's also got blunt square-shaped nails. The veins that run on the backs of his hands, going up to his wrists, are thick and bumpy.

And then there are his forearms. Muscled and moon-kissed skin with a dusting of dark hair that thins out as you go up while his muscles become thick and hilly and strong.

These are the hands that hold back my hair when I throw up. They rub circles on my back as I'm heaving over the toilet bowl. These are the hands that then bring me saltines and ginger tea.

He also warms up my dinner every night after school because my tiredness knows no bounds.

Before, he could pick me up and drop me off and leave, but now things have gotten so bad that he stays.

He has to.

He has to come inside the house that he arranged for me to live in.

He has to stay with me all through dinner, which if I'm very lucky I get to keep inside. Then he has to stay while I do my homework on the couch — he usually does his work from the office that he hates — or try to. Because I always end up falling asleep in the middle of it.

Then with those same arms, he carries me to the bed.

And sleeps on the couch.

To do everything all over again the next day. Because he wouldn't let anyone else do this for me. He and my brothers had an argument about who'd watch over me. But there was no contest.

Reed Roman Jackson won that one with one fiercely spoken statement. "She's carrying my baby in her body. So I'll be the one taking care of her if her body is giving her a hard time."

Anyway, these are the hands that I hold on to when I go for my doctor's appointments.

Like the first time, Reed doesn't let me hold on to the examination table. He makes me let go of it and wraps his fingers around mine. He lets me dig my nails into his skin when things become uncomfortable for me. He doesn't even flinch under the force of my grip, simply keeps his eyes on me and lends me all his strength.

And he always asks for copies of the blurry ultrasound pictures.

Of her.

That he then puts into his pocket with those very hands.

With those hands, he makes lists of questions he wants to ask our doctor. And those same hands curl into fists when her answers remain the same for the next couple of appointments.

My raging morning sickness will hopefully vanish when I enter my second trimester. It's normal for me to feel tired and lethargic as my body changes and yes, second trimester should be better than the first.

And it is.

God, it is.

When February comes around and I enter my second trimester, I start to feel normal.

I start to feel like a human being. The days aren't blurry and I'm not so tired anymore. I can bear the school days, the homework, the snickering, the looks, which still haven't faded.

But it's fine.

I've got my girls and they're on my side. So I don't care what the rest of the world thinks about me. I have so many other things to worry about anyway, and so I'm letting it go.

I can talk to people when they visit me, like my brothers, especially Conrad. Ledger comes down from New York as much as he can. Shepard and Stellan try to make it too.

And I'm so glad that I'm feeling more like myself now when a week into my second trimester, one of my favorite people in the whole world visits me: Tempest.

She comes down from New York for the weekend and I'm so excited about it.

Because I missed her so much.

I've been talking to her over the phone since I don't have any time limits now, or on the number of calls that I can make. But I'm so glad that I get to see her.

"Oh my God, you're going to be a mommy," she squeals as soon as she arrives in her car, carrying what looks like everything from every store in New York City.

She dumps it all on the driveway and runs over to give me a

big hug, her gray eyes cheerful.

I laugh, squeezing her tightly. "What have you done? What are all these bags for?"

She squeezes me tightly back. "It's for the baby. Because hello, I'm going to be an aunt. And trust me, I'm going to be the most fun aunt ever. And for you."

"For me?"

She moves away and tells me all excitedly, "Yarn for your knitting. I still don't know how you do that stuff. But I know you love it so I brought you tons of it."

"You did?" My eyes tear up; that hasn't gone anywhere, my hypersensitivity. "Aww, thanks. I've been dying to knit."

Now that I'm healthy again, I have been thinking about making little hats and socks for my baby girl. There is no way I'm going to have her wear store-bought knits.

When her mommy's an expert, she doesn't have to wear subpar stuff.

Tempest waves my thanks away. "And maternity clothes."

"Maternity clothes?"

"Duh. Look at you." She looks down at me and her smile knows no bounds. "You're showing."

My hand goes to my teeny tiny baby bump and I smile too. "Very little. I can't believe you can see it through my baggy clothes."

"Oh, you mean through the hoodie that you're wearing. That belongs to my jerk brother." She raises her eyebrows. "I can see it."

Oh right.

I don't wear my own clothes anymore. His hoodies are so comfy.

And I do have maternity clothes — Reed bought me some and then my brothers bought me some and yes, it was like the cell phone and the groceries, the tug of war between my four overprotective older brothers and the guy whose baby I'm carrying.

Even my girls bought me stuff. So I have tons of maternity clothes.

Even so, I usually wear his clothes. Mostly hoodies and t-shirts, and I've been doing this for so many weeks now that it has become normal for me.

It's not.

Not for other people.

I tug on the hem of his hoodie. "It's only because of his scent. He has this amazing fabric softener and —"

"Ew." She shakes her head. "I don't need to hear about my brother's scent. Although, I do wanna hear about why you're blushing right now."

"I'm not."

Am I?

Laughing, she hugs me again and then I help her with all her shopping bags and usher her inside.

We spend the day like we used to back when I was free and lived in Bardstown.

We talk and gossip and laugh. We watch movies together while we eat popcorn and the Peanut Butter Blossoms she brought for me. She shows me all her purchases too.

Even though I'm assuming it's a girl and Reed seems to be on board, we really don't know what we're having and we won't until our fifth ultrasound appointment, which is still six weeks away.

So Tempest bought everything gender neutral. And it's all so pretty and cute that I start crying, freaking her out. But I tell her that these days I cry at everything.

Soon it's dinnertime and that's when I hear him.

I hear his Mustang arrive in the driveway and my heart starts racing.

He'd texted me earlier in the day that he had a meeting at the office but he'd be home for dinner. And I have to admit that throughout the day, while hanging out with Tempest, I was thinking about her brother.

I was waiting for him.

And he's here now.

My stomach flutters and I have to press a hand on it to calm it down, her down. She always does this.

Every day when he comes to pick me up from school or brings groceries over the weekend or asks me how I'm doing, she goes crazy inside my belly.

And yes, I still know that it's scientifically impossible for those flutters to be her. But I'm a mom-to-be, I'm allowed my quirks.

So every day she wakes up at the sight of him, all happy and cheerful. Excited.

I, on the other hand, have tried to stay unaffected.

I have tried my best to deny the rush, the warmth, the goosebumps from invading my skin. I try to deny that my breaths scatter at the sight of him.

In fact, all I've done in the past weeks, aside from being sick and tired, is deny and remember.

Remember what he did.

How he used me and lied to me. How he made me fall in love with him only to cast me aside when it suited him.

I have tried to hold on to it, to the past and his crimes.

To the hands that broke my heart.

But these days when I see those very hands, I remember them holding my hair back, making me tea, rubbing my spine as he soothes me while being tired himself. Because of his work all day and my sickness all night. I remember them driving me to and from school.

I remember them bringing groceries, underlining things in the pregnancy books even though he thinks that books can go fuck themselves, noting down things when Dr. May talks about handling ballet and pregnancy, fixing a leaking tap in the bathroom so it doesn't get worse later.

These days whenever I see his hands, I get tired. A different type of tired and exhausted.

The kind where holding on to the past has become increasingly difficult.

The loud sound of the car door shutting breaks my thoughts. That and Tempest's squeals as she jumps up from the couch and runs to the front door, throwing it open.

Even though my ballerina heart is spinning in my chest at his arrival, I slowly rise from the couch and approach the door.

The winter sky has darkened early but it doesn't matter.

It never does when it comes to him.

He burns so brightly that the night can't hide him.

Wearing a white dress shirt that's wrinkled after his day in the office and hair that's long and messy, he glows as he emerges from his Mustang. Tempest is right there when he does and like two years ago at the party that changed my life forever, I see him envelop her in a big hug.

I see him chuckle at her as he asks her how her ride in was and if she was speeding. And what has she been doing to her car. Because it looks like shit and he's going to take a look at it later, see if it needs a tune-up.

When Tempest answers all of his questions and asks some of her own, he looks up.

And I have to hold on to the edge of the door at the impact of his gaze on me.

His dark, dark possessive gaze.

Like he's looking at something that belongs to him.

I mean, technically the hoodie that I'm wearing, white and creamy and cozy, does belong to him, yes. Not to mention, the baby inside my body.

The body that has grown and swelled — only slightly but still — in the past weeks.

And all of it has happened under his wolf eyes.

And so this dark possession has only grown over the past weeks.

Before it made my skin coarse with goosebumps, but now it burns me.

It makes me curl my extremities and part my lips.

Now it makes me, actually makes me, put a hand on my belly. Not that it's a hardship; I love touching my belly, but still.

The moment I do, he lets Tempest go and his animal eyes fall on my expanded abdomen. He stares at it for a few beats as if checking that my — our — baby girl is all safe inside of me. As if he can confirm this just by looking at me like that.

Then he lifts up his eyes and moves toward me.

With every step he takes toward me, he does his thing.

Checking to make sure that I'm okay, that nothing bad has happened to me while I was safely ensconced in this cozy house, spending a relaxed day with his sister.

His steps echo as he climbs the porch steps and I dig my fingers into my belly.

When he reaches me, he dips his face and I crane my neck up.

"Hi," I say, doing my thing, glancing at the tired lines around his eyes, his mouth.

The sharpness of his cheekbones, his jaw, the creases on his forehead.

As if that place where he works chisels him down, brings out his blade-like edges, and I hate that.

I absolutely hate it.

"You okay?" he asks instead of greeting me back.

"Yeah. You? You look tired. Was it a hard day?"

"I'm fine." He dismisses my concern over him and it bugs me even more but I keep my mouth shut for now. "You throw up at all?"

"No, not even once," I whisper. "Remember what the doctor said? I won't. Not anymore."

At the mention of our doctor, his stubbled jaw clenches. "Well, the doctor can go fuck herself."

"Reed," I warn. "Don't say that. It's not her fault that my morning sickness was so bad."

"But it was her fucking job to make it better, wasn't it?"

I sigh. "You know, you shouldn't curse so much, Reed."

His eyes flash, making me blush.

Then he asks gruffly, "Pest give you a hard time?"

"Of course not. She's my best friend. We had tons of fun. We saw movies. We gossiped. We had pizza and popcorn. And cheesy fries. Also cupcakes."

Aside from my nausea being gone, my hunger is back. I still can't do meat. But God, give me all the fried stuff.

His lips twitch. "Peanut Butter Blossoms."

Gosh, those cupcakes will be the death of me.

Because every time I eat them, I think about his mouth. I know I'm not supposed to but I do. I do think about his taste. And it doesn't help that I'm surrounded by his scent, his clothes. Him.

I bite my lip, nodding. "And she bought me stuff."

"Stuff."

"Yeah. She got me tons of yarn and…"

Something flashes through his eyes then and I realize what I said. What it means.

I made him a sweater once. Took me weeks to work on that

intarsia for him. I worked late into the night, trying to get it finished for his championship game.

My fingers hurt with the phantom pain now.

The pain over the fact that he must've thrown it away.

Because it didn't mean anything to him.

But more than that, there's pain in my hands from holding on to the past so tightly.

"To knit," he says in a low voice, his gaze piercing into mine.

"Yeah. I wanna make her socks. And hats."

"Sweaters."

I swallow, still cradling my belly. "I wanna make her those too. But I'm afraid."

"Of what?"

"What if… What if she doesn't like them? My sweaters."

A muscle on his cheek pulses. "She'd love them."

My heart jumps. "You think so?"

"I fucking know so."

I like it…

That's what he said back when I gave him the sweater and I was so happy that he did. But he was lying. I know.

I also know that he isn't lying now.

And his next fiercely-spoken words prove it. "Because you'll make it. And for once you'll make it for someone who actually deserves your perfectly made things and your first attempts at intarsia."

"Reed, I…"

I trail off because I don't know what I was going to say. I don't know what I wanted to say.

What did I want to say to him?

It doesn't matter anyway because Tempest decides to tell us both, from where she's still standing by Reed's Mustang, that she's hungry and that we should finish making googly eyes at each other later.

And then I'm so embarrassed that I was, in fact, making googly eyes at him, I don't even look at Reed all throughout dinner. Although I can feel his eyes on me and also on Tempest, whom I think he's glaring at.

After we're done, we have a debate on who's going to do what in terms of cleaning up. Reed wants to do everything himself but I tell him no. I tell him that I'm fine now and I can do stuff. Plus he's tired from work anyway. So I clean up the table, put away all the food, and Reed does the dishes.

Tempest watches it all with her gray eyes that never ever seem to stop laughing.

When we're done, she pulls me out of the kitchen without even a word to Reed and drags me to my room, closing the door.

"So?" Tempest goes when she's got the door locked.

"So?"

Wide-eyed, she asks, "Are you going to tell me?"

"Tell you what?"

"You've told me everything. Except one thing."

"What is that?"

She sighs, looking at me, and her always smiling eyes go dim and grave. "Are you still mad at him? For what he did to you."

My heart starts to thump in my chest. "I... I'm..."

She grabs my hand in hers and squeezes it. "Because if you are, then it's okay. I support you."

I squeeze it back. "A-and what if I'm not?"

"Then I support you too. Duh."

"He's your brother, Temp," I remind her.

"I know. And I love him and he's my BFF. But you're my BFF too and I saw how you were that night. I saw what he did to you, Callie. I was there. He broke you." She scoffs. "You're the biggest good girl I've ever met and look what he made you do."

My eyes sting.

I can't believe this girl. I don't know what I would've done if she hadn't been with me. Not only that night but also throughout that summer.

I mean, she's my partner in crime.

"So? Are you?" she prods.

And the only reason I can tell her is because not only do I love her but I also can't keep it inside anymore. "I think... I think I'm tired now."

"Of what?"

"Of being angry at him. Of holding on to the past. I try. I do. I... make myself remember and it was easy before. So easy but..." A tear falls down my cheek. "But I... it's hard. He makes it so hard. Do you think I'm weak? For not being angry at him anymore. For letting go of the past."

She has tears in her eyes too as she says, "God, Callie, you're not weak. You're one of the strongest people I know. You're a survivor, okay? You survived your first heartbreak. You survived my brother. So no, it doesn't make you weak. Moving on is not weakness. It's a choice that we make when the time is right. It's a choice that we make to cut that toxic, hurtful part out of our lives. So we can be free. We can have closure. You're getting closure, Callie. You're choosing not to hurt."

I'm choosing not to hurt. I'm choosing closure.

That's what I wanted, right? I wanted to move on.

I wanted to stop the hurt, the pain.

And it has stopped.

I haven't felt that anger in such a long time. I've been trying to but it's gone now.

He made it go away. He did it.

He did what I asked him to do that night.

He made it stop hurting.

"Closure," I whisper, a light bulb going off in my head. "I've wanted that. That's what I wanted."

"And you have it now."

I wipe the tears off my face and nod. "Yeah."

"And besides, not being mad at him doesn't mean you can't make him pay," Tempest says with raised eyebrows, wiping her own tears.

"What?"

She winks. "Watch this."

Letting go of me, she opens the door and peeks her head out, shouting, "Reed, Callie's feet hurt." My eyes bug out and I tug on her arm to stop her but she doesn't. "Get in here, bro. She says her feet hurt because of what you did to her. You knocked her up, didn't you? And now her ankles are swollen and my best friend can't stand. All because of you, Reed." Then, she turns to me. "Wait, is it feet or ankles? What happens to pregnant women?"

A shock of laughter bursts out of me. "Uh, everything."

She laughs too and I decide that as soon as I get a chance, I'm introducing her to all my St. Mary's girls. She's going to get along great with them, especially Poe.

That's how Reed finds us, giggling like lunatics. His frown says all about what he thinks of that. Pair of silly teenage girls. This is exactly how he used to look at us back then, when Tempest and I would hang out together.

When Tempest leaves us alone, he asks, looking down at my ballerina feet, "What the fuck is she talking about? What's wrong with your feet?"

I study his face.

His bruises are long gone now. His arched cheekbones, his straight pretty nose, those eyelashes, that V-shaped jaw dotted with stubble that he scratches in irritation.

"You really hate your stubble, don't you?" I ask instead.

He frowns. "What the hell is wrong with your feet, Fae?"

"I like it, your stubble," I keep going without answering him. "Always have. And your longish hair."

His eyes pierce mine. "You like my longish hair."

"Yes." I eye his long, dark strands that are brushing against the collar of his shirt. "Technically you need a haircut. But I don't want you to get one."

He studies me a beat. "Fine."

"Fine what?"

"I won't get one."

"You won't get a haircut."

"That's what I said."

I raise my eyebrows. "Because I said so."

He tightens his jaw for a second before he almost growls, "Are we done chit-chatting? What the fuck is wrong with your feet?"

"Why, are you going to massage them?"

"If I have to."

I bite my lip, circling my eyes over his face, my heart thumping in my chest. "You're crazy."

"And you're pregnant."

"With your baby," I whisper.

Something washes over his beautiful but concerned features. Something heated and bright and possessive. And his eyes home in on my tiny bump that, to be honest, is not even visible under his hoodie, but still.

"Yeah, you are," he whispers back, gruffly. "So are you going to tell me?"

When I put my other hand on my stomach, he swallows, fisting his own hands.

The hands that I'm so entranced by.

The hands that I can completely admit I want on me. God, so much.

"I'm just pregnant, Reed. That's all," I tell him. "You don't have to treat me like a princess. And no, nothing's wrong with my feet. Tempest was just messing with you."

"Tempest and I are going to have words." He bends down slightly. "And I'm not."

"What?"

"Treating you like a princess. Because you're not a princess, are you?"

"No."

He looks me up and down, my short body in his large hoodie, my daisy-printed pajama pants, my loose braid, my ballerina toes. "What are you then?"

My toes go up at his question and I whisper, "A fairy."

His wolf eyes glow. "Yeah, my Fae."

And I know what I have to do.

I know.

Chapter 20

Today's the day.

That I'm going to do what I've decided.

It's not a special day per se. It's a Monday after Tempest's visit and everything's been the same.

The school, the teachers, my supportive gang of girls.

Reed.

He's been the same too, crazy protective and crazy caring, dropping me off at school, picking me up. Glaring at the lingering girls through the black metal gate. Helping me with the dishes and cleaning up after dinner.

In fact, that's what he's doing right now.

He stands beside me in his white dress shirt putting away the dishes that I'm giving him. And I'm doing the same thing that I always do these days, watching his strong beautiful hands, his veins, the tiny drops of water decorating his marble skin.

"Fae."

I blink and look up. "What?"

He looks at me slightly impatiently. "The fucking dish."

"Right."

I hand him the rinsed dish I am holding and when he wipes it down and puts it up in the cupboard, I blurt out, "Reed, I..."

"You what?"

You what, Callie? Say it.

Tell him.

"I have a name," I blurt out instead for some reason.

"What?"

"For her."

He goes alert then. "You have a name for her."

Biting my lip, I smile slightly. "Yes."

Even though this wasn't what I was going to say to him, I'm glad I did. Now that my mind isn't muddled with exhaustion, I've been looking at names.

Or rather, paying attention in English lit class about character names and such.

And today I heard a name that I absolutely loved.

His wolf eyes sharpen with interest. "What is it?"

"Okay, so," I begin, my voice buzzing with excitement as I close the tap and turn to him. "Today in class we were reading this story and there was a name that jumped out at me. It completely blew my mind."

"Completely."

"Yes. Like it changed how I looked at that name, you know. And I think it's very rare. I don't think I've ever —"

"Fae."

"What?"

"What the fuck is the name?"

"Right, okay. Listen to this: Miya. With a Y."

I grin then.

Because isn't it wonderful? Who would have thought?

I mean, you either go with Mia or Maya. But Miya with a Y is so exotic and different and as soon as I heard it, I knew I was going to name her Miya.

He hasn't said anything though.

He's simply looking at me with a blank face, leaning against the counter in his open-collared office shirt, his arms folded across his chest.

So I prompt him as I keep grinning because I can't contain the excitement. "So? What do you think? Miya with a Y, huh? I think this has completely changed how we think of the name Mia."

"No."

"What?"

"It hasn't completely changed how we think of the name Mia."

"What, why?"

"Because we still think Mia is a shitty name."

"Excuse me?"

"And adding a Y in is not going to change that."

I gasp. "Are you serious right now?"

"Do I look like I'm joking?"

"Then you're insane, Reed," I tell him, raising my chin. "Mia is a wonderful name, okay? Adding a Y makes it even more wonderful."

He shrugs then. "All right. I'm still not naming her Miya with a fucking Y."

"You're not naming her?"

"That's what I said."

I purse my lips at him. "First of all, you're not going to name her anything. We're going to do that. And second of all, I really don't think you should curse, Reed. And third —"

"Why?"

"What?"

He unfolds his arms, straightening up, his eyes flashing. "You keep saying that. That I shouldn't curse."

I'm confused. "Yeah…"

"Why shouldn't I?"

I tuck my loose strands behind my ears. "Because you shouldn't."

He takes a step toward me. "Yeah, you said that. Why?"

I automatically take a step back. "Because it's bad manners."

"And you're a good girl."

"Yes."

"Yeah, you are." He smirks slightly, taking me in, my braid, his hoodie, my bare toes.

I realize that I haven't seen his smirk on him in so long. I haven't seen him this cocky, this arrogant in so long either.

This predatory.

He's glorious like this. Gorgeous.

As gorgeous as he is when he's my protector.

Because he's both, isn't he?

He's my protector, the one who takes care of me and treats me like I'm the most fragile thing ever, his Fae. But he's also a predator, the one who broke my heart and who's stalking toward me in all his dark glory.

"And what else?" he continues.

"I don't like it."

"Yeah, you do."

"I don't."

"You always did," he rasps, as he keeps coming toward me and as I keep moving back.

Until I can't.

Because the small of my back has hit the counter and I come to a jerking halt.

Unlike my heart that's pounding like crazy, because he's right.

I do like it when he curses.

I do like it when he talks to me so unapologetically. In a way that's so raw and intimate and… dirty. I've always liked it.

"Ask me how I know that," he says when he reaches me, the predatory quality in his tone so thick that I can taste it.

"How?"

"Because you blush," he rasps, watching me, his face dipped. "Now ask me why I do it. Why I talk dirty to you."

I grab hold of the counter at my hips. "W-why?"

"So you can tell me not to and get all hot and bothered, while blushing like a daisy-fresh schoolgirl."

I don't know what to say to that.

I don't know how to respond because my heart is right there, in the back of my mouth, beating and beating. And then, he decides to send it to the tip of my tongue.

Where it sits precariously, on the edge of a deep and deadly fall.

When he raises his hand, the hand that I've been so fascinated with, and runs a rough finger down my cheek.

I feel something swirling in my blood. Heat. So much of it.

A current, a pulse.

But more than that, I feel relief, because this is the moment when I also realize that along with letting his predatory side sleep, he also hasn't touched me.

It's been weeks, actually, since he's touched me like this.

I mean he has touched me, of course. But it has mostly been out of necessity, protection, an arm around my waist to help me stand up after a bout of nausea or a hand on the small of my back to usher me inside the exam room.

But not like this. Not since that night in his Mustang back in October.

He's been holding himself back.

It's all clear as day. When I see the relief that I've been feeling on his face. In his loosened shoulders, his parted lips. In the way his eyes home in on my cheek.

And God, I have to tell him. I have to say it to him now.

So he'll touch me more.

"I liked that," he whispers, breaking my urgent thoughts.

"What?"

"When you laughed. This weekend. With Pest."

His finger is on my parted lips now. "Oh."

"Haven't seen you laugh like that in a long time," he murmurs, still watching his finger. "Back when you'd come over to the house. And you and Pest would be gabbing about something in her room and suddenly you'd burst out laughing." He pauses and a muscle jumps out on his cheek. "I'd hear you and I'd stop whatever I was doing and I'd think…"

I don't know how I manage to string words together but I do and I whisper, "You'd think what?"

He looks into my eyes, his finger tracing the curve of my lips. "She laughs like a fairy too."

My stomach hollows out and I grab onto his wrist with both hands as I say, my body melting, "I forgive you."

He, on the other hand, goes rigid. "What?"

That's what I wanted to say to him. That's what I'd decided this weekend.

That I'd tell him that.

And so I do, even though he's gone all rigid, all unforgiving. "I-I forgive you. For everything."

He studies my face with a gaze that has hardened, much like his body. "Everything."

I was afraid before, to say it.

To actually say the words and make them real.

But I'm not afraid anymore.

I'm not afraid to tell him that I've forgiven him because it is the truth. It has been the truth for some time now. Even though he doesn't look too happy about it. He doesn't look like he wants to hear it.

I dig my nails into his wrist. "Yeah. I forgive you for breaking my heart two years ago. For lying to me. For using me. For breaking your promises to me and for choosing your vendetta against your dad over me. I forgive you for all that."

This time his silence is much, much longer.

During which the muscle in his cheek beats like my own heart. It beats like it will rip out of his skin like my heart will rip out of my chest.

"Why?" he asks after a while, somehow with his finger still on my lip, still as tender as ever, so in contrast to his harsh demeanor.

"Because my heart doesn't hurt anymore," I whisper, staring into his pretty eyes. "Because ever since you broke it, my heart, two years ago, I've been in pain. I've been in so much pain, and that's why I stole your car, to stop it. That's why I asked you for closure the night when... when we had sex. For the last two years, all I've wanted was for the pain to stop. I just wanted my heart to stop hurting and it has. I don't feel it anymore. The pain. It's gone."

"Why?" he asks again. "Why is it gone?"

I go up on my tiptoes to reach him because he looks so far away right now. "Because you took it away. You made it go away. I asked you to do it and you did."

Isn't it ironic though?

That the guy who gave me this pain is also the one who took it away. He's the one who soothed it.

But it only seems to push him further away.

So much so that he breaks out of my hold. He takes his touch away from me and steps back.

The touch that he'd given after weeks, he takes it back in a matter of seconds and my knees feel weak without it.

My body goes cold. My legs tremble.

He stares at me with angry eyes, his stubbled jaw ticking. "And I'm assuming all this forgiveness is because of what I'm doing, is that correct? For driving you around, for bringing you groceries, for taking you to that useless fucking doctor. You think I'm doing this for your forgiveness?"

I don't know how I can be so calm when he's like this. Agitated and angry. Callous.

Old Callie would be freaking out. She'd be trembling and maybe even crying at his cold behavior. But I'm not that Callie anymore.

Because of him.

Because I've met the villain once and I've survived.

That's what Tempest said and she was right.

I survived him. And I'm stronger now, a lot better for it.

"No," I say, shaking my head. "I know you're doing all this because you want to. You're doing this because of her." I cradle my belly and say something that I know in my heart. "Because you love her."

That throws him.

That makes him take another step back. The word 'love.'

So along with 'protect' and 'save,' love is another one of his triggers.

"Don't you?" I prod, digging my fingers in my bump. "You love her."

His features ripple with surprise as if this is such news. When it has been apparent to me, to my brothers even, since day one.

That he wants her. Genuinely.

He loves her — as much as I do — and he doesn't even know

if it's a her yet.

I know he thinks that he doesn't love anything, that he has no space for love, but he loves her.

His chest is not barren after all. There's at least one flower in it. For her.

For our baby.

He stares at my belly really hard before looking up. "Yes, I do."

"I know."

"She's mine."

My eyes sting with happy tears. "She is."

See? How can I be mad at him anymore for what he did two years ago?

How can I be mad that he never loved me when he loves her?

When he loves our baby.

I can't. I'm done.

I thought that nothing he could do would make me forgive him. But turns out, all he had to do was love her.

Love this accidental, wonderful gift he's given me.

I'm done living in the past and thinking of him as my villain. The predator who fed on my heart and left me to die. When he's also a hero. Her hero, her protector.

He's both, a gorgeous villain and a haunted hero.

"But that doesn't mean anything," he snaps, plowing his fingers through his dark overgrown hair. "That doesn't mean I want your forgiveness. I don't. You can fucking keep it. Throw it out the window for all I care."

I don't even flinch when he says that.

In fact, I take a step closer to him as I ask, "Why?"

"What?"

I take another step closer. "Why don't you want it?"

He watches my feet with a thick frown. "What the fuck are

you doing?"

"Tell me why you don't want it."

He watches me take another step toward him and his fists clench. "Are you trying to scare me, Fae? Because I'm not in a mood to laugh."

I reach him and tilt my head back to look at his beautiful face. "No. I'm asking a question. Tell me."

His chest moves up and down with his sweet but agitated breath. His nostrils flare as he glances around the room. And it looks like I've cornered him. Which is so crazy, because there's no way I can hold him here or overpower him.

Not him.

The one who's as tall and broad as the mountains. As wild as a mustang.

"Because I didn't protect you, all right," he bursts out. "I couldn't protect you two years ago and I couldn't protect you now. Do you understand that? Do you understand what I did to you? I didn't only break your heart, you had to be caged because of me. Caged. Because I made you steal my car. In a shithole school. When you should've been out there, free, dancing like you were born to do. But that's not all, is it? I stole from you. I stole your virginity. I took it from you. I tore it out of your body until you bled. You fucking bled on my dick and I was too fucked in the head to understand that. I was too fucked and blind and jealous to figure out that the pussy I was plowing into was untouched. And then, I got you pregnant. You're having my baby, Fae. And it's so brutal on you and I can't do anything about it. The fucking doctor can't do anything about it."

"But I'm fine now," I say in a determined voice.

"Yeah. But you weren't, were you? You couldn't keep anything down. Not even fucking water."

Oh yeah, that night was brutal.

I think my stomach was all upset and even the water was making me throw up. And he was up with me all night. But he was tired too, I remember. He had a meeting at work the next day and I remember him not getting a wink of sleep, same as me.

I know I was going through a hard time but he went through it too.

But he doesn't let me speak as he continues, "So I don't want your fucking forgiveness. Because there isn't any. For what I did. For breaking my fairy. For putting her in a cage, for taking her dream away from her. For hurting her body, making her bleed, and I wasn't even there to make it better. I —"

"Do it, then."

"What?"

Yeah. What?

What did I just say?

But I take a moment to study him then. His messy hair, his stubble. His wrinkled shirt. The fierce expression on his face. The regret that is apparent in his every gesture, his closed fists, his wildly breathing chest.

And I realize I had to say it. I had to.

Not because I need him to make it better. Because he already did it.

But because he needs to.

He needs to make it better and I can't not give it to him, what he wants.

I swallow. "You said, back at the bar, that you'd... you'd make it better. You'd apologize. To her. To my... pussy. Because you made her bleed. Because you're so big and I'm so small. So..." I swallow again, clutching the hem of his hoodie. "So do it then. Make it better."

By the time I finish, a throb has started up between my legs.

A throb that I've been feeling for days now. But I always

pushed it aside. First, it was my sickness and then it was the fact that I shouldn't have been feeling it in the first place.

But now there's nothing stopping me.

I don't want anything to stop me. From feeling it. From feeling him, inside of me. Even though he's only been there once, I remember it so well.

I remember all the dirty, intimate things he did. All the dirty, intimate things he said to me.

His eyes glint, his high cheekbones going flushed and I know he remembers them as well.

I think he shudders too, licking his ruby red lips, and I have to press my thighs against each other.

"Are you fucking with me, Fae?" he growls. "Because I told you I'm not in the mood for it."

"No, I'm not."

In fact, I reach out and take his hand. And I put it where I know he wants to touch me but hasn't because he's been keeping himself away. I put his hand on my slightly swollen stomach as I go on. "I don't want you to apologize anymore. I'm done, Reed and I mean it. But if you need to do it anyway, if you need to apologize or make it better, then I want you to. I want you to apologize and take my hurt away."

And then I let his hand go but his fingers latch on.

His long strong fingers latch onto my baby bump and I know, for sure this time, that he shudders. His chest vibrates, his fingers too, on my belly.

And his gaze drops down to where he's touching me.

I look down as well and my own breaths shake when I see how his big hand covers it all. My tiny bump. How he's cradling it and how his fingers sport a slight tremble.

"I wanted to…" he rasps with a slight crease between his eyebrows.

I reach up to smooth it. "I know. You wanted to touch it but you never did."

He swallows. "For a long time."

"You can touch it. Whenever you want. I want you to."

He looks up, the color of his eyes one that I've never seen on him before.

All melting and liquid. Molten mercury.

"It's warm," he says.

My eyes become wide in excitement as I bring my hands to grab the sleeves of his shirt. "Isn't it? I feel it too."

"Yeah."

"I thought I was crazy," I tell him. "I haven't read this in any of the books yet but I —"

"Books can go fuck themselves."

I bite my lip to stop my smile. I can't stop my blush though and his wolf eyes sparkle at that. There's my predator. My gorgeous villain.

"You shouldn't curse, Reed," I whisper, looking up at him with smiling eyes.

His fingers on my belly tighten. "Yeah? Maybe I should apologize for that then."

"You should." I fist his sleeves even tighter. "I'm a good girl and all you ever do is talk filthy to me."

"What a fucking asshole am I, yeah?"

"And you make me hurt."

His nostrils flare again on a long breath. "Tell me where I hurt you."

I have to open my mouth as well because breathing is getting harder. "In my pussy."

"My fucking dick is an asshole too."

My channel pulses, waking up, remembering everything from that night. "And also here."

This I can't say.

But I will show him.

I will show him all the places that hurt so he can do whatever he wants to them. So he can make it better and lose all his regret.

So he can see that I've already forgiven him.

I take his hand again, the one that's clutching my swollen belly, and drag it up.

Up and up.

Until his hand is right there. On my breast.

I know my cheeks are all pink now. Red and burning. But still I peek at him from under my eyelashes. "This. It hurts here too. Sometimes."

His fingers twitch on the fabric and like he grabbed hold of my pregnant belly, he palms my breast too and my toes inch up.

Because God, I've never known my breasts to be so sensitive.

I've never known them to be so soft and tender. So heavy.

And it's all getting worse because he's watching them.

Even through his soft, thick hoodie, I can feel his gaze on them, on my bare skin. Not to mention his hand covers all of it, like it did my belly, and that makes me so breathless that I squeeze his wrist tightly, making him look up.

"They hurt," he whispers thickly.

"Yes," I whisper back.

"Tell me how."

"They're all sensitive and tender and… and big. Bigger than before, and my nipples…"

"What about them?"

"They ache sometimes. They throb. I-I think it's because I'm changing. My body is."

His jaw clenches, making the peaks of his face harsher, painted with a deep flush. "Your body is changing. Because of what I did."

"Because of the baby."

His fingers squeeze my breast, just one squeeze but it's enough to make me moan slightly and he watches it all. With his heated eyes.

"My baby," he whispers as if correcting me.

"Yours."

"And it's only going to get worse, isn't it? Your tits," he says, squeezing my breast again.

This time the force is harder and I have to arch my back and he's right there. To give me support.

To let me use his body, all big and muscled and strong, to lean against, and when I do, my relief is complete. My breaths are easier, far, far easier than they've been in a long time.

Since two years ago.

But he doesn't let me stay that way, all relaxed and loosened up.

He decides to keep me on my toes when he squeezes my breast again, his thumb swiping over my tender nipple. "I can't stop picturing it."

"What?"

"I can't stop picturing you. Every time we go for a doctor's appointment and she makes you lie down. She puts that gel on your stomach, I think about it. Every time I see you wearing your schoolgirl uniform or my hoodie, I fucking think about it."

"Think about what?"

Finally, he looks up and answers. "You, pregnant with my baby. Your belly swelling up, getting bigger. Your tits." His palm has grown bolder now and he starts to knead my tender flesh, making me moan and gasp. "Getting all soft and creamy. Ripe. I picture you walking around, barefoot and pregnant. In those daisy dresses, your belly all swollen up, your tits squished together, jiggling with every step you take. And every five seconds you'll cradle it, your pregnant belly, like it's the most precious treasure in the world and it is, isn't it?"

"Yes."

"Yeah, she is. She fucking is. She's the only right thing in all this. In every fucked-up thing that I've done."

"Reed —"

"So there you are, lying on the exam table, grabbing onto my arm because it's uncomfortable and scary and all I do is stand there like a useless bastard. A horny bastard, picturing all this. I get hard thinking about this like a motherfucking perv. Like a proud motherfucking perv though. Because this is the only good thing I've done, blowing my load inside your fairy pussy. But I made her hurt, didn't I? And now your tits hurt too. Because your body's changing for my baby. Your body is preparing and I have to apologize. I have to apologize for doing this to you, for putting a baby in you like the villain I am and I will, you understand?

"I will spend all my days apologizing, on my knees, with my mouth on your sweet snatch. And when I'm not apologizing to your cunt, I'll put my mouth on these." He squeezes my breast again, rhythmically, driving me crazy. "On your creamy tits. And I'll say sorry to them with my tongue and my mouth. For making them all sore and heavy. For stretching them out. And then lusting after them like an asshole. And you, Fae. I'll apologize to you too. For making you go through all this. Because I didn't protect you enough. I didn't think clearly enough. But I want you to know something, okay?"

His fierce eyes make me ask, "What?"

"That I'll protect you now. I will. I will do anything and everything in my power, beyond my power even, to protect you and her. No one will touch you. Or her. Not now. Not ever. I promise, and I'll die before I break this promise to you. Tell me you believe me."

My heart is spinning and spinning in my chest and my toes, which are carrying all my weight, tremble.

At the gravity of his tone and words.

"Yes, I do," I whisper because I do.

I do believe him.

He studies me for a second with those fierce eyes and when he realizes the truth in my words, a small breath escapes him. Before he does what he told me he would.

He apologizes.

With his lips.

He captures my mouth in a hot kiss, bending down over me. So that I don't have to stretch up to get to him. So my legs don't have to shake to carry my weight.

He'll do it all for me, make it easier to breathe, to kiss and be kissed.

And I'm dying and aching. In pain once again.

But this is a different kind of pain.

A restless kind.

And it only grows with every suck of his mouth and every flick of his thumb on my nipple. Every time I rub myself against him, his hard body, I hurt.

It's as if someone has made a fist and is pressing down on my stomach, pressing down on my pussy.

In my tits.

All swollen and creamy because he got me pregnant.

And then he breaks our kiss, making it even worse, taking away my lifeline, and my hands on his shoulders grow insistent. They want to pull him back but he doesn't come to me.

Instead, he brings me to him.

He picks me up and puts my thighs around his hips. I'm so gone over his lips, with the need for his lips, that all I remember to do is hold on when he starts walking.

All I remember to do is press my mouth to his when he cradles the back of my head and pulls me to him.

I bury my fingers in his thick rich hair as he takes me places. I don't even care where, really. As long as he keeps kissing me like that.

Although again, he breaks the kiss, and this time I'm all ready to claw at his skin and bring him back.

But he turns my world upside down when he puts me on the bed.

The bed that I sleep in.

The bed he used to put me down on back when I used to be so sick. But he's never gotten into it. He looms over me now. His shirt made even more wrinkled by my fisting fingers, his lips appearing wet and swollen due to my kisses and his eyes all burned with lust for me.

Burned with all the things that he thinks about.

Because I'm pregnant and my body's changing.

And so when he kneels at the foot of the bed and goes for the waistband of my pajama pants, I don't stop him. I don't feel shy when he strips them off my legs and goes for the zipper in his hoodie.

He lowers it, all hastily now, without any finesse, and I know it's because he's excited.

He's excited and eager to see me in my new body.

But when he reaches to the bottom of the zipper and his fingers grab the hoodie to part it so he can see my naked skin, his jaw clenches. And I know it's because he hates it at the same time.

He hates this eagerness because he's making my body change.

He's responsible for my swollen belly and my aching tits.

So I grab hold of his hands that are fisted in the fabric and make him do it. Make him part the hoodie that's covering me from his eyes. So he can see.

So he can revel in what he did to me.

And he does, I think.

He does when his body moves with his breaths and when his lips part and his eyes grow hooded. He revels in my slightly bigger belly and wider hips. My swollen, rounded breasts and darker nipples, as I lie there on my back with his hoodie parted and spread, my braid almost undone and fanning over my head.

But then I realize that he's never even seen them before.

My naked body, let alone my naked tits.

So I tell him, "I… I used to be smaller." I swallow when his eyes lift up. "My breasts. Even smaller than this, and my nipples were… were a lighter shade of pink. My hips were smaller too. I'm not… I'm not your tight little ballerina anymore."

The bones of his wrists that I'm still holding flex. "No, you're not. You're my gorgeous, glorious, pregnant Fae. And you're perfect. You're so fucking perfect that it hurts. Here." And he puts his fist on his chest to show me like I showed him.

All I can do is go lax on the bed and whisper his name. "Reed."

"Show me where I hurt you," he demands, his eyes piercing.

And I do it.

I have no shame when I let go of his wrists and creep my one hand up to my breasts and squeeze one. "Here." My other hand goes down my swollen belly and touches my pussy.

I don't stop there though.

I don't just touch it, I rub my lips, wet and soft, making my hips jerk under his eyes. I part those lips like he parted my hoodie to show him my fairy hole, like he calls it, and whisper again, "And here."

Making him growl.

There's no mistaking the sound that emerges from him.

He growls at the sight of my spread-open pussy, the pussy that he thinks is hurting because of him, and I see determination wash over his gorgeous features.

He brings his eyes, all dark and predatory and protective, to mine as he grabs my naked thighs. As he makes my legs fold up at the knees and hooks the arches of my feet to the edge of the bed.

Then without taking his eyes off me, he moves his hands.

He gets them under my butt and picks me up off the bed. I fist my hands on the sheet when he fits his broad shoulders between my spread thighs and settles himself at my raised pelvis.

And then with his eyes on me, he puts his mouth right there.

On my pussy.

On the hole that I showed him, and sucks my lips into his mouth.

The growl that emerges from him then is the fiercest one I've ever heard. And I can't help but think — again — that he has turned into an animal. Like he did that night when he came for my scent and sniffed the column of my throat, wanting to see if I smelled the same.

And God, I love that.

I love how I change him.

Because he changes me too.

He makes me shameless and I writhe my hips on his mouth, moaning. Which only makes him growl louder and suck harder, as if he's sucking and drinking from a cup or a wedge of a fruit with his big hands raising it up to his mouth.

After that I don't have the strength to look into his horny animal eyes.

I close mine and give myself to him.

I curl my fingers in the sheet, my toes in the air, and I let him apologize to me.

I let him talk to my pussy, tell her how sorry he is. How he was an asshole to her that night. How he should've known. He should've known that she was tight and untouched. She was innocent and daisy fresh before he plowed into her. Before he destroyed her and trashed her and made her cry. Made her bleed.

How he knocked her up.

And then with his long pulls and sucks on my clit, he tells her that he'll apologize to her for the rest of his life if he has to. He'll eat her and suck on her and lick her until she can't stand it anymore, until she can't stand the pleasure.

He'll pamper her until she comes and comes on his tongue.

And she does.

I do.

My channel pulses and I undulate my hips in the air. I twist them, shake my ass in his hands as I come in his mouth. As my pussy ripples on his tongue.

As he sucks on my clit and licks my fairy hole. As he moves his mouth up and down and side to side, growling and apologizing and soothing and hurting me.

I come and come and come. I flow into his mouth, douse his tongue with my juices as I chant his name over and over and over.

I chant the name of the guy who's asking for my forgiveness on his knees, with his mouth on my pussy.

The guy I've already forgiven. Who then brings me down to the bed, carefully, tenderly before he bends over and places a reverent kiss on my pregnant belly.

He moves up to my swollen tits and kisses them too, finally going up to my forehead to breathe me in, to place soft kisses in my hair.

Only to leave me all alone in my bed.

Chapter 21

The Hero

"She's forgiven me," I say to Pete, barging into his office.

An hour later, after I've put her to sleep in the bed.

I couldn't sleep though. I couldn't stay there either.

At the scene of my crime.

At the scene where I touched her with my dirty hands. Touched her pregnant, warm belly and her soft, swollen tits. I touched her pussy.

I touched my gorgeous, glorious, pregnant Fae when I'd promised myself that I wouldn't.

I promised myself that I wouldn't touch her, make her all dirty.

"Isn't that a good thing?" Pete asks from his beat-up office without me having to give him any context.

An office with a table that's overrun with files. A cabinet that hardly organizes anything for him and a computer screen that he was squinting into because like me he can't sleep either, until I interrupted him.

It's a tiny place, much smaller than my father's office, and Pete has had this as long as I've known him.

But this doesn't suffocate me.

It doesn't choke my breaths.

"Fuck no," I spit out.

"And how's that?" he asks, settling into his cheap leather chair that squeaks and is bad for his back. That I've told him a million times to replace. But he won't.

It was a gift from Mimi.

He can be such a sucker.

I plow both my hands through my hair. "I don't deserve it."

"Well, that's not your call to make now, is it?"

"It fucking should be."

"But it's not. You wronged her and she moved on. You need to move on too. That's how it works. An apology, making it up to someone."

My chest contracts. My fingers flex.

The fingers that touched her because she tempted me.

She wouldn't let me keep my fucking hands to myself.

I've been aching, dying to touch her ever since she told me she was carrying my baby. I was fucking craving to touch her body, her belly that she so freely touches and every time she does, my blood heats up. My fingers hurt for not getting to touch her skin, the life inside of her.

And she fucking took advantage of that.

"What if…" I burst out but then trail off, pacing in his office.

"First, sit down. You're giving me a headache. And second, what if what?"

I don't.

I come to a halt though and grab the back of the chair in front of his desk. The chair that's better than the one he's sitting in but he won't replace it because he still loves his dead wife.

What is with people and love?

Seriously though, why is it such a big deal?

"Thanks. But I'll stand," I tell him.

He studies my face before shaking his head. "You know what you are?"

"What?"

"A rabid dog."

I narrow my eyes at him. "Thanks, Pete. I feel much better now. I'm glad I came."

"Good, because you are. You're like a vicious wild animal that bites the hand that dares to pet you. Because that's all you've ever known. Biting and snapping your teeth at the world. But as Mimi would say, it's not your fault. It's the world's fault. Because the world has bitten you back."

I clench my teeth. "Are we done here? Because I've got a fucking problem."

"What is your problem, boy?"

"My problem, old man, is what if it happens again?"

"What happens again?"

I don't even know what I'm doing here. I don't even know why I came.

I don't know why I keep coming to Pete whenever I've got a problem. I went to him when my father fucked her over two years ago. I went to him when I found out I fucked her over again and got her pregnant.

And I'm here tonight too.

He never helps.

But the thing is that I've got no place to go. And if that doesn't burn, that the only place I can go to is a fucking garage and the only person I can talk to is a fucking old man who's still in love with his wife and needs a beard trim, then I don't know what will.

I swallow, curling my fingers into the chair. "What if she falls in love with me again?"

"Why's loving you such a bad thing?"

"Aside from the fact that one time she did, and I broke her heart because I was too wrapped up in my shit?" I swallow, my throat feeling tight. "And then my father used her to get back at me. In case you didn't know, my father is still alive. As much as I'd like to kill him, I'm not going to do that because that might also kill my mother. Who somehow still loves that sick fuck. So nothing's changed. She needs to stay away from me, from us. From Jackson men. We don't know a thing about love or being decent human beings."

Pete stares at me for a moment, rubbing his bushy white moustache, before muttering, "You know why your father used her to get to you?"

"Because he's a psychopath who only cares about what he wants and because he saw it as an opportunity."

"Yes. But he's also smart," Pete tells me. "He was smart enough to know that you'd do anything for that girl. You'd give up soccer. You'd give up your scholarship, your whole plan of getting into the pros to stick it to him. He knew that."

"Yeah, so?"

"So you'd give up your fucking soul for that girl. And your father knew that. So what does that tell you?"

I raise my eyebrows at him. "Why don't you explain it to me?"

Pete smiles. "It tells you that you might know a thing or two about love after all, you clueless bastard."

My chest contracts again. Like a boulder is sitting on it.

A giant fucking wrecking ball. A ticking time bomb that's going to explode.

But I ignore it. I ignore it all and scoff at Pete. "I made that deal with my father because she didn't deserve to be used. Not again. She didn't deserve to be punished for something that she did because she was hurting. Because I hurt her. Not everything is about love."

"Whatever helps you sleep at night, kid."

You love her, don't you? You love our baby.

The pressure on my chest increases at her words but I ignore that too.

It doesn't matter if I love our baby or not.

She's a part of me. Of course I love our baby.

But that doesn't mean I'm free to love anyone else. I don't have time for it when I have to protect Fae, protect both of them, from my father.

That's why I'm doing all this, aren't I?

That's why I'm working for him. That's why I go every time he calls. I attend every goddamn meeting. I sit in on every conference call he makes like a good boy.

I'm giving him every little thing his villainous, corrupt heart desires because I want him to be happy enough to back off, to leave me alone.

I never want him to find out about Fae and our baby. I know he'll use them as pawns if and when he can.

And it has worked.

He's a psychopathic toddler. You give him what he wants and he'll move on to something else.

My father has no clue. He doesn't know what I do with my time off. He doesn't care as long as I show up for work and give him what he wants.

But you know what? I don't know why I'm freaking the fuck out right now.

Nothing has changed.

I promised that I'd protect her from my father and me and that's what I'm going to do. Unlike last time, I'm going to keep her heart safe from me.

Because no matter what she believes, I can't love.

I am that rabid fucking animal that bites. Because that's all I know. That's how I've survived this world. That's how I've survived the man who brought me into this world.

"Thanks for nothing," I say to Pete, stepping back from the chair, ready to leave. "And I'm buying you a new chair that won't kill your back. That fucking thing you have right now needs to go to the dump."

And then I turn around and walk out.

But not before I hear his laughing words. "I'll throw it in the dump the day you throw away that sweater of yours. The one with that fucking mustang on it that you still keep in the trunk of your car."

Asshole.

Chapter 22

All the girls at my school are in love with him.

Which is nothing new because every girl at Bardstown High loved him too.

And his dark magic is still alive at St. Mary's School for Troubled Teenagers.

They are in love with him, with his Mustang.

His sparkling vampire skin and his long dark hair. They think his gunmetal gray eyes are so cool, and the way he walks with long, effortless steps makes them swoon.

Even though they watch us with giggling eyes and snickering lips. Even more so now than before because my belly's showing. And well, I've had to make uniform adjustments. Meaning, I don't wear one because those skirts are not made for expanding bellies.

Anyway, I know they love it that he drops me off and picks me up from school. I heard a bunch of them talking during lunch one day.

My girls especially love that. That he waits.

"Oh look, our gorgeous villain is here," Poe sing-songs. "Waiting for his Fae."

My breath catches in my throat. Because I was talking to Wyn about our English lit homework as we were climbing down the steps after finishing for the day and I hadn't seen him yet.

Although to be honest, I should've known.

He's somehow never late, even though he comes straight from work.

I narrow my eyes at Poe though. "Don't make me regret telling you that."

I don't even know why I did.

Since I don't live with them anymore, we try to catch up as much as we can during lunch and any other free time that we get. And since Reed Roman Jackson is such a big topic, all our conversations circle around him, and since I'm an idiot, I let it slip one day that he calls me Fae.

And well, since then they haven't let it go.

Poe sticks her tongue out at me and I do the same in return.

While Salem, our doomed-in-love turned happy-in-love friend, sighs. "I'm so jealous. Like, it's so cute I wanna die. You know what? I'm going to make Arrow write me another poem next time he calls. Just to make up for all this cuteness."

Arrow and Salem are still going strong. Not that I ever doubted that they would.

He's crazy about her. Every visitation weekend, he makes sure to fly over from California, where he lives to visit Salem. The rest of the time, they talk on the phone on Saturdays, email each other. Even write love letters.

I don't know what she's complaining about because her thing is beyond cute.

I raise my eyebrows at Salem. "Make him?"

She raises hers back, smiling slyly. "Yeah. I can make him do things."

Poe jumps in. "What kind of things?"

Salem shrugs. "Things your virgin ears won't be able to hear without blushing."

"I don't blush. Ever." She throws us a coy smile then. "And who says I'm a virgin?"

"Poe, you are a virgin, okay?" I tell her, rolling my eyes. "We know that. So stop trying to be all mysterious."

"Fine. I'm a virgin." She sticks her tongue out at me again and I do the same. "And I hate you. I hate both of you for having sex before me. I want to have sex too. And you know why I haven't had sex yet?"

"We know," Salem says.

"You do?"

"Yes," I reply. "It's because of your tweed-jacket-with-elbow-patches-wearing guardian. Who sent you here."

As expected, Poe's face scrunches up with fury. "Exactly. Everything wrong in my life is because of him. Everything. Ugh. I can't wait to kill him and dance on his grave and then have sex with the first guy I meet." She turns to Salem then. "Until then you're gonna have to tell me everything. So I can live vicariously through you."

As Poe harasses Salem to give up all the dirty details, I turn to Wyn, who I realize hasn't spoken a word in all of this. And the reason for that is that she's staring at something with a slight frown.

Wyn has always been the quietest of us all but these days she's been quieter than usual. And I hate that I don't share a room with her or I'd prod for every single detail during our midnight chats.

I miss her so much. Her and her dream man stories.

Anyway, when I follow her gaze, I see nothing that's worth much attention though.

There's a group of girls, wearing mustard-colored sweaters and blazers, sitting on the concrete benches under the late February sun before the light goes out in the winter sky.

Oh, and there's a group of teachers right behind them that includes my brother, Conrad. Who's been the new soccer coach since last November. Since I sit out soccer games because of my condition, I haven't had much of a chance to be coached by my legendary soccer coach brother. But he does check in with me a couple of times during the day, including lunch, when he brings me all the fried stuff that I've been craving ever since I got my appetite back.

Ugh, and right by my brother stands our history teacher, Miss Halsey, who has made no secret that she's in love with him and would do anything to have him.

Even now, she's almost draped on his arm, looking up at Con like he's the most amazing man she's ever met.

I mean, he is — he's the best man and brother ever — but I hate that Miss Halsey thinks so too. I never liked her before and I don't like her now.

But that's not the point.

My friend needs me so I look away and bump her shoulder. "Hey, what's up?"

She blinks as if waking up. "What?"

"What are you looking at?"

"Nothing," she says quickly.

I frown. "Are you sure? You were staring pretty hard at something."

She ducks her head and tucks her hair behind her ears. "Uh, no. I was just… thinking about something."

"About what?" I prod. "You know, you've been pretty quiet these days. Is something going on, Wyn? You can tell me, you know that, right? I mean, you have to know that. I love you."

She smiles at me but sadness still lingers in her eyes. "I know. It's just I'm stressing about art school applications. It's end of February now and I haven't heard anything back. So I don't know if they liked my sketches or not."

I get her nerves. I haven't heard back from Juilliard myself but she has to know that she's beyond talented and hard working and she'll get in.

"Are you crazy? You're the best artist I know." I grab her shoulders. "Wyn, you're so talented. So, so, so talented. You make me cry with your talent, okay? Cry."

She chuckles. "But you're pregnant. You cry at everything."

"Ha. Ha. I've always cried at your sketches. Because they're awesome. And everyone will love them. You'll see. You'll hear back from them, trust me."

Salem and Poe say the same thing before hugging me goodbye and telling me yet again — Wyn joins in this time — how amazing it is that my gorgeous villain is waiting for me in his Mustang.

So my girls are definitely in love with him.

And although I wouldn't ever say that my brothers are in love with him, they too have somewhat warmed up. Stellan doesn't glare at him all that much and Shepard doesn't respond to everything that Reed does with sarcasm.

Last week Conrad even gave him a short nod through the black gates when Reed came to pick me up after school.

Even Ledger isn't always biting Reed's head off. And vice versa.

Last weekend it was my brothers' turn to bring groceries and Ledger brought tons.

Reed was also there because he came around to fix the gutter up on the roof. Because when it had rained a couple of days ago, the water didn't go down smoothly, whatever that meant.

When I told him that I didn't notice anything and that he was crazy to worry about the littlest things and that he should relax and enjoy things like rain because it's pretty and cozy to watch from the glass house, he shot me a flat look. Then he said that I should let him handle things beyond my ken.

"Beyond my ken. That's offensive, Reed."

He set the ladder against the siding of the house and murmured, without glancing at me, "Yeah? I hadn't noticed."

I put my hands on my hips. "It's not only offensive, it's also misogynistic to imply that women don't know anything about house maintenance."

"Well, they don't if they think rainwater clogging on the roof is cause for celebration."

"You're —"

"Are you bothering my sister?" Ledger asked, appearing out of nowhere.

Reed threw him an irritated look. "I'd be happy to start something with you but I'm a little busy here."

"Yeah, with what?"

I jumped in before Reed could make matters worse. "He's cleaning the gutters or whatever. And when I told him he shouldn't bother because everything was fine and that he should enjoy things in life like pretty rain instead of worrying about everything, he said I didn't know anything about house maintenance."

Ledger turned to me. "Pretty?"

"Yes. That's all. Relax."

Ledger frowned at me before turning to Reed. "She tell you that it was pretty?"

"Also cozy."

They both looked at each other, sporting the same look. The look that said I was crazy, that all women in the world are crazy for suggesting that rain is pretty.

Ledger turned back to me. "Callie, it's not going to be pretty or cozy or whatever the fuck when your roof starts leaking and there's water damage. Let him do his thing." And then, just to annoy me — I know it — he added, "You should go inside and bake cookies instead and see if the purple leprechauns that live under your bed want some."

My eyes went wide. "You moron. I can't believe you said that. Especially when you know that I'm pregnant and my hormones are all messed up."

They are.

Along with making me cry, they make me angry and hot and just… so irritated.

So much so that I punched my brother in the chest that day, which only made him snicker. And when I noticed that Reed's lips were twitching, I punched him too.

"You know what, I am going to make cookies. Oatmeal raisin, Ledger. But you don't get any."

"Hey!" Ledger protested. "Now, that's a little hasty. Who loves you the most, huh?"

"Not you." Then I turned to Reed who was watching me with amused eyes and declared, "You too. I know you like them too. But you don't get to have any either."

So yeah.

Apparently, ever since Reed and Ledger ganged up on me, Ledge doesn't openly glare at Reed anymore either.

Which is great but I hate that there's so much testosterone around me.

The only person that I know who does glare at him is my ballet teacher, Miss Petrova.

Aside from forcing her to apologize to me all those months ago, Reed gets on her nerves. Because he likes to watch my lessons and Miss Petrova thinks it's disruptive.

But of course Reed doesn't listen.

He still sits there and still watches me awkwardly hold my poses and heave and pant as my pregnancy progresses and my bigger belly messes with my balance. But my doctor has said that as long as I don't exert myself too much and do it all under professional supervision, it should be fine.

"You know, you're starting to creep out other girls too. That you sit there and watch me and don't even listen to our teacher," I tell him when he opens the door to his Mustang to drive me back home after class one evening.

"And I should care about that why?"

"Because they might call the cops on you," I reply, raising my eyebrows. "Because you're acting like a stalker."

He narrows his predator animal eyes. "I know all the cops, remember?"

"So what, you're going to keep stalking me then? Like a criminal."

"No, like a villain. And you're pregnant with my baby." He flicks his eyes over me, over my bun and sweaty neck, my white leotard and ice blue tutu that hides my pregnant belly. "It's my fucking job to stalk you."

I run my hands over my tutu, cradling my belly. "But —"

His eyes follow the gesture as usual before he murmurs, cutting me off, "Besides, you should tell your Miss Petrova that this isn't the first time I've stalked you in a ballet class. So she should really stop gasping every time she sees me watching you."

"What?"

His wolf eyes that I know are going to be the death of me sparkle then. They glow like his beautiful vampire skin as his lips tip up in a smirk. "Long before I made you spin for me in the woods, I used to watch you spin on your toes at Blue Madonna. I used to watch you leap and jump across the dance floor while your fucking Miss Petrova smiled at you proudly."

My skin wakes up in goosebumps but I know it's not the winter breeze that's making it happen. It's him.

"You used to watch me?" I whisper, looking up at him. "Before the woods."

"Why do you think I blackmailed you into dancing for me that night?"

"B-because that's what you do. That's your thing."

His smirks changes into a lazy, languid smile as he confesses, "Yeah, that. But also because you were my tight little ballerina long before you knew it."

My heart goes up on its tiptoes and I do too. "But you never said anything."

"If I'd wanted you to know, Fae, I would've told you. Now get in the car."

This is crazy and incredible and exactly like the pregnancy book, isn't it? That he was trying to hide that day.

And I can't help but ask, "Why do you hide it, the things that... that might make someone like you?"

I don't know where the question came from but now that I've asked it, it feels like the most important thing I could ask him. The most important thing that he could tell me.

"If you think watching a girl dance through the window like a creepy stalker is something worth liking, then you need to reevaluate your whole thinking, Fae," he says with a tight jaw. "And I don't want people to like me. I'm pretty happy being hated. Now, for the last time: get in the car."

And I do.

With a spinning heart and heaving breaths.

With something moving and melting inside of me. With my stomach fluttering, and I know she's melting inside of me too.

At him.

At her daddy.

Melting and melting like thick raindrops on the windows, on the roof for which he cleaned those gutters last week.

Melting like the honey when he makes me come.

Because he does.

He does make me come every night.

And God, when he does, stars explode in my veins. I feel it in my stomach, my womb, my trembling thighs and my ballerina toes.

Ever since I forgave him and he apologized to me and my body on his knees three weeks ago, he does it every night. He apologizes with his hands and his mouth. With his warm and wet and sucking kisses.

His kisses that taste like cupcakes, my favorite dessert in the world, the most addicting dessert in the world. So is it any wonder that I've become addicted to his kisses? To his mouth.

To him.

Some of it could be my hormones again because God, I'm horny all the time. But I know that majority of the credit goes to him and his sexiness.

In fact, I can't even go to sleep without him.

Before when I was really sick, I'd pass out in the bed and the only way I knew that he stayed with me in the same house, not in the same room or bed, was because he'd always be there if and when I woke up during the night to throw up again.

These days though, I remember everything.

I remember how he puts me to sleep. How after making me come, he kisses my pregnant belly and my forehead before cuddling with me.

Gosh, his cuddles.

My gorgeous villain gives the best cuddles ever.

Maybe because he's so much larger in comparison to me. So when he spoons me, he covers my entire body. When he settles his muscular arm on my waist and presses his splayed palm on my belly where our baby sleeps, he spans my entire torso.

And when I close my eyes at night, I feel safe.

I feel replete and satisfied.

But I know he doesn't.

I know that.

Because that's all he ever does.

He makes me come but he never takes his own pleasure.

He doesn't ever ask anything from me. He doesn't ever fuck me, and yes, I know it's a bad word. But I don't care. I'm bad for him. I always have been.

And yes, I know that fucking will make everything complicated. But I feel so restless without him. I feel so achy. My belly is filled with his baby but I'm so empty.

So what's a little dirty talk if it means he'll do it? He'll do me and put himself out of this misery. And me too.

I don't even know why he's holding back.

I've forgiven him, haven't I? He gets to touch me everywhere, every night. So why would he torture himself like this? Why wouldn't he take that final step?

Especially when every day he comes to pick me up at school, I see how tense he is. How after a long day of work when he comes home for dinner, how agitated he appears.

That job is killing him and he doesn't even talk about it; I tried one more time, just casually, to strike up a conversation but he shut me down. So I'm at my wit's end.

I don't know what to do, how to give him relief.

So I try this.

I try to make him take me, tempt him as much as I can.

In fact, one night when he's kissing me on the bed, I make the bold move of pressing my hand on his dick. "You're hard."

He is.

He is rubbing me right there, right where my pussy is, his cock.

It's making a small hill inside his jeans. And it's so thick and swollen that he always has to pop the button of his jeans to let it breathe. If I focus hard enough I can see the dark shadow of his cock pressing up against the edge of his pants.

"Shut up, Fae," he growls, taking my hand off his cock and putting it up above my head on the pillow.

Glancing up at him, I say, "But it's hurting you."

He grabs my hand harder. "It's fine."

"I can help."

"I don't need your help."

I lick my lips. "I can suck on it like you suck on me."

"Stop talking."

"Or I can jack you off," I say from under him, moving my bare pregnant belly against his hard t-shirt-covered abs; because he doesn't even take his clothes off while he strips me and makes me lose my mind. "I can use my hands. I've never done it but if you teach me what to do I —"

"Stop fucking talking."

"Or you could... you could put it in me." I arch up, rubbing my bare tits on his chest. "In my pussy. And this time you won't even..."

"I won't even what?"

God, I'm shameless.

So shameless to tempt him like this.

But I can't stop. I won't.

I need him to stop torturing himself. I need him to give me what I want.

"You won't even have to pull out," I say and his eyes become slits. "You could come inside me, inside my pussy. You could give me all your pain, all your hurt. Because I won't get pregnant."

"Yeah, because you already are," he says, in a guttural voice, his one hand holding mine over my head and the other buried in my hair, all tight and punishing.

"Yes."

"Because I already did that. I already blew my wad inside you before I had the sense to pull out and knocked you up."

Biting my lip, I nod. "So you can come inside me all you want now, can't you? You can fill me up, Reed. Until I'm flowing with you. Until my pussy is all creamy with your cum and leaking and —"

"Stop. Fucking. Talking."

And then he kills my words himself with his lips as he kisses me and doesn't stop.

Not until he's completely overpowered me and made me come again and again.

Until I forget everything.

By the time my twenty-week appointment comes around and they tell us the sex of the baby, I don't think Reed will ever end this torture on himself.

And I don't think I'll ever stop crying, because I get what I always wanted.

It's a girl.

I'm having a baby girl.

"It's a girl," someone whispers, and I think it's me. And when I do, I feel a pressure on my hand. Because the guy whose hand I'm holding, lying on the exam table, has squeezed my fingers.

He's wrapped his long, strong fingers that I adore around mine tightly.

I look up and my ballerina heart skips a beat.

I've never seen him happier than this. It's not an outright, bright happiness though. It's a subtle thing.

The lines around his wolf eyes are crinkled slightly and the ones around his ruby red lips are loose and relaxed. And there's this glint in his gaze and an easiness in his posture that usually disappears in the evening after work.

"We're having a girl," I tell him as if he doesn't know.

"With blonde hair and blue eyes," he whispers back, staring down at me.

"Or maybe dark hair and gray eyes," I whisper back and this time I say the words out loud that I'd thought the day I told him I was pregnant. "Like her daddy."

His stubbled, messy, beautiful jaw tics as a strong emotion overcomes him, and I squeeze his hand back because I know he needs it.

When the appointment is done and we walk to his Mustang to go back home, Reed doesn't let me sit in the front seat. He opens the back door and ushers me inside before getting inside himself. He then lets me crawl into his lap and I start crying again.

I drench the collar of his shirt as he rocks me in his arms.

When I get control of myself enough that I'm not a blubbering mess, I look up at him. "She's going to be perfect."

His eyes are my favorite color right now, liquid mercury. "She is."

Sniffling, I curl the ends of his longish hair that he wasn't ready to cut but I made him trim at least because it was starting to poke him in his wolf eyes. "We have to protect her, Reed. We have to take care of her. She'll be so small and she won't know anything at all. We have to be there for her. Promise me."

He swallows, his eyes growing even more liquid if possible, his arms around me flexing and squeezing. "We will."

"And we have to love her. She has to know that. She has to know that Mommy and Daddy love her the most and that we'd do anything for her."

His jaw tics a couple of time before he reaches up and wipes off my tears, promising again, "She will know it."

***

"Why won't you do it?"

I can't believe I asked him that.

But I don't know what else to do anymore. Except ask him point blank.

He's at the door of the glass house, his white shirt wrinkled, his suit jacket hanging from his arm. He was about to leave. Since I don't get sick anymore, he leaves after making me lose my mind over him and putting me to sleep.

And I was asleep, but maybe it's the whole emotional upheaval of the day because we just found out the sex of the baby, or maybe I'm just so tired of him denying himself, that I woke up as soon as he rolled out of bed.

I'm standing in the hallway and I approach him, my bare feet silent on the hardwood floor.

Still, somehow he hears them, my silent feet, and he turns around.

His shoulders sigh at the sight of me. "Go back to bed."

I keep walking toward him. "Not until you tell me."

"Tell you what?"

I reach him and I see that he fists his hand at his sides, as if bracing himself. "Why won't you fuck me?"

His eyes narrow, flashing bright in the dim lighting of the living room. "Fuck you?"

I swallow. "Yes. Why won't you?"

Something falls over his features, a coldness. "Is that the first time you're using that word?"

The same coldness I saw that night two years ago.

The same coldness I saw the night I forgave him.

So I'm not going to be deterred.

I fist my hands too. "No. I used it the night you did fuck me. In your Mustang."

He hates my comeback. I can see it on his rigid features, his V-shaped jaw. "So what, you're an expert now? I fucked you once and you think you can use that word whenever you feel like it?"

I raise my chin. "I can use that word whenever I feel like it. In case you've forgotten, I'm free to do whatever I fucking want."

He exhales a sharp breath. "Well, in that case feel free to go back to bed."

"No," I tell him because I've had it. "Not until you tell me why you won't fuck me. I know you want to. I know that. I can feel it. I can feel you, all hard and horny and needy. I feel you, Reed. So why won't you do it? Why would you torture yourself like this? Is it still about punishing yourself? I've forgiven you, okay? I don't want you to punish yourself anymore."

"Yeah, it's about that. It's about punishing myself. You happy now? Now go back to bed. I'll see you tomorrow."

Instead of backing off like he wants me to, I go up to him.

I bump his stupid shoes with my ugly cut-up ballerina toes. "I told you I'm not going until you tell me why. Why are you doing this, Reed? Why are you making yourself suffer?"

He clenches his jaw, his eyes brimming with something.

Something frustrating and angry and agonizing that I don't understand.

But then he makes me.

He makes me understand all of it as he asks, "You want to know why? You want to know why I won't fuck you? It's because of you."

"What?"

"It's because of this," he spits out, looking me up and down with a coldness that still has the power to chill my bones. "It's because you just won't let it go. It's because you won't stop begging."

I draw back from him. "Begging."

But he bends down to cover the distance that I've created between us. "What else do you think you're doing? You forgave me even when I didn't deserve it, fine. I gave you a couple of mind-blowing orgasms. I rocked your world. But now you're back to begging. Now you're back to thinking that I'm a fucking hero. A fucking hero who you can let inside your body. A hero who can fuck you. Where does this end, Fae? If I fuck you, are you going to fall in love with me again? Because if you are, tell me right now so I can go hide my fucking Mustang. Because I'm only going to break your heart again."

"Get out."

I say it calmly, evenly.

So much so that I don't even think that I've said it. I think I've whispered it. Whispered it to the wind so it can carry my words to him.

The guy who's standing only a few feet away from me.

But we might as well be miles apart. Millions of them.

He might as well be in a different dimension because of what he just said.

Because of what he just stupidly, callously said.

"Get out," I say again, this time loudly, more determinedly. "Now."

I don't know if I'm imagining it or what but something flashes through his features. A wave of anguish, and he swallows before throwing me a short nod. "Fine."

He turns around and leaves then.

I watch him bound down the porch stairs and stride toward his car that glints in the night. I watch him jerk the door open and get inside before peeling out of the driveway.

I watch him and watch him and when I can't see him anymore, my eyes fill with tears.

A sob catches in my throat.

But I don't let it out.

I won't.

I refuse to cry for him anymore. I refuse to waste even a single tear on him. After all the progress we've made, all the tender and intimate moments that we've shared, he goes and does this. He hurts me like this.

Asshole.

God, he's an asshole. A cruel fucking asshole. A villain.

And yet I'm crying for him.

I can't stop the tears that I just promised myself that I will never shed for him. What is wrong with me?

What is wrong with you, Callie?

What is wrong with you that you lo...

No.

No, no, no.

I can't. I won't.

And suddenly I'm so angry at myself. So angry at him for pulling this, for being so cold, that I pant and heave. I march to the glass door and slam it shut.

And lock it.

I turn every lock on the door as if I'm keeping something out, and I am.

I'm keeping him out.

Even though I know he has a key and it's his friend's house — I still don't know who — and he can get in any time he wants, I won't let him.

As irrational as it is, I won't let him come inside.

As soon as I'm done, my knees give out though and I slide

down to the floor. And I completely smash the promise that I just made myself. Propped up against the locked glass door, I let myself go and cry.

I hug my knees and I sob.

I hate him. I hate him. I hate him.

I hate him so much and the thought of it makes me cry all over again because it's a lie.

I don't hate him. That's the problem.

Because I'm still stupid.

Because even though all I wanted to do was forgive him and move on, I know that I haven't. Not completely. Not how I wanted.

Because all I have moved on from is the past, not him.

I've already committed the crime.

He's right.

It's done and I can't... I can't bear it.

And so I sob and sob for hours and days and an age.

Until I hear a sound.

A screech.

Tires burning the gravel that dulls out the sounds of my broken sobs. And then comes a flood of light pouring through the glass door and chasing away the shadows.

I spring up from where I'm sitting on the floor and spin around to find his Mustang coming to a jerking stop.

Out of which he climbs.

My gorgeous villain.

Chapter 23

He's here.

A glowing silhouette. A dark shadow.

Tall and broad as he stands by his Mustang. A dream. A beautiful nightmare.

I have to squint against the headlights so I can't really tell the details of his face, but when the light goes off and he bangs the door shut, taking a step toward the house, I do the opposite.

I take a step back and away from the door.

And I keep doing that. I keep moving away from him. For every step that brings him closer to the house, to the door, to me, I take a step back.

Until he's at the door and my legs touch the back of the cozy white couch, feet and feet away from him.

He watches me through the thick glass, his chest heaving up and down, his mouth slightly parted, his wolf eyes glowing.

Hungry.

And despite everything, I clench my thighs together. The thighs that are still wet with my juices and his mouth.

I clench them harder when he runs those heated eyes all over my body. From my loose hair to my rapidly breathing chest and his hoodie that I'm wearing over my floral-printed pajama pants. His eyes stop at my belly for a second or two, the outline of which is now visible through his baggy hoodie.

Only slightly though, but still.

She flutters inside me and I cradle it under his scrutiny.

His eyes narrow when he notices it and his hands that were fisted by his sides unfurl. He grabs the knob then and turns it.

Or tries to.

But it doesn't budge.

He looks up, something dark and possessive flashing through his gorgeous features, and I raise my trembling chin up.

There. Take that. I locked the door.

When he understands my silent answer, he says, "Open the door."

He commands it really and his order, given in a thick rough voice, makes me press my hand on my belly and clench my wet, needy thighs again. "No."

His cheekbones jut out in anger. "Open the fucking door."

My heart is thudding in my chest and I shake my head. "No."

His chest pushes out on a long breath. "If you don't open it right the fuck now, Fae, I'm going to break it down."

I sniffle. "Do it. It's your friend's house. You're the one who's going to have to explain why his door is broken."

He studies my face, watches me wipe my tears, and his anger mounts. Putting both his hands on the glass door, he says gutturally, "You're fucking crying, Fae, and I can't get to you. I'm losing it, okay? So open this fucking door so I can make it better."

Gah.

Why does he have to sound so anguished and so agonized over

the fact that I'm crying? He's the one who made me cry in the first place. He doesn't get to make it better.

And I tell him that, even though my heart is twisting in my chest and I have to curl my toes to stop myself from going to the door. "You don't get to make it better. Not after how cruel and mean you were. Go away."

I would've done a lot more.

I would've turned around and given him my back but I feel something.

In my belly.

And I have to bring my other hand up too. I have to bring it up to my pregnant belly and press it with both hands. I have to bend down and look away from Reed. I have to look at my trembling fingers.

Oh God.

What is... what is happening?

Because something is happening.

Something... something that I've never felt before and oh my God, I clutch my belly harder when I feel it again.

It's not pain exactly, but it's something, and I gasp when it happens for the third time and something, a little thing, kicks into my hand. As if pressing back from the inside, and that's when I know.

That's when I know it's her.

She's kicking back.

My baby girl is kicking back.

She's moving inside of me — something that I've waited for so long and it feels so different than what I expected it to be, and from those flutters that I've been feeling for weeks now — and the euphoria is so great that my knees give out for the second time tonight and I plop down on the couch.

She's kicking inside of me and I'm about to tell him that.

The one person I want to tell everything to, her daddy, but I hear a crash.

A shattering sound, and before I can blink away my tears and figure out the source of it, he's here.

He's kneeling on the floor in front of me, both his hands on my hands that are still on my belly. "What... what's happening?"

I notice the splotches of blood on his knuckles and I let go of my belly to grab his hand. "What happened? What did you..." Glancing up, I see that the door is open and there's broken glass all over the floor. "Oh my God, Reed —"

"What the fuck is happening, Fae?" he cuts me off. "Should I call the doctor? No, of course I should. Of course. I just need to figure out where the fuck my phone is and —"

I put my hand on his lips to make him stop.

He's rambling. He never rambles.

I stare into his panicked gaze and tell him, "Everything is fine. I just got scared for a second." His breathing is still haphazard on my palm so I put my other hand on his and make it press on my belly. "It's her. She moved, I think. I've never felt anything like that before. It's kind of like the flutters but not really and —"

My eyes go wide and his breath stops altogether.

Because she moves again.

And his hand on my belly comes alive. The pads of his fingers dig into my flesh that has become harder now that she's growing inside of me. When she kicks again, I see his eyes flaring for a second before crinkling slightly and so I take my hand off his mouth to reveal the most beautiful smile I've ever seen on him.

When she does it again, he chuckles slightly, his eyes on my belly, and I bite my lip at how gorgeous he looks.

"That's my girl," he whispers.

Goosebumps rise on my skin at his possessive tone and she kicks again as if at his voice, to say hi to him. "She's feisty."

He lifts his eyes. "Like her mommy."

That's the first time he's said that, mommy, and my heart skips a beat.

It races in the next second when he continues, "Halo."

I frown at his reverent whisper. "What?"

"Her name."

"Her name?"

"Yeah," he whispers again, his fingers glued to my belly. "Like the circle of light on an angel. Or a fairy."

A rush goes through my chest. A big huge rush of warmth.

Halo.

My baby girl. Our baby girl.

"It's perfect," I whisper back, my eyes stinging again but this time with happy tears.

"Halo Jackson."

"Did you think of it just now?"

"No." He shakes his head slowly. "I've always known."

"You have?"

"Yeah."

I've been proposing name after name that he kept rejecting. And we've had countless arguments about it. Well, I have argued. He's simply looked at me with amused eyes and twitching lips.

And now I know why.

Because he always had a name.

He always knew she was Halo.

I frown. "Well, why didn't you tell me then?"

"Because it was more fun to watch you get all excited about stupid names before I shot them down."

And then I have to ask him again, "Why do you hide the things that might make someone like you?"

That might make me like you...

His eyes move back and forth between mine, his fingers on my belly flex and, swallowing, he rasps, "Because I don't want to be liked."

Not by you...

I hear his unspoken words, and the heart that was already twisting in my chest squeezes even more. So much so that I feel like all my vessels and chambers will burst and explode and he'll kill me with everything that I feel for him.

Despite my better judgement. Despite history teaching me.

Despite him.

"Listen, Fae, about earlier —"

I don't let him talk though. I grab his wrist and take his hand off my belly. When I stand up, I take him with me and drag him to the bathroom. He goes without a word.

I guess he knows what I'm going to do.

He knows that I'm going to clean and bandage his cuts.

He hits the lights in the bathroom and I let go of his hand to get all the stuff together. When it's all out on the counter, I grab his bleeding hand again.

I keep my eyes on the task but I know he's watching me.

"Where's your key?" I ask.

"Threw it away."

"Why?"

"So I don't get to you. When I want to. So you're safe from me."

My heart twists again and I bite my lip at how much it must sting him when I run the cotton swab over his scrapes, but he doesn't move a muscle.

"Did you punch the door?" I ask then.

"No."

"Then?"

"Found a rock. Busted the glass with it."

I shake my head, still looking at his hand as I wrap a bandage around it. "I was mad at you. Am mad at you."

"I know."

"But I was fine. She — Halo — was fine."

"It didn't look like that from where I was standing."

I sigh sharply, finishing up. "What you said to me was rude. It was uncalled for and it was mean."

"That's why I said it."

I look up then. "What?"

His eyes are all dark and intense. "Because I wanted you to understand something."

"And what is that?"

He comes closer to me, as if now that I've gotten my way and I've cleaned his wounds, it's his turn now. To talk. To do things. To grab me.

Which he does.

He grabs my thickening waist with one hand and my face with the other. He even pulls me to him as if he doesn't want a single thing separating us.

Especially after how I kept us apart by barring the door on him.

So he eliminates every little thing that stands between him and me, presses my short body to his tall one, and I hate that my hands clutch his shirt at the waist.

I hate that as soon as our bodies touch, my achy, tender breasts to his ribs and my swollen belly to his pelvis, my lips part on a trembling, relieved breath.

He dips that body over me then, and cranes my neck up as he growls, "First things first, you're pregnant with my baby. You're pregnant. And you need to understand that if I want to get to you, you're going to let me. It doesn't matter that you're angry at me or I've been an asshole to you. You are going to let me. Because if something happens to you, Fae, if something happens to her, Halo, I don't even know what I'm going to do. So if you ever lock your door or bar the windows or whatever the fuck you want to do to keep me out, remember that I'll break it all down. I will destroy every single thing you put in my way in order to get to you. Do you understand that? Tell me you understand that."

I do.

I do understand that.

He told me this once when I was sixteen, that he'd climb every tower, bust through every window to get to me. And today he did.

So I get that and I nod. "Yes."

"You fucking scared me." His fingers on my body are urgent and pulling. "You scared me."

I fist his shirt and stretch my neck even more. "But you were so…"

He presses his forehead to mine, his eyes flashing. "I know. I know I was cruel. What I said was uncalled for, but you need to re-member something. You need to remember that I'm not made for love. I don't do love. Some people can. Some people can fall in love, have a family, live in a big fucking house decorated with flowers and stuff. Some people stay together for the rest of their lives. And when one of them dies, the other one dies too. Or lives while praying for death. I'm not one of them. I didn't grow up like that. I didn't… I never saw stuff like that, you understand? All I've known is how to fight, how to go to war, how to win wars.

"And you won't get that because you've always had it. Love. You've always had brothers who loved you, who cared for you, who protected you. And you bake fucking cupcakes and you knit and you dance like a fairy. You are a fairy. But I've always been alone. I don't have friends. Except for a sixty-year-old man who sucks at giving advice. I don't have a family to speak of. I've got a shitty father and a mother who doesn't care. I've got Pest but she's more dependent on me than anything. I don't expect you to understand any of this though. But I want you to understand this: I want you to understand that you can't fall in love with me. Not again. You can't fucking fall, Fae. You can't. You can't get your feelings mixed up again if I fuck you, you got that?"

"What?"

"I've got a sister who's pretty fucking emotional. And you're that too. Girls can be emotional about this stuff. But I don't want you to be, okay? I don't want you to get involved emotionally if we have sex. Because I'm only going to hurt you. And I've done that before and it fucking sucked. It sucked. It tore me apart for two years and I pretended that it didn't. But it did. And even though it might destroy me to hurt you again, I will. You saw what I did just now, didn't you? So I know that I will. Because that's all I know."

That's all he knows.

How to hurt and how to be cruel.

How to be a villain.

A villain who doesn't want to hurt me but will. Because I'll get emotionally involved if we have sex.

This should do it then, shouldn't it? Kill my love. Once and for all. Besides this isn't the first time he's said that he can't love or that he'll break my heart if I give it to him again.

So this should make me move on.

But it only makes me fall more. The thing he doesn't want me to do.

It only makes me fall deeper and deeper, so deep that I'll never come out. I'll never come up for air. I don't even need air.

I only need him.

This lonely boy.

Because I'm a girl in love.

"Promise me," he rasps, begging, when all I do is stare up at him. "Promise me that you won't fall in love with me. You need to promise me that, Fae."

His features have the same urgency that they did when he asked me to hold on to my dress two years ago. When he asked me to protect myself, my virginity, my body, from him. Because if he saw what was between my legs, he would take it. He would rip it from me.

I did what he asked me to do back then.

But I can't do it now.

I can't not love him.

"If I promise, will you fuck me?" I whisper like I did back then.

If I promise, will you kiss me?

At my words, he lets it show. His need. The need that he's been hiding for weeks now.

The need that darkens his features, sharpens them. Makes them all points and peaks and edges. Unsafe and dangerous.

Villainous.

And I know his answer is going to be the same as it was two years ago on that rainy night. "Fuck yeah."

My breaths shouldn't come so easy now but they do.

My lungs are happy. My heart is happy too. Because I get to be his and he gets to be mine. Secretly but still.

"I promise," I lie and seal my fate.

His villainous, beautiful features ripple. "You do."

I nod. "Yes. I won't fall in love with you."

Because I already have.

I already fell in love with him, two years ago, and now I know that I never fell out of it. Even when he broke my heart and I hated him. Even when I wanted to move on.

I never stopped loving him.

And now I don't have to stop. I can keep loving him for eternity. I can keep loving my villain even if I can't tell him. Even if he doesn't want me to.

Then his hand on my face goes up to my hair. He tugs my head back, primal, savage hunger evident in every line of his face, and bends down even more, seeking something. Seeking me. And I go up on my ballerina toes.

I grab his shirt and crane my neck up, give myself to him.

Because if I don't, I think the hunger will eat him alive. This hunger that's been building up inside of him for weeks.

And I can't let that happen. I can't let him suffer any longer now that he's captured me, my heart.

So I offer my mouth to him to feed on.

But it's not as if I'm shy. That all I do is let him take, no.

I take things from him too.

It's important, see.

It's important to take because I'm hungry too. In fact, my hunger matches his. This hunger to love him, and if I can't say it with words, then I will let my body talk.

I will let my lips speak for me when they open for him and they suck on his lips. When my tongue licks his and my teeth clack with his. And when his hands tug at my hair and his hoodie that I'm wearing, my hands come alive too. They tug on his shirt, pull at his buttons.

Soon though Reed has to break the kiss to divest himself of his shirt, throwing it away. But he doesn't stop there.

He takes off the hoodie I'm wearing too. Not only that, he goes down on his knees to take off my pajama pants. And it all happens so fast and yet so slow that by the time I'm naked and he comes back up, I'm dying to put my mouth on him.

And then we don't break even when he picks me up. I'm heavier now but he doesn't even pant or blink an eye.

I suck on his cupcake lips as he walks out of the bathroom, strides down the hallway and reaches my bedroom, lowering me onto the bed and inevitably breaking our kiss.

I prop myself up on my elbows and watch him, standing at the foot of the bed, his thick cock making a tent in his pants. And as enticing as it is, my eyes don't stop there.

Because God, he's bare-chested.

This is the first time I've seen him like this.

It's crazy, isn't it?

So freaking insane that I've loved him for two years and I'm pregnant with his baby but I have never ever seen him naked. I've never ever seen that vampire skin mold over the broad muscular shoulders, those jutting collar bones. Or that sparkling skin stretching over his taut arched pecs.

I've never seen his light brown nipples that I want to flick with my fingers. Or his taut ribs. That stomach, all muscular and dense with a ladder of abs. His sleek waist and his belly button that I want to dip my tongue in.

I don't even know how to describe him except to say, "You're gorgeous."

"But a villain," he whispers, and I look up to find his eyes on fire, his eyes roving over me, over my swollen belly, my bigger tits, the wet gash between my thighs.

I don't care. I don't care if you're a villain.

I don't say that though.

Instead, I demand with wide eyes, "I wanna see."

"See what?"

I lick my lips. "Your cock."

Something about my shamelessness makes him chuckle, his

stomach hollowing, throwing his corrugated muscles into stark relief. "You want to see my dick, Fae?"

I nod, glancing down at the bump in his jeans. "Yes."

"Because you've never seen him, have you?"

I bite my lip, slide my leg up and down the bed. "No."

"And he's been inside of you."

I swallow, looking back at his face because I don't know where to look, at his wolf eyes or his hard-on. "Uh-huh."

His hands go to his button and my breath hitches when he pops it. I clench the sheet when he lowers the zipper. "And he gave you this. Your swollen belly."

At his words, that swollen belly flutters. But I know the difference now. I know it's not Halo. She's sleeping safely inside my body.

I know it's him. It's my love for him that flutters, that has been fluttering all this time, spreading its wings, wanting to fly.

I've had it caged until tonight.

But I let it fly now.

I let my love for him fly and flow through my veins and I nod. "Yes. And it's unfair. That I haven't seen him yet."

He nods with a tight jaw. "Yeah. It is. When I get to see her every night, your fairy pussy. When I get to lick her and suck on her and play with her. When I get to see how fucking pink she is. How soft and pretty. How tiny and daisy fresh. Just like my Fae."

I grip the sheets tighter, squirming my hips. "But she's not. She's not daisy fresh anymore."

He chuckles again, this time only a puff of breath that makes him shudder. He still doesn't show it to me though. He only massages his hard dick over his jeans and rasps, "He saw to that, didn't he? I saw to that."

"Yes," I whisper.

He comes closer then, puts his hand on the bed and bends

over me, and stares at my prone form intensely. "I made sure that this time when I caught you in my evil clutches, I made you pay. That I left my mark, didn't leave you unscathed."

My elbows give out and I fall on the bed, all writhing and needy. "You did."

And that gives him permission to get on the bed. To hang over me like a thrilling, threatening shadow. "Yeah. Maybe you should call the cops on me then. You should tell them how I cornered you in the woods. How I carried you screaming and kicking in my arms and put you in my Mustang. You should tell them how I tore at your clothes, your pretty white dress, to get at you. To get at your pussy. Your virgin pussy, wasn't it? How I didn't even care if she was a virgin. How I took one look at her, all pink and swollen shut and I lost my mind. I lost my fucking mind and rammed inside of you. How I made you cry. I made you bleed. You should tell them that, Fae. You should tell them that this motherfucking villain didn't even care that he was fucking you raw. That his dick was banging into your sweet pussy without rubber and when he got enough sense to pull out, it was already too late."

God, I'm a mess.

I'm a writhing, sweating mess and I'm tearing at the sheets. I'm tearing at them and rocking and I know my pussy is so wet for him.

For the villain that's hanging over me, telling me these filthy tales.

False tales though.

"But I wasn't," I whisper almost incoherently.

"You weren't what?"

"I wasn't k-kicking and screaming."

"Ah, so you wanted it then."

I nod. "Yes."

"My Fae wanted to be fucked by a villain."

"Uh-huh."

He crawls over me even more and my thighs, even in my mindlessness, part for him. They make space for his large body. When he's directly above me, his biceps straining and sweaty now, he says gruffly, "So you won't call the cops on me, baby?"

I shake my head, shuddering, almost orgasming at his 'baby.'

"No? Not even to tell them that you just went out for a walk. An innocent fucking walk when he took you, that villain. When he captured you in his dirty hands and fucked you so hard that he sowed a baby inside of you."

My hands leave the sheet and go to him.

My nails make homes in the meat of his biceps and dig in, making him shudder over me. "No. God, Reed. Please."

He lowers himself on me, his taut abs touching my pregnant belly, and I arch my back. I bring my thighs around his waist, my core seeking his cock.

"Please what, Fae?" he asks, framing my face with his hands, rubbing his jean-covered cock right at the notch of my thighs. "'Please, show me your dick, Reed.' Is that what you're saying?"

I undulate with him, chasing that friction. "Yes."

"What about now?" He chuckles, teasing me, moving against me, giving me that friction that he gives me every night, but I want something more tonight. I want his cock. "You want to call them now? You want to tell them that this asshole won't even show you his dick. His big, fat dick that made your pussy cry and got her pregnant."

I push at his biceps and claw at his skin. "God, Roman, you're —"

Sense slams into me then.

It jars me.

It opens my eyes, clears my foggy vision and I see him.

I see his flushed cheekbones, the sweat dotting his brows. His stubble-covered jaw that's sharp but still. His entire body is still. Hard like a rock. So much so that digging my nails into his muscles is a hardship now.

My heart pounds in my chest as I lie beneath him, naked, with parted thighs.

"What'd you just say?" he asks in a voice that barely reaches me even though I'm almost wrapped around him.

I swallow. "R-Roman."

He stares at me for a few beats and I don't know what he's thinking.

I don't know what he'll do.

"I've been…" he says again in that low voice. "I didn't… I didn't think that you'd ever call me that. I thought…"

"You thought what?"

His eyes pierce into mine, so many emotions running through them, and his Adam's apple jerks. "I thought that I'd lost it. Lost the privilege of you calling me that."

My hands fly to his face then, my palms rubbing his stubble. "You didn't. You didn't lose it."

His jaw tics under my palm, his eyes burning me. "Say it again."

Tears prick my eyes but I blink and obey him. "Roman."

"Again."

"Roman."

"Again."

"Roman."

But this time, I don't stop. I chant it for him, so he can absorb it, the name that I gave him two years ago. So he can tuck it inside all his empty spaces.

So this name that I gave him in love warms him up.

It warms his winter blood, his chilled bones, his cold soul.

I chant it until I can't anymore.

Because his mouth is covering me. Because his mouth is drinking that name from my lips, swallowing it down like an elixir. An antidote to all the hurt, the pain inside of him.

And then he isn't kissing me anymore.

He's broken that kiss and left me to get rid of his jeans. And again, he's done it all so fast and yet so slow that by the time he gets back to me and settles himself over me again, I'm hurting.

My lust is hurting me.

It's hurting him too, but still he frames my face in his large hands and stares into me. "I don't... I don't have a condom. I didn't exactly plan this. But if you need me to, Fae, I'll go get some, okay? I'll —"

I shake my head, clutching onto his muscled obliques, rubbing my heels over the backs of his naked thighs. "I don't care. I don't want anything between us."

God, not anymore. I'm tired of being apart from him.

But he has more to say. He has more to tell me when I want him inside of me.

"I'm still cl —"

I put my hand on his lips then. "I know."

We're way, way past that now.

And he's relieved to see that bit of trust in my eyes because his breaths puff out on my palm and then he does what I've been wanting him to do for weeks now.

He fucks me.

Or prepares to.

Staring into my eyes, he grips his cock and lines it up with my core before dipping his slippery head in. I grip his shoulders and wait for him to breach me, and in the next breath, he does.

Not all the way though.

Like he did the last time, all blind and raging in his jealousy.

He gives me only an inch but even that stretches me out. Even that makes me throw my head back and moan, makes my thighs slip around his hips.

Reed pulls out then, grunting, and on his next push, gains another inch.

Another inch that makes me moan and stretches me out like a rubber band. So much so that I take my hand off his shoulder and bite on my finger.

I take it between my teeth and bite on it hard, trying to adjust to the pain, to the largeness of him, the girth and the width.

My villain's invasion.

But as always, Reed doesn't like it when I bite or claw on things when I'm uncomfortable.

Especially when that discomfort is something he thinks he's responsible for.

So breathing heavily, still half stuck out of my body, he makes me take my finger out of my mouth and gives me his. He gives me his thumb, and as always I latch onto it like it's my lifeline.

I grab his wrist with both hands and suck on his thumb, bite on it, and just like that my pain goes away.

His magical, fascinating hand makes everything easier.

He pulls out again, his body vibrates before pushing back in. All the way in.

And the stretch is not so bad.

The stretch is sweet.

So sweet that I suck on his thumb harder and I arch myself under him and open my legs wider. I stretch them on either side of his body, like I'm doing a split, getting ready to spin on my toes and dance for him.

He gets so deep that I feel him in my pregnant womb and the moan that I emit is my loudest so far.

But I'm not alone.

He makes noises too.

Especially when he watches my big lusty blue eyes staring up at him and my pink lips sucking on his digit.

A long growl escapes him as he drops down on me, not all the way though. He's careful of the baby but enough that his forehead falls on the crook of my neck.

But I've gotten so messy now, so wet between my legs that I don't feel any pain, only delicious pleasure when he starts to move and sets up a rhythm.

A rhythm that drives me crazy. That gets his cock all the way in and all the way out. That makes me juice up more so he can hasten it.

Hasten that rhythm so his hips slam into me.

His hips shake my body and I grab onto his sleek skin as I moan.

As he grunts too, in my neck. As he sucks on the skin there, leaving yet another mark on me.

The mark of my gorgeous villain.

And God, he's so deep now.

So deep and so high up there that my thighs, which had gone back around his waist after he gained full entry into my body, inch up. They slide up and down his sweaty sides.

That somehow makes him go even deeper when I thought there was no space for him.

But that's the thing about him, isn't it?

He always creeps up on me. He always makes space for himself in my heart, in my body.

Even when I don't want him to.

Even when I knew I was wrong to obsess over him back at Bardstown High because he was my brother's rival, he lived in my heart, in my thoughts.

Tonight I want him in there. I crave him, so when he gets deeper and deeper and his pumps grow feral and faster so that he has to pull himself up and away from me, so he can look down at my jiggling body, at my pregnant belly, I come.

My womb contracts and I come all over his dick.

I come even harder when he puts a hand on my swollen belly, as if he wants to feel the life he's given.

The life I wasn't expecting him to give me that night but he gave me anyway.

In turn binding us for life.

Maybe he's thinking the same thing, that love or not we're bound for life, when his eyes snap shut and he comes too. His back arches and the beautiful lines of his face drip agony as his dick lurches inside of me and spews cum.

It lashes it as I'm still coming.

As my pussy is still fluttering around his rod and I put my hand over his on my belly.

As he grabs my hand and joins our fingers, squeezing, and when he's done, he opens his shining wolf eyes. He opens them to show me his stark possessiveness, his stark satisfaction that he's got me now.

That I'm his.

Not forever, no. But for as long as he wants me.

And then he comes back down and kisses me softly on the forehead.

Chapter 24

Some girls in love don't get their happy ending.

The men they love don't love them back. The men they love can't love them back. And so they are forever blue.

They're forever sad and aching.

They're forever longing.

But my Halo won't be one of them. My Halo will be loved.

By the first man she'll ever love.

The man with sparkling vampire skin and glinting wolf eyes. Her daddy.

He will carry her in his muscular arms, play with her with those fascinating hands. He'll even put her on his shoulders so she feels like she's at the top of the world. He'll make her smile and laugh. He'll wipe her tears off, bandage her scrapes. Maybe teach her to ride a bicycle.

He'll protect her from everything bad. Or at least he'll try to.

I know that.

I know that he'll lose sleep over how to protect her, how to make her life easier, how to give her everything. How to make all her dreams come true.

I'll take my happiness in that.

I'll watch them together, our baby and him, and all the blue inside of me will fade for a while.

For now though, I'll let myself cry.

In the shower, at school during lunch, when I'm shut up in the restroom. Even in class, sitting in the last row while teachers are explaining to a bunch of uninterested, delinquent girls how a heart functions or why Romeo and Juliet is the greatest Shakespeare play ever written.

It's not.

It's tragic and painful. There is nothing great about tragedy.

There is nothing epic in keeping two people who love each other apart.

Heartbreak is not glorious. It's not poetic or an inspiration for generations to come.

Stupid, sadistic, sick Shakespeare.

Although crying in class is much harder, not because my teacher cares that a pregnant girl is sitting with her head down all the way in the back, possibly not paying attention. But because my girls are there and they worry over me. Especially Salem, who always sits right adjacent to me. Something that accidentally happened in the beginning of the year and that's how our friendship started.

But I tell her and the other two that it's the pregnancy.

That's my excuse for everything.

I'm crying because I'm hormonal.

And I am.

The only good thing is that I can eat meat now; as soon as I entered my twenty-third week, something shifted and I started craving meat again. So peanut butter ice cream with beef jerky bits on top? That's the food of the gods. That's like my pregnancy anthem.

Other people don't think so though.

Especially the guy who got me pregnant in the first place.

Scooping a spoonful of my ice cream, I put it in my mouth and look up to find him watching me. With my mouth full, I ask, "What?"

As he stands by the door, his wolf eyes rove over my face, my ballooned-up cheeks, my propped-up form on the bed, surrounded by pillows. It's only late March but I get so hot these days that I've ditched his hoodies — though I keep them close if I want to smell him and he's not around to lend me his sexy body — and started to wear all the maternity stuff that people have gotten for me.

So I'm wearing a white, frilly, sleeveless nightie that goes down to the middle of my calves.

He spends a lot of time on that, on studying my nightie and my baby bump.

When he comes back to my face, I swallow the ice cream and glare at him. "You think it's weird, isn't it? That I'm eating this. You think peanut butter and beef jerky is weird." I stab my spoon at him when all he does is stare at me with amused eyes and lips that are on the verge of smiling at me. "But let me tell you something: you are weird. You, Roman. For not liking it. For thinking that my ice cream is weird. And it's not as if it's my fault that I like it, okay? Halo likes it. She wants it all the time and everybody thinks I'm crazy. And it's all your fault. Your fault, yes. You're the one who got me pregnant and now I'm eating weird ice cream and I'm fat and my ankles are always swollen and my…"

I trail off because he's moved.

He was leaning against the door, his arms folded. But now he's straightened up, his hands at his sides, his eyes on my verge-of-crying face as he approaches the bed.

He still has his work clothes on, white shirt and dark dress pants, and suddenly I don't want to cry anymore.

I want to kiss him.

I want him to kiss me because God, he's so sexy. All masculine and strong and tall. And pretty.

So pretty that I'm breathless by the time he reaches me, which only takes him about three seconds, but still. And when he does, he bends over and grabs my face. "And what?"

I lean up to his touch. "What?"

"Your ankles are swollen and what?"

"My fingers. They're swollen too."

He glances down at my hands. One is holding my ice cream tub with the spoon in it but the other's free and he grabs it. "These fingers?"

Sniffling, I nod. "Yes."

And without taking his eyes off me, he goes on to kiss every single one of them, making me curl my toes and squirm. "Roman..."

That's all I can say. His name.

I've been saying that a lot these days. Ever since I realized he missed it, missed me calling him that.

So now I call him that all the time. Without occasion, without reason. Just like that.

"And your ice cream is weird, huh?" he rasps, still bending over me.

I nod. "Poe laughed at me."

"Yeah?"

He knows all about my St. Mary's friends now.

"Yes. And Salem too. Even Wyn. And she never laughs at anyone. People think I'm weird, Roman."

His eyes have that same melting color that I've come to like, liquid mercury. "But you're not, are you?"

I shake my head. "No."

"Then what are you?"

My heart spins in my chest as I whisper, "Your fairy."

Possessiveness flickers through his features when I say that. "Fuck yeah, you are. My glorious, gorgeous, pregnant fairy."

"And hot. I'm always hot. And I have to pee like all the time," I whisper, almost accusingly, wet between my legs. "You did that."

This pregnancy thing is hard.

He breathes me in, smells my hair, kisses my forehead. "My poor, sweet fairy."

"I'm fat too. All slow and awkward. I'm an awkward, clumsy ballerina, Roman."

I can't dance anymore though. It's become more difficult.

But Miss Petrova, despite being super angry at Reed still, helps me with stretches and exercises. Which is good and will keep me in the loop.

Oh, and I've also started Lamaze classes, and of course, Reed goes with me. And of course I cry in class when I see all the happy, cuddly couples. And when I do and Reed wipes my tears with a concerned, clueless frown, I tell him it's the hormones.

I sniffle, continuing, "You did this to me."

"Yeah, and this too." His arm reaches out and he spreads his fingers over my belly, rubbing his palm, and Halo kicks back, making his eyes go tender. "Made my sweet fairy all swollen and ripe. And horny. You horny, Fae? You want my cock?"

God yes, I'm horny.

I'm horny, horny, horny.

I've become a devourer. I eat and eat and I need his cock. I need him. My Roman.

All the time.

"Yes. Give it to me, Roman. Make it all better," I order and he does.

He bends down to kiss me. He bends down to lick the peanut butter ice cream off my mouth and eat it himself. To keep kissing me until I forget everything else.

The ice cream, my hormones, the fact that I'm heartbroken.

When he plays with my lips and my body, he makes me forget about my heartbreak.

Which means nights are better for me.

The time when all heartbroken and lovelorn girls cry in their pillows, I cry different kinds of tears. I cry in his arms, his body covering me.

Ever since we had sex a few weeks ago, Reed has been insatiable.

He has been a fiend.

It's like something has been unlocked inside of him, years of pent-up desire, years of lust, and he doesn't know what to do with it.

My gorgeous villain has no clue what to do with me, with the fairy that he's finally captured.

So he does everything.

Whatever he wants to do. Bite, suck, fuck, love.

Some nights he makes me come — once, twice, three times — with his mouth between my legs and his large hand covering my swollen belly. As if to make sure that our baby is safe and sleeping while at the same time reveling in the fact that he did this to me.

That my body is his wonderland, his playground, and he's changed the landscape of my bones and muscles.

When he touches me like this, I don't feel fat. I don't feel ungainly and awkward.

I feel beautiful.

He makes me feel beautiful with his hand on my belly.

After he's satisfied, when he's finally had his fill of my pussy, he emerges from between my legs, all naked and glowing, my juices running down his chin, his stubbly throat, his muscular chest.

He settles himself between my spread and languid thighs before giving me what I crave the most.

His cock.

He enters me in one easy stroke and why wouldn't he? He's made my pussy all wet, pounded it with his tongue, trashed it with his mouth so much that she opens herself to him easily now.

Like a flower. A daisy.

He pounds her with his big cock, beats her up, looms over me, his beautiful muscles tightened and standing up. His face is doused in lust, his wet-with-my-juices lips pulled back and his teeth showing and snapping like he's really an animal.

Part human, part wolf.

I've always thought that, and it has never been clearer than when he's fucking me like this.

All beautifully and tenderly and savagely.

Lovingly.

And I come.

I come so easily these days. So viciously and violently.

It's like as soon as he touches my pussy, I don't stop coming and he takes advantage of that. He keeps fucking me, he keeps making my pussy come as it flutters and ripples around his rod.

And then it's his turn.

To come, I mean.

Some nights he fills up my pussy so that I flow with him. So that I feel him leaking out of me as I toss and turn in the bed, as I go to school the next day and sit in class with sticky, wet panties.

But some nights he likes to come on my body.

On my tits that he loves so much.

Or my swollen belly.

God, he loves my swollen belly. He's always touching it, rubbing it. And he likes to come on it too.

He likes to kneel over my prone, satisfied body, all sweaty and panting, and jerk his cock until he lashes his cum on my belly, the muscles of his abdomen straining, his biceps flexing.

When he's done, I rub it all over my skin like his cum is one of those rare body oils that I love so much and he watches me with hooded, villainous eyes.

His pregnant, captured fairy rubbing his scent all over her skin.

So even if I manage to break free from him, he can smell me in the night, follow my trail and bring me back to his evil lair.

So yeah, nights are easier.

Because at night, it feels like we'll never be apart. When he cuddles with me after it feels like love.

Other times though, I try to keep myself busy.

With school, with baking, with my large family of friends and brothers.

Who all come over when I finally get my acceptance letter from Juilliard.

I thought it would never come and that it was too late.

Everyone already knows what they're doing after graduation, including Wyn, who also got her acceptance letter to one of her dream art schools in New York. Salem is going to California for youth soccer camp and to be with her Arrow. And Poe, well, she is still deciding what her next move will be after she kills her guardian.

Anyway, after I get my acceptance letter, I decide to invite everyone over for a little get-together.

All my brothers, Tempest and my St. Mary's friends, who all got day passes via Conrad, even Salem and Poe. We're all gathered out in the backyard, against the backdrop of woods and dangerous cliffs.

And it's a happy occasion, or at least, it's supposed to be.

First, there are my brothers and Reed.

As I said, they have thawed toward him slightly. But still, all of them together in one place is not without some glares or awkward pauses and sarcasm. All courtesy of Shepard and Ledger, my two rowdy brothers. Reed doesn't care or looks like he doesn't. He keeps his cool and his barbs to a minimum.

Then there's Tempest, whose usually laughing gray eyes appear sad. Not a lot though — I bet she's trying to hide her sadness from her own brother, Reed; I would do the same thing for my brothers if I were her — but I can tell.

And I can also tell that it's because of Ledger.

How he's hardly paying her any attention and how all his attention is on my St. Mary's group of friends, especially my quiet, dreamer friend, Wyn.

I know Tempest and I haven't talked about him in years because of our no brothers rule. But I can tell now that her crush on my idiot brother hasn't gone anywhere.

You know what, I'm going to give Ledger a piece of my mind as soon as I get a chance. First, he needs to be careful of Tempest's feelings. And second, he needs to leave Wyn alone; she's innocent and sweet as opposed to his player ways.

And sad.

Yeah, Wyn is sad too.

Again, not a lot but I can tell. I don't know what's bothering her and she doesn't tell me — absolutely refuses to tell me — when I ask. But I know it can't be art school anymore; she already got in, as we all knew she would.

Oh, and there's another person who looks slightly upset.

Okay, a lot upset. A lot. About something. My oldest brother, Conrad.

I have no idea what's happening and I know that he will never tell me either. But about an hour ago, he disappeared into the house for something and when he came back out, he was glowering.

At nothing in particular, but he was glowering.

Finally there's me.

And the fact that I've done something that all my brothers never wanted me to do. Not again.

I don't know how they'll react if they find out.

That I'm in love with him. That I never fell out of love with him.

So I've decided that I won't tell them. I won't tell anyone.

I'm already not telling Reed. I've already promised him that I won't love him. So there's no reason for anyone to find out what I've done.

Although this time around, it's hard.

Harder than the first time even.

The first time, I wanted to be good. I wanted to not lie or hide from my brothers. I was ashamed at what I was doing, falling in love with someone despite all the warnings.

This time, I don't want to keep it from people like it's a dirty little secret. This time, I'm not ashamed. I don't think I'm doing anything wrong by loving him.

This time, I'm not naïve either.

I know he's a villain. I know he has all the power to hurt me.

But I also know that he can be a hero if he wants to be. He can be a protector, a lonely protector.

So I don't know if this whole get-together was a good idea. Because not only do I have to hide my love for Reed, I also have to pretend to be happy about going to Juilliard.

I thought I would be.

That I would be so, so happy about going to the place where I've wanted to go ever since I was five.

But I'm not.

As people around me, my brothers especially, make plans about what's going to happen after Halo is born, all I want to do is cry.

My brothers tell me that they have thought it all through: I'm going to live with Ledger, Stellan and Shepard, who all share an apartment in New York. They have also begun baby shopping and clearing out a room for me. And since Reed lives here now because he works for his dad's company, he can visit whenever he wants to.

I expect Reed to say something then.

I expect him to object and declare that he'll be moving to New York with me. Or as crazy as it is, that I'm not going anywhere without him. Mostly because he's buying stuff for Halo too and hoarding it all in the spare bedroom as if he means for us to stay.

But he doesn't.

He doesn't say a word. He doesn't tell us that he has a plan. He simply stands there with a tight jaw and shuttered eyes.

Again, I try to tell myself that it doesn't matter.

If he'll visit Halo and be there for her, then that's enough for me.

But I can't help but want to sob and sob and sob.

Anyway, after that miserable party, when I'm not sobbing, I'm knitting.

Oh, I knit like crazy these days.

Tempest bought me so much yarn that I can knit well into next year. I knit Halo everything that I can think of: socks, booties, hats, scarves. Even sweaters.

When I complete the first sweater, baby blue with little white wings and a white halo above it, and I show it to Reed, he doesn't say anything for a minute.

A whole minute.

I sit in the bed, propped up on my pillows as usual and count the seconds.

When I can't take the suspense anymore, I ask, fearfully, "You don't like it?"

Sitting beside me, he looks up then; he's been staring silently at the sweater all this time and my heart squeezes in my chest at the look in his eyes. All molten and intense.

Then he speaks, his voice so rough and guttural that my heart bleeds in my chest. "I like it."

"This is my second attempt," I whisper, clutching my nightie. "At intarsia."

His jaw, as usual stubbled at night, moves back and forth. "It's perfect. Just like the first."

Again, I want to ask him.

I want to ask him what he did with the sweater that I made him. But I can't.

I'm still too afraid.

I'm afraid that he will break my heart even more. I'm afraid that even though he'll tell me that he's thrown it away, that maybe he doesn't even remember where he put it because it was so inconsequential to him, I'll make him another sweater.

I'll keep knitting for him and storing them away somewhere like the brokenhearted girl that I am.

So I don't and he doesn't tell me.

What he does do is love me.

That night he's the most tender he has ever been. He clutches my belly, cradles it as he moves inside of me. And when we come together, he cuddles with me tightly.

He can't stop kissing my forehead.

He can't stop smelling me, rubbing his nose in the crook of my neck. And then he does the sweetest thing ever. He spreads that tiny sweater over my naked bump and kisses it.

In fact, he sets up camp there, near my swollen belly, lying on his stomach and propped up on his elbows as he keeps staring at the sweater, at my belly. Deep in thought, he keeps tracing my veins over my distended belly.

"No boys," he says, suddenly.

I was playing with his hair, my other hand cradling my bump, but I stop now. "What?"

He looks up with a fierce frown, his bare chest tight, his shoulders brittle. "No boys. Ever."

Halo kicks in my stomach. "For Halo?"

"Yeah. Boys are fucking assholes."

I chuckle, tugging on his hair. "Takes one to know one."

His frown thickens. "Exactly. No one gets to break her heart."

"What if she falls in love with one?"

"She won't," he declares as if he can control that. "And if she does, I'm going to kill him. So problem solved."

I can't help it then. I laugh. "You're going to kill the boy Halo falls in love with."

"If that's what it takes to protect her, yes."

I study his outraged features, his longish hair brushing his strong, muscular shoulders, his hand on my belly, the hand of a protector, a predator.

Her hero. My villain.

"You're crazy," I murmur.

"She's mine."

I smile, my eyes all wet. "She is."

"No one gets to hurt her."

See?

My Halo will get her happy ending and so as her mom I'll take my happiness there.

As her mom, I'll ignore my own heartbreak.

I'll ignore that her hero is my gorgeous villain.

***

Late-May, in my seventh month of pregnancy, I get what I want.

So all this time, I've been trying to figure out how to help Reed. How to set him free from the job he hates, from his dad and that company that's sucking the soul out of him. When he leaves for the office after dropping me off at school in the morning, he's all smooth and polished but by the time the day ends, it's like he's been in a war.

He, of course, does not want to talk about it.

I've even discussed it with Tempest but she says the same thing. That her brother has always been like this. He won't talk about it. He won't discuss it. He won't let anyone know what he's feeling. It's just best to leave him alone because he'll bite your head off if you show even a little bit of sympathy or try to help him.

But I can't leave it alone.

Flawed and destructive and gorgeous, he's the love of my life.

I have to help him. I have to find a way to get him free.

So I've been mulling it over and over about what to do.

But then a miracle happens.

I get to meet Pete.

Reed's sixty-year-old friend who sucks at giving advice.

The only reason I get to meet him is because I've annoyed Reed so much by asking about him ever since he revealed that piece of information to me. And because I told him if he won't talk about his job, then I at least get to meet his one and only friend, Pete.

Besides, he's met all my friends. He knows my entire family.

Why is he being such a jerk about me wanting to meet his one and only friend?

So after a lot of debate, today we're going to meet Pete.

Through my poking and prodding, I have at least found out that he's the owner of Auto Alpha, where Reed used to work back in Bardstown High. And he was the one who taught Reed everything about cars.

I'm so excited to meet him.

In fact, I go all out in preparation.

I've baked him chocolate chip cookies and vanilla cupcakes with cream cheese frosting. To thank him for being Reed's friend when my villain never had anyone. I wanted to bake Pete something different and fancier. But idiot Reed won't tell me what Pete likes so I've gone with the safest choices.

Reed glares at the cupcake boxes in my hands as I emerge out of the glass house before taking them from me and depositing them inside his Mustang.

I know his mood is off for the reason only he understands. I mean, we're going to go meet his friend. How bad can it be?

Even so, I smile up at him. "I'm excited."

His frown only deepens as he stares at my smiling lips. Then jerking his smooth jaw up, he asks, "What's this one called?"

I touch my lips. "Oh. Uh, Queen of the Bards."

It's dark-green lipstick, almost black, and I've paired it with a lime green maternity dress with black printed flowers and black flats.

I've given a lot of thought to my appearance. This is the first time I'll be meeting a friend of the guy I love and I'm trying to make a good impression.

"Why?" he asks.

"Because of Bardstown. Our town. I love it."

"Good," he almost growls.

I frown. "Good what?"

"To know the name of the lipstick that I'm going to wipe off your lips."

And then he does just that.

He grabs my face and leans down to kiss me. I've gotten a lot heavier now but I'm still a ballerina and my toes jump up so I can meet him halfway.

When he's done, he lifts his head and I open my eyes to find him wiping my lipstick off his mouth with the back of his hand. "Why did you do that?"

His fingers flex on my face and on the small of my back. "Because I draw the line at cupcakes."

"What line?"

"The line of what I'll let you do for other men."

I fist his hoodie; he's back in my favorite outfit ever, his white hoodie and dark jeans. "What you'll let me do."

"Yes," he growls again. "You baked him cupcakes and that's it. You're not going to wear lipstick for him too."

I stretch up my toes even more. "Roman, it's Pete. Your friend. He's old."

He flexes his grip on my body again. "He has eyes, doesn't he?"

"Is that why you've been a grumpy bear all day? Because I was baking him cupcakes?"

"Cookies too. Besides, you shouldn't be working at all anyway. You're fucking pregnant."

Yes, I know.

And if he had his way, he wouldn't even let me get out of bed.

I shake my head at him and Halo chooses that moment to wake up and kick. Which he feels, obviously, because he has me plastered to his body.

"See? She agrees with me," I tell him. "She thinks Daddy's crazy too."

His gaze pierces me then, all dark and dangerous. "Daddy's

crazy because her mommy makes him that way."

My breasts are all squished into his chest, heavy and achy, and my thighs clench and unclench with every breath I take. But I can't get distracted. I have to go meet his friend.

"It'll be fun. I promise," I whisper up to him and with one last heated and agitated look at me, he lets me go and we go see Pete.

And it is fun.

Pete is like Santa Claus. Bushy white beard, beer belly and a loud good-natured laugh.

He's happy to see me. He says that he's heard a lot about me and he was dying to meet the girl who stole Reed's Mustang and drowned it in the lake.

"Serves him right for being an asshole to such a pretty girl," he says, laughing. "He had to work on it all summer."

I shoot Reed a guilty look and he flips Pete the bird, which makes Pete laugh even harder.

Pete practically inhales all my cupcakes as we chat. Because he says my cupcakes taste exactly like how his wife, Mimi, used to make them before she died a few years ago.

And then Pete and Reed start arguing over Pete's accounts.

Reed sits at the computer at Pete's desk and tells Pete that he needs to take better care with his finances. That from the looks of it there are some pending invoices that customers haven't paid yet. Pete tells Reed not to tell him how to run his business. Then Reed tells Pete that Pete won't even have a business if he keeps going like this and that Pete should move aside and let Reed fix stuff for him.

And to get back at Reed, Pete tells me stuff about Reed's Bardstown High years, how Reed used to spend all night up in the garage, how he'd be so interested in everything but tried to pretend that he wasn't. Pete also says that Reed is some kind of a genius with cars.

At which point, a customer appears and Reed chooses to disappear, making me realize that Pete's compliment was what sent him away. I saw his face, all tight and somehow shaken up.

I realize that their bond is so precious, Pete and Reed's. Like father and son. And I'm so grateful that Pete was there for him when he had no one.

But that's not the end of it. I realize something else too.

I realize that Reed loves cars.

I mean, he would have to, to build one of his own, but this is something else.

He's at ease here, in his element.

Among the cars, checking them out, looking under the hood, sliding under one's body, working with tools. Tools I don't even know the names of. All I know is that while sitting inside Pete's tiny office, watching Reed talk to customers and other employees, I've never seen him happier.

Not even when he was playing soccer.

I mean, back when he played, he was fantastic. But he was also super competitive, super wrapped up in winning and goading others, my brother especially. It brought out the worst in him.

It brought out the villain.

But this is different.

He loves this. He has a passion for it.

Halo moves inside me and I rub my stomach, trying to calm her down.

There's Daddy, I tell her. Look how happy he is here.

"He loves it," I murmur, watching Reed bent over a sleek black car.

"He does," Pete says from his chair, pulling my attention back to him.

"I've never seen him like this. So relaxed and at ease."

His smile is fond. "That boy loves cars, yeah."

I wring my hands in my lap. "Do you think… Do you think he can come back and work for you?"

His smile wavers slightly but still remains on his lips. "You'll have to ask him."

I swallow. "He won't talk to me."

He chuckles then, his beer belly shaking. "Yeah, that sounds like him."

With emotions pressing into my throat, making my voice all wobbly, I say, "I'm guessing the house that I live in is yours. He said it belonged to a friend and you're his only friend."

Pete nods. "Yeah. He wouldn't ask but I offered. It was something Mimi wanted. A vacation home but not really out of town. Just close to the cliffs and secluded. Something we could escape to when we wanted. Anyway, he was going to rent an apartment but I told him to take it. After Mimi, it was sitting there empty anyway. How are you liking Dr. May?"

My eyes widen when I realize that Pete was the one who recommended her. "I… You recommended Dr. May too?"

"Well, the boy was freaking out. Showed up at the garage with a mountain of books, saying he didn't know the first thing about any of this." Pete chuckles again fondly. "He was a sight to see that night. Told me he needed a doctor, a good doctor, a fucking excellent one for his Fae but someone out of town and so I hooked him up with Mimi's old doctor. We never had kids but we did try and Mimi seemed to like her."

Then I blurt out, "Thank you. For being his friend. I-I grew up in a big family. I mean, my parents were never there but I grew up with four brothers who took care of me. They still do. And I was so scared when I found out about…" I rub my belly. "But I had friends, and even though my brothers were mad, I knew I could count on them. But he… didn't have anyone. To talk to. He pretended he was fine. He always does that, but yeah. So thanks. For helping him."

At this, moisture coats Pete's eyes. "He's a pain in the ass with his crap about computers and things but I love that kid." When I smile, he says, "Like you."

I swallow again, this time thickly, painfully. "Please don't tell him. I've made him a promise."

"He's a clueless asshole, isn't he? Making such a sweet girl cry for him." He shakes his head. "I won't say anything. Even if I did, I doubt it'd get through his thick head. But you, Callie, you don't be afraid to push him. Don't be afraid to do what needs to be done to make that bastard see sense." Then with a twinkle in his kind eyes, he says, "And when you get a chance, ask him what he keeps in the trunk of that fucking Mustang of his."

That was confusing. But okay.

I take Pete's advice and tuck it inside my heart as we leave.

He's right.

I need to push Reed to make him see that this is his dream. This garage, his cars. The Mustang he built when he was in high school. That's what he wants to do.

He's always talking about my dream of being a ballerina, but what about him?

What about what he wants?

I need to give him that. After everything he's given me, after everything he hides from me.

And I need to give him what he wants right now too. He wants relief, I know.

I can see it in the tight lines of his body as he drives us back to the glass house. I can see that I've tortured him enough. By pushing him for a meeting with Pete, by baking cupcakes and cookies for someone else.

He was fine while he was working at the garage but I know he's back to feeling antsy.

While I'd never ever regret pushing and well, I'm going to push him more, I can at least calm him down. I can at least make things better for him.

So as soon as we get back home, I whisper, "Help me down on my knees." When he only stares at me with a frown, I add, "Please, Roman."

And he does that.

He helps my heavy body so I can drop down on my knees and get to work.

But first he takes off his hoodie and spreads it on the floor so I can rest my knees on something soft instead of hardwood.

My hands go for his jeans and I open them with eager, expert hands.

He's not the only one who knows how to play with my body. I know how to play with his as well. He's taught me and I want to play with him now.

I want to bring out his dick and suck on it.

I already know it's big, his cock. But when I unzip him and bring it out, I feel like I'm seeing it for the first time.

It's angry right now.

All thick and hard and huge, sticking out of his body.

Mean looking, villainous.

Because I tortured him. Because I drove him crazy.

I look up at him, his face that looks as mean as his arousal. "Sorry I made cupcakes for someone else."

His jaw clenches and he grips his dick in his large hand. "So are you going to apologize to me?"

I nod, rubbing my palms up and down his jean-covered thighs. "Yes."

He tugs on his rod, his face becoming meaner. "What else though? What else are you going to apologize for?"

Eyeing his thick rod and its slippery head, I whisper, "For putting on lipstick for someone else."

"Damn right. And for laughing with someone else. For giving someone else your sweet fairy smile. For making all those people fucking look at you back at the shop."

My breaths are harsh. "I didn't... I didn't know someone was looking at me."

His free hand goes for my braid then and he uses it to tug my head back and bend down over me. "Because you never know, do you? Because you live in your fucking la-la land, your rosy tits jiggling in your rosy dresses when you walk. Your sweet pregnant belly sticking out, all ripe and juicy."

I dig my nails in his thighs. "Roman —"

His eyes are all mean too, predatory. "You know, I thought you're pregnant now. My Fae is pregnant, her belly's swollen and right there for all the world to see. For all the men to keep away from. But no, that's not the case, is it?" His teeth clench, his fingers in my hair tightening. "They still look at you. They still want to sniff around your skirt. They want to know what's under it. They want your creamy tits and your big belly. They want you for themselves, my pregnant ballerina, and fuck yeah, it drives me fucking crazy. It drives me to kill. You drive me to kill. Are you going to apologize for that, Fae? For making me want to kill every man who looks at you."

I arch my neck up even more. "Yes. I will. For everything."

His chest is moving up and down with his noisy, growling breaths. "Then you better take off your dress. You better show me that pregnant belly where my baby sleeps. While you suck on the thing that got you pregnant."

And so I take off my dress for him and cradle the precious belly he gave me, making his eyes flash with primitive possessiveness, making him growl deep in his chest.

Then I take him in my mouth.

I suck on his dick.

That never ever fits in my mouth.

His monster, villainous, tasty dick, dick that got me pregnant, that never fits in my good girl, fairy mouth.

I go for it anyway and he grunts and curses.

Even his knees tremble, my big, bad villain.

And that's such a happy thought, such a satisfying thought that soon I'm taking him all in.

I'm taking him in my throat.

I wonder if my slender throat swells up with his huge dick. If he can see it. If he can see that his pretty and mean cock is inside of me and stretching my throat.

I hope he can.

I really do.

I hope he can feel how much I love him.

And when he comes in my mouth and I swallow what he gives me, I hope he can feel that I'm going to do anything to give him the dream that he doesn't even know he has.

Chapter 25

The Hero

I know something is off.

Something has to be for my father to call me into his study.

He hasn't called me in here in months.

Usually we see each other at the office and that's all we can take of each other. Besides, I've been right under his nose every day so I thought I was free.

Of this suffocating office at least.

But apparently not, because he's called me in on Sunday morning. It's fine though.

Fae's at the school library; she has finals and she's planning on spending the day studying. I'm supposed to go pick her up in a few hours. If her admission to Juilliard wasn't conditional, based on her graduating high school, I wouldn't even let her go.

She gets tired easily these days and I wasn't very gentle with her yesterday after we came back from Pete's.

What can I say, I'm a jealous motherfucker.

I'm jealous. I'm possessive. I'm afraid.

I'm fucking afraid, all right.

I'm afraid that time's running out. That Halo will be here soon. That Fae will leave for Juilliard.

Which is ridiculous.

I've wanted her to get out of St. Mary's. I've wanted her to go to Juilliard and away from my father. And as much as it fucking scares me that I'll actually be a father in a few weeks, I want Halo.

I want the life I accidentally made with Fae.

Especially on the night she wanted to end things.

And now it's all happening and I don't know what the fuck my problem is.

But anyway, back to my father and the reason he's called me into his office. Which he states as soon as I enter the room.

"This belongs to you, I take it."

And as soon as I hear those words, I forget to breathe.

I forget to move.

I forget that I ever knew the meaning of being afraid.

I didn't know. I never knew.

Not until this moment.

Not until I see what he has in his hands.

A square photo. A black and white blurry picture from the last doctor's appointment.

Of Halo.

I snap my eyes up to my father's face and there's a slight triumphant smirk on his mouth. "It looks like you've been keeping a secret from me."

With a conscious effort, I breathe deep.

I breathe to calm down the terror inside my body, the chill.

It's like my bones are freezing over.

But still, I unhinge my jaw and say, "I don't know what you're talking about."

He grazes the edge of the photo with his finger. "I think you know. I think you know exactly what I'm talking about. Although, I'm a little hurt."

The sight of my father's dirty, villainous hands touching something so pure is making me want to leap across the space and snatch it from him.

It's making me want to rip his fingers off his body.

But I stay put. I try to sound nonchalant. "Didn't know you were capable of being hurt."

"Well, I am. I'm a sensitive man. And this is such big news. The biggest." His smile appears wolfish, his gray eyes flashing with cruelty as he throws the photo away and threads his fingers. "My new secretary, Linda — you've met her — she found it on the floor by your desk and well, she let it slip in one of her, let's say, weak moments."

Even though he's not touching Halo anymore and that brings a bit of relief, I still fist my hands.

I still dig my nails into my flesh.

That he found out. That my plan, my promise, failed.

"You mean, when you were fucking her," I say.

He shrugs, sitting in his throne-like chair. "I was trying to be tactful."

"Don't start on my account."

He smiles again, watching me. "You're going to be a father, huh? That's a big job. Being a father."

"Yeah, you'd know a lot about it, wouldn't you?"

"Come on." He laughs, making my skin crawl. "Don't be that way, son. I should be the one who's mad. You hid it from me. You hid that I'm going to be a grandpa. And you did a good job of it, I must say. I never had a clue. Not one single clue. I feel foolish, to be frank."

"You should. You're not exactly bright."

Anger flashes through his eyes but he chooses to let my dig go.

He has something bigger up his sleeve, I know. I can feel it.

He wants revenge.

He wants to put me in my place for hiding things from him, for playing him. Like he did two years ago when he had Fae arrested just because he wanted to get to me.

To punish me for years of taunting him with soccer.

He settles back in his chair then. "I can't help but think why. Why would you hide something so big from your own father? You don't think I mean your future child any harm, do you?"

"You —"

"You don't think I mean her harm," he says, tilting his head to the side to look at the photo again, reading off it, "Calliope Thorne."

"Don't," I snap with clenched teeth, "say her name."

He laughs again. "She must be one special girl, this Calliope." I clench my jaw again when he says it. "Well, she's already proven herself to be so useful. A fucking goldmine, I have to say, and I haven't even met her yet. She —"

"Stop talking about her," I snap again, and this time, I move.

I stride over to his desk with violence running in my veins, and when I reach it, I put my hands on the wood, bend over and growl, "What the fuck do you want?"

His wolfish smile grows.

He knows he's got me.

He knows I'm going to do whatever the fuck he wants me to do.

"Nothing really. Just wanted to see it with my own eyes."

"See what?"

He chuckles. "If you're still whipped. What is it about her

though, I wonder? Is it because she's a dancer?"

"What?"

He smiles, his eyes flashing. "What, you thought I wouldn't find out everything, every fucking thing, about the mother of my grandchild?" He chuckles again. "She's a ballerina, huh? A good one from what I've heard. And she's got her little heart set on Juilliard. My, my. Apparently, it's one of the best schools and apparently, they're pretty fucking lucky to have her. At least, that's what he said when I talked to him, the dean. Turns out, I know him. I've asked him to take good care of her. She's family now, isn't she? You saw to that. And unlike you, the girl's got ambition. She wants to dance for the New York City Ballet Company. I think I like her more than I ever liked you."

My fingers vibrate on the desk, with fear, with dread, as he takes a pause to let his words sink in.

As he makes all my nightmares come true.

"But then, are you sure you want to give her that much freedom? Maybe she's better off, staying home, taking care of your sweet little kid, who I very much hope takes after its mommy rather than its useless fucking daddy."

"You fucking –"

Finally, his façade breaks and my father becomes the villain he is. "Watch your fucking tone with me, boy. You don't want to piss me off. You don't want to get me upset. Not right now, you fucking piece of shit." His jaw clenches. "You think you can keep things from me, huh? You think you're so clever keeping things from your old man, taunting him, rebelling against him. I tolerated that back when you were growing up. With your goddamn soccer and your teenage rebellion and little revenge plans. I let it go but those days are over. Those fucking days are over. You know what you are now? You're my bitch. You do what I tell you to do. I ask you to jump, you ask how high. I ask you to get down on your knees in front of me, you better be prepared to not only get down on your knees but to lick my fucking boots. And if you don't, I'll take your happy little family and crush them under those same fucking boots, you understand, you shithead. Don't ever keep anything from me or try to pull one on me or I'd be happy to remind you, Roman. I'd be happy to remind you who the boss is."

Bile surges up my throat.

He's the only one who calls me that. Roman. And I've fucking hated that name for as long as I can remember.

Until her.

Until she chose to call me that, cleansing it with her voice.

Until she baptized that name with her candy lips and gave it a new life.

"How did you know?"

The question is out before I can stop it and now it hangs in the air like a time bomb. The one that I feel lives in my chest these days.

"How did I know what?"

You'd give up your fucking soul for that girl. Your father knew that.

I look at the man I've hated all my life, the one who brought me into this world, whose face looks like mine and who's taught me everything I know, every cruel, mean, bad thing I know.

"How did you know I'd do it? I'd do everything. For her."

My father stares back at me, his gray eyes hard. "I didn't. I took a shot. I didn't even think it was going to work. Because for all your tantrums, you're exactly like me. You never cared for anything, much less a girl. But then she goes and steals your car, the car that you love so much, and you do nothing. Not a single thing. Made me curious, but again, I wasn't sure it was gonna pan out. But it did. When you barged into my office that night, begging me to let her go. That's when I knew. That's when I knew that my son is a pussy. He's a pathetic, weak, lovesick pussy. But I underestimated her charms, didn't I? Because apparently, you're still a pathetic, weak, lovesick pussy. Now get the fuck out of my office."

Love.

There's that word again.

The time bomb that I think lives in my chest starts ticking again. It starts ticking and ticking but then my father breaks into my panicked thoughts.

"Actually, take this with you."

He opens the desk drawer and retrieves a file.

He throws it on the desk and it skates over to me; I don't look at it though. I'm staring at him, waiting for him to speak.

He tips his chin to the file. "There's a piece of land I've got my eye on for a long time. I've let it be for some reason. I guess I was saving it for the right opportunity and now I want you to get it for me."

I look at the file then.

I reach out and open it and the terror that I've been feeling turns into anger.

It turns into fury. Violence and outrage.

So much of it.

But at the heel of it comes despair. Frustration, helplessness. This is exactly how I felt on the day of the championship game. When I broke her heart.

When I had to break her heart because my father left me no choice with his demands. With his threats.

Because it was a war and I had no choice but to fight it and win.

That's exactly how I feel when I see the name of Pete's garage on the top of the page.

"You want me to get it for you," I say in a low voice.

"Yes. Now the man who owns this has been hesitant. We've given him plenty of opportunities to come around but people can be stupid, sentimental. I'm sure you could relate." He chuckles. "So now you're going to do your thing and take it from him."

My heart is beating in my ears, in my teeth.

I exhale a long breath, a long shaky, terror filled, helpless breath. Because he wants me to do what I always do, destroy people.

This time however, the person he's chosen for me to destroy is Pete.

My father wants me to take something from Pete that he's built with his own hands, that is his entire life's work.

"Is there a problem?" he asks.

"No."

"Good boy. Get the fuck out."

I pick up the file from the desk because I'm going to do it.

I'm going to destroy Pete and serve him on a platter to my dad. Because I'll do anything for her.

Chapter 26

I'm going to talk to his dad.

I decided that right after we got back from Pete's.

Reed loves Pete's garage. He loves cars. He loves working there and he should.

He should be able to do that.

I know he doesn't want me to interfere. He doesn't want me to go anywhere near his dad and well, rightfully so. The man must hate me for what I did to his son's car. But it was two years ago and I'm not going to ask his dad to forget it. I'm only going to ask Mr. Jackson to let his son go.

To punish me instead.

I'm not stupid though. I know his dad is not a good man. I mean, look at what he forced Reed to do in exchange for my freedom. Plus Tempest has told me often enough about how crappy their dad is.

But I have to talk to him. I have to convince him somehow.

I can't stand by and watch Reed work in a place that he hates.

I've decided that this is going to be my gift to him: his dream. I can't tell him I love him because I've already made him that stupid promise but I can give him this.

Like he gave me my dream.

And yeah, I'm miserable about it because it will take me away from him, but still.

So I make a plan with my girls at the school library; it's Sunday and I'm studying for finals. Or at least, I should be, but I'm planning and I'm nervous.

And the girls are not helping.

They don't want me to talk to his dad because of what he did to me.

They think he's dangerous and maybe I should talk to Reed first and then figure out a plan. But I tell them that I've tried. I've been trying for months but he doesn't say anything and I'm getting impatient.

"I love him, okay?" I say, looking at all three of them before fixing my eyes on Salem. "Wouldn't you do the same for him? For Arrow."

Her golden eyes fill with sympathy and also determination on my behalf. "I'd do anything for him."

And so it's decided.

Not that they were going to change my mind but still.

But there's one thing that I think is a bad sign. Halo is restless.

She's been kicking and moving and making a ruckus inside my womb ever since Reed dropped me off at the library. And she's yet to calm down. I rub my belly, rock my body in the chair, take a walk around the library – which is not a hardship because I have to get up to pee every five minutes anyway; stupid bladder – but to no avail.

By the time I'm done, I've had it with her.

But then as soon as I see Reed, she quiets down.

She goes back to sleep and oh God, I'm so relieved. I'm so re-lieved to see him that I can't stop my smile as I walk through the black metal gates to meet him.

"Hi," I say, smiling. "Oh, I'm so glad to see you."

His frown is immediate. "What happened?"

"Nothing happened," I tell him, rolling my eyes, before grabbing his hand and putting it on my belly. "Halo was being such a brat, Roman. All day. And look, now that you're here she's fine. I don't like that she's chosen teams."

I was expecting a chuckle. Or if not that then at least a small smile.

But he doesn't give me any of that.

Even though he does grab my belly like he always does, his fingers splaying over the bump, but his wolf eyes that always shine or glint when he touches her don't come alive.

They're shuttered.

"What's wrong?" I ask, squeezing his hand.

"Nothing. Let's go," he says and tries to take his hand off my belly.

But I stop him. "Roman, what's going on? What happened?"

His jaw tics. "Nothing happened."

Something must have.

Because I know he's coming back from work.

He was supposed to drop me off at school to study before going back to his hotel room — where he still lives despite spending the majority of his time at the glass house — to get changed and go to work.

Because he got called in, which I completely hated.

It only made me more determined to take matters into my own hands.

That and the fact that after I worshipped his cock in the foyer yesterday, he drew me a bath. He washed my hair for me, rubbed lotion on my belly, massaged my back, my knees, my feet.

How can I not give him what he so obviously wants then?

When he can be so tender and loving.

"You're upset about something. I know. Tell me." I inch closer to him, to his rigid body. "Just tell me, please. You never tell me anything, Roman. And I know you're coming back from work. Something must've happened. You need to —"

"Fae," he growls, speaking over me as something flashes through his eyes. "Not now. Not fucking now."

That flash of something, something dark, tortured, makes me nod.

I wasn't going to do it.

But that light of utter anguish makes me agree. Like it pains him right now to be asked questions.

"Okay."

He gives me a short nod and takes me to his Mustang, helping me gently inside despite his harsh demeanor.

I watch him from the corner of my eye as he drives.

I watch the tight lines of his shoulders, the way his jaw is ticking. The way it doesn't even look like he's in the car with me.

As if he's somewhere far away in his thoughts.

As if he's in a trance.

I don't know what's going on but whatever it is, it's bad.

It's worse than his daily battles at the office. It's worse than him going into that place every day. Worse than anything I've seen in the past months.

I don't know what to do.

I don't know how to make it better, how to reach him right now.

All I know is that I'm not going to let it go on for long. I'm not going to let him suffer like this.

This time I have a plan and I'm going to make it happen.

I'm going to set the guy I love free.

The guy who's just taken a turn and I realize that we're not going home.

He isn't taking us to the glass house in Wuthering Garden.

He's taking us to our town, Bardstown. And from the looks of it, he's taking us back to the woods.

The woods where I first danced for him. Where he first kissed me.

Where I fell in love with him.

I'm not sure if it's a conscious decision on his part, driving us back to this place from our past, but as soon as we arrive, my heart starts spinning in my chest.

My heart starts remembering.

I haven't been in these woods in two years, not since the night he kissed me and told me to hold on to my dress, but I remember everything.

All those nights when he took me out here for a ride and I danced for him.

We're back here and I've forgotten how to breathe.

I've forgotten everything except him.

Except how to love him, how to adore him, how to be his.

In jerky movements, Reed climbs out of the car and walks around to help me. Again, despite all the turmoil in him, he's gentle. He's oh so careful as he helps me out of his Mustang but that's it.

That's where his gentleness ends.

He slams the door shut and steps back, his breaths noisy.

He turns around and walks a few paces away, his shoulders moving up and down harshly, the muscles of his back so bunched up that I can see them through his cozy hoodie.

"Roman," I call out.

His back tenses for a second before he turns back around to

face me.

Before his wolf eyes home in on me, his vampire skin sparkling in the summer sun.

I watch him stride toward me with an unknown purpose. A purpose only he knows but I get myself ready for whatever it is.

Whatever it is he'll give me.

He reaches me, his eyes agitated. "You're done."

"What?"

"You're not going back to that school."

"What? Why?"

He bends his body down, bringing all his intimidating bulk closer to me. "Because I said so. Because I don't want you going back to that shithole school. Actually I don't want you going anywhere."

I don't understand what's happening.

"Roman, what are you talking about?"

"I'm taking you home," he declares. "And I'm locking you up. I'm not letting you run around town unprotected. You're not going anywhere without me."

"But… But there's just a couple of weeks of school left. I have my finals and then —"

"Fuck finals."

"What?"

"Fuck the fucking finals," he repeats in a savage tone. "A lot can happen in a couple of weeks. A lot can fucking happen, all right? And I'm not taking any chances. Not when you're pregnant. What if something happens and I can't get to you, huh? What if something terrible happens to you or to Halo and I'm not…"

He trails off because he has to swallow.

Because something gets stuck in his throat. Something that makes his cheekbones all harsh and his eyes all intense and liquid.

And then I realize that I don't even want to know what the

cause of all this is. I don't even want to know why he's being all paranoid and panicky.

I can find out the cause later.

I need to make it better now.

I need to take this look away from him. This look of anger and
panic and frustration. And the anxiety of something happening to me
or to Halo.

So I get closer to him, as close as I can get.

I raise my hands and grab his face. I go up on my tired tiptoes
and look him in the eyes. "Nothing's happening to me, okay? Nothing
is happening to Halo. We're fine. We're —"

His hands come to grab my waist, or whatever is left of it due
to the pregnancy. His fingers fist my summer maternity dress. "You
don't know that. You don't fucking know that. There are things that
can harm you. People, you understand? There are people who could do
things to you, Fae. Who could do things to her, to Halo and —"

"Hey, hey," I speak over him, pressing my hands on his gorgeous, agitated face. "Look at me. Look at me, okay? I'm fine right
now. In this moment, Roman, no one is coming to harm me. No one
is coming to harm Halo." I grab his wrist and make him touch my belly
then. "Here, feel her. She's safe. She's sleeping, see?" His fingers grab
on to my belly again. "I swear, she's been acting up all morning. Ever
since you left. But she's fine now. She knows you're here. She knows
her daddy's here."

Reed swallows again, his hand moving over my abdomen.

"No one is coming here, Roman, okay? We're safe."

He presses his fingers in my belly for a second, staring into my
eyes. And slowly his wolf eyes lose the panicked look. Slowly, his eyes
fill with determination.

With a different kind of ferocity.

A mix of possession and protectiveness.

Before he does something that he's only ever done once before. Two years ago.

In his driveway when he took me out for my first Mustang ride at night. When I asked him to take me on a ride. A good girl asking a gorgeous villain to take her away.

Turns out though, I'm not that much of a good girl and he's not all villainous.

Right in front of my eyes, Reed comes down on his knees.

His knees hit the ground, his bones crunching the leaves into the earth, and the sound of it echoes in my body.

In my heart.

Then he presses his open mouth on my swollen belly, the belly he gave me and where his baby is sleeping now that he's here. He presses his lips onto it and, closing his eyes, he simply breathes.

Slowly and methodically, as if calming himself.

As if breathing like this, gulping air with his open mouth on my pregnant belly, is the only way he'll live.

And I let him do that.

I let him do whatever he wants, whatever he needs to relax. I rake my fingers through his thick, dark hair. I rub his back, his shoulders. I caress his jaw. I let him be.

I love him with my fingers as he gets his breath back.

My gorgeous villain.

A few moments later, he lifts his head, his eyes burning. "You know I'll do anything to protect you, don't you? To protect her."

I nod my head. "I know. I already know that."

"I'll turn this world upside down, Fae. I'll destroy anything, anyone, I don't care. I don't fucking care."

I put my forehead against his, smiling slightly. "I know you will. But you don't have to. Because we're safe."

Something emerges in his gaze again, that panic that I saw,

but it's not as dominant now that he's touching me and our baby. Now that he's studying my face from this close, his body so tall that he's right there, up to my eye level.

"I made you dance for me," he says in a low voice. "Here, for the first time."

My heart flutters. "You did."

"And you called me a villain."

I caress his face again. "That's because you were acting like one."

"I was, yeah."

"And the song you chose was offensive."

It was.

About a ballerina who dances for him like a stripper. It reeked of sex.

His kind of sex, all dirty and filthy and oh so good.

A puff of air escapes him as he chuckles. "I know."

"So you did it on purpose, then?"

He licks his lips. "Fuck yeah. I'd been dreaming about you spinning on your toes for me to that song."

"You'd been dreaming about me?"

"Yes, Fae. I'd see you spinning at Blue Madonna, pink cheeks and heaving chest. In your frilly tutus, looking all pretty and fairy-like. And I'd go home and jerk off to making that fairy dance dirty for me."

God.

God.

One day I'm going to find out all his secrets. All the things that he hides from me.

All the things that make me fall in love with him more and more.

Things that are both my salvation and damnation.

"I loved it," I whisper, curling my ballerina toes in my flats.

"That song."

"Yeah, you loved dancing dirty for me?"

My hands have come down to his shoulders and I fist his hoodie. "Yes."

A puff of air escapes him again as he chuckles slightly, his eyes intense. "God, Fae, you kill me, you know that?"

"Is that why you brought me here?" I whisper breathily. "Because I danced for you in this place?"

"Tell me what else happened here," he rasps instead of answering me.

I don't even have to think about all the things that happened in these woods. They are written in my soul, in the chambers of my heart.

I see them in my dreams.

"You kissed me in the rain," I reply.

"Yeah, for the first time."

"And you let me go after."

His eyes glint then. "I did. I let you escape my evil clutches unscathed."

Goosebumps wake upon my skin as I say, "You're not going to this time, are you?"

He slowly shakes his head. "No."

A current goes through my channel. A thick, pulsing current.

A current that makes me needy and makes me clench my thighs when he continues, "Tell me what's going to happen to you now. Here."

Somehow he's grown even closer or maybe I'm losing my mind, I don't know.

But I feel his words on my chest, on the lacy neck of my summer dress showing a slight cleavage. My swollen breasts and my nipples perk up.

"You're going to fuck me."

A flush of arousal appears on his features. "Yeah. Tell me where."

I don't know how it's possible for him to look so large and looming and inevitable like fate when he's on his knees, but he does look like that.

He does look like my destiny.

He does look unstoppable, written in the stars, and I bite my lip for a second before saying, "In my pussy."

His fingers twist my dress. "Yeah, in your tight little pregnant pussy. But tell me, Fae. Tell me if you think I'll stop there."

The lust in his eyes makes me squirm and somehow I know the answer. "You won't."

"No, I won't. I want something else, don't I?"

I nod, fisting his hoodie even tighter. "You do."

"Tell me what. Tell me what I want, Fae." His one hand creeps up and wraps itself around the back of my neck in a possessive hold. "Tell me what you'll give me for the first time. Here."

I know. I know.

I know what he wants from me. What he's wanted for months now but for some reason, he won't take it. For some reason, he's always held himself back.

He's always said that I wasn't ready.

And God, I've told him a million times that I was ready.

That when he touched me there with his finger, grazed it or popped his thumb inside while fucking me doggy style, it felt so good. It made me explode and I wanted his cock in there too.

So when I tell him, I'm all breathless and wet between the legs. "My ass."

His fingers squeeze my neck and his other hand slides away from my waist too, to go down to my ass and give that a big squeeze, making me go up on my tiptoes.

"Yeah, I want this." Another squeeze. "I want your ass. I'm going to fuck it here, in these woods. Where you danced for me. Where I've imagined fucking you a million times."

Just like that he gives me another piece of information, and I latch onto it. "You did?"

He kneads my ass again, rubbing the cheek through the fabric of my dress, inching it up, making it all wrinkled and messy. "Yeah, every time you danced for me. Every time you spun on your toes for me, I wanted to grab you. I wanted to grab your waist, bend you over my Mustang and flip up your dress. I wanted to stick my cock in you and fuck that fairy hole until you screamed. And no one would've heard you, if you had. No one would've come to save you if I wanted to fuck you and fuck you and come inside your sweet, innocent, sacred body. I've wanted to do that a million times, Fae. Here, in these woods. I've wanted to trash that tight little temple between your legs and send you home to your four overprotective older brothers with my cum leaking out of it. To send them a message, see. To tell them that you're mine. That tight little prize between your ballerina legs belongs to me. Fuck soccer. Fuck everything else. I just want that prized pussy for myself. That's why I brought you here."

I arch my body into his. I can't help it.

I stick my tits out and rub my belly against his torso because he's making me crazy now, gasping, "Roman."

And he takes advantage of that.

He presses his stubbled face in between my breasts, rubs the soft skin with his jaw, sucks on it, sinks his teeth in the meat, leaving little love bites.

"That's why," he growls when he's played out with them, when my breasts are all tender and achy and begging to be sucked on again. "Because I've thought about fucking you here a million times and I'm going to do it today. I'm going to take your virgin ass here. In these woods. Out in the open. Tell me you understand."

I jerk out a nod, my fingers in his hair and my tits in his face. "Yes."

"Tell me you'll let me."

God, is that even a question?

"Yes, I'll let you."

He buries his face in my tits again, this time pulling on the bodice of my dress and my bra until my nipple is showing and he sucks it into his mouth, growling at the taste.

"God, Roman," I moan, arching into his mouth even more.

"I'm going to spread you on my Mustang, Fae," he whispers over my breasts. "And then I'm going to fuck you in your ass, but first, I'll fuck you in your pussy. I'm a bad guy but I'm not a savage. I took your virginity without a care but I've put a lot of thought into this. I'll make you all loose and horny first. I'll make your pregnant snatch gush cum over my dick. So it's all lubed up, Fae, before I put it in your tightest hole. Do you understand what I'm saying to you? I'll grease it up real good before I put my big cock in your ass so it's easier for you to take. So it doesn't hurt you as much, because I'll lose my mind if it hurts you."

"It won't," I say even though I know it will.

His big cock in my ass will hurt but I don't care about that.

I want him in there. I need him.

"And then I'll fuck you real nice and slow. Real careful. As I rub your swollen belly. You know how much I love it, don't you? Your pregnant belly, your pregnant tits. I love it all, Fae. I love that I gave it to you. Me. Even though I had no right to. Even though I never had the privilege."

"You did. You —"

"And I'll do all that until you come again and I come in your last hole because your ass won't quit squeezing me. The only hole I haven't had yet. In this place where you danced for me and where you called me a villain. That's why I brought you here, Fae. Because that's what I am, a villain. And this is what a villain does, doesn't he? He spreads his girl on the hood of his car and goes to town on her ass. Out in the open with her pregnant belly sticking out and her tits jiggling. This is what a villain does to the girl he wants."

He is right.

This is what a villain does.

He fucks the girl he wants out in the open for the whole world to see. He not only fucks her, he takes her virginity that way.

On his Mustang, in the woods where he first captured her.

And the girl he's captured, she has no qualms about it.

She doesn't care if the world sees her. They can see if they want to.

That she's got his baby in her belly and his cock in her ass.

But I have to tell him something. Something very important. Something that I want him to know and to understand. That this is not why he brought me here.

He didn't bring me here because he's a villain.

He might be that, yes. But his reasons were different.

And when he spreads me over the hood of his Mustang — on his cozy hoodie though; he's not a savage as he told me — and parts my legs, his cock all lined up with my leaking pussy, I put a hand on his bare stomach where he's inched up his t-shirt to have a clear view of what he's doing to me.

I stop him and whisper, "This isn't why you brought me here."

He frowns. "What?"

"You didn't bring me here because you're a villain." I dig my nails in his abs. "You brought me here because this place is special. This place is ours. You brought me here, Roman, because in this place, there's no heartbreak. In these woods, I'm still sixteen and you're the guy who watches me dance. I'm your Fae and you're my Roman. That's why. Because this place is us."

Isn't it?

This place, these woods are before.

Before the tragedy struck and he broke my heart. Before he became haunted and I became broken. Before I found out that he's just a lonely boy and I'm just a girl in love.

In this place, we're magical, him and I.

We're timeless. We're frozen.

In this place, I'm still his dancing fairy and he's my wild mustang.

That's why my gorgeous villain brought me here.

And when I tell him that, his eyes flare for a second like this is only occurring to him right now. Just like when he realized that he loves our baby, our Halo.

God, he's so clueless. So lost.

My sweet, sweet villain.

But then his eyes turn predatory and full of desire.

Full of something that looks a lot like love.

But I know better.

I know better than to read into things. He's taught me well.

So when he enters my body, I don't think it's love. Even though it feels like it.

It feels like this might be how my Roman shows his love, by driving me back to our special place and taking the last thing on my body that he hasn't taken. By leaving his mark everywhere.

By building a shrine on my body, turning it into his love letter.

I would think about this more, but he chooses that moment to rub my clit and make me come.

And then he does everything as he told me he would.

He greases up his cock with my juices so he can put it in my ass. So he can dip his slippery head inside my tightest hole and make me arch and moan. And when it still doesn't go in smoothly, he spits on it.

He spits on his cock like a beautiful, vulgar beast and rubs it all over his length, mixing his spit with my juices before trying again.

Before gaining an inch or two with his short thrusts.

I help him further by inching up my bare thighs on the hood of his Mustang and grabbing the cheeks of my ass to widen my hole. To present it to him like a gift, that prize he's always wanted to trash and fuck.

And then there's no turning back.

Yes, it's painful and yes, I've never felt this kind of a stretch before.

But then I've never felt this kind of love either.

A love that makes me fly and makes me hurt. A love that feels like life one second and death the next.

A love that only grows and expands as I look into the wolf eyes of the guy who's fucking my ass, who's bent over me, his gaze tender and carnal and piercing, his big hand on my stomach, protecting our baby.

And the other hand in my mouth so I can suck on his fingers and not feel even a lick of pain.

Who's grunting with every thrust and every time I squeeze my ass over his length.

And who tells me, "You're so fucking beautiful, Fae. So fucking gorgeous. You're a wonder."

Popping his thumb out, I cradle his face, his tight jaw. "You are too."

Before his mouth descends on me and I inch up slightly to help him put his lips on mine.

And as soon as he does, I crash and burn and come.

My pussy contracts and my ass flutters, forcing him to come as well, to come together. As one.

Making him fill my ass with his cream and conquer that last hole of mine.

Making him even more entrenched in my heart. A heart that says, I love you, Roman.

And somehow a heart that hears, I love you, Fae.

Chapter 27

"Gregory Jackson."

The name echoes in the house, clashes with the soft blue walls.

But I know that I'm only imagining it because his voice is in my ears, coming through the phone.

Him being Reed's dad.

I got his number from Tempest, who also warned me against calling their dad. She told me that Reed would flip the fuck out, her exact words.

But I told her what I told my girls at St. Mary's.

That I'm not going to stand by any longer and let him suffer.

So yeah, after getting back from the woods and having dinner, I decided to send Reed on a grocery store run for that ice cream I like so I could call his dad.

I'm sitting down for this.

And good thing because I'm quaking, quaking, on the inside.

But I grab the edge of the cozy couch and say in a calm and de-termined voice, "Mr. Jackson, hi. You probably don't remember me but I'm a friend of your daughter." I cringe; great introduction. "And also

Reed. My name is Callie Thorne and I was hoping that I could talk —"

"Calliope."

I cringe again. Because no one has called me that in like forever.

But it's not exactly the fact that he's called me by my full name. It's how he's done it.

With so much interest. And I'm not going to lie, that creeps me out a little bit.

That intense interest.

Even so, I'm glad he knows who I am. It might save me from telling him the whole sordid tale from two years ago.

"Yes, I —"

He speaks over me. "How nice of you to call. I've been meaning to have a conversation with you."

Mr. Jackson's voice is smooth and deep, like his son's, but there's a quality in it that I find… slimy. Halo finds it slimy too I think because she kicks in my belly angrily and I have to rub the spot to make her go back to sleep.

Not now, honey.

Before I can respond to that, he continues, "I hear congratulations are in order."

"You know?" I blurt out before I can stop myself.

I didn't think he knew.

Reed has been so adamant about not letting me go anywhere near his dad or getting him involved in my pregnancy in any way that it comes as a surprise.

As a shock actually.

Unpleasant and vexing.

Something that gets my heart rate up.

"Of course," he says in that slimy, deep voice of his. "Of course I know. I've only recently found out, actually. My son did the best he could to hide it from me. I wonder why, however. I wonder why he wouldn't share such happy news with his own father. It hurt me, to be honest with you. But anyway, I'm glad I found out. Please accept my greatest congratulations."

There's nothing wrong with what he's saying.

In fact, it's all polite and polished and pleasant.

But something is off.

Something is very much off and it's not just the fact that he told me that he's only recently found out despite Reed's efforts not to tell him.

Again, it's okay.

It doesn't matter. That's not why I'm calling anyway.

I rub my belly again to calm Halo down so I can focus. "Uh, thank you."

"So," he asks magnanimously. "What can I do for you?"

Okay, this is it.

I sit up straighter on the couch and say, "I actually wanted to apologize."

"Apologize. For what?"

"For what I did two years ago. I never got a chance to apologize to you before and I want you to know that I regret it. I'm not..." I pause to gather myself. "I wasn't myself that night and if I were, I never would've done it. But that's not an excuse and I know that. I'm not exactly hoping that you forgive me but I'd like to say that I'm sorry."

"Forgive you?" He laughs, and this time I'm definitely, definitely creeped out.

His laugh is somehow both booming and screeching, like nails dragging across a chalkboard and you get the feeling that whatever is making him happy is coming at the expense of someone else.

Someone innocent.

God, and Reed has had to endure this all his life.

Reed has to endure this every day when he goes to work for his dad.

My heart is both racing and clenching in my chest. I need to make this happen. I need to get Reed's freedom.

His laughter trails off on a chuckle and he says, "I can see now what my son sees in you. Sweet and innocent. Begging for my forgiveness so sweetly. I regret that we haven't met yet. I'd very much like to meet you, Calliope. One day. If my son stops being stubborn. In fact, I'm going to insist to him that we meet. I can be very persuasive when I want to be. I'm sure my son must have told you all about that. But anyway, it would be a pleasure to meet the girl who sounds so sweet over the phone."

My skin is crawling right now.

Crawling.

At his slimy tone, his creepy laugh.

It makes me feel unsafe and disgusted.

It makes me want Reed. I want him to come back and chase away this chill in my bones.

And I know he will do it too.

He will do anything to make me feel safe and so I have to do this for him.

I have to be strong.

"Listen, Mr. Jackson, thanks for congratulating me and for all the compliments that I wasn't expecting. At all. But that's not why I'm calling," I say sternly. "I've heard a lot about you over the years and I have to admit that very little of that has been flattering. So maybe I'm making a mistake in calling you but I had to. I had to because I want to ask you something. I want to ask you to let Reed go."

"Let him go," he repeats. "Interesting choice of words. You don't think I'm holding him prisoner, do you?"

I swallow. "I'm not sure what you're doing but he's your son.

I'm a lot younger than you and I don't know everything you know, but I'm going to have a child soon. And I know that I'll love her. In fact, I already do. I already want to hold her in my arms and protect her from everything." I cradle my belly where she's sleeping. "I already know that I want to give her her every wish, every dream, every little hope. I want to know every beat of her heart. I want to ease every little breath she takes. I want to do that for her. Every parent wants to do that for their child, Mr. Jackson. And yes, we're not perfect and we make mistakes and there are times when our children hate us but that doesn't mean that we ever stop loving them or wanting what's best for them. So that's what I'm asking you, Mr. Jackson. I'm asking you to give your son what he wants. I know that you know that working at your company is not what Reed wants, and I know that you forced him into it. Because of me. Because of what I did. But it's been two years now and I want you to find it in your heart to let him out. You can punish me if you want. But please let him go."

"Okay."

He doesn't even think about it. He says it as soon as I finish what I wanted to say. And somehow I know that he's bluffing. He's completely bluffing.

He thinks I'm sweet and naïve, and I might be but I'm not that naïve.

So I insert steel in my voice when I say, "You will let him go."

It's not a question at all.

But he answers me anyway. "Yes. I will. You've made an excellent point here. So I'll let my son go and do what he wants to do, whatever that might be. Dreams are important to me. That's how I built this company. You have a dream too, don't you?"

"Yeah," I tell him hesitantly.

"Juilliard. Very ambitious," he murmurs. "I told this to my son too. But if you need any help, I'd be happy to be of assistance. I know quite many people there. And you're family, aren't you?"

I don't care about Juilliard right now. I don't.

Even though his words are filling me with dread.

"So you're going to let him go?"

"Yes. In fact, this will be his last job. The job I gave him today."

"Job."

"Yes, to sieze this lovely garage for me."

My heart thunders in my chest at his words.

Halo moves in my belly again. Just like she was doing this morning, restless and angry and agitated.

Through all the chaos happening inside my body, I ask him, "What garage?"

And when he answers me, I know.

I know he's the real villain.

He's the real evil, the real threat, the real danger.

Reed's father.

I sit there on the couch long after the call is done, my bones shaking. My breaths scattered.

It feels like an age.

Exactly like the night we had that fight and he made me promise that I'd never fall for him because he'd only break my heart.

The night I realized that I'd already fallen.

And exactly like that night, I hear the tires screeching in the driveway when he comes back. The sound of his Mustang door banging shut, his footsteps bounding up the porch stairs.

Tonight though, I haven't locked the door.

I haven't barricaded myself or erected barriers. Or walls.

I'm cut open and vulnerable as he enters through the door, carrying my favorite ice cream in a brown bag in his arms and I rise from the couch.

My phone slipping through my fingers and falling on the floor with a loud clatter that echoes around the house.

The glass house.

That belongs to his friend, Pete.

Reed glances down at the phone before looking up, "Fae, what —"

"I talked to your dad."

I hit him with these words. Punch him.

Because he draws back.

For a second, that's his only response, being pushed back slightly.

Before things happen.

Things like a flash of panic in his wolf eyes. The same one that I saw this morning, which confirms what I already knew after talking to his dad.

That is why Reed was so paranoid, panicked.

Because his father found out about me and Halo.

But the panic is only momentary. It's replaced by anger.

Great, mighty anger that makes his arms loosen for a second so that paper bag slips out, before tightening up every inch of his body. Every single inch of his muscle, every bone and tendon and vein that I can see tightens up, stands out.

"What?" he spits out, his wolf eyes deadly.

"I… After we came back from Pete's, I realized what your dream was. I realized that even you didn't know. Or even if you did, you didn't think you could have it. What you wanted. So I wanted to give it to you. I wanted you to have it, Roman, your dream. And so I got your dad's number from Tempest and… and I called him."

His vampire skin is stark white, leached of all color like his blood has frozen over.

Like there's a chill inside of him.

That perpetual winter that makes him wear hoodies all the

time.

White and pure and pristine hoodies that he loves so much.

"You called my dad," he repeats in a low voice.

"Yes."

He takes a step toward me. "After I told you not to."

I clutch my dress, white, his favorite. "Yes."

"After I made it clear that I didn't want you anywhere near him," he pushes out through clenched teeth, taking another step toward me. "After I made it crystal fucking clear that you're not supposed to even think about it. You're not supposed to interfere."

I swallow. "You did but I had to."

"Yeah, why?"

"Because you're killing yourself by working there. You don't want to work there. You want something else." And then, I can't keep it in any longer, I have to say it to him, I have to beg him not to do it.

So I go to him. I meet him halfway.

I clutch his hoodie. "Don't do it, Roman. Don't do what your dad asked you to do. Don't destroy Pete's garage. Please."

His jaw tics, his eyes violent and aggressive. "Do you have any idea how dangerous my father is? How big of a psychopath he is? He's a fucking criminal, okay? A goddamn criminal. And I have done everything in my power to keep you safe from him."

"Tell me," I say as I grab onto the opening he's given me. "Tell me what you've done. Tell me everything."

Reed bends down, his face vicious. "You wanna know, Fae? You wanna know what I've done and what my dad can do?"

"Yes."

"All right. You think he pressed those charges against you because he was trying to punish you, don't you? Because you stole his precious son's car. Isn't that correct, Fae? Isn't that what you think?"

"Yeah," I say, fear clutching my heart.

"He didn't. He doesn't give a fuck that you stole my car or that you tried to destroy his son's property. He doesn't give a fuck," he snaps, looming even closer. "He doesn't give a fuck about you. He doesn't care who you are or what you did. He pressed those charges against you because he wanted to get to me. Because he wanted to punish me, not you. He wanted to punish me for years of defying him, for taunting him with soccer. For taunting him with my scholarship, with my inevitable career in the pros. Yeah, he doesn't give a fuck about you, Fae."

He takes a moment to grind his teeth. "When I told him that I wouldn't do his bidding if he didn't make all the charges disappear and set you free. He, in turn, told me that I had no leg to stand on. Because if I didn't quit soccer and come work for him, you'd go to juvie and he'd make sure that you stayed buried in there. So he doesn't care about you or your little family. All he cares about is me. His rebellious, disobedient son who fucking hates him. Controlling me, making me his bitch, making me do things that I don't want to do. It's fun for him. Do you understand that? It's fun for him to toy with people. He's done it all his life. Me, my sister, my mother. In business. So he was toying with you to get to me."

I let him go then.

I unfurl my fingers from his hoodie and ask him with my heart beating in my ears, "And now that I'm pregnant?"

His nostrils flare. "He'll use that too. He'll use Halo. He'll use Juilliard too, your dream, if he has to."

"Against you."

His response is a muscle on his cheek that comes to life and throbs.

"So…" I have to take a moment here to gather myself. "So you'll do his bidding for the rest of your life?"

"Yes, if that's what it takes to keep you safe. To keep Halo safe."

That's what he's been doing for the past two years. That's what he'll keep doing.

I fist my hands. "What about Pete?"

"What about him?"

"Are you going to take his garage from him and give it to your dad?"

His features ripple and I know, I know, that it's pain.

He's hurting at the thought of harming Pete. His one and only friend, the man who's been more of a father to Reed than his own.

"He'll get over it," Reed says, trying to sound nonchalant, but his rigid body gives him away.

"Will you?"

"What?"

"Will you get over it, Roman? For screwing over your friend. The friend that you love."

At this, his features scrunch up and he plows his fingers through his hair as he scoffs. "Jesus Christ, you don't give up, do you? Why does everything have to be love? I don't love anything. I don't have time to love anything. My life is already plenty screwed up without it, you understand? So yeah, I'll get over it. I got over hurting you, didn't I?"

No, he didn't.

He hasn't.

He still apologizes to me. He still feels bad about what he did two years ago.

The other day he bought me daisies. Both flowers and dresses with daisies printed on them. Because I told him that I'd buried all the dresses from two years ago somewhere deep in my closet so I never look at them. Because they remind me of him.

And then I told him that I missed sitting in his Mustang with him, listening to music with the windows down and our eyes closed. So he recreated that whole moment last weekend in our driveway.

He even apologizes for the things that weren't his fault to begin with.

Like getting me pregnant.

It takes two people to do that, doesn't it?

But he doesn't care.

He isn't over that either. He shows it to me every single day by
pampering me like I'm the most precious treasure in the world. Like
I'm the first girl to get pregnant. Ever.

Like I'm a wonder. His wonder.

You're a wonder…

"And what about you?" I ask, sounding all calm when I want
to shake him and make him understand that he can't live like this.

He can't keep hurting people he cares about because his father
is a villain.

"What about me?"

"Don't you see? You love cars, Roman. You love them. You
have a passion for them. I watched you yesterday. You were so happy.
Working at that garage gives you joy. It gives you peace and it sets your
soul on fire. That's your dream, Roman. That garage is your dream.
Like ballet is mine. Don't you deserve at least a shot at it? At your
dream."

His chest moves with a violent breath as he snaps, "Fuck
dreams. I don't care about dreams. I don't want any dreams. Do you
think I'm any better than my father, Fae, huh? I did the same thing he
did, didn't I? I used you. I took advantage of you. I lied to you. I broke
promises to you. And you're not the only one. I've used people. I've
used Ledger, his anger, against him. I've cheated just to win at soccer.
I've lied to people to get my way. I've blackmailed them. I'm my father's
son. Everything I've learned, I've learned from him. What makes you
think I deserve my dreams? Or a happy ending of any sort?"

Because he's regretful.

Because he has remorse. Because he wants to do better.

That's the difference between him and his father, the true villain.

My Roman wants to be better.

"And if that's the price to pay to keep you safe, to keep Halo safe, I'll do it. I'll keep working for my dad. I'll keep doing what he asks me to do. I told you that, didn't I? I told you that I'll destroy anything and anyone if it means you're safe. And I'm not going to apologize for it."

Yeah, that's what he said.

He said that he'll destroy the world, burn it down to protect me. To protect Halo.

But he's not burning down the world, is he? He's not destroying someone else.

He's destroying himself.

He's hell-bent on destroying himself because he wants to keep me safe.

Because that's what will happen if he screws over Pete.

And suddenly, I have to ask him.

I have to ask what Pete told me to yesterday. It confused me then but somehow things are clear.

Things are so clear and vivid and my heart can't stop spinning in my chest.

I look up at him, into his wolf eyes that are watching me defiantly, agitatedly. "What do you..." I swallow, trying to steady my voice, my breaths. "What do you keep in the trunk of your Mustang?"

Reed's breaths, however, seize as his brows snap together. "What?"

"Tell me what you keep in the trunk of your car."

"Pete tell you to ask me that?"

"Yes. Tell me."

His chest shudders as he plows his fingers through his hair again, almost ripping it out. "I'm going to fucking kill him."

I raise my voice. "Tell me, Roman."

I have to.

To make him answer. To make my own heart stop beating so loudly.

He hates it. Having to answer me.

But he does even though there's violence in every word of his. "The sweater you gave me, all right?"

"The sweater."

"Yes," he pushes out. "I keep the sweater you gave me, wrapped up in a bag, in the trunk of my car."

"Why?"

"Because that's the only place I know it will be safe. The only way I know it will be with me wherever I go."

My sweater.

The one I made for him because I loved him. Because I knew that he was always cold and I wanted him to have something warm and cozy when I wasn't there to wrap him into my arms.

He keeps that sweater, my love letter to him, safe in his Mustang. Again, something he never told me and probably never would've if I hadn't pushed him.

He keeps the thing I made for him with love, in the only thing he says he loves.

But I know that's not true.

I know he loves his sister. He loves Pete despite what he says. I know he loves Halo.

And now I know he loves me.

He loves me.

Reed is in love with me. He's been in love with me for a long time now.

And you know what? He loved me two years ago too.

What I felt back then was real. He loved me.

That's why he did everything.

He protected my virginity. He got those charges reduced at his expense. And I know that he broke my heart that day but he loved me even then. He did it because he thought he had no choice. He did it because of his father.

And more than anything, I know when he broke my heart, he broke his heart too.

Like his heart is breaking right now.

And God, I thought… I thought if I ever found out that Reed was in love with me too, then I'd be the happiest girl in the world. I'd be the luckiest girl.

Because the guy I fell in love with when I was almost sixteen loves me back. I'm not sure if he realizes that he loves me but he does love me back.

Reed Roman Jackson.

The love of my life. The beat of my ballerina heart.

Loves me back.

But I'm not.

I'm not happy. I'm not happy because he's destroying himself for this love.

He's tearing himself apart for this. For Halo. For my dream that he thinks his father will destroy if he doesn't give that vile man everything.

Just look at him.

Look at his messy hair, his pretty eyes all red and ferocious. That jaw all rough and clenched. His tall, broad body tight and alert in a battle stance.

And so I take a deep breath and try for the last time to make him understand.

That this isn't the only way to love. He's free to love in a hundred different ways.

Halo, Tempest, Pete... me.

"You're regretting it now, aren't you?" he asks in a guttural voice. "Forgiving me. Forgiving a guy like me."

"No. Because there's a difference," I say, looking into his eyes. "Between you and him."

"What?"

"I know you think that you're like him. I know that. And you might be. You came from him, right? He's your father. Of course you share similarities. You grew up with him. You grew up fighting with him, hating him and yet learning things from him. Because that's what we do. We learn things from our surroundings, from our parents. But through some miracle, you learned new things. Different things. Things that he didn't teach you, Roman. Because your father is incapable of those things. I talked to him. I could feel it. And I believe you when you say that your father is dangerous. And he's that way because he's incapable of remorse. He's incapable of love. But you're not. I know you want to believe that you don't love anything and I'm not going to push you to believe otherwise. Not again. But I also know that you love Halo at least."

I put my hand on my belly and she kicks into it. And as always, his eyes, so pretty, so anguished, fall to my hand.

"I know that you love her. You love our baby. And you know what else, Roman? She loves you back. She hasn't even met you yet but she loves you. You know why? Because you're her daddy. You're going to protect her. You're going to teach her so many things. Riding a bike or doing a math problem. Or throwing around a ball. Maybe climbing a tree. And you're going to put her on your shoulders and she's going to feel like she's on the top of the world. She's going to love her daddy. I can see it.

"I can see that she's going to look up to you for everything. You're going to be her favorite. Even more than me. I know that, Roman. She's going to come to you for everything. Because you're going to be her hero. You already are her hero. She perks up whenever you're close. She goes to sleep if she's restless. She hears your voice and I can feel her smiling inside of me, being all happy. But if you do this, Roman, if you do this thing for your father, then you're going to break her heart. You're going to break our baby girl's heart because then you'll be like everything else that you want to protect her from. You'll be a villain.

"Don't be a villain, Roman. I know you think you don't have a choice. I know you think you have to do this. But you don't. You always have a choice. Always. Choose the right thing. Choose the protector in you. You always wanted to be out of your father's control, right? You can be. All you have to do is choose. Please. Choose what you want, what you've always wanted. And do it for Halo. Don't break her heart before she's even born, Roman. Before you've even held her in your arms. But more than that, choose what you want for yourself. Choose it because if you hurt the man who's always been a father to you, for the man who's never cared about you, you'll break your heart. You'll break your own heart, Roman, like you did two years ago. Stop breaking your own heart. Please."

I've begged him now. As much as I can.

I've begged him and I've pleaded with him and I don't know what he's thinking.

I don't know because he's not showing me.

His body is a statue, made of beautiful marble, and his eyes are inscrutable. And even if he had any expression in them, I wouldn't be able to see it anyway.

Because my own eyes are filled with tears. My own body is trembling.

I want him to say something, anything, and he does.

He shifts on his feet, takes a step back and says, "Don't wait up."

With that, he spins around and leaves.

He goes out the door he came in only a little while ago.

Even though he told me not to wait up for him, I do.

I wait for him but he doesn't come back.

He doesn't come the next morning either. Conrad comes to pick me up for school, says that Reed had texted him and asked him to drop me off.

Even though I know that I won't see him until the end of the school day, I still wait for him.

I wait and wait and wait.

Until I'm climbing down the stairs at St. Mary's, switching to my next class, tired and achy and so in love with the guy who I haven't seen in hours now, that I slip.

My foot slips.

And I stumble.

I try to hold on to the metal banister but I can't.

I can't hold on and I fall.

I roll down the stairs and a blinding pain grips me, my back, my ankle.

But more than that, a blinding pain grips my abdomen.

Where my Halo is sleeping.

Mine and his.

Chapter 28

The Hero

I open the door to my father's study and enter the four-hundred-square-foot space that I've always hated.

He's sitting in his throne-like chair and I know I've shocked him with my sudden intrusion.

I've actually never seen him shocked, now that I think about it.

I've seen him happy and gleeful and furious and in the fucking throes of passion but no, I've never seen him shocked. His gray eyes, so much like mine, flare slightly.

And I realize his eyes are too big for his face.

Thank God or whoever the fuck is responsible for these things that I didn't get this trait from him, cartoonish eyes.

He opens his mouth to say something but I'm not interested. And I'm not staying long anyway.

So for the first time ever, without reservations or hesitations, I stride over to his desk and throw something at it. It skids all the way over to my father's side, loose papers spilling across the polished desk.

It's the file he gave me.

Like before, I put both my hands on his desk and look him in those eyes.

Eyes that have never been warm or affectionate.

"You wanted to teach me a lesson about keeping secrets, yeah?" I begin. "Well, here's a little secret for you: I'm good with cars. Pretty fucking good. Fantastic, actually. Have you ever wondered why I love my Mustang so much?"

His features tighten up but I don't give him a chance to speak. "You probably haven't. Given how amazingly self-absorbed you are. I love it so much, Dad, because I built it myself. With my own hands. I didn't buy it at a showroom, didn't buy it with your money. It's completely mine. Surprised you, didn't I? Yeah, me too. Never thought I had that sort of talent. I mean, soccer's easy. Soccer's a piece of cake, but this stuff takes some real genius. And as I said, I'm pretty fantastic. So I've come to a conclusion: If I love it so much, building cars I mean, I should probably do it for a living, don't you think?"

His malice-filled eyes narrow. But again, I don't give him a chance to speak.

His speaking days are over.

"So here's another little surprise for you: I bought the garage. On that piece of land that you wanted. That's mine now. That I unfortunately had to buy with your money, or the money I earned working for you so technically it's mine, but still. It made my skin crawl. But I guess it was for a good cause, huh? And now I think congratulations are in order, aren't they? Because you're never getting that piece of land."

Now I give him a chance to speak. And he does, with clenched teeth. "You're a little piece of shit, aren't you, son?"

"I am, yeah. But I don't think I can take all the credit for that. Some of it goes to you." Then, "Oh, and that guy we usually use to mess with people? Who was going to fuck with Pete's bank accounts? Yeah, he's indisposed. Somebody broke into his house and broke all his bones. Now who would do such a cruel thing? I'd say a real piece of shit."

"Looks like you need a little reminder about who's the boss, don't you?"

"I leave that up to your judgement, actually. If I need a reminder or not."

My father leans toward me. "You sure you want to? Because from where I'm standing, it looks like you've got a lot more to lose this time."

I clench my jaw, showing him all my hate, all of the pent-up loathing inside of me, all the fury, all the mayhem I'll rain down on him if he dares to talk about her.

My Fae. Or Halo.

Yesterday I choked on my fear. I choked on what he could do.

But I never thought about what I could do.

What I'm capable of.

"Yeah, I do," I tell him, keeping my gaze steady. "I do have a lot more to lose. And I thought about it last night. And I think I've got another little surprise for you."

"What's that?"

I press my hands on the desk harder, my fingers almost digging through the expensive wood. "You don't want me to lose those. The things I've got to lose now. Because those are the only things standing between you and me. Between what I can do to you if you so much as even think about hurting her and my baby. Which is ironic. Don't you think? The things you want to hurt in order to make me your bitch are the very things keeping you safe from me."

"Are you fucking threatening me, Roman?"

I expect my skin to crawl again.

I expect to feel the phantom noose around my neck tightening up as it has in the past two years.

But nothing happens.

My breaths are harsh but it's my fury, my anger, my own violence that's making them so.

"No, of course not. This is not a threat. It's a fact, and I mean it in the sincerest way possible. If you even look at my family, I'm going to rip your heart out. The only reason I haven't done that yet — and believe me, I've thought about it a million times in the last two years — is because I thought I had no choice. I had no choice but to do your bidding. I had no choice but to be like you. Because we're both assholes, aren't we? But whaddya know, I do have a choice. And I would very much like to see where that choice takes me. If I get to fuck you up in the process, it would be icing on the cake. So be very careful about what you do next. You don't want me to turn into a man who's got nothing to lose. Because then there'd be no stopping me."

With that, I straighten up.

I watch his furious eyes, so much like mine, that have a hint of terror in them.

The terror that I felt all day yesterday.

Ever since he found out about Halo and Fae's Juilliard.

Not going to lie, I love seeing that.

I love seeing my father, sitting in his throne-like chair, afraid of his own son. I memorize it, that look and file it away for future use as I walk out of that study for the last time.

As I breathe the toxic fucking air of that toxic fucking space for the last time.

And Jesus Christ, I've never felt lighter.

I've never felt more… relieved. More like I could breathe now.

And it's all because I've got a choice.

I never thought I had a choice, actually.

I had a shitty father who wanted to control me, who wanted to treat me like a possession. Who never cared about me or my sister or my mother. Or people in general. So I had no choice but to hate him. I had no choice but to rebel, to fight. To stick it to him.

I had no choice but to go to war with him.

Every action, every reaction in my life has been born out of the fact that I never had a choice.

But then... then she said that I did. That you always do.

No one's ever said that to me before. No one's ever said to me that I had a choice, that I could pick the life that I wanted for myself.

So I thought about it. I thought about if I had a choice, what would I want?

What are the things that I want?

Turns out, I want a lot of things. And they were buried inside of me just waiting to come out.

I'd want a mother who cared about me and Pest. Who didn't love a villain like my father. Who was happy and carefree.

I'd want Pete as my father.

The man who taught me everything about cars and showed me what my passion was. The man who I went to last night, after driving around for hours, and told everything to. And his response was that he was done with the garage anyway. That he wanted to travel now, visit all the places he went to with Mimi, and he was ready to give it up but only if I'd promise to take care of it.

Well, his exact words were, I was waiting for you to wake the fuck up and get your head out of your ass so I could hand you this damn shop and retire.

So I took it. Because if I had a choice, I'd pick working in a garage over playing soccer any day.

It's mine now. My dream.

Because a dream is something that gives you peace and sets your soul on fire at the same time.

That's what she said to me.

The girl because of whom all of this is happening. The girl who showed me that I could take my life back from my father, if I wanted. I could build my own life. The kind of a life, the kind of a father that my baby girl would be proud of like I was never proud of my own father.

The girl who showed me that I could be different, good, someone I like – but wait a second.

Wait a fucking second.

She isn't the girl who finally made me realize that I do have a dream and what it means to have one, no. Or that I could choose to be a different person.

At least, she's not just that, is she?

She's more.

She's my... She's my dream itself.

Because she gives me peace. And she sets me on fire.

Holy fucking Christ.

Fae does that for me. Every time she smiles at me. Every time she touches me. Or she tells me something that she's read in a pregnancy book or she bakes for me. Or looks at me with her pretty eyes or blushes for me.

Every time she lets me inside her body so I can worship her, ruin her, sate myself in her.

Every fucking time she dances.

That's why I used to be so eager to watch her spin on her toes in the woods or back at Bardstown High. Because she gave me peace. Because she took away my stress of soccer and rivalry and my dad.

Because when I saw her, all I could think about was her.

Jesus Christ, Fae is my dream.

The biggest one I've ever had. The most precious one.

Isn't she?

My tight little ballerina who's glorious and gorgeous and pregnant with my baby.

I'm outside now, in the driveway of my posh house and I have to take a second. I have to plow my fingers through my hair and just breathe.

At the realization.

At the fact that I've been such a fucking idiot.

All this time, all this fucking time, Pete kept telling me. My own fucking father kept telling me and I…

I've been too bogged down and wrapped up in my own self to recognize it. To recognize that I love her. That I could love her.

I had so much hate inside my heart that I never thought I could. I never thought I was capable of it. But she kept telling me too, didn't she?

She kept telling me that I could love.

That if I love Halo – I do; I fucking do – then that means I can love other things as well. But I kept ignoring her like I kept ignoring everyone else.

I straighten up then, an urgency flowing through my veins.

I have to go to her. I have to fucking tell her.

She needs to know. She deserves to know.

How I feel. How I've been a big fucking idiot. Especially after how I left things with her last night.

I know she's at school right now. But that's fine. I'm going to stand outside of those fucking black metal gates and wait for her until she comes out.

But as I begin to stride toward my Mustang, I realize I have a text. My phone's been on silent all night long and I've got multiple missed calls and texts.

From Conrad, Pest. Even Ledger.

And then for the second time in twenty-four hours, a panic like no other grips me. It chokes the life out of me, keeling me over.

But I don't have the time for that. I don't have the time to panic or to breathe even because she needs me. My Fae and Halo. And I have to get to them.

I break all speed limits and lights as I race toward the hospital. It's in the town of St. Mary's, miles away from Bardstown and my father. Something that would've made me happy. To have Fae and the baby away from the clutches of my father.

Not so much now.

Now I'm panicking. I'm angry and frustrated and helpless.

So goddamn helpless.

By the time I reach the hospital, I'm shaking. My body is cold. My bones can't be contained within it.

I'm not sure where I'm going or who even helps me get there but thank fucking God, I end up at the right place. Because I see the tall form of Conrad, standing, his eyes immediately falling on me as I enter the space.

"Where is she?" I ask, pushing through the panic. "Where the fuck is she?"

Conrad stares at me with grave eyes. "She fell down the stairs at school. It was an accident. We brought her in—"

I don't think.

I get up in his face and grab his collar. "What do you mean she fell down the stairs at school? Where the fuck were you? Why weren't you keeping an eye on her?"

"Reed —"

"She's pregnant, for God's sake," I shout. "She can be slow and clumsy and does no one…" Suddenly, the winter in my body becomes even chillier. "Halo. What… Is she…"

"Callie's in surgery right now. The fall induced labor and…" He swallows and I see the same terror reflected in his blue eyes. "And we won't know for a few hours if Halo… We won't know until they come out of surgery."

We won't know.

We won't know if Halo is fine. If my Fae…

My fingers come loose from Conrad's collar.

My hands fall limp as I take a silent step back.

As the initial adrenaline of panic and terror is overtaken by the heaviness of them. The weight of fear.

The gravity that we're here. In this stark white waiting room with doctors and nurses and patients bustling around, something that I'd blocked up until now.

But it's rushing back, along with the vivid realization that my Fae fell down the stairs at school and now she's in surgery with Halo.

And they both might not… be okay.

"We've been trying to reach you all morning," Conrad says. "Where were you? Why couldn't you drop her off this morning?"

I texted him early this morning that I wouldn't be able to drop her off at school today because I had something to take care of. Something that I know he doesn't care about and I never wanted him to.

Because it was my responsibility, my father.

So I tell him, my chest burning, every bone in my body hurting. "It's over. With my father."

Even though his gaze is dipped in the same gravity and fear as mine, I can see a tiny bit of approval in his eyes as well. "Good."

And then, I can't help but say, "I love her."

"I know. I could see. It's good that you can see it now too."

"I've been an asshole."

"Yes. But I was wrong about you. I don't like to be wrong but I'm glad I was." Then the look in his eyes get shuttered. "And I'm sorry

I wasn't there. To save her when she…"

Fell.

***

Halo Jackson comes into the world at exactly 3:27 PM on a Monday.

She shouldn't have though.

She's approximately six weeks early. All the books say that a normal pregnancy lasts up to forty weeks. Any babies born between thirty-seven and forty-two weeks are considered full term. Any born before are premature.

Halo is premature at thirty-one weeks.

She weighs 4.6 pounds and she has a ninety-five chance of survival with no ill effects.

But we need to keep her in the NICU. In an incubator because premature babies don't know how to regulate their body temperature. They might have excessive weight loss. Their vital signs may be unstable.

Not that these things might happen to Halo because she comes under the mild category of premature, as the doctor who performed the surgery told me. Which went smoothly. They were afraid that the fall might have caused some internal bleeding of sorts but it didn't.

My Fae and Halo were lucky.

But they're not taking any chances. Hence the incubator.

I know all this because they told me.

But I know some other things too.

I know that she has dark hair like me. And blue eyes like her.

And I know that she's small. She's so very, very, dangerously small. I don't know how I'll keep her safe. I don't know how anyone can keep a baby safe when they're so small and fragile.

So breakable.

And it looks like Halo might break if I touched her even with a finger.

Good thing I haven't.

Not yet, seeing as they took her straight to the NICU after surgery and stuck her with all these tubes. So I haven't gotten to hold my daughter yet.

My daughter.

She's my daughter. I have a daughter.

Over the past months, I thought I was preparing myself. I had questions. I asked them. I had a list of things to buy for her. The list of things she'll need when she arrives.

And yes, I've been afraid.

Of course I have been. Of what kind of a father I'll be. Given I always had a shitty one.

But I never thought I'd feel so incompetent. So blind as to what to do next.

What am I supposed to do now? With her.

How am I supposed to contain all this love? All this rush of love that I've never felt before.

Not this kind of love.

It's like I'll burst. My skin will fall apart with the kind of love I feel for my baby.

So yeah, I don't know.

Except the only thing, the only person in this whole world, that has the power to calm me down, to give me peace, is sleeping. Doctors say that she's doing great.

Except the normal post-op pain and recovery and the weakness that she'll feel.

Oh, and her ankle's sprained from the fall.

And I know she's going to be fine but with her eyes closed and her blonde hair fanned over the white pillow, she looks just as fragile as Halo.

Just as beautiful and small and mine.

But then those eyes flutter and open, pure and shining blue, and my heart skips a beat.

"Hey," I whisper, leaning over from my chair by her bed and squeezing her hand that I've been holding for the better part of the last two hours.

She smiles, those fairy-like eyes roving over my face. "Hey." Then she frowns slightly. "You look completely destroyed."

A tired chuckle escapes me. "And you look like a fairy." She chuckles slightly too and I swallow. "How do you... how do you feel?"

"Good. I had a dream."

"Yeah?"

"Yes. About the championship game. I'm at the stadium, watching your game," she whispers, squeezing my hand back, making something prickle in my throat. "And I'm all dressed up in my tutu and my wings and I'm smiling because I know you're gonna score the goal. But then, you look up from the field. You look directly at me and you smile too and I want to tell you that you need to keep your eye on the ball or you'll lose but I'm so happy. So happy that you looked at me, that you didn't care about the game and the world and you just looked at me in the crowd. And then, I felt Halo in my belly and..." Her breaths hasten, her eyes filling with realization and her free hand flies over to her belly. "Halo. What... where's..."

"Hey, hey." I squeeze her hand, trying to get her attention. "She's fine. She's here. She's —"

"But she wasn't supposed to be... I fell, Roman." She looks at me with teary, panicked eyes. "I fell at school and there was so much pain. And I was waiting for you but you never came and Halo... where's Halo?"

"Hey, look at me, Fae. Look at me. I'm here, okay? I'm not going anywhere. I'm not leaving." I squeeze her hand again. I keep squeezing it as if trying to pump her heart back to life, as if to tell her lungs to breathe, just breathe. "And Halo's fine. She's fine. A little premature but she's doing great, okay? There's nothing to worry about. I promise. I promise, Fae."

Tears are falling from her eyes, disappearing into her hair. "You promise?"

"Yeah. Yeah, I do. She's fine. You're fine too."

Finally her breaths calm down. "Okay, I trust you. I need..." But with her ease comes exhaustion and her eyes are fluttering closed. "I need to see her. Take me... take me to her... she must be alone and... afraid. She must be..."

I caress her hair, rub my thumb over her almost completely shut eyelids.

And when she goes back to sleep, her breathing calm, easy, I kiss her forehead, smell her sweet scent and promise, "I won't let her be. I won't let Halo be afraid. Or you. Ever."

Chapter 29

Halo Cora Jackson is beautiful.

She's the most beautiful baby to ever be born. I know I'm biased because I'm her mom, but I don't care. She's got the darkest hair and the bluest eyes, even bluer than mine, and she has the rosiest cheeks.

And she's small.

Even now, four weeks later.

She was small to begin with. Because she wasn't supposed to arrive so early, see. She was supposed to be here in July but she came in May.

But I'm not complaining.

I'm not complaining at all.

Even though she had to spend the first four weeks of her life in the NICU.

We didn't expect that however. Because even though she came early because of my accident, the delivery was more or less without complications. And the doctors were hopeful that we might be able to go home within a week.

But then she developed breathing problems and her body temperature would fluctuate. So they decided to keep her and somehow my baby had to stay in her incubator for four weeks.

Those were the longest four weeks of my life.

The longest and the toughest.

Every second of which I spent hoping and praying and wishing to God that it was me. That I was the one who needed to stay at the hospital, rather than my baby who's just so... small and precious and innocent.

That it was my body they were sticking all those tubes into instead of her fragile one.

But it wasn't.

I've only been a mother for four weeks but I think I'm going to spend the rest of my life now, wishing for the same thing. That if something bad were to happen to Halo, I wish it would happen to me instead.

I was sent home after three days with a bunch of information about post-op care that I really didn't pay attention to because I was leaving the most precious thing behind, my baby.

But there's one person who remembered.

Him.

He remembered that I had stitches on my stomach. The stomach that was once tight and smooth but now will have a scar where they cut Halo out of me.

He remembered that I couldn't take a bath until my incision was healed, only showers. Or that I couldn't lift anything heavy; he didn't let me lift anything heavy when Halo was inside of me anyway so this wasn't anything new. Plus my ankle was twisted, so he wouldn't let me carry anything, period.

Not to mention, he remembered that my scar would hurt in the weeks to come.

And so he made a note to stock up on all the over-the-counter pain medications that are safe for me to take. He made a note to help me move around the glass house and stretch my muscles.

Oh, and he made a note to help me. When I initially breastfed Halo and I didn't know how to hold her and find a comfortable position that wouldn't hurt my stomach.

He made a note of everything.

He's not here right now though, at the glass house.

Even though he wanted to be because today's Halo's first day out of the hospital and he wanted to be here for every single second of it.

And he was here for most of it, before he got called away.

We went to the hospital together; brought her back to the house together. The house that was decorated to the fullest, courtesy of all Halo's aunts and uncles.

God, she has a lot of them.

Four uncles who're going to be as overprotective as they were — are — of me, Conrad, Stellan, Shepard and Ledger. Four aunts too, actually. My St. Mary's girls, Salem, Poe and Wyn, and of course, my oldest best friend and Reed's sister, Tempest.

And together, they all decorated the house to welcome Halo home.

She slept through most of it though.

All the festivities and all the laughter.

But then they started to hold her. One by one.

First went Shepard. Because according to Shep, he's going to be her favorite uncle. Ledger objected to that of course. But then Shep said that Ledge didn't have a say in it because first, Shep is older and so he had authority over these things. And second, look at how Halo was already smiling up at him.

When I told him that Halo's only a month old, she can't smile right now, Shep told me that I was jealous that my baby was smiling at him instead of me.

Anyway.

After Shep came Tempest. Somehow Ledger was okay backing off for her; isn't that interesting, that my rowdy, angry brother backed off for a Jackson?

Then it was my St. Mary's girls' turn, especially Wyn, because my oldest brother, Conrad, declared that ladies would go first and then the guys. Also interesting that Con would tell everyone to back off so Bronwyn — that's what he calls her — could have her turn. Not to mention, he keeps staring at her.

But anyway, somewhere between Poe and Salem, my sweet baby had decided that she'd had enough so she started wailing.

I rushed over to grab her, but someone else was there first.

Again, the guy who's been there for everything since the beginning.

He'd been standing off to the side, letting everyone have their turn with Halo while he kept an eye on things. But as soon as Halo started crying, he broke into action.

And then I got to see a sight that I die to see every day. I crave to see it. My little ballerina heart waits and craves and aches to see it.

Him holding our baby.

And he does it so well, too.

Like he knew right away, right from the beginning, how to angle his arm, how to hunch his shoulder, how careful he should be with her neck, how wide he should splay his fingers on her teeny tiny body to give her the maximum support and protection.

Maximum safety.

Her protector. Her hero.

Anyway, as soon as he took our Halo in his arms, she calmed down. She started flailing her fists too, making noises, kicking her tiny feet in those booties I'd made for her.

Like she used to do whenever he was near, even when she was still in my belly.

You know what, Shepard and Ledger and everyone else can go suck it.

I know, as I've always known, he is going to be her favorite.

There's magic in him. Dark magic. All girls, including my four-week-old baby, can't resist him. The one with the vampire skin and wolf eyes.

Reed Roman Jackson.

The guy who gave me Halo. She looks like him, actually. Except for my eyes, Halo got everything from him. Her hair, her nose, her chin. Her forehead. Even her ears.

She's a carbon copy of her daddy.

And he's just pulled into the driveway.

As usual, I hear the screech of his tires before his car door bangs shut. It's not his Mustang though. He got a new, baby-proof car from the shop, his shop.

Auto Alpha.

Oh yeah, he told me.

The very next day, when I finally woke up and had enough sense to ask things and hear things and go see Halo. He told me that he bought the garage. It's his now and he's going to work there and I guess I was so emotional about everything, I started crying.

I sobbed and sobbed in happiness that Reed is free now.

He's free of his dad. He has what he wanted. He has his dream.

He chose his dream. He chose the right thing.

That's where he goes when he leaves for work every day. And that's where he went today because they called him about some parts that were wrongly delivered.

So I'm happy now.

I have Halo. She's finally at home and healthy. Reed doesn't have to work for his dad anymore.

Extremely, excessively happy.

Happy, happy, happy.

So happy that when I hear his bounding footsteps on the porch stairs, I stand up from the cozy couch that I was sitting on and leave the room.

I go to the kitchen and busy myself with something.

Although there's nothing that needs doing around here. Because the people who were here, my family and friends, cleaned up everything before they left. Because they didn't want to bother me or stress me out with the new baby at home.

Ugh.

I hate this.

I hate that I have nothing to do and that my heart is spinning and spinning in my chest because he's now inside the house. He's just closed the door and he's probably three seconds away from me.

I almost hope, almost, that he doesn't come in here.

In the kitchen.

Where I'm hiding away from him.

Although to be very honest, this isn't a good hiding place. I should've probably chosen the bedroom and locked the door. Barred the windows. Not that it would keep him out, but I'm too angry at him right now to do it anyway.

Yes, I'm angry.

I'm so angry that I could...

I spin around when I feel him at the threshold. His tall, big presence overwhelms everything else, and as soon as I see him, the space that was bright turns darker.

So much so that the only thing that shines bright is him in his light-colored t-shirt and dark jeans. There's a strip of grease on his left bicep and also a smaller spot on his left wrist that makes my stomach clench, my chest heave with longing.

He's usually super careful about washing up at work before he comes home. Something about not wanting to dirty things up. But sometimes he misses spots and I don't know what it is about them, but I find them so masculine, so very, very sexy.

And I want them on me, those dirty, greasy, fascinating hands.

I clench my fists because it only makes me angrier.

When I look back at his face, I find that his eyes are taking me in.

They are glowing as he takes in my braid, my daisy-printed white dress.

I chose this dress today because it makes me feel like a fairy — courtesy of the guy I'm mad at — and since I was bringing my Halo home, I wanted to feel like one.

When he's done, his gaze lingering on my stomach that's more pouchy than flat for a second too long, and his eyes come back to mine, I blurt out, "Everybody left."

"I see that."

Of course he does and of course he'd use a voice, all deep and smooth, that goes down my spine like warm honey.

I clutch my dress and blurt out again, "Halo's sleeping."

It's true.

She is sleeping. I just fed her, changed her and now she's out. Which won't last long because she'll need another feeding soon but for now, my baby's sleeping and hopefully dreaming of magical things.

Meanwhile I have no idea what I'm doing except that I'm very, very mad at him and if he doesn't do anything about it soon, I'll punch him.

I will.

"I know," he says as if he heard what I was thinking.

"What?"

"That she's sleeping."

"How do you know?" I ask uselessly, belligerently.

And a very subtle sparkle of amusement enters his eyes. "Because I know her schedule. Because I've known it for the last four weeks."

I know he knows it.

He knows everything, doesn't he?

Then how come he doesn't know that I'm so mad at him right now? That I've been slowly getting madder and madder over the past few days?

And maybe I shouldn't be but I can't help it.

I inhale sharply and wipe my trembling, sweaty hands over my thighs. "Well then, I'll go catch some sleep too. Because all the books always say that I should sleep when Halo sleeps." I nod to emphasize it. "So I'll leave the kitchen now and —"

"Not so fast."

My breaths falter then.

My ballerina heart skips a beat because suddenly all his gorgeous features sharpen. His cheekbones become more chiseled and his jaw, stubbled and obviously irritating to him, morphs into a sleeker V.

God, he's so beautiful like this.

Despite my anger at him, I can't stop admiring his gorgeous, predatory face. I press my spine against the counter, all thrilled and breathless. "What?"

At my question, he finally steps over the threshold and I swallow.

His long legs prowl toward me with a lazy and yet somehow determined quality and oh my God, is he going to?

Is he going to finally tell me now?

When he reaches me, which doesn't take more than three seconds anyway, he dips his head and asks in that voice again, "How's the pain?"

The pain.

He's asking me about the pain?

To be fair, he asks me every day. He asks me if my stitches hurt, if I'm okay to move around more. If I'm tired more than usual and all that.

But I've been getting better and I thought…

I thought he'd do it. He'd finally tell me.

Because it's been four weeks.

Four weeks, okay?

Since I found out that he loves me after all. That he's loved me for two years. Since I found out that he still keeps that sweater I made for him in the trunk of his Mustang.

And yes, things have been rocky for us with Halo. Some nights I felt like I would die without her. My body felt so empty and my heart felt so empty too and I'd cry and cry, hugging her little booties and her sweaters that she hadn't gotten to wear yet.

Reed felt the same way.

He would hold me in bed and I'd burrow my face in his chest and wet his t-shirts with my tears. He'd kiss my forehead, caress my hair, rub my back and I know he never cried but I felt his chest shudder. I felt him swallow and gulp down his emotions with every breath he took.

But for the past week, she's been on the mend and we could finally see the light at the end of the tunnel. We at last knew that the wait was over and we could bring her home.

But the wait isn't over, is it?

Not when it comes to me and him.

He hasn't said anything. He hasn't even hinted at anything. He knows that I'm leaving for Juilliard in a few weeks but again, he hasn't mentioned it at all. He still lives at the hotel even though he spends all his time at the glass house and in this moment, I realize that maybe it will never be over.

This wait.

Maybe he will never say anything. Maybe he'll never realize.

And just like that all my anger goes away and is replaced by so much misery and heartbreak. Despite telling myself a million times over the past months that I'll take my happiness in the fact that he loves Halo, I just want to curl into a ball and disappear.

"It's fine," I reply, looking down at his collarbone, his stubbly throat. "It's much better than when you asked me yesterday. And much, much better than the day before when you also asked me. I'm getting better every day, Roman. You don't have to worry so much about me. Now can I go please?"

"No."

I sigh, keeping my eyes on his throat. "Fine, what do you want?"

The sooner he tells me, the sooner I can go and try to get myself under control. So I'm ready and back to myself when Halo wakes up hungry. Maybe I can take a long, hot shower and cry there so I'm all cried out for a few hours while I take care of Halo.

"You."

I fist my hands for a second as the longing hits me the hardest at his answer. But I unfurl my fingers and say, "Me what?"

"To listen."

I look up then.

Like a fool.

He's only said two words but I can't not. Look at him, ask him. "Listen to what?"

His eyes are my favorite color right now, molten mercury, even as they carry hints of frustration. "I've been trying to hold back. Because of everything. I've been trying to be a good guy but it's fucking hard. It's so fucking hard, Fae. When it comes to you."

"What's hard?"

He doesn't answer me.

Instead, his V-shaped jaw tics and his eyes look far away. As if he's having a conversation with himself. And when he's done, he sighs, his broad chest pushing out and a determination falling over his features.

"I wanted to give you a week…" he pauses, before saying, "all right, a day. I wanted to give you at least a day after we brought Halo home but I am an asshole. I can't wait any longer. I can't wait any longer to…"

My heart is banging in my chest. "To what?"

Again, he doesn't answer but responds with something else completely. "You always say I don't tell you things, right?"

"Yes."

"Well, I'm going to now. I'm going to tell you everything. From the beginning."

"Beginning?"

His jaw tightens up for a second and he swallows thickly before saying, "The first time I saw you, I was nine and you were six."

I wasn't prepared for this.

I wasn't expecting this at all and so I breathe out, "I-I'm sorry?"

"You were dancing, spinning on the playground and God, you looked so pretty," he says gruffly, again his eyes both burning into me and seeming so far away. "You had a pink tutu and your blonde pigtails were flying as you spun. And I thought… I thought, I have to touch her. I have to touch her just once to make sure she's real. Because you came out of nowhere and I don't even know what I was doing but suddenly there you were. There this girl was, so pretty and…"

He swallows again. "So clean. Like a fairy or something. And so I had to touch her to see if someone like her could be real, and I did. I did get to touch her. I had to, actually. Because one second you were spinning and the next, you were about to fall and I was there to catch you. But I ruined your dress. I remember that very well. I left muddy fingerprints on it because my hands were dirty. And I wanted to let you go but you made me feel so clean, so filled with fucking light that I didn't want to, and I wouldn't have if not for your brothers. They came and they pushed me away and yeah. So that was that.

"And then the next time I saw you, I was eleven and you were eight. I saw you through the window at Buttery Blossoms. You were with Conrad, and by that time, I fucking hated him. I hated him because he got to touch you freely. He got to be with you, him and your other three brothers. They got to talk to you and you probably smiled at them all the time and danced for them. And yeah, I hated them for it. Anyway, I kept watching you through the window. You were taking a fuck-ton of time deciding on what you wanted to get and I thought, if she were mine, I'd buy her the whole fucking shop so she never had to choose."

He chuckles. "I was loaded. Or my dad was, and back then, I loved his money if not him. So I thought, I'd buy her everything. I'd get her whatever she wanted. And in my head, I was already better than your brother who was making you choose. And so I kept watching and maybe you felt me, I don't know. Maybe you felt a creep watching you through the window and you turned around so quickly that you stumbled. Again. And I wanted to get to you. I wanted to bust through the glass window and catch you but your fucking brother caught you. It made me so angry. That I didn't get to do that. I didn't get to save you. But anyway, I thought… this is what I do. This is what I do to her, my fairy, I make her fall. I make her dirty. So it's better if I stay away, and I did.

"I fucking did, trust me. I'd see you somewhere around town,

I'd turn around and walk away. I wouldn't even pause, not even for a second. But then one day, I saw you at that store. The one you always go to, the girly one, with all those dresses…"

"Anti-social Butterfly?" I offer, as if in a trance.

It's one of my favorite stores in Bardstown. They have such feminine and lacy and floral things that I'd spend hours there, just browsing if not buying.

"Yeah. That's the one."

"Y-you saw me there?"

He nods slowly, his eyes all filled with memories, glinting, looking so intense. "It was before you were about to start at Bardstown High. I was counting the days, actually. When you'd get to my school. I mean, I knew Ledger would be a bitch about it, but at least you'd be there. Where I was. At least I could see you every day. But anyway, I saw you at that store and you were picking out dresses and laughing with your friend or whatever and I had to go in. I had to see you. Just for a little while. So I did, and I watched you come out of the dressing room, showing off your daisy fresh dresses to your friend. And you looked so pretty in every one of them and I wanted to buy you the whole fucking store. I wanted to… give you everything you ever wanted. But anyway, nothing happened that time. You didn't stumble. I didn't make you dirty, so I thought it was all in my head and Jesus Christ, I was so fucking happy. I was so ecstatic, like I'd won something. That I didn't have to be away from you anymore. I mean, except for your brothers, but fuck them, you know?

"But then on the first day of school, you were getting out of Ledger's truck and I think you saw me, my Mustang, and you squinted your eyes against the glare maybe and the next second I knew, you stumbled again. And I thought to myself, 'Fuck you, Jackson. Why can't you stop hurting her? Why can't you just… stop? She's not for you.' So after that, there was no turning back. After that I always, always made sure to stay hidden, to not look at you more than normal. Even when I watched you at Blue Madonna, because fuck me but I couldn't help myself, I made sure you never saw me. You never felt me. Because if you did, I'd hurt you again. I'd make you dirty.

"And then you... you showed up at my party and despite all the promises that I made myself, all the good fucking intentions, I couldn't stop myself from going after you. And God, you were so... innocent and pretty and so fucking gorgeous when you danced for me. I felt guilty. I felt so guilty for making you do that, for watching you like that, for wanting to kiss the fuck out of you when your brothers showed up just to make them understand that I wouldn't stay away from you. I wouldn't."

His hands are clenched now, his voice tight and angry as if he's reliving that moment back in the woods. And I want to go to him and tell him that...

I don't know what I want to tell him except that I love him.

I love him so much and I didn't expect this. I didn't know and God, please can I just tell him?

I don't care if he says it back to me or if he hasn't realized it yet or if he never realizes it. I just want to love him and he looks so lonely and angry and defiant standing there with his fists clenched and I...

He swallows again and his eyes, wolfish and pretty, flash with something. "Anyway, you know everything that happened after that. Except... except the night you gave me that sweater. The one that I never wore — I couldn't after what I did — but I keep it. I keep it close and I think that was the night that I felt something. I felt a pain, a longing. That was the night when, instead of bringing you back to your brothers, I wanted to take you away. I wanted to keep you for myself. My fairy. Who made such a beautiful gift for me. No one had ever given me anything before that. I didn't know what to do with it... I... That was the night, yeah. That was the night I wanted to take you away and…"

"Roman?"

My voice brings him back to the moment. It makes him focus on me.

Even though he's been looking at me all this time, I know he wasn't really seeing me but now he does. He does see me and his features arrange themselves.

They arrange themselves in a look that's even more determined than before and yet, there's this openness in them. An openness like he's exposing something.

His thoughts, yes.

But more than that. His soul maybe.

"I never tell you anything because I don't know how," he says thickly. "I've never really told things before. I've never really shared things with people. I never had anyone I could share things with. And that has been okay with me. Because I was always bogged down by other things. I was always too wrapped up in my own shit to… take a second. To stop and to take a breath, but I want you to know this. I want you to know the thoughts in my head, Fae. Because you have the right. Only you have the right to know."

"Know what?"

"All my life I've felt suffocated and angry and hateful. I've felt like I had no choice but to do the things that I was doing. I had no choice but to hurt people and fight with people and lie and cheat and be the bad guy. But then every time I saw you, every time I see you, Fae, you destroy a piece of me. A dirty piece, you understand. This thing inside of me that makes me a villain, you destroy it, Fae. You kill it and you cleanse me. You make me better. You make me breathe. I can breathe with you and I've never been able to breathe so freely as I do with you.

"And every time you do that, every time you fill my lungs with sweet life, I want to destroy anything and everything that hurts you. I want to burn down the world so I can keep you safe. Every time you slay my dragons, I want to slay yours. I want to be your hero, Fae. I want that. I know you told me that I'm Halo's hero and I am. I will be. For the rest of my life. I will love her and protect her and keep her safe. She's mine. She's ours. But I also want to be your hero. I also want to keep you safe. I want that job for myself. And so I want to give you something. Something that I never put much stock in. I laughed at people when they talked about it. I scoffed. I thought they were crazy. Until now."

My eyes are wet. They sting but I don't let my tears fall. I don't let my vision become blurry because I want to see him. I want to see him clearly and vividly.

But it gets so difficult now when I whisper, "What?"

He clenches his jaw for a second before whispering back, "My heart."

"Your heart."

"Yes. I want to give it to you."

"Why?"

He chuckles harshly, brokenly. "Because when you gave me yours, I broke it. I didn't protect it like I should have. I hurt you and I'll regret that for the rest of my life. So my heart is yours. It has been since I saw you on that playground. Something that I've only realized in the past few weeks. Because you made me realize it. You made me realize that my heart could be filled with something other than hate. Something like love."

"L-love."

He throws out an imperceptible nod. "Yeah. I love you, Fae. I've loved you for a very, very long time now. Ever since the playground, I think. The things I feel for you, I never knew they could be love. But they are love. I'm in fucking love with you. And so I want to tell you that you have my heart. I want you to do whatever you want with it. You can do with it what I did to yours. You can break it, Fae. You can break my heart. I want you to. I'm putting it in your hands. I'm putting it under your ballerina feet that you think are ugly but they're the prettiest feet I've ever seen."

His heart.

And then I have to look at it, his chest.

I have to look away from his gorgeous face even though it's hard. Because I think… I think if I focused enough, I probably would be able to see his beating heart inside his chest.

That he wants me to have.

The chest I once thought was barren and infertile. That no flower could ever grow there. He proved me wrong when he said that he loved Halo but now I think I was wrong about that too.

He doesn't just have a flower, he has a garden.

My Roman has a secret garden of daisies in his chest. For me, and then I can't stop my tears at all, even though they make it hard for me to see him. But I shouldn't have worried about not seeing him because one second, he's standing all the way over there and the next, he's touching me.

He's putting his hands on my wet cheeks and tilting my face up. He's wiping those tears off, kissing my forehead. "Don't cry, Fae. I keep making you cry."

"Y-you want me to break your heart?"

He kisses my forehead again. "If you want to."

I shake my head, grasping his wrists. "But I already did that."

"What?"

I move my hands to his cheeks then, his beautifully harsh jaw. "I already broke your heart. Two years ago. My tears, my pain. My heartbreak. They broke your heart, didn't they?"

His jaw moves under my fingers. "Yeah."

"Every time I cried in my bedroom, you were lying awake in yours, weren't you?"

He throws out a short nod.

"And every time I felt all broken and hurt and alone in my town, you felt hopeless and miserable in your city."

"I did."

"So I don't wanna break your heart anymore. I want to heal it. Like you did mine. I want to keep it. Safe and protected and warm because you get cold so easily. I want to make you sweaters that you wear. And I want to dance for you. So you don't have to stalk me at the studio anymore. I want to make you cupcakes and I want to laugh. For you. I want to be for you, Roman. So you don't have to look at me from a distance. So you don't have to get angry when I fall if you're not there to catch me. And..."

I take his hand off my face and without taking my eyes off him, I drag that hand down, the one that has a grease stain on the inside of his wrist. And still watching him, I rub that wrist on the side of my neck, painting my skin with dirt.

"And I don't want you to stop touching me just because you think you'll get me a little dirty."

His eyes flare at the mark; his stomach contracts.

"I'm not afraid of a little dirt, Roman. I never was. Or falling. I'm not afraid of all that. You know why? Because I survived you. Because I survived the heartbreak you gave me and I kicked your ass. You survived it too. And I'm done, okay? I'm done hurting each other. All I've ever wanted, ever since I danced for you, was for you to love me. That's all. All I've ever wanted was for you to keep me. I want you to keep me with you. Forever."

"Forever."

I nod. "Yes. Ask me why."

He swallows. "Why?"

"Because I love you too, you idiot."

He goes still, only his eyes are moving, going back and forth between mine. "You... you love me."

God.

What am I going to do with him?

Why is he so... crazy and adorable and such a big, clueless idiot?

I dig my fingertips into his unforgiving jaw. "Yes, Roman. I love you. I've loved you for two years now, okay? I loved you when we were at Bardstown High and you were my sweet Roman. I loved you when you became a jerk and broke my heart that night and I stole your car. And I loved you for the two years after that even when I shouldn't have. And I love you now. Every time I see you with Halo, I love you more. Every time I see how you love her, I fall in love with you more. Every time, Roman."

"Holy fucking... Christ. I didn't think... after everything. I didn't..."

"I do, because I never stopped. Even though I'm very angry at you."

"Angry."

"Yes." I sniffle. "Because you made me wait."

He frowns. "Made you wait for what?"

"For this?" I purse my lips. "For telling me all this. And just so you know, I figured it out four weeks ago."

"Figured out what?"

"That you're in love with me."

His eyes pierce into mine. "You figured it out."

"Yes."

"How?"

I go up on my tiptoes. "Because I'm smarter than you."

Finally his lips twitch. "You are."

"And because you told me that you had my sweater in the trunk of your car. You know who would do such a thing?"

"Who?"

"A guy in love. A guy who's obsessed with me. You're obsessed with me, Roman."

Those twitching lips of his break into a lopsided smile, a smile that makes him look boyish. "I am."

I move my hands and tug at his hair then. "And you never said anything. As usual. But it's worse, isn't it?"

His own hands move and his fingers go into my hair, burying themselves, and his body loses its rigid quality, sliding against me. "How is it worse?"

I shake my head at him, letting my anger show. "Because you've been obsessed with me for the past thirteen years. Since you saw me at that playground. And I don't even remember that day."

Not that my anger is making a dent on his amusement, no.

He's all relaxed now, totally opposite of how he was only a few moments ago and yes, I want to be relaxed too that he told me. And I've been waiting for it.

But I'm not.

Because my anger is catching up to me.

"You don't, huh?" he rasps, massaging my scalp.

I don't let his magic fingers deter me though. "No. And now I want you to tell me every single detail about that day. Every single thing, Roman. The weather, the time. What were you wearing? And what I said to you and —"

"You said thank you," he interrupts me, his small smile still in place, his fingers slowly working their magic on me. "Like a good girl. I dirtied your dress and you gave me your big blue eyes and said thank you."

My breath hitches at the tenderness, the heat in his tone.

"From now on, I want you to tell me everything. Everything. All your secrets and your fears and your desires. Your dreams. Everything."

At this, his eyes go grave. "I will."

"Promise me."

"I promise."

At last, my ire lessens. "I'm going to be your best friend, Roman. And you can't stop me."

Those wolf eyes of his flash. "You want to be my friend, Fae?"

My heart races. "Yes."

"Yeah, I don't think that's possible."

"Why not?"

"Because I don't know what kind of a friend I'd be when all I'd ever think about is talking dirty to you and making you blush. And kissing those lipstick lips."

My lips tingle and I bite them as I whisper, "A bad one. You'd be a bad friend."

He smirks, his vampire skin heating up and his wolf eyes looking so pretty and predatory. "Which one is that?"

My mouth tingles harder. "Blueberry Fairy."

I have to admit that I only bought it for the name but the color turned out pretty good too with its dark blue shades.

He wraps his wrist around my braid, tugging my head back. "Why?"

"Because I'm a fairy."

"Yeah, you are," he whispers. "My fairy."

"Ever since I was six."

"Ever since you were six."

"And you're my Roman."

"I am."

"Ever since you were nine," I tell him. "So will you keep me then?"

His body shudders with emotion. "Fuck yeah, I will. And I will love you and Halo. And I will make all your dreams come true, Fae. I want you to know that. I know you're going to Juilliard and I'm not going to stand in your way and —"

I put a hand on his mouth to stop him. "Why don't you let me worry about Juilliard?" He frowns and I press those fingers harder. "For now, tell me you love me."

I move my fingers and he rasps, "I fucking love you."

I smile, winding my arms around his neck. "I love you too. Tell me again that you love Halo."

"I fucking love Halo."

"Tell me that we'll stay together. Forever."

He swallows. "We'll stay together forever. Because we're a family now."

My eyes fill with happy tears. "Family. Yeah. Now kiss me."

Chuckling, he does exactly that. He captures my lips in a kiss. As if he couldn't wait any longer. I couldn't either.

I can't believe I waited for this for thirteen years. I didn't even know that I was waiting.

But I was.

Because how could I not?

How could I not have felt what he felt? Maybe that's why he made me want to dance whenever I saw him play, the Wild Mustang. Maybe that's why I couldn't stay away from him, couldn't stop thinking about him despite all the warnings.

Because I was his dancing fairy long before I knew it.

And yes, I have to tell him about Juilliard. About how I got my admission deferred for a year and talked to Miss Petrova about teaching ballet at Baby Blues for the next year. Everyone did so much while I was pregnant and now it's my turn. And so I've got a year before I go after my dream.

A year to be Halo's mom, to watch her grow up, to adjust to this new life, to be close to all my brothers because I wasn't for the last two years. And now I've got a year where I get to be his. I get to watch him with Halo, him being the best daddy in the whole wide world. I get to watch him go for his dream and I get to watch him love me.

But first I'll let him kiss me.

Everything else can wait.

Epilogue

One year later…

She has pretty blue eyes and they're widened in excitement.

Actually, her whole body seems excited.

Sitting in her high chair, she's flailing her arms in the air, her tiny fists pumping, as she swings her cute chubby legs. And don't even talk about the noises she's making.

I'm convinced that her laughter and her coos, her excited squealing can melt any heart in this world and fill all the empty spaces with joy.

But maybe that's just me because I'm her mommy.

To be honest though, my Halo is the most joyous baby ever.

Like, she smiles at strangers. She waves at them. If someone waves back — which pretty much all of them do because hello, Halo is adorable — she completely freaks out with happiness, practically dancing either in my arms or in her stroller.

Oh and she loves dogs. Puppies are her favorite in particular.

If she sees one in the park, we have to go and say hi. We have to pet him and let him lick our faces or our hands at least, and we have to tell him how much we love him.

Which I do obviously.

Because Halo can't talk but she does tell me what to say.

She nods her head at me, which in Halo talk means 'tell him that I love him.' If she's waving her little fists and squealing, then that means 'tell him he's the cutest puppy ever.' But if she also tries to get out of my arms to go crawling over to him, then that means 'tell him I wanna take him home.'

I keep telling Halo that we can't take someone else's dog but she's yet to believe me on that.

So then we get into this whole mess where she cries and gets angry. Snot runs down her nose and she gets all red-faced, breaking my little mommy heart.

But you know, kids need to learn that they can't get their way every time they cry and throw a tantrum.

Even though it's super hard when my baby girl's voice has gone all hoarse from crying and she looks at me with accusing eyes, I try to stay stern.

Not someone else though, no.

Someone else is a complete sucker.

Oh God, is he a sucker.

A slight tremble on her rosy lips and his frown comes out to play. If she points her finger at a toy in the store, he lunges to get it off the shelf. In case someone else gets their hand on it. Even though we can clearly see that they have that toy in stock, like tens of them sitting on that shelf.

And God forbid if a tear rolls down her pink cheeks, his wrath will not be contained. He'll pace and stomp and won't settle down until his Halo girl has what she wants.

And so after a long, long debate and discussion, we're giving her a puppy. Because as I said, he's a sucker and tomorrow's my baby girl's first birthday.

Of course, she doesn't know that.

Not about the birthday — I think she knows; I've told it to her a million times now and I think she totally understands me. But about the puppy.

It's supposed to be a surprise.

The one who can't see his Halo girl cry, her daddy, is going to pick it up after work.

Anyway in this moment, my baby's excitement is due to something else altogether.

It's because we're baking. And Halo loves baking as well.

She has to be present in the kitchen when I bake. She has to sit in that high chair and help me put the butter in the mixing bowl and measure out cups of sugar, add in a pinch of salt and everything.

And every time she does, we have little high fives.

But her favorite part is frosting.

I think she loves the colors. The brighter, the better.

And so I'm leaning across the island, flipping pages of an amazing baking recipe book that I found online, showing her all the pretty colors that she wants to see.

They have some elaborate decorations on their cupcakes. I'm an amateur baker; I can't do all that but I at least know how to whip up some amazing shades so I'm asking her, "Okay, this one?"

Her answer is to chew on her teething ring we bought her a few months back when her first teeth started to come in and she was miserable, she still loves it, and scrunch her nose.

"Hmm... so not this one then." I flip the page and show her a pretty green cake. "What about this one?" I ask excitedly. "How green it is. Look! So pretty. Like Mommy's dress. See?"

I'm wearing a light green sundress with white flowers that Halo sees but instantly dismisses by shaking her head and making protesting noises.

"What? You don't like Mommy's dress?" I pout and she shakes her head again.

Narrowing my eyes at her, which only makes her giggle and chew on her toy, I say, "All right, girlfriend, I'll remember this. I'll remember what you said about Mommy's dress. But for now we need to figure this thing out. We need to figure out what to color those cupcakes we made for Daddy and…"

I stop talking because that just gets her to another level of excitement, Daddy.

He's not the only one crazy about his Halo girl actually. She's crazy about him too.

You can't say 'Daddy' in front of her, without her getting super excited. She'll flap her chubby arms, wiggle her tiny body and laugh and chuckle and squeal, fill the room with her happiness and joy at the mention of him.

Like she's doing right now.

And she'll say random baby syllables. "Da da… Da da da…"

"I know," I say, leaning further over to nuzzle my nose in her sweet smelling hair. "We made cupcakes for Daddy. He's gonna love it, right?"

She wiggles her little body even more, opening and closing her fists, as if calling for him. "Da da… da da…"

I kiss her cheek. "Aww, I know. I miss him too. He'll be back soon though. And then you can tell him all about your day. About how you made cookies with Mommy earlier and your birthday cake. And how we went to the park in the morning and when we came back, we picked out our outfit for tomorrow's birthday party." I widen my eyes and she does it too. "And oh my God, it's so pretty, right? It's pink!"

More random baby syllables and nodding.

I nod too to show her how excited I am, which I totally am. Because it is a cute outfit. It's a frilly tutu-style dress and I got my baby some cute little pointe shoes to go with them.

Along with her love of baking and puppies and her daddy, Halo loves ballet too.

She loves to watch me dance. Sometimes I'll do a twirl just to make her laugh. She especially loves it when I don the whole costume, leotard and tutu.

"Yeah, it is," I continue, talking to her excitedly. "It's pink and it's pretty and it's so cute. Just like Halo. And my Halo's gonna look like a little ballerina tomorrow, right? Just like Mommy."

She keeps nodding and I kiss her cheek again, making her laugh.

"Okay, but we need to focus, honey, all right?" I tell her. "We need to pick out a color for Daddy's cupcakes before he gets here, okay? So I can make it all pretty for him and we can surprise him later."

At this, Halo jerks out a nod, completely getting my meaning and going serious so she can pick out a color for her daddy.

And of course, she picks out her favorite color for him.

I shake my head at myself.

Because duh, I should've known. My precious baby thinks that the whole world loves what she loves. Anyway, I spend the next hour, making the frosting, putting it on cupcakes and getting the surprise ready for him.

I'm putting everything away, when I hear it.

The screech of the tires.

Followed by the typical bang of his car door shutting and then my favorite sound in the world, his thumping footsteps, bounding over the porch stairs before he clicks the door open.

Through all this, my heart is racing.

My ballerina heart is spinning in my chest, taking leaps and twirling.

He still does that to me.

His arrival. His impending nearness. The fact that I'll get to see him in maybe about five seconds. The fact that he'll be deliciously rumpled and sexily worn out after his long day at Auto Alpha, his garage.

Back when he was working with his dad and hated every second of it, I'd always get this anxiety in my stomach when he came home. Because I knew I'd see the atrocious toll the day must have taken on him.

Now though, all my anxiety is gone.

Even though his days are still just as long, the toll of them is different.

These days his tiredness comes from a good day's work. A good day spent doing something he's passionate about, something he loves.

My thoughts break when he at last appears at the threshold of the kitchen.

All tall and burly, in his navy blue overalls. His hair, which he keeps sort of long-ish because I love it that way, is rumpled and his beautiful V-shaped jaw is covered in stubble that still irritates him. Even after I've spent hours and days, licking it and kissing it and caressing it.

And his eyes, wolfish and pretty, are on me. As always.

Smiling, I bite my lip and they glint and I can't wait to properly welcome him back home.

But I'll have to. Just a little bit.

Because there's someone else who wants to welcome him home first.

The little girl we accidentally made together on a rainy night almost two years ago. Who's just as excited as I am at the arrival of the man she loves, her daddy.

The only difference is that she's going all out to show how happy she is to see him by squealing in her high chair and flailing her arms.

As soon as his eyes land on Halo, my whole body sighs and my thighs clench because I'm about to see the most beautiful thing in the world.

The thing that's going to make me fall in love with him all over again.

First, it's his eyes.

Those pretty animal eyes of his melt and his ruby red lips stretch up in a small but tender smile. Then, he goes to her and bending down slightly, he picks her up in his arms, his biceps flexing under the sleeves of his overall.

And then, he says, in a voice that's so deep and smooth and so fond that my skin wakes up in goosebumps. "Hey, Halo girl. I missed you."

Okay, I was wrong.

This is my favorite sound in the whole wide world.

When he talks to her in that soothing voice of his.

God, I don't even know how many times he's been able to calm her down by just talking to her like that. Or managed to put her to sleep on the nights when she's fussy and won't listen to me at all. And I'm so tired and irritable that I don't know what to do.

Sometimes I envy him that, the magical powers he has.

But right now, I'm totally falling for them. Just as my baby girl.

Because at his voice, she laughs and squeals again, kicking her chubby legs at his chest and clapping, making him chuckle and kiss her forehead.

But the show's not over yet.

The next part is my favorite part. Even though I always roll my eyes at it.

Halo raises her arm then, tugs on her hair barrette — this one's white and shaped like a daisy — and gives it to him. Which he dutifully takes from her small hands. Before he sets her down on the island, her legs dangling off the edge, and combs her dark hair with his large, beautiful fingers, putting it back on.

She nods at him. Like this is such serious business, putting a hair barrette on, and he nods back like he agrees.

Like how Mommy did it before was wrong and only Daddy knows how to do it.

I'm about to roll my eyes at their cuteness when he looks up.

He smirks at me and I narrow my eyes at him, mouthing, I hate you.

Which only makes him chuckle and wink, meaning, No, you don't.

Ugh.

No, I don't. I can't hate him. I've never been able to. And these days, he's even more irresistible with how playful and amazing he is with Halo.

Who wants his attention back on her so she waves her hand in his face, tapping his jaw and addressing him in random syllables. He picks her back up and with a last heated look at me, he takes her into the living room like he always does.

He's going to play with her for a bit, keep her occupied so I can work on dinner in peace. It's a routine we came up with in the beginning of this whole parenting thing, which I think is working out great for the most part.

Before coming to me.

Which he does about thirty minutes later.

I feel an arm sliding around my waist and his hard body settling against my back. I close the tap where I was washing the lettuce for the salad. Wiping my hands, I raise my arm and caress his stubble, sagging against him.

It's my turn now.

"Hi," I whisper, smelling his delicious scent of woods and wildflowers.

Also cars.

Spicy and masculine and so freaking sexy.

Reed hums, rubbing his jaw in my hair as he takes a breath, his chest undulating against my spine. Like breathing my scent calms him. It calms me too.

Knowing that I give it to him.

"Did you bring it?" I whisper, talking about the puppy, burying my fingers in his thick stubble.

"Yeah."

"Is it cute?"

A puff of air escapes him. "Fuck knows. Pete liked it though. He'll bring it over tomorrow, at the party."

I'm glad Pete's here for Halo's party.

After giving his garage to Reed, he took off for a while. He traveled to all the places he wanted to go because they reminded him of his late wife, Mimi.

When he came back, I told him he should take the glass house back and live here. Especially when this was a special place for him and his Mimi. But he said that this house was ours now, Reed's and mine, because it brought us together.

And so it belongs to us.

I chuckle. "You know what, Roman?"

"What?"

"You're a sucker."

He flexes his arm around my belly before spinning me around

and crowding me against the counter, his arms on both sides of my body, making a cage. "I'm a sucker."

I tilt my neck up, my fingers clutching his sleeves at his biceps because there he is.

My predator.

The one with the glinting wolf eyes and the sparkling vampire skin.

The love of my life. My hero.

"Uh-huh," I say. "For Halo."

His eyes narrow. "And why's that?"

"Because you got her a puppy."

"And?"

"I don't know if you know this, Roman, but you don't have to give her everything she wants. You can say no to her."

"Why would I say no to her when I want to give her everything she wants?"

He looks so outraged right now. Like the thought of not giving Halo something is offensive to him and it makes me chuckle.

It also makes me go up on my tiptoes to kiss his jaw. "That's the very definition of a sucker actually."

That's when he grabs my braid, pulling my head back, making my breaths scatter. He even goes so far as to press his hard body against my soft one and sighing, I sink myself into his harsh places.

He shudders and I shiver. Something that happens every time we touch and align ourselves with each other after a long day.

Keeping a firm grip on me, he flicks his wolf eyes over my features. "You okay?"

God.

Sometimes I think he wants to kill me. That's why he does this, doesn't he?

That's why even when he's holding me captive like this, like he's really a villain, he has to go all protective over me and ask me about my day. He has to melt me with his mean fingers and tender voice.

He used to do this, ask me about my day, look me over to make sure that I was okay, back when I was pregnant. I thought after Halo came, his protectiveness would go down a notch. But I was wrong.

He still does this.

Because pregnant or not, I'm precious to him, to my villain.

I'm the love of his life. His Fae.

"Yeah," I whisper, looking him over myself, looking at the tired but happy lines around his eyes and his gorgeous mouth.

"Halo was okay too?"

"Yes. It was a fun day. We went to the park. We prepped for the party. Halo loves her outfit for tomorrow."

It's a Saturday and usually Reed's home. But they're working on this vintage car that I don't even know the name of and they're on sort of a deadline to get it done for this rich guy from New York so he had to go in.

"How was your day?" I ask then.

He shrugs. "Good. Tiring. But we got the car ready."

My eyes go wide in happiness. "You did?" I grin. "That's way before the deadline. Yay!"

That's awesome.

Not that I had any doubts. My Roman knows his cars. But more than that it's the fact that he told me. It's the fact that he tells me things now.

Like he promised me he would. The day he told me he loved me. That he'd loved me for years.

At first, it was hard though. For him to share things.

After burying things inside of him for years, it was new and difficult for him to open up. But slowly, though my prodding and poking and his willingness to share, even though he didn't know how to, we made progress.

He told me things about his childhood, about how his dad was the only one to call him Roman and how he hated that name until I started calling him that. And I'm not going to lie, there were times when I was so angry on his behalf.

But then I channeled that anger. Into love.

Into showing him that he has a safe place in me. A safe place in his fairy.

He hums again, bringing me back to the moment.

Then, "So I'm a sucker, huh. For bringing Halo a puppy."

I nod. "Yup."

"Or maybe you're just jealous."

I frown. "Why would I be jealous?"

He flexes his grip on my hair. "Because I brought a present. For a girl."

"And?"

Smirking, he replies, "And that girl is not you."

I raise my eyebrows at him and his smirk only becomes more devilish.

Just to be a brat, I bite my lip. "Well, you got me. I am jealous. Because I thought I was your main girl."

"My main girl."

"Yes. See this?" I let go of his bicep and show him my left hand, the one sporting a wedding ring. "This proves that I'm your main girl. For the rest of your life. So what do you have to say for yourself, husband?"

He eyes my hand for a second, a flash of possessiveness flickering through his features.

The same one he had on the day he put that ring on my finger almost a year ago.

It was exactly a week after we brought Halo home.

He took me out on a ride in his Mustang and popped the question in the woods where I used to dance for him. He said that he wanted to do it right but he couldn't wait. I told him that he'd made me wait long enough so this was perfect. And then, we laid on the hood of his Mustang, his engagement ring on my finger and watched the stars for a bit before going home to Halo.

Who luckily had been super good for Conrad and my brothers.

Who in turn already knew what Reed was going to do and they were completely on board.

Good.

Not that it would've changed anything – I loved Reed and I was going to marry him no matter what – but I was glad that my brothers approved.

A week later, we got married in our backyard with all my friends and brothers in attendance. Pete couldn't be there because he was traveling but he did call. It was small and intimate and absolutely perfect.

Reed's eyes come back to me, the look in them all heavy and intense as he murmurs, "That. Right. My bad then."

"It is," I say primly before winding my arms around his neck. "So where's my present?"

He puts his other hand on my waist and tightens his grip on my braid with the other. "Outside."

"What?"

"It's a Porsche 911."

My mouth falls open for a second before I sputter, "But wait, wasn't... wasn't that the car you were restoring for that guy? The car that you finished today."

Now that he said the name of it, I remember.

He shrugs. "I lied."

"You lied."

"That's sort of what I do."

I can't help it. A shocked laugh bursts out of me.

He doesn't actually.

Except that one time when he broke my heart, Reed has never lied to me and I can't believe that he lied to me now. I mean, it's not a bad lie but oh my God.

A car?

We don't need any more cars. We've got his Mustang that usually sits in the garage because we have Halo. And Reed, my sexy, badass husband, is super adamant about driving the minivan that he got last year because it's the most kid friendly.

And now this, a Porsche?

I shake my head. "But Roman, we already have two cars and I don't... I don't need a car. I..."

"Yes, you do," he tells me. "For Juilliard."

Juilliard. Right.

So after deferring for a year, I'll finally be going this coming fall. It's going to be a huge change but I think I'm ready. I'm excited at least and well, nervous.

This past year has been great though.

I did everything that I wanted to do. I got to be with Halo and Reed. I got to see my brothers as much as I could. I got to teach at the Baby Blues and I discovered something about myself.

That I love kids.

I absolutely love them. I love, love, love being a mother. I love, love, love teaching little kids and seeing wonder on their faces when they do a pose correctly or when they simply twirl for fun.

It just makes my heart so happy.

So that's what I'm going to do. After I graduate from Juilliard,

I'm going to teach kids. Letting go of my other dream of dancing with the New York City Ballet Company is the easiest thing I've ever done.

But first, I've got to get through this amazing program.

Our plan is to move out of the glass house for the duration of it and live in an apartment we found that's midway between Wuthering Garden and New York City. So I can do my classes and Reed can work at the garage. And I was going to take the bus to the city.

It's not going to be easy but a lot of people do it so I can do it too.

But apparently not. Because I have a car.

"But I... it's too much."

He squeezes my waist. "Look, it's fast. It's safe. You've got a few weeks to try it out before you actually have to go. And it'll get you there twice as fast than a fucking bus would. And what in the world gave you the indication that I'd ever let you ride on a bus?"

I squeeze my own arms that are still around his neck. "Let me?"

"Yeah. You're my main girl, aren't you? And she doesn't ride on a bus."

I purse my lips. "That's extremely archaic but I'm gonna let it slide. Because you're kind of being sweet right now." I reach up and kiss his jaw again. "Thank you. I really appreciate it. Even more than I appreciate you letting my brothers win tomorrow."

He goes alert then. "What?"

"At soccer."

"You want me to let your brothers win tomorrow. At soccer."

I peek at him through my eyelashes. "Please."

So tomorrow, along with Halo's birthday party, we also have a soccer game. A friendly soccer game.

After the get together from last year to celebrate my acceptance to Juilliard, I also discovered that I love doing little parties and lunches. Even though that get together was sort of disastrous with all the hidden tensions and whatnot.

But anyway, it's a regular thing now, these get togethers.

I try to do one every three to four months depending on everyone's schedule.

I cook and bake and we have a fun time in the backyard. The people who attend are usually the same: my brothers; my St. Mary's friends plus the loves of their life; of course Tempest. Sometimes Pete makes it too.

Oh and I made two new friends in the past year, Jupiter and Isadora or Dora. I adore both of these girls and it works out because they're dating my brothers.

Yeah, they're dating the twins and I'm not gonna lie, seeing Shep, the player, totally whipped makes my day every time.

Anyway, as fun as these get togethers are, some time last year, they were also turned into soccer games.

I'm not sure whose idea it was but whenever all my brothers and Reed are together, they split into teams and play each other. Sometimes Arrow joins in, even Salem.

Reed usually ends up with Shep because they're great friends now. Because well, my brother loves cars and Reed is sort of a car expert.

Their games are pretty low key and for the most part, friendly. Except Ledger and Reed sometimes still butt heads. Not like before though, thank God.

But the fact that Ledger's little sister, me, is married to Reed, is still a point of contention between the two.

Anyway, I try to keep the peace as much as I can.

Hence the request that Reed let Ledger win tomorrow.

Not that he cares about the game, no.

In fact, he watches me from the field more than he watches the ball. Which pisses Shep off because they miss shots that way. But he doesn't have much leg to stand on, my brother. Because he watches his girl from the field just as much.

Anyway, I'm making this request because as I said, Reed and Ledger still butt heads. And along with me being married to Reed, the other point of contention between them is that my brother is dating my husband's sister, Tempest.

Which came as a relief after months of Ledge being an idiot about it.

But yeah, I don't think Ledger and Reed will be best friends any time soon.

Reed bends down then, his features sharp and wolfish. "What do I get in return?"

My heart skips a beat. "What do you want?"

"You."

"Me what?"

His eyes sweep over my features again. But this time, there's no sign of the good, noble protector. This time when Reed looks me over, he's doing it with that predatory, villanous intent that I love so much.

"I hear you're a ballerina," he drawls.

I bite my lip to stop my smile and nod. "I am."

He pretends to think about it, all the while squeezing my waist, flexing his fingers in my braid. "So I want you to spin like one. For me."

I pretend to be shocked as I play with the ends of his soft hair. "You want me to dance for you?"

"Fuck yeah," he rasps. "You promise to dance for me like the pretty blonde ballerina you are and I'll think about letting your brothers win tomorrow."

God, I love him.

So much.

"And if I don't?"

"Then I'll have fun wiping the floor with them."

I can't stop my smile then as I shake my head. "You're a villain, aren't you?"

"I am." He pulls me even closer if possible, tugging my neck back. "And you're my fairy."

"I am."

"For the rest of our lives."

"Until the end of time."

His jaw clenches with emotion and I can't help but whisper, "I love you, Roman."

He swallows. "I fucking love you too, Fae."

At last, he bends all the way down and I stretch myself all the way up so we can kiss after a long, long day of being apart.

Because this is my life now, see?

This wonderful, lovely life where I get to kiss my villain whenever I want. Where I get to tell him that I love him freely, without hesitation.

Where I get to dance for him.

Which I'll do tonight.

Like always.

And like always, he'll get impatient and grab me before the song's done. He'll take my clothes off and kiss every inch of my skin. Even though I'm not the same after the pregnancy. I've got ugly stretch marks and the scar where they cut Halo out of me still lingers.

But it won't matter.

Because it's him and he still kisses my belly like it carries precious life.

For now though, we'll eat dinner.

Later, Halo and I will show him the surprise we made for him — cupcakes with 'Halo + Mommy loves Daddy' spelled out in pink frosting.

Which I know he's going to love.

I also know that he's going to choke up a little like he always does when Halo and I make him something. Like he thinks he doesn't deserve it.

But it's okay.

I'll keep making him things until he believes it.

It will be bath time for Halo then. Which is all handled by Reed because she won't let anyone do this but him, not even Mommy. Followed by story time, which Reed is in charge of again.

And then I'll get to witness another beautiful thing: Halo sleeping on a bare chested and drowsy Reed.

When I've had my fill of watching the two loves of my life, we'll put her in her crib, and I'll drag him to our bedroom. So I can dance for him.

Because I'm still his dancing fairy and he's my wild mustang.

And as I said, this is our wonderful and gorgeous life.

THE END
(For Callie and Reed)

Bronwyn

When: *Callie's Juilliard celebration party during her pregnancy*
Where: *The glass house*

His eyes are pretty.

And so are his hair and his face.

I think if I wanted to, I could draw him.

I'm an artist; I draw things. I see things as a piece of art. As lines and angles. As colors and shades. It's just something I've done all my life.

And I'm not going to lie, he is a piece of art.

He has a broad face, a square jaw and high cheekbones. His lashes are curled and dark, almost forest-y, furry. And his hair's dark too. With shades of brown, just like his eyes.

Brown of the earth.

Ledger Thorne is handsome and worthy of any artist's time and attention. Especially when he's looking at you like that. With so much focus and intensity.

Although I don't know what I did to catch his eye.

I'm not an attention worthy girl.

I'm usually pretty quiet and shy. I like to stand away from the crowd, in the back of a room, close to a wall. I'm a wallflower, if you will. People don't generally notice me. As they shouldn't.

Because I'm the artist here. I should notice them.

I do have one quirk though.

I love jewelry. Nothing expensive or fancy. Just cute, quirky stuff. Like toe rings and thumb rings. Ankle bracelets, belly chains, necklaces, leg chains and stuff. You could say that I clink when I walk or move because I usually have at least five pieces of jewelry on my body at any given time.

So maybe there's that.

Maybe I clinked in his vicinity because I have an arm chain on my right arm, sort of in a butterfly shape with yellow stones. I'm wearing two long necklaces — again made of yellow stones — to match my bohemian looking yellow maxi dress. Not to mention, I've got a pair of tinkling earrings and a belly chain under my dress, which is invisible of course but has star like charms that rustle against my skin and my dress when I move.

So yeah, maybe that's why.

That's why he had to take notice of me. Because of my crazy love of jewelry.

Because other than that, I can't think of any other reason as to why he'd follow me in here. Especially when I think there's something between him and Reed's sister, Tempest. Whom we've all just met and I think who could be Poe's troublemaking soul mate.

Anyway, by follow me in here I mean, inside this house made of glass.

This is where Callie lives now that she's pregnant with her sort of ex-boyfriend's, Reed, baby. She's having a small get together today because she just got her acceptance letter to Juilliard and we're all super duper excited.

These days, nothing excites me. Nothing feels right. Not the colors, the sketches I keep drawing because I don't know what else to do. Not the woods behind our school or green rolling grounds. Things I usually loved because they inspired me to draw.

But I'm really, genuinely happy for her.

My friend deserves all the good things in life. Including the guy she's in love with and from the looks of it, that guy loves her too. Not sure if he realizes it but still.

Anyway, I've gone off topic here.

I have to solve this mystery first.

Mystery being why does Callie's brother keep looking at me? He has been staring at me ever since the get together started. And why did he follow me in here, the kitchen, where I came to get away from the crowd for a few minutes, from the backyard where everyone's currently gathered?

But then he speaks and the mystery gets even more... confusing.

"I'd like to take you out on a date," he says.

Okay, I think I heard him wrong.

Did he say a date?

"I'm sorry?"

"A date," he says in a deep voice, standing casually against the marble island, his arms folded. "With you. I'd like that very much."

"You'd like to take me out on a date?"

"Yes."

I'm standing by the counter, holding a glass of water and my fingers around it tremble. Hugging it to my midsection, I reply, "I'm not... what?"

Something like amusement flickers through his beautiful eyes.

"You're allowed to go on dates, right? I mean, at St. Mary's. Over the weekend. Or whenever you're allowed out."

"Um, yes. I can get my day pass."

He smiles then, all confident and arrogant. "And you've been on dates before?"

"Yes."

Sort of.

I mean, as I said, I'm not an attention worthy girl. I usually stick to the shadows and pass by without making any sort of ripples. And where I come from, Wuthering Garden, the town of the rich, people don't generally notice girls with weird taste in jewelry who wear bohemian dresses and have messy, uncombed looking hair and a sketch pad in hand.

Even so, I have been on dates.

With guys in my art classes, back at my old school, before St. Mary's.

And then there have been dates where I...

Okay, don't think about it, Wyn. Don't think about your non-date dates. Especially not in front of him.

"So yeah, you and me," he says, his eyes taking in my arm chains, his lips twitching with a smirk. "What do you think?"

What do I think?

I think it's all kinds of wrong. And not only because he's Callie's brother. But because Ledger is his brother and oh my God, I can't even fathom going out with his brother.

Not that he would mind. He doesn't care and he...

I clear my throat to break my own thoughts and try to appear calm. "Oh, I don't... I'm sorry but I don't think so."

It doesn't faze him at all.

In fact, it looks like he was anticipating it.

"Why not?" he asks, still standing casually, only a few feet away from me.

"Because I don't think we're each other's type. Besides you're Callie's brother and I..."

"You what?"

I press the glass to my stomach even harder. "It would be inappropriate."

Yes, definitely.

Only it doesn't feel inappropriate when it's him.

God, I'm a bad friend.

"You know what, I think I should..." I trail off when he moves.

Ledger unfolds his arms, which I have to admit are extremely corded and sexy but do nothing for me. Nothing at all. They don't even stir my creativity like his arms do.

He closes the gap between us and I swallow thickly, my eyes wide. His eyes, on the other hand, are calm and relaxed and serious.

"Look, I'm not the best guy, I'll tell you that right away," he says, his gaze flicking all over my face. "I've been a player. I've been an asshole too. To girls, I mean. And I'm pretty sure Callie would freak out at the thought of you and me. Not because she wouldn't want you to be with her brother. But because she wouldn't want her asshole brother, me, to be with one of her innocent friends, you. Despite that, I'd very much like to take you out on a date. I think you're interesting. You're quiet and maybe sad and I think I could get you to smile. Even though we're not each other's type. But then who made the rule that you can only go out with someone your type, right? I'd like to break the rules for you, if you'd let me. So this is me breaking all the rules and asking you out. What do you say?"

Oh that was... good.

I swallow again. "You'd like to break the rules for me?"

He nods slowly, his expression earnest. "Yes. You should think about that too, breaking the rules."

I would laugh if I could.

That's what I've thought about, breaking the rules. Ever since he came to St. Mary's, back in November. Not Ledger but someone else.

Him.

I've broken a million rules for him since then, for his love and all of this would be funny, his brother asking me to break the rules, if it wasn't so painful.

If he was willing to break the rules for me too.

Maybe I should say yes. I mean, how long am I going to be hung up on someone who's not hung up on me. Who will never be hung up on me.

But I can't.

Because I have to ask Ledger and with a sigh, I do. "What about her though?"

"What about who?"

I look him in his pretty brown eyes. "Tempest."

That gets me a reaction. A pretty fierce one.

His brows snap together and his square jaw goes tight. His entire body goes tight as he replies, "What about her?"

"I thought... she was important to you. I mean, the way you were pretending to not stare at her and —"

"Tempest is nothing."

And I know he's lying.

He's lying in the way I lie. To myself I mean.

When I'm angry at myself. For wanting him.

For wanting a man who doesn't want me back.

Finally I also know why he followed me in here. Maybe he was trying to get away from the crowd too. From her, Tempest.

I smile at him sadly and say, "You know, it would be a great idea to go on a date. But you're..."

But I trail off because I notice a movement behind Ledger's shoulders. A flash of dark hair and stricken gray eyes. Tempest.

She's standing at the kitchen threshold and from the looks of it, she heard everything. When she spins around and leaves, my heart twists for her, for the disdain and rejection she must've heard in Ledger's voice.

I'm about to go after her, maybe help her understand what's going on in Ledger's head, but I freeze.

Because she isn't the only one who heard things.

Someone else did too.

Someone who lives in my dreams. Has been living in my dreams ever since I accidentally met him on a summer night. Ever since he told me to follow my dreams before becoming a dream himself.

He stands at the threshold too, all tall and muscular.

His navy blue eyes taking in the scene before him, taking in the closeness between me and his brother. His chest broad and his fists closed at his sides.

When our eyes clash, my lips part to exhale a trembling breath.

He looks at them for a second before he snaps his gaze up and leaves. Just like Tempest did.

And this time my heart twists so fiercely, so forcefully that I know it doesn't matter.

It doesn't matter that my dream man, who also happens to be Callie's oldest brother and our soccer coach at St. Mary's, doesn't want me.

Because I want him.

I want Conrad Thorne.

I love Conrad Thorne.

I love him even though he loves someone else...

ABOUT THE AUTHOR

Writer of bad romances. Aspiring Lana Del Rey of the Book World.

Saffron A. Kent is a USA Today Bestselling Author of Contemporary and New Adult romance.

She has an MFA in Creative Writing and she lives in New York City with her nerdy and supportive husband, along with a million and one books.

She also blogs. Her musings related to life, writing, books and everything in between can be found in her JOURNAL on her website.
www.thesaffronkent.com

Printed in the USA
CPSIA information can be obtained
at www.ICGtesting.com
LVHW041737280823
756543LV00010B/294